The
Carpenter and *His Bride*

How wonderful that Paula K. Parker has delivered yet another biblical era masterpiece, even surpassing her well-crafted and captivating *Sisters of Lazarus* series. Once again, this gifted writer takes her readers back more than 2,000 years, deftly weaving into the narrative enlightening historical information while never losing the flow of the story. Thank you, Paula, for portraying Mary and Joseph as living, breathing human beings who willingly accepted the greatest responsibility of all time.

~Marian Rizzo
award-winning author of *The Leper*

Most of us are familiar with the story of Mary as told by the Sunday School play each Christmas. A neat and clean version with little hardship or doubt. Paula Parker pulls back the curtain and shows us what may have really happened for Mary and Joseph. Paula's meticulous research gives historical and cultural details for more realism. A retelling of this important story to give all readers, believers and non-believers alike, a new appreciation for Jesus's parents.

~Susan K. Stewart
author of *Donkey Devos: Listen When God Speaks*

In *The Carpenter and his Bride* Paula Parker reveals an ancient world and culture that, because humans are involved, is relatable to our own today. Mary and Joseph: just a boy and a girl who one day fell in love, having no idea of the journey God had laid ahead of them. But that's not where it stops. As with all God-stories, this is only the starting point of an amazing adventure!

~Mary-Kathryn
internationally acclaimed recording artist

Captivating! In true Parker style, a story for the ages has been brought to life in a way in which the reader actually becomes immersed as a part within it. Paula shares her gift of making it possible for us to get to know the characters in a real way and experience what they do. Brilliant and a must read.

~Donna Williams, Vice President
EPIC Ministries, Inc.

Like the work of a fine jeweler, crafting a novel from the Bible's pages requires a delicate touch. Paula K. Parker has once again brought a novel to the beauty of a fine gem. Paula's deep historic research, her reverence for the Holy Scriptures combined with her wordcraft has given readers a beautiful stirring account of Joseph and Mary as they walk the journey of complete obedience to God's plan of salvation to humanity through His Son.

Following Joseph's work not only in Nazareth but the huge construction of Herod's capital city and palace, the reader delights in his growing love for Mary. Mary's esthete nature, revealing beauty to her in various ways and her natural acclivity to things artistic is woven amongst her life at home, dealing with difficulties and rejoicing in Jewish holidays while focusing on her love for God and her servant heart towards those she loves.

The adventure that awaits *The Carpenter and His Bride* is an exciting tale. Paula weaves in characters, circumstances and historic events that bring aspects of this very familiar story to a place that invites the reader to relish every moment that comes next; from surprising to thought provoking, to joyful moments of laughter and times of deep reflection.

Having read Paula's previous books, I can say she has created another masterpiece in *The Carpenter and His Bride*. Reading this book will bring this beloved and well known story and the familiar characters in it to a priceless treasure in your heart and in your personal library.

~Tracy H Sugg,
sculptor

Beauty Unveiled: Sisters of Lazarus Book 1 is a fun and meaningful read, offering the best of what biblical fiction provides—a tale built around beloved scriptural figures. But Paula Parker goes deeper than just creating an entertaining story featuring Mary and Martha, she explores the eternal question of what it means to be truly beautiful.

~Roma Downey
Actress, *Touch by an Angel*
Executive producer of *The Bible* miniseries

Beauty Unveiled gives us a wonderful glimpse into the lives of the New Testament women, Mary and Martha. It's as though we get an exclusive peek beyond the veil, surveying what their lives might have been like back then, as they walk through the challenges of life and love. This story explores the heart of one sister, Martha, who struggles to embrace her true beauty while Mary must learn her outward attractiveness is not the only beauty worth cultivating. This story is touching, heartfelt, and humorous, and brings these biblical characters to life.

~Cheryl McKay
Author of *Finally the Bride*

Paula K. Parker captivates her readers with an intimate look at a miraculous and timeless story of true beauty. *Beauty Unveiled: Sisters of Lazarus Book 1* not only gives a unique perspective on what it must have been like to walk with Jesus and bask in His love, but the Bible comes alive giving the reader a new appreciation for the story of Mary, Martha, and Lazarus—unveiling a beautiful story that has never been told!

~Holly McClure
producer, film critic

I just read the last word of *Glory Revealed: Sisters of Lazarus, Book 2*. I remain mesmerized by the world Paula Parker's words evoked. I feel as though I visited the family of Lazarus and experienced the final, earth-bound days of Jesus along with them. To sum up my reaction, I have only one word: masterpiece! Or in this case, the Master's peace is all over this book! I highly recommend this book to any who wish to rekindle their first love with the lover of our souls, Jesus of Nazareth, the Messiah, the heavenly bridegroom awaiting His bride.

~Brenda Noel
Audie Award-winning production supervisor of
The Word of Promise: Next Generation

Paula K. Parker offers an artistic tale of intersecting lives, fractured self-worth, hearts held prisoner to their legalistic perspectives, and in the middle of it all is Jesus. Though she tells a story set centuries ago, it is no different from our stories today. And she offers us the same hope. The hope that Jesus is in the middle of our 'stuff' too.

~Denise Hildreth Jones
Author of Reclaiming Your Heart

In today's modern world value and self-esteem issue abound. It's as if a cruel joke has been played on humankind whereby the traits that are really valuable have been diminished and the outward, temporal things have been inflated beyond measure. As I read *Beauty Unveiled: Sisters of Lazarus Book 1* I saw this reality in a new way. I traded my 'I'm not worth much' tag for 'I'm extremely valuable to God.'

This book is captivating—I couldn't put it down—and brings to life that which is most important.

~Monica Schmelter
General Manager, WHTN-TV

In *Beauty Unveiled: Sisters of Lazarus Boook 1*, Paula K. Parker pens a riveting story of love, longing and faith. Parker's novels bear the profoundly satisfying mark of her gift as a playwright. She combines masterful storytelling with well-crafted dialogue. The result is a cast of Biblical characters fresh and human and real.

Through the eyes of Lazarus, Mary, and Martha the reader eagerly connects with three siblings from a normal, dysfunctional family. Gone are the dusty, unapproachable characters of Sunday school. Set in Bethany, 2,000 years ago, Parker breaks the time barrier with her brilliant use of cultural detail. The veil lifts, and we are brought face to face with flesh and blood people who jump off the pages and into our 21st century world. We resonate with their struggles, dreams, delights, disappointments, and the unpredictable ways God continually touches the human heart. Thank you Paula for giving powerful new voice to another ageless story.

~Bonnie Keen
Dove Award winning recording artist

Having thoroughly enjoyed the first two books in this series, *Beauty Unveiled* and *Glory Revealed*, I was more than excited to hear that Paula would be completing the trilogy with **Grace Extended.** I was then deeply honored to be given the opportunity to get a first look at the anxiously awaited manuscript. Oh my—it did not disappoint! Though it may sound strange, I have to say, **Grace Extended**—in my opinion—is more painting than book. Vibrant strokes of beauty, pain, loss, and betrayal kiss the gently muted hues of love, forgiveness, and ultimately, redemption, creating something so real you want to reach out and touch the virtual landscape. Paula's skillful mastery of word and (seemingly endless) knowledge of period, language, histories, and human nuance, add depth, texture, and breath to the page, making you read a little faster than intended, so great is your need to see what happens next.

From beginning to end, I found myself drawn deeply into her expert brush work, and in the end felt I had been left with something quite breathtaking. I genuinely wanted to stand back, hands clasped behind my back and quietly ponder—as one might in the Louvre when spending time with a work they love and are reluctant to leave.

When I closed the book and stepped away, my final thought was—Monet's *Water Lilies*...in word. Simply lovely.

I cannot wait to see her next work.

~Barbie Loflin
Executive Pastor, Springhouse Church
author of *I Wish Someone Had Told Me*

The *Carpenter* and *His Bride*

The Birth of Hope

a novel

Paula K. Parker

WordCrafts Press

There must be Despair
before there can be a
A Birth of Hope

The people living in darkness
have seen a great light;
on those living in the land of the shadow of death
a light has dawned.

~Matthew 4:16

Part I

Chapter 1

21 Nissan 3757
The week following Passover

*N*issan called to Mary. Since childhood, spring—sometimes as short as a few weeks in the months of Nissan and Iyar—had always been her favorite season. She never knew what to expect; the weather could be warm one day and chilly the next. She never knew when she might get caught in an unexpected shower, as if the earth was trying to quench its thirst before the heat of summer declared, "That is enough moisture!" Even though she was four-teen—old enough to be a wife—the fleeting spring lured Mary outside to run through grass the shade of young olives, climb amidst the branches of ancient trees, and drink in the sight of blossoms bursting in a rainbow of colors with a perfume that would defy King David's skilled pen.

She closed her eyes, listening to the songs of the birds, seeing hues of green, rose, blue, yellow, and purple sparkle behind her eyelids. *This must have been what Father Adam and Mother Eve experienced in Yahweh's first garden.*

"Aunt Mary."

The birds' song lilted, lifting her spirit, calling her upwards.

"Aunt Mary."

She raised her face, her spirit soaring in response to the color, song, and fragrance of rebirth.

"Aunt Mary!"

The tug on her garment accompanying the insistent demand drew Mary's attention earth-ward. She looked down to the coun-tenance of her young nephew, John. Even at five years of age, his determined nature was evident; black curls brushed brows furrowed above deep brown eyes. One little hand grasped her tunic; the other held an olive leaf.

"Aunt Mary!" He tugged again. "Help me!"

"Help you?" Mary smiled, crouching to be eye-level with the child. "John, what do you need help with?"

"That," he let go of her tunic to point to some shaky lines in the ground near his feet. "I tried to draw this," he lifted the leaf to her face, "but I cannot make it look like right." The creases in John's forehead deepened.

"John!" James, Mary's other nephew, stomped up; anyone who looked at him could tell he and John were related. James folded his arms, his countenance exuding the superiority that came from being three years older than his brother. "We do not have time to waste with your *scribblings*."

John lifted his chin and folded his arms, his chubby fist squashing the leaf in question. "They are not *scribblings,* James. I want to draw like Aunt Mary showed us."

"It is alright, James," Mary said. She glanced toward the sun climbing in the azure-blue sky over Nazareth. "We have a little time before you two have to be at the synagogue." Tucking a wayward black curl into her cream head covering, she folded her tunic—the color of the leaves in the trees around them—to pad her knees and knelt next to her younger nephew. "Let me see if I can help, John.

"First, for a drawing in the ground to work, you have to make sure the dirt is soft." She picked up a stick. Scratching and digging, she loosened the hardened dirt, breaking up clumps with her fingers, before smoothing it flat with her hand.

"Now, let us look at your olive leaf." She took the silver-green leaf from her nephew and turned it over. "On the back, it has lines you can feel," she ran a finger down the spine of the leaf, "like the bones in your body. Do you feel it?"

John traced the leaf with a grubby finger. He nodded.

"Good. Now, turn it over and lay it on top of the soft dirt."

The child knelt next to her and put the narrow leaf on the dirt.

"That is right. Now, lay your hands on the leaf and *press* down, firmly but not so hard as to damage the leaf…Yes…Hold it there a little longer…Now, gently grasp the stem of the leaf and lift it carefully straight up…Just like that. Now," Mary pointed, "look at what you have done."

In the dirt before them was a perfect imprint of the leaf.

"Now," Mary held John's forefinger, "trace the pattern of the leaf." She began slowly moving his finger around the imprint. After a moment, she gently removed her hand.

John continued tracing the leaf, his tongue protruding from the side of his mouth, his brow furrowed in concentration.

"Yes," Mary whispered. "Yes…Like that…You are almost finished. Look!" She smiled at him. "You have drawn a perfect leaf!"

The child's mouth spread in a wide grin. "I did it!" He threw his arms around Mary's neck. "Thank you, Aunt Mary!"

Sandal-clad feet beneath the hem of a brown robe stopped in front of them.

"Mary bat Eli! What are you doing?"

Mary and John jumped up, eyes lowered, to avoid Grandmother Tzipora's blistering gaze.

"Look at me!"

Mary did not have to lift her eyes very high to obey her grandmother. How the older woman could loom when she was shorter than everyone was a question Mary often pondered.

Yet loom Grandmother did, the frown deepening the wrinkles in her face. As long as Mary could remember, Grandmother Tzipora's face had been covered with wrinkles. As long as Mary could remember, Grandmother Tzipora was always frowning. The gaze from her black eyes could peel away your skin. Plump arms folded across the brown tunic covering an ample body with hips that rolled when she walked. Not one wisp of thick white hair dared escape the cream head cloth. The cloth-covered basket hanging over the crook of her elbow contained items purchased from the marketplace.

Out of the side of her eye, Mary noted John trying to pat the dirt from his tunic, dust flying around him. *Do not move, John. Grandmother will notice. Ah…too late.*

When Grandmother's razor gaze shifted to the boy, Mary

grasped the sides of her own tunic and, holding her breath, gently shook it.

The searing gaze darted back to her, noting—Mary was sure—every speck of dust on her clothing. "Mary bat Eli, you were supposed to be walking with James and John to the synagogue, then go to the rabbi's house, not wandering through the olive grove outside of Nazareth. I repeat my question: What are you doing?"

Mary paused. Over her grandmother's shoulder, she saw James step behind a nearby olive tree. *Does he really think he can easily escape Grandmother's notice?*

"Answer me!"

Mary lifted a hand, palm up, indicating the sky. "Grandmother Tzipora, it was so beautiful today, I thought James and John might enjoy the spring day."

John lifted the leaf. "Great-Grandmother Tzipora, Aunt Mary was showing me how to draw a leaf." He pointed to the ground, smiling. "Look."

The older woman lowered her eyes to stare at the outline of the leaf. Her mouth pulled down as if she had tasted a morsel of week-old fish. "Idols!" she rasped. *"You shall not make for yourself an image in the shape of anything in heaven above or on the earth beneath or in the waters below.* This was the commandment Yahweh gave to Moses." Lifting her foot, the elderly woman stomped on the drawing; twisting her sandal, she smeared the sketch beyond recognition.

Mary's heart ached at the tears forming in the corners of John's eyes. Grandmother had never understood Mary's love for the beauty she saw and heard around her, or her desire to capture it, whether drawing in the dirt, or in story, or in song. Grandmother only understood cleaning, sewing, cooking; things she believed would make Mary a good wife and mother.

Her younger nephew sniffed, wiping his nose with the sleeve of his tunic. Grandmother Tzipora opened her mouth—Mary was certain—to scold the child further. Before she could speak, Mary said, "Grandmother, that is not all Yahweh said to Moses."

Wrinkles stretched taut across the older woman's face; she gaped as if she had swallowed her tongue.

Mary rushed on, "The rest of the commandment says, *You shall not bow down to them or worship them.* Yahweh's command was not against *making* the images; it was against *worshipping* the images. Why else would Yahweh give Bezalel, Oholiah—and all those people who worked with them—the skills to be engravers, designers, embroiderers, and weavers in colorful linen in order to decorate the Tabernacle Yahweh commanded Moses to build?"

Grandmother's countenance turned the hue of blood. "How do you, a mere girl," her nostrils flared like an angry bull, "—who should be focused on cooking and cleaning, and other things that will prepare you to be a wife—know what Yahweh intended in His commands to Moses?"

"I told her, Tzipora bat Leui."

Chapter 2

Grandmother Tzipora startled, whirling around to face the man approaching them. The basket over her arm swung upwards, the cloth flapping, the contents threatening to spill out.

Mary bit her lip. Not that she wanted to laugh at her grandmother; it was simply rare to see her out of countenance.

"R-R-Ra-b-b-i Boaz bar Penuel," Grandmother flushed, dusting her robe, and then reaching up to adjust her head cloth. "Greetings."

Mary could not hold back a tiny smile at her grandmother's unnecessary response. *Nothing—not even being startled by Rabbi Boaz—would ever cause Grandmother's clothes to need straightening.*

Of average height and build, with hints of gray in his dark beard and hair waving above brown eyes, there was nothing about the rabbi's appearance that would cause people to take note of him. Yet, people took note of Rabbi Boaz.

"It is his smile," Mary's friend Adina—and the rabbi's only child—had told her. "Father smiles as if he knows things no one else knows." She sighed. "It has been my downfall whenever I have tried to hide things from him."

"Greetings, Tzipora bat Leui," he smiled at Mary, "Mary bat Eli," and grinned at the two boys, "James, John, sons of Zebedee; how are you all today?"

Grandmother *harrumphed* at the rabbi's greeting of the children. "Late," her eyebrows lowered to their perpetual state. "The boys are late to synagogue, although it is not their fault." She looked from the boys to Mary. "*Someone* was supposed to escort them there, before attending to her own responsibilities."

Mary felt color wash over her cheeks. She looked at the ground. "Grandmother is speaking of me, Rabbi Boaz. I was to walk the boys to the synagogue and then go to your house to help Adina. I was…" she lifted a hand half-heartedly, "*distracted* by the beautiful day."

"It is easy to see how one could be *distracted*," the rabbi said. "To speak truth; I am late as well. I met with some of the elders in the gate this morning before I was to go to the synagogue. Coming home, I too was…*distracted*… by the day." He extended his arms wide. "Who could not be distracted by the beauty of the season of rebirth? One can see the promises of Yahweh everywhere you look." He looked at the older woman…and smiled. "Do you not agree, Tzipora bat Leui?"

Grandmother Tzipora blinked in surprise. "Uh, yes; Rabbi Boaz. You are right." She glanced around. "Yahweh's promises are…obvious." Her gaze met Mary's smiling eyes. Her eyes darkened, brows lowering as she filled her lungs. "But Rabbi, what is this Mary spoke about Yahweh approving of people making graven images? And why was she speaking with you about matters that should be left to men?"

"Grandmother," Mary started to speak, "I said—" but was silenced by her grandmother's upraised forefinger a mere handbreath from her face.

The rabbi's smile never shifted. "Tzipora bat Leui, Mary did not have the opportunity to explain how she heard me speak of this matter.

"Two weeks ago, she was at the synagogue helping Adina prepare for the Passover Week." He smiled at Mary. "Even though Adina can do most of the work caring for our home and the synagogue, there are areas where she still needs help. Your consistent help and friendship to my daughter is a blessing to her and to me."

Mary returned his smile. "Adina is more than a friend to me, Rabbi. We are *heart-sisters*."

"*Heart-sisters!*" Grandmother Tzipora snorted. "What nonsense!"

"I do not agree, Tzipora bat Leui. Love between friends has great value," Rabbi Boaz replied. "The prophet Samuel wrote that when David was in the service of King Saul, he had a covenant relationship with Saul's son Jonathan. Their relationship went beyond mere *friendship*."

"King David was a special person, chosen by Yahweh," Grandmother said. "My granddaughter is just a girl from Nazareth. That does not, however, answer my question. We were speaking of Mary telling me what Yahweh meant."

"Ah, forgive me, Tzipora bat Leui; the desire to teach is hard to suppress," the rabbi's smile remained. "As I was explaining, the other week, Mary was helping Adina clean the synagogue while John and James," he grinned at the boys, "were there with the other boys of Nazareth, studying the writings of Moses.

"We had read Yahweh's commandment you quoted, and John asked a question." Squatting, he looked into the youngster's face. "Do you remember what you asked?"

John glanced sideways at his great-grandmother, who nodded.

"Answer Rabbi Boaz," she said.

"I asked," the child scrunched his face in concentration, "if Yahweh commanded Moses not to make images in the shape of anything in heaven or on earth or beneath the waters, why did He give the instructions for the Tabernacle to be decorated with images of plants and animals?" The child grinned under the encouraging gaze of the rabbi. "And even the Ark of the Covenant has two golden carvings of cherubim on the lid."

"You are right, John ben Zebedee," Rabbi Boaz put a gentle hand on the boy's shoulder. "Do you recall my answer?"

John glanced at his elderly relative, who nodded again. "What Aunt Mary told Great-Grandmother; you said Yahweh's command was not against *making* the images. It was against *worshipping* them."

James stepped closer to the rabbi. "You explained that many Gentiles bow down and worship these images, because they believe their gods inhabit trees or rocks or animals or the even graven images they make."

"This is correct, James." The rabbi straightened, smiling at the older boy before turning back to the elderly woman. "You see, Tzipora bat Leui; Mary and Adina were nearby and overheard this conversation. It appears Yahweh has blessed Mary with a hunger and mind to know Him—and His creation—better." He grinned at the two boys. "It would please me if all my students felt as she does."

He squinted at the sun. "It has been delightful talking with you, Tzipora bat Leui, but we are late. I will escort James and John to the synagogue. Mary," he smiled at her, "I believe Adina has plans for the two of you to bake honey cakes for my students, *if*," he cocked an eyebrow toward the boys rubbing their hands together and licking their lips, "they are attentive to their lessons."

Chapter 3

I have *never* left my Grandmother's presence without her permission, but your father provided an unavoidable reason for me to go." Mary dried a dish with a cloth and set it on the worktable, "I tried to not be obvious, but I glanced back as we walked away."

Adina lifted a dish from the pan of water and handed it to Mary. "What was your grandmother doing?"

"She was standing as still as a pillar in the synagogue, staring," Mary dropped her jaw and widened her eyes, "as if she had just met King David or one of the prophets of Yahweh." She giggled. "I love and respect my grandmother, but Rabbi Boaz is the only person I know who can put her out of countenance. And he does it in such a way that she behaves as if he has honored her."

"Which is exactly what he *is* doing," Adina said. "Father frequently reminds me," Adina lifted a hand to stroke her chin and pitched her voice deeper, "As Job told his friends, *Is not wisdom found among the aged and does not long-life bring understanding?*" She burst out laughing.

Mary joined her friend's laughter. "You sound just like Rabbi Boaz. He treats everyone with love and honor, no matter what their age or station in life." She picked up the dried dishes and set them on the shelf above the worktable.

"He does indeed," Adina's dark eyes twinkled. "He says we must treat people as those whom Yahweh created. There, the dishes are done." She dried her hands on a cloth and laid it on the edge of the table. "It is time to make the honey cakes." Pushing away from where she leaned against the worktable, she shook her tunic—the color of ripened wheat—and reached for a staff set against the nearby wall.

Like Abraham and Sarah of old, Rabbi Boaz and his wife Devorah bat Lael were barren for many years before she conceived. The joy of this blessing was soon overcome with sadness; Devorah died giving birth to Adina. Beyond being motherless from her first breath, the babe was born with one foot that twisted inward and downward.

Rabbi Boaz did not know what to do. He did not have family in Nazareth, and he knew nothing about caring for an infant.

The women of Nazareth swooped in to care for the grieving man, cleaning, and cooking.

Many women brought their unmarried daughters with them, in the hopes one of them might catch the rabbi's eye. It did not matter that the rabbi was old enough to be their father; a husband is a husband. Many a girl had heard their parents remind them, *If a woman's husband be as lowly as an ant, her seat is placed among the noble women.*

It was fortuitous for Rabbi Boaz that Anne bat Samuel—wife of Eli bat Matthat, the local blacksmith—had just given birth to their second daughter, Mary. Anne took Adina home, raising both infants as if they were twins.

When Adina was still a babe, Rabbi Boaz had spoken with Mary's parents about her twisted foot. Nazareth was too small to have a trained physician, but with the rabbi's aid, Anne sent a letter to her mother's cousin, Elizabeth bat Shelomoh and Elizabeth's husband, Zechariah bar Barach.

All who knew Elizabeth and Zechariah loved them. They were a kind and generous couple devoted to serving Yahweh and those around them. However, despite their dedication to Yahweh, their one prayer—to have a child—had never been answered. Instead of becoming bitter, they turned their love for children toward the children of their family and friends.

The couple lived in Ein Kerem, a town in the hill country of Judah. Being located five miles from Jerusalem made it easy for Zechariah—who was a priest in the division of Abijah—to travel to the City of David when it was his turn to serve in the Temple.

Knowing there would be men trained in medicine in Jerusalem,

Anne asked her cousin's husband if he would consult with a physician on Adina's behalf, to see if there was anything that could be done for the infant's twisted foot.

Within a short time, Zechariah wrote back, with suggestions from a physician in Jerusalem who had discovered a treatment for Adina's foot in the writings of the ancient Greek physician Hippocrates of Kos. The renowned physician had recommended to, *"manipulate the foot as if holding a wax model, not by force, but gently."*

Rabbi Boaz spoke with Haran ben Reuel—a cobbler and leatherworker—and commissioned him make a pair of sandals for his daughter similar to those Romans wore. One sandal was normal in shape and construction. The other was longer—reaching almost to the infant's knees—with many laces that could be adjusted as needed. Anne wrapped Adina's feet and legs with soft cloths to pad them against the leather straps. When Adina was older, this sandal—along with the help of a small staff the carpenter Jacob ben Matthan had made for her—helped Adina to walk. As the years passed and Adina grew, Haran, Jacob—and later Jacob's son Joseph—created larger sandals and staffs for her.

"Is this your new staff?" Mary asked.

Adina nodded, extending it to Mary. "Joseph ben Jacob brought it last evening."

Mary ran her hand down the smooth, finely grain wood. "Olive wood?"

"Yes. Do you remember the old olive tree that fell during the storm last month?"

Mary nodded.

"Joseph took one of the branches from the tree to carve this staff."

"He did a fine job," Mary said, handing the staff to Adina. "It is beautiful."

"Mary," her friend laughed, "except for Joseph and his father, you are one of the few people who would find the beauty in a simple walking staff."

"I am certain Mother would consider this beautiful." Mary followed her friend across the kitchen area to the worktable near the fire pit.

Adina smiled. "As Father always says, *'Ewe follows ewe; as the acts of the mother so are the acts of the daughter.'* It does not surprise me that our *heart-mother* would agree with you."

Even after Adina was old enough to return to her father, the two girls spent most of their days between their two homes. Neither Adina nor Mary considered this to be anything unusual, until the day Sarai bat Zebah—the daughter of the weaver and seller of purple—told Adina that she did not have a mother.

Adina hobbled crying to Anne bat Samuel, who wiped away the child's tears and explained, no, she did not have *a* mother; she had *two* mothers.

Anne laid a hand on her own abdomen. "You were not the daughter of my body," she told Adina and moved her hand to her chest, "but you are the daughter of my heart."

Mary, who had followed Adina into the house, wrapped her arms around her mother and her friend. "If you are Adina's *heart-mother*, that makes us *heart-sisters!*"

From that moment, Adina began calling Anne her *heart-mother*, and the two girls referred to each other as *heart-sisters*.

Although raised as if they were twins, just as Jacob and Esau of old, they looked nothing alike. Slight of figure, Adina was almost Mary's height, but that was hidden by the fact that she was crippled and walked with the help of a staff. Her black hair was long, thick, and straight—her smile sweet, like her father's. The only thing similar to Mary were Adina's onyx eyes fringed by thick lashes.

"I confess I am thankful Joseph ben Jacob's skills go beyond practicality. As you, I enjoy beautiful things." Adina glanced toward the sun, hand shielding her eyes. "If we start now, we should have enough time to make the honey cakes before the boys are released from their lessons. I made the dough this morning; it is in the kneading bowl." Adina pointed to a cloth-covered bowl on a work-table near the far wall of the courtyard. "If you bring the bowl, I will build up the fire."

Some homes in Nazareth—including Mary's—had a fire pit made from a ring of rocks. In these homes, the women would balance a large, flat stone over the edge of the fire pit and cook loaves of bread—or meat, when they had celebrations—on the hot stone. Because Adina was unable to lift and move such a stone, Rabbi Boaz had the potter, Ephraim bar Ovid, build a low domed oven of hardened clay with an opening in the center.

While Mary crossed the courtyard to get the bowl of dough and a wooden platter for the finished cakes, Adina used her staff to lower herself beside a flat stone next to the oven. She picked up a stick lying near the stone and stoked the embers sleeping in the oven, blowing gently until small flames began dancing among the reddened coals.

Baking bread—whether loaves or cakes—was something every girl learned almost as soon as she was weaned; but it was not an easy task. It requires grinding the grain into flour; mixing in the proper amounts of seasonings, leavening, and liquids; kneading the dough, letting it rest, shaping it, and then baking. A wrong step along the way—inaccurate amounts of ingredients; insufficient kneading; not allowing time for it to rise; not attending while the dough baked—and the bread was ruined. Only when it was finished would the cook know if she had been successful.

Just as Anne bat Samuel had taught Mary's older sister, Salome—who was James' and John's mother—the skills needed to run a household, she had also taught Adina and Mary. Adina easily learned all her *heart-mother* taught them; she had a natural gift for cooking and would frequently create new recipes. Her honey cakes were a favorite among many Nazareth residents.

Mary sat across from Adina, placed the bowl beside the flat rock, and removed the cloth. The dough was the shade of cream with a shiny, smooth appearance. "It looks perfect," she smiled at her friend, "as always."

Adina grinned at Mary, lightly pressing the dough with a finger; the indentation quickly sprung back. "It is ready."

Taking handfuls of dough, the girls pressed them between their palms into flattened rounds. Once all the cakes were fashioned, they took a few rounds and, leaning over the oven, carefully slapped the dough against the inside of the curved wall. After a few moments, thin tendrils of smoke wafted through the air, carrying the smell of warm, sweetened cakes. When the dough turned a golden brown, they removed the cakes to the flat stone to cool and quickly slapped more dough onto the oven walls.

When the last of the cakes were baking, Mary carried the bowl to the worktable and washed it while Adina moved the cakes to the platter and covered them with the cloth. After wiping the bowl and setting it on the shelf, Mary brought two damp cloths and handed one to Adina. "Baking is hot work; I thought this would be cooling. Also," she pointed to her own nose, "you have bits of dough on your nose."

"Thank you," Adina laughed. "It does not matter how careful I am, I am a messy cook." She wiped her face and hands, as well as the flattened stone, and then set the cloth aside. "It is time to take the cakes to the synagogue. Father should be finished teaching the boys."

Mary helped Adina to stand. "I know John and James will be happy to see you, and—" she lifted the covered platter, "—they will be happy to see these cakes."

"It is always a joy to see your nephews," Adina adjusted the thick padding on the staff's handle before placing it beneath her arm. "I believe there is someone else who will be happy to see you."

Mary blinked in surprise. "Who would be happy to see me?"

"Yared bar Arieh."

Mary's eyes widened. "Why would the *hazzan* be happy to see me?"

"I heard him tell Father that he loves to hear you sing during Sabbath assembly. He said you have the voice of a sunbird."

Mary felt heat rush to her cheeks. She avoided her friend's gaze. "That was…*kind*…of him."

"Yared is indeed kind," Adina's tone was dry. "He is a hard worker and studious, which Father appreciates as he is training him in the hopes the village elders will one day select him to take over as Leader of the Synagogue. Yared is tall as a cedar and as handsome as Absalom and, like you, he has a beautiful singing voice. Yet, for all of that, he is neither vain nor boastful. I have heard my father say if anyone asked him what he thought Father Adam must have looked like, he would point to Yared."

Chapter 4

*I*f anyone were to ask me what I think Father Adam looked like, I would point to Yared bar Arieh," Rabbi Boaz said. The older man leaned against the stone wall near Joseph, arms folded, watching the carpenter repair the synagogue's door frame. "Do you not agree, Joseph?"

"Hm." *Thunk.* Joseph placed another wooden dowel in the tip of hole on the corner of the door frame—he had used a bradawl to drill the holes—and lifted the mallet with his other hand.

"Yahweh has blessed Yared with many gifts. The sound rising from his singing is ethereal," Rabbi Boaz continued, "as if it were birthed in another realm. Greetings, Jesse bar Naum, Haran ben Reuel," he straightened as he nodded to the men leading two donkeys walked past the synagogue. "Yahweh has blessed us with a lovely day, do you not agree?"

"Greetings Rabbi Boaz bar Penuel, Joseph ben Jacob," the men bowed their heads in response to the rabbi. "It is a lovely day."

Joseph swallowed a sigh as he lowered his mallet and turned to greet the two men. Even though the morning was well advanced—*I have much work left to do*—it would be rude to work in the presence of village elders.

After Rabbi Boaz and the two elders had exchanged pleasantries common to older men—the health of their families, the news in the village, the purpose of their going toward the marketplace—the two elders continued down the street. Rabbi Boaz folded his arms again and leaned against the wall of the synagogue.

Joseph turned his attention back to his work, adjusting the dowel in the hole and lifting his mallet.

"Do you not agree, Joseph?"

"Hm? What is that Rabbi?" *Thunk.* The mallet hit the dowel, driving it securely into the hole. He placed another dowel in the hole on the opposite side of the door frame.

"Yared bar Arieh, our hazzan. Do you not agree that his gift in song is amazing?"

"Hm."

Thunk! Joseph reached down for another dowel.

"If you close your eyes and listen to Yared sing," Rabbi Boaz said, "you could easily imagine yourself in the presence of King David himself. Do you not agree?"

"Hm."

Thunk! The wood vibrated under the impact of the mallet. He placed another dowel and drew back his hand.

"Ah, here come my beloved daughter Adina and Mary bat Eli."

THUNK! "Eoww!" Pain exploded in Joseph's thumb, shot through his palm, and up his arm. He dropped the mallet and jumped up, shaking his hand as if the action would alleviate the pain.

"Joseph, I am so sorry. Is your hand alright?" The rabbi's tone was consolatory, but his eyes crinkled with suppressed laughter.

Before Joseph could respond, Adina and Mary reached the door to the synagogue. "Greetings Father, Joseph ben Jacob," Adina said.

Mary echoed her friend's greeting.

Adina looked between the two men. "What has happened?"

"Ah, Joseph ben Jacob was repairing the door of the synagogue when he hit his thumb with his mallet," the rabbi explained. "I am afraid it was my fault. I was talking to him and," he favored Joseph with a smile, in which sympathy and humor were nicely mixed, "I said something that distracted him."

"Oh, Joseph ben Jacob," Mary said. "I am sorry. I hope it is not bleeding."

Joseph stared into Mary's eyes. *Eyes as deep as woods in autumn.* "Joseph?"

Mary's nearness shot through Joseph like a wandering star in the dark sky of a new moon.

"His hand is fine," Rabbi Boaz said. He laid a hand on Joseph's shoulder and squeezed. "Is it not, Joseph?"

The rabbi's sharp pinch brought Joseph to himself. "No, uh…I mean yes," Joseph corrected himself quickly. He blushed, realizing that he had been gaping at Mary.

"I am glad to hear that," Mary said.

"I am glad, too," Adina echoed her father's grin. "Father did not mention you would be here today. I thought you spent your days in Zippori, helping to build King Herod's new capital."

Located a little over three miles north-west of Nazareth, Zippori was a center of commerce and travel. After the Romans conquered Israel, they built several important roads that connected Zippori with the major cities in Galilee. Herod, son of Antipater the Idumaean, was selected first as governor of Galilee by the Roman Senate who would later give him the title, "King of the Jews." He started several building projects throughout the land, earning him the name, "Herod the Great." These projects including fortresses, aqueducts, theatres, and other public buildings, as well as several palaces for himself. He also built or improved select cities, including Zippori, designing his Galilean capital as a luxurious Grecian city.

"I am in Zippori most days, working on King Herod's palace," Joseph said, "along with many craftsmen and artisans from Nazareth and other nearby villages. I would be there today, save that Rabbi Boaz needed to have the door frame for the synagogue repaired. I explained to Lucius Septimus, the Roman overseer at Zippori, that I needed to work here in Nazareth. As he has hired me to make decorative trim for the doors and windows of *his own* house in Zippori, he was willing to let me stay in Nazareth today. After I am finished here, I will work on the pieces for his house.

"That reminds me; Mary bat Eli, when you return home, would you please tell your father I will be coming to his shop later today? I need to purchase more nails for Lucius Septimus' house before I go to Zippori tomorrow."

"I will tell him, Joseph ben Jacob," she smiled at him. "I am certain the Roman overseer will be pleased with your work. The new walking staff you made for Adina is beautiful."

Joseph was mesmerized by Mary's smile. *Lips like a scarlet ribbon. Your mouth is lovely.*

"*Ahem*!" Rabbi Joseph cleared his throat.

Joseph shook his head. "Uh…thank you." His would have gulped, except his throat had grown too parched to even produce spittle as he realized his thoughts about Mary's lips came from the love song King Solomon wrote to his bride.

"Working for Romans cannot be easy," Adina lifted the cloth covering the platter Mary carried. "Here, have some of these honey cakes. Mary and I made them for the boys; there are plenty and they will give you energy to complete your work."

Joseph grinned as he took a cake. "Thank you, Adina bat Boaz," he looked at Mary, his grin softening into a smile, "Thank you, Mary bat Eli." He took a bite. "It is delicious."

Mary returned his smile. "You are welcome, Joseph ben Jacob; but the true skill was not mine." She nodded toward Adina, "Adina made the dough for the honey cakes; all I did was help with baking."

"The dough is only half of making bread," Adina grinned at Mary. "Baking is an important part as well."

"Oh, I-I…uh…," Joseph stammered, looking between the girls, "I meant no offense."

"I took no offense. I knew…*exactly* what you meant." Adina's glance slanted toward her friend, who was offering the rabbi a honey cake.

Joseph's cheeks burned under Adina's knowing gaze. *Does everyone see I am drawn to Mary?* Before he could reply, Rabbi Boaz spoke up.

"Adina, you and Mary should take these cakes in to Yared and the boys before Joseph and I eat all of them."

"Yes, Father. Fare you well, Joseph ben Jacob." Adina turned to walk into the synagogue.

"Fare you well, Joseph ben Jacob," Mary said. "I hope your hand recovers."

"Thank you." Joseph watched Mary follow Adina inside the synagogue. A moment later a cheer rose from inside the synagogue.

Rabbi Boaz laughed. "It is obvious the boys consider the needs of their stomachs over their studies." He slanted a glance at Joseph. "As some appears to consider the needs of their *heart* over their work."

"*What?*" Joseph startled, looking at the older man. "What…do you mean, Rabbi Boaz?"

"Ah, Joseph," the rabbi wagged a finger at him. "I might be old, but I am not yet blind to see that *someone* is drawn to my daughter's friend."

Chapter 5

*T*he sound of feminine laughter floated from the synagogue. The two men looked through the door to see Mary and Adina smiling and laughing with the hazzan.

Joseph had often seen how Yared affected the women—young and old—of Nazareth. Of an age with Joseph, and taller than most men, the hazzan's chiseled features looked more Greek than Jewish. One dark wavy lock of hair brushed over a noble forehead and eyes the shade of ebony. The young man's full lips spread into a slow smile as he bit into a cake. He leaned in toward Mary and Adina to speak to them; even over the babble of the boys, his voice carried deep and resonate.

Joseph ground his teeth at the girls' laughing response.

"Joseph?"

Yared is especially attentive to Mary.

"Joseph?"

Look at how he leans just a handbreath closer to Mary. If he gets any closer…

"Joseph?"

A sharp elbow in his side, followed by a soft chuckle, re-focused Joseph's attention. Turning, he saw the rabbi lifting a shaggy eyebrow at him. Flushing, Joseph cleared his throat. "Pardon, Rabbi Boaz; I was…" he hesitated, at a loss what to say.

"…distracted by the delicious cakes," the rabbi finished for him. The older man took a bite of his cake and smiled. "I understand how they could distract a man." He glanced beyond Joseph's shoulder into the synagogue. "Yared appears to enjoy the cakes as well, does he not?" the rabbi asked.

Joseph clinched his fist, crumbling his cake.

"Yes. He does appear to enjoy…the cakes."

"Nazareth is blessed to have Yared bar Arieh as our hazzan. He is a hard worker, a talented singer, and he is studious," the rabbi said. "This is a blessing to me, as I hope the village elders will one day choose him to take over my position as Leader of the Synagogue.

"I have overheard some men in the village complain about Yared drawing the attention of the women. Yet for all his skill," he slanted a glance at Joseph, "he does not appear concerned with that nor boastful of his appearance. He is the kind of man some men would wish to hate…or to be like…but they just cannot do either."

The rabbi dusted the crumbs from his hands and looked at the door of the synagogue. "Joseph, you are nearly finished repairing this door. What a fine job you have done."

Joseph filled his lungs and blew out the air. "Thank you, Rabbi, for your kind words. Yes, I am nearly finished." He turned his attention back to his work. Lifting a dowel, he placed it in the hole and lifted his mallet. *Thunk.*

The older man folded his arms and leaned back against the wall of the synagogue. "Yahweh has indeed blessed Nazareth. Not every village can boast of having a family of skilled carpenters. Not only do you work on the synagogue itself, but you have built the chests that hold the scrolls of Holy Scripture. You are valuable to us."

"Thank you, Rabbi." *You* are *valuable*, he reminded himself, *and would make a good husband to Mary.* Joseph placed another dowel and lifted his mallet. *You do not have to be…concerned…over Yared.* He refused to name what he felt toward Yared as jealousy.

"Do you not agree, Joseph?"

"Hm? What did you say, Rabbi?" *Thunk.* The mallet hit the dowel, driving it securely into the hole. *I am not* jealous *of Yared.* He placed another dowel in the door frame. *Thunk!*

"I was talking about the hazzan. As I have often told my beloved daughter Adina, if anyone were to ask me what I thought Father Adam must have looked like, I would point to Yared bar Arieh."

Chapter 6

*T*he golden sun hung midway in the sky as Joseph hurried from the synagogue. He hated feeling rushed, especially with work left to do for the day. As his father always reminded him, "According to the effort is the reward." Generally, Joseph planned his days by this proverb, making certain to allow sufficient time to complete each task properly.

The fault is your own, he thought, lengthening his stride. *You did not have to spend extra time at the synagogue. The work was not arduous*, although he *might* have made it appear thus. *I wanted to be there*, he acknowledged. *It was Mary.* Mary was there, and where she was, he wanted to be.

After Mary and Adina had entered the synagogue, he continued working on the door frame, his attention divided between his work and Rabbi Boaz's sharp-witted comments—*Does everyone in Nazareth know how I feel about Mary?*—while straining to hear the interaction between the two girls and the hazzan. When the repairs were completed, Rabbi Boaz thanked him, complimented his work again, offered to pay him—which Joseph refused, stating that it was his family's honor to care for the synagogue. Rabbi Boaz did not press the matter but thanked him once more before inviting him inside for a cool drink of water.

Joseph had hurriedly put his mallet, bradawl, and extra dowels in his bag. He had to restrain himself from rushing ahead of the elderly man into the synagogue.

The synagogue was the largest structure in Nazareth, built to accommodate all the residents in the little village. On the main floor, it had a large inner room where the men and older boys would stand or sit on step-like benches placed along the four walls, and a loft above where the women and younger children would gather. In the center was the *bimah,* a raised platform, with a reading desk where the scrolls of Holy Scripture would be placed during synagogue assemblies. This arrangement allowed all the people's attention to be focused on whomever was reading or speaking—generally Rabbi Boaz—or on Yared, who always led the people in singing songs of worship to Yahweh.

Joseph waited politely as the rabbi brought two cups of water. He took the cup with a quiet word of thanks and forced himself to drink it slowly, his eyes wandering to where Mary and Adina were offering cakes to the group of young boys who daily came to the synagogue for their lessons with Rabbi Boaz or Yared.

He heard the hazzan say, "Today, the boys learned some of our history." Yared turned to the boys. "Tell Adina bat Boaz and Mary bat Eli what you learned."

"We learned about *reaping,*" seven-year-old Adriel ben Elon said around a mouthful of cake.

"Reaping?" Adina lifted an eyebrow. "You learned about *harvesting?*"

"Not *reaping,*" Mary's nephew James laughed. "He means *reading.* Adriel should not be speaking when he is chewing. As King Solomon said, 'The hearts of the wise make their mouths prudent and they do not speak without first thinking.'"

Adriel's cheeks reddened as he dropped his face beneath the echo of James' laughter.

"Ah, James ben Zebedee, some might agree *if* you had correctly quoted King Solomon's proverb." Rabbi Boaz set down his cup and crossed the floor to lay a hand on Adriel's shoulder, "Solomon wrote, *'The hearts of the wise make their mouths prudent, and their lips promote instruction.'*"

James gaped, his cheeks turning as red as Adriel's, as the rabbi continued. "King Solomon went on to write, *'Gracious words are a honeycomb, sweet to the soul and healing to the bones.'* I do not believe your words toward Adriel were meant to be gracious, wise, sweet, or healing. Were they?"

With each word the rabbi spoke, Mary's older nephew dropped his gaze until he too was staring at the floor. He gave a minute shake of his head. "No, Rabbi Boaz," he glanced at the other boy. "I am sorry, Adriel. My words were unkind. Please forgive me."

Adriel moved to place a hand on James' forearm. "I forgive you, James. You were correct on one part; I should have finished eating my cake instead of being anxious to be the first to speak."

James lifted his gaze to Adriel's grin. He nodded, smiling.

Adriel turned toward Mary and Adina. "We learned why every Jewish boy is instructed how to read and write. It was because of the Maccabean queen Salome Alexandra." He looked at the hazzan, who nodded encouragement for him to continue. "She was Israel's only queen regent."

"Athaliah bat Ahab was queen, too," John added, but Adriel was quick to continue,

"But Athaliah was a *usurper* and *not* the proper queen, like Salome Alexandra. She…"

"Adriel," Yared lifted a forefinger, "I do not think the women are interested in a history lesson. Please just answer my question." He followed the admonition with a gentle smile.

The youngster blushed but continued. "Queen Salome Alexandra ruled as regent after her husband King Alexander Jannaeus died, leaving the kingdom to her. She was wise and her reign peaceful, considered to be one of prosperity for our land. Among the things she did was to make reading and writing compulsory for all Jewish boys."

"Thank you, Adriel," Yared laid his opened hand against his chest. "It is comforting for a teacher to see that *at least a few of his students*," he glanced at the other boys, "listened to the lesson. Of course, there is wisdom in knowing," he lifted his cake, took a bite, and swallowed, "what is *truly* important."

All those present looked from the hazzan to the rabbi. Without blinking, the older man took a cake from his daughter, lifted it to his mouth, and took a bite.

The boys erupted into laughter, followed by Yared, Adina, and Mary. Even Joseph found himself grinning at the hazzan's wit. From the exuberant chatter of the boys, it was obvious to Joseph that Yared's joke—as well as Adina and Mary's cakes—made for a satisfactory ending to the day's lesson.

Chapter 7

*T*he sun cast long shadows by the time Joseph arrived home; He had stopped by Eli ben Matthat's forge to purchase nails. Joseph hoped the blacksmith did not mistake his haste as rudeness. He would not wish to offend Mary's father.

Once home, Joseph paused long enough to greet his mother and younger sister Sarah—who were gathering mallow and mustard leaves from their garden—before hurrying to his family's workshop to complete the cornice, the decorative molding Lucius Septimus had commissioned him to make for the front door of his home in Zippori.

The carpenter's shop where Joseph worked with his father, his older brother Clopas, and—when he felt strong enough—his Grandfather Matthan was located on the front corner of their home. The large room was filled with items to be built or repaired; furniture—including tables, chairs, beds, and stools—as well as plows, carts, yokes, and other tools needed by the men of Nazareth. Hanging on the walls or placed on tables were chisels, mallets, adzes, blow-drills, saws, awls, sharpening stones, and other implements used by Joseph and his family. In the far corner were stacks of various types of wood; almug, tamarisk, cypress, walnut, and olive.

Slipping on an apron—Joseph never understood how his mother and grandmother noticed every speck of sawdust he carried into the house on his clothes—he picked up the smallest chisel and sharpened its edge before crossing to the other side of the room where, on the table beneath the window, was the wooden cornice for Lucius Septimus' home in Zippori.

The Roman overseer had explained that he wanted Joseph to

carve a *dentil* into the *bed-mold*, the decorative trim at the bottom part of the cornice.

Joseph smiled, remembering his confusion with the overseer's instructions.

"Dentil?" he had asked the Roman. "Does that not mean teeth*? You want teeth carved into your cornice?"*

"No, no," the overseer had laughed. "Not teeth." Tall and heavy, Lucius Septimus' close-cropped hair and lack of beard clearly set the Roman apart from the Jewish artisans and workers he supervised. For an overseer, Septimus was pleasant, laughing often. For a Roman, he was fair; he did not hesitate to notice those who worked hard or chivy those who were lazy. He also had an eye for those—like Joseph—who were skilled artisans.

"Forgive me, Joseph ben Jacob. You are so well-trained in your craft that I forget you do not speak Latin. Yes, dentil *comes from the word* dens, *which means tooth. Let me show you what I mean."*

He stooped to pick up a stick and drew a line of connected blocks in the dirt. "This pattern is called a 'dentil.'"

"Ahh…" Joseph smiled, "because it looks like the teeth in a mouth."

"You are correct," Lucius Septimus straightened. "My wife misses Rome." He turned to point to the area above the door of his house. "I thought it would please her to have a dentil in the bed-mold of the door under the cornice, where the wall and ceiling meet. Something to remind her of home."

Joseph smiled. "How thoughtful to wish to please your wife. As my Grandfather Matthan always says, 'A man who seeks to please his wife sows peace in the garden of his home.' I will take special care to carve these," he stretched his mouth into a toothy grin, "'teeth' into the bed-mold."

Joseph opened the shutters on the window, to allow light to shine onto the cornice. It was nearly finished, but he wanted to go over it once more before with the smallest of his chisels, to smooth away rough pieces. His hands fell into work, allowing his mind to go back to the morning; of being near Mary.

As far back as he could remember—even when, as a young boy, he thought girls were a plague to be avoided—he had noticed Mary bat Eli.

Mary was not like any other girl in Nazareth. She was not loud like Rachel bat Daniel or vain and determined to be the center of attention like Sarai bat Zebah. She had none of the other irritating attributes young boys associated with young girls.

No; Mary had always been kind, gentle, an obedient daughter, a good friend to Adina bat Boaz, and—most important—faithful in her devotion to Yahweh. When she laughed—as she had that morning—it was never at the expense of someone's heart. She might be quiet—as though her thoughts were in another place— but she did not shrink into the background and would converse easily with everyone.

He knew she was drawn to beauty, whether it was the walking staff he had made for Adina, the beauty found in the Holy Scriptures, or—he forced himself to admit—to the beauty of music. Such as what had happened that morning in the synagogue.

While the young boys finished devouring Mary and Adina's cakes, the hazzan had crossed to where he was standing with Rabbi Boaz.

"They are good boys," the rabbi had said, "and appear to be learning their lessons. You are to be commended as a teacher, Yared. As King Solomon wrote, Hold on to instruction, do not let it go; guard it well, for it is your life." *He grinned as he took another bite of cake, "I believe these boys will remember today's lesson."*

The hazzan laughed. "Thank you, Rabbi. Your approval is like these cakes," he took another bite, "sweet and satisfying. Greetings Joseph ben Jacob," Yared had looked at him. "I have not had an opportunity to thank you for finishing my kinnor. *King David mentions the lyre and harp in so many of his psalms. I have always wanted to learn to play a stringed instrument as he did."*

"A kinnor?" *Mary turned toward them. "Truly? Adina, did you hear? Yared has a harp."*

"I heard." Adina and Mary crossed to the men.

"Is the kinnor nearby?" Mary asked. "I have always wanted to see one."
"It is in my guest chamber. I shall get it." He crossed the main room
of the synagogue to walk down a corridor.

Besides the main room and upper loft for the women, the synagogue
had four other rooms. One was used for storing the chests that held
the scrolls of Holy Scriptures and another was a mikvah, a bath
used as part of religious ritual cleansing. Although the synagogue's
primary use was as a house of gathering, Rabbi Boaz had turned the
other two small rooms into guest chambers, furnished with a small
table, a stool, and a thick sleeping pallet with coverings woven by
Adina and Mary. These guest chambers were to be used by pilgrims
who were making their way to Jerusalem and needed a place to
wash and rest during their journey. As Nazareth was not on the
main road toward Jerusalem, these guest rooms were rarely used.

The people of Nazareth did not pay Yared for being the hazzan.
In lieu of wages—and to allow him easy access to train under Rabbi
Boaz—when a guest chamber was empty—Yared would stay in one
on the day before holy days, or whenever his training ended late at
night. As his family's home was outside the confines of Nazareth,
during the times Yared stayed the night in a guest chamber, he
shared meals with Rabbi Boaz and Adina.

A few moments later, Yared had returned, carrying a kinnor. "Would
you like to hold it?" he extended the instrument to Mary.

Mary took the small harp, holding it as if it were a newborn infant.
She ran her hand along the two arms at the top—one longer than the
other—from which ten strings extended to the soundboard at the bottom.
"Yared, this is beautiful." She looked at Joseph, "You made this from olive
wood? Like Alina's walking staff?"

"Yes," Joseph smiled. "There was enough wood for both the staff and
the kinnor."

"I love olive wood," Mary smiled. "I recall Rabbi Boaz reading
from the prophet Hosea: His splendor will be like an olive tree, his

fragrance like a cedar of Lebanon." *She looked at the Adina's father,* *"I believe you said the prophet was speaking of Israel?"*

"I did," the rabbi smiled at her before slanting a glance at the boys. *"If other people remembered what Yared and I said, it would make our task as teachers easier."*

The boys looked away, their faces flushing.

"Father," Adina's frown was softened by the twinkle in her eye. "How can you expect your students to remember what you say when the lessons linger, and their stomachs grow empty? Here," she extended the plate of cakes to the boys, "there are a few cakes left."

Rabbi Boaz grinned as the boys gathered around Adina. "My daughter is wise."

Mary set the kinnor against her right shoulder, placed her forefinger on the longest string at the bottom of the instrument, and pulled her hand back, drawing her finger up and across the strings. A rippling, ethereal sound filled the room; even the boys stopped, mouths gaping, to listen.

"I did not know you played a kinnor," Yared said.

"I have never played an instrument of any kind. To speak truth, this is the first time I have ever seen an instrument of music." Mary plucked several of the strings. "It just felt right to play it thus." She handed the kinnor back to the hazzan. "I often imagine King David as a shepherd boy, playing such an instrument."

"It appears that, like King David, you have a natural sense for music. I have been practicing for our synagogue assemblies." Yared cradled the kinnor's soundboard against of his chest. Lifting his other hand to place his fingers against the strings, he began closing his fingers, plucking the strings, creating a melodic tune. After a moment, he closed his eyes and sang:

"Sing joyfully to the Lord, you righteous; it is fitting for the upright to praise Him.

Praise the Lord with the harp; make music to Him on the ten-stringed lyre."

Mary joined in, her pure, lilting voice blending with Yared's rich, mellow voice:

"Sing to Him a new song; play skillfully, and shout for joy. For the Word of the Lord is right and true; He is faithful in all He does. The Lord loves righteousness and justice; the earth is full of His unfailing love."

All were silent as the room echoed with the fading song. After a moment, Rabbi Boaz spoke. "King David wrote about the eternal joy of being in Yahweh's presence. Mary, Yared; I believe we have just experienced what that must feel like."

Joseph noticed delicate color washing Mary's face at the rabbi's compliment. She thanked him, adding, "I was drawn to King David's psalm. And to this kinnor. Joseph," she had turned to him, smiling, "you have created a beautiful instrument."

His heart raced as he recalled her words…her face…her eyes… *her nearness.* Then he ground his teeth, recalling how the boys, the rabbi, and Adina had surrounded Mary and Yared, praising the hazzan's playing as well as his and Mary's singing.

When I sing, I sound like a donkey braying. Joseph stomped to the other side of the room to put down his chisel. Grabbing a cloth from a basket and a skin filled with olive oil, he carried them back to the table. He opened the skin, poured a small amount of oil onto the cloth, and began rubbing it into the cornice with more force than necessary.

Mary loves beauty. Beauty in nature, beauty in music, even the beauty found in the Holy Scriptures. I cannot sing. I cannot play an instrument. I cannot write a psalm. He picked up the skin, but lost his grasp, spilling oil over himself and the cornice.

"Arrrrgh!" he growled. "And I am clumsy as a Syrian bear." He crossed to the basket, grabbed another cloth to wipe his soiled tunic. "I am a simple carpenter. Nothing more. The only thing of beauty I can create is woodwork, and the main reason I take the effort to make it beautiful is because I know it will please Mary."

He filled his lungs and blew out the air. He lowered his voice, as if someone were close enough to hear. "And to earn enough money for the *mohar,* for the bride price."

Although imperial law allowed a Roman soldier to compel a Jewish civilian to carry his baggage or armor for one mile, that law did not apply to the Roman overseer. Lucius Septimus could not compel the Jewish workers and artisans in Zippori to do extra work.

Most of the Jewish workers did only what was required of them and nothing more.

Joseph, however, readily agreed when the overseer approached him about the work on his house; the price the Roman offered was more than fair.

Joseph returned to the table and began rubbing the wood of the cornice again. He knew the hazzan, like most people in Nazareth, did not have much money. Although he did not rejoice in someone's lack, Joseph was secretly relieved to know he had *something* Yared did not.

"Once I finish this cornice," he smiled, "I will have enough money to ask my father to approach Mary's father with a proposal of marriage."

Chapter 8

*M*ary placed a bowl of lentils and a platter of bread—still warm from the oven—on the low dining table next to Grandfather Matthat. She picked up another bowl of lentils and platter of bread from the tall narrow table at the back of the room and crossed to place them between her father and brother-in-law, Zebedee ben Kalev.

Similar to most houses in Nazareth, Mary's home was a rectangle with an open courtyard in the center, where her father's forge, the cooking area, cistern, and small stable for their cow, donkeys, and handful of chickens were located. Along the sides and back of the house were bed chambers for her father's parents—Grandfather Matthat and Grandmother Tzipora—for Mary's parents and—since the time she had reached the age for marriage—a small bed chamber for herself.

There was also a bed chamber for her sister, Salome, her brother-in-law Zebedee, and their boys James and John. The previous year, Zebedee had taken Salome and their boys to visit his relatives in Capernaum when an earthquake hit Nazareth. Mary's home suffered damage, but the home of Zebedee's family was destroyed, killing everyone in the house. Mary's family had welcomed Salome, Zebedee, and their boys into their home, offering them a place to live while they grieved and contemplated their future.

On either side of the home's front door were two large rooms. The room to the left, near the forge, was the blacksmith's shop where her father, Zebedee, and—when he was able—Grandfather Matthat worked.

The room to the right side of the front door was where the family gathered for meals. In the center was the dining table—a long, low table with cushions beneath for people to sit or recline on while dining. In the corners of the room lamps filled with oil were placed on stands. A long window covered with a lattice shutter faced the street. On the back wall—next to the door leading to the courtyard—was the table for the bowls and platters of food and a stone jar filled with water, milk or—during Passover or other holy feasts—wine.

Once Grandmother Tzipora was satisfied that the meal was ready, she nodded to Mary's mother Anne, to Salome, and to Mary. Grandmother crossed to sit next to Grandfather Matthat at the head of the table; the other women moved to her side of the table opposite the men. As the youngest female in the family, Mary's place was at the end, opposite her two nephews.

Mary smiled at Salome as she smoothed her tunic and sat on the cushion next to her sister. Younger than Salome by nine years, she and her sister looked like their mother, Anne. The three women were short in stature, with soft curves, long wavy black hair—although their mother had hints of grey—onyx eyes with thick lashes, gentle smiles, and soft voices.

Mary bowed her head as Grandfather Matthat spoke the blessing:

"Blessed are You, Yahweh, Lord our God, Ruler of the Universe, Who brings forth bread from the earth."

With her grandfather's first spoken word, Mary heard a melody, deep and rich as a shofar. As Grandfather continued to pray, the music grew, accompanying him.

"Blessed are You, Yahweh, Lord our God, Ruler of the Universe, Who creates the fruit of the tree.

"Blessed are You, Yahweh, Lord our God, Ruler of the Universe, Who creates the fruit of the ground.

"Blessed are You, Yahweh, Lord our God, Ruler of the Universe, Who creates varieties of nourishment.

"Blessed are You, Yahweh, Lord our God, Ruler of the Universe, at Whose word all came to be."

The music faded as Mary joined the family in speaking, "Amen." Mary smiled as she offered a bowl of cucumbers to her sister.

"Mary, why are you smiling?" Grandmother Tzipora snapped. "Was there something humorous in your grandfather's prayers?"

"Not humorous, Grandmother. I enjoy hearing Grandfather Matthat pray," Mary smiled at the family's patriarch. "His voice is as rich and melodic as a yellowhammer. Listening to him speak the blessing is a joy."

She did not add that she *heard* a song behind her grandfather's words, lest her family think she was insane.

As far back as Mary could remember, she heard music when no one else could. Sometimes it was prompted by words, or colors, or even smells. When she was younger than John's age, she had commented to her mother that the blooms on the Rose of Sharon sang a lovely song.

"What do you mean, Mary?" Her mother's brow had furrowed. "Flowers do not sing."

It was then she realized that others did not hear music or sounds, or see colors, as she did. She was careful never to mention it again.

"Thank you, my child," the older man grinned. "Being compared to that beautiful songbird is a compliment for this old man. I know some would wish my prayers shorter," he looked at James and John, "as their stomachs are *always* empty, and they wish to eat.

"However, prayers are important for me. It is the time to acknowledge Yahweh's blessing on our family."

"You speak truth, Husband," Grandmother Tzipora nodded, extending the platter of bread to him.

"It is also," he slanted a glance at his wife, "one of the few times when I am allowed to speak uninterrupted."

His grin broadened as the children's jaws dropped, their wide eyes shifting between him and his wife.

Grandmother Tzipora gaped at her husband and, in one smooth movement, removed the platter from beneath his outstretched hand and turned, handing it to her daughter-in-law. Lifting her chin, Grandmother wrapped her robe—and shredded dignity—around her. "I do not know of what you speak, Husband," she huffed, staring at the far wall.

Grandfather grinned at the children, before sliding another glance at his wife, and *nudged* her with his elbow.

Grandmother startled, turning to see his face lowered, as if studying his empty plate. Then, turning his head, he raised his gaze to hers…and wiggled bushy eyebrows.

She tightened her crossed arms. Lifted her chin. Looked at her husband…and burst out laughing.

That action stunned her family; until Grandfather joined her. Then laughter filled the room; James and John holding their sides as they rocked back and forth.

"Husband," Grandmother Tzipora used the edge of her head covering to wipe her eyes, "you are incorrigible."

"And you, my bride," he took her hand and carried it to his lips, "are as beautiful today as the day we met."

Mary's eyes widened as her Grandmother *blushed* beneath Grandfather Matthat's warm gaze. She quickly smoothed her expression—*I would not want Grandmother Tzipora to catch me staring at her*—but she was not fast enough.

"Beauty!" Grandmother huffed. "As King Solomon wrote in his proverb, *"Beauty is fleeting and charm is deceptive."* The older lady frowned. "Mary bat Eli, spends excessive time focused on," she sneered, *"beautiful* things." She looked at Mary's parents. "She was supposed to take James and John to the synagogue this morning. Instead, I found her in the olive grove outside Nazareth, *kneeling* in the ground."

"Kneeling?" Mary's mother looked at her. "Mary, why were you kneeling?"

Mary opened her mouth, but John spoke first.

"She was helping me, Grandmother Anne." He paused under the blistering stare of his great-grandmother, but took a deep breath and continued. "I had asked Aunt Mary to show me how to draw a leaf." He placed his hand on the table, pressing down on the wood. "You press a leaf in the dirt," lifting his hand, he extended his forefinger, and began moving it in a leaf-like pattern, his excitement growing, "and then trace it with your finger."

"That is nice, John," his mother Salome said.

"Nice?" Grandmother Tzipora's white brows slanted downwards. "Salome bat Eli; is it not bad enough that your sister *draws things,*" her mouth pursed as if eating a rotten persimmon, "something that—if it were known—would bring shame on our family. Now you consider your son drawing idols to be *nice?*"

"It was not an *idol!*" John jumped up, fists planted on his hips.

John, please, Mary cringed, but her nephew could not hear Mary's thoughts.

"Rabbi Boaz told you it was *not* an idol! He said he *agreed* with Aunt Mary."

Please, John. Mary wished the boy would look at her. *Please do not say it.*

"Rabbi Boaz said that he too was," his brow furrowed trying to remember, "*distracted* by the beauty of the day. He said that, like Aunt Mary, he could see the promises of Yahweh everywhere he looked." The child lifted his chin and smiled.

The room was quiet as a tomb. All eyes were either on the matriarch of the family or the young boy.

Mary watched as her nephew's countenance changed from triumph to chagrin. *He realizes what he said and to whom he is speaking.*

"Leave." Grandmother rose to her feet, pointing to the door, "Leave the table," her voice picking up strength with each word. Her color was rising ominously. "Leave the room."

Mary glanced between her sister and brother-in-law; both were flushed, their eyebrows slanted down. Even though they were family, in truth they were guests in the home; it would be unheard of for them to speak against Grandmother Tzipora. However, Zebedee was opening his mouth when Grandfather Matthat spoke.

"No."

"What?" Her grandmother spun toward her husband, sputtering. "You heard what John said to me!"

"I did." Her grandfather planted his hands on the table and pushed up to stand. He towered over his wife by nearly a cubit. "John told you what the rabbi said."

"But the tone of his voice…"

"…was enthusiastic, but *not* disrespectful." Grandfather shot a glance at John, who quickly sat down, before he continued. "Tzipora, the fact that John not only remembered the rabbi's words but applied them to…*life*…means he is learning what he has been taught about Yahweh." He laid his hand gently on his wife's shoulder. "Beloved, is that not what we want for our children and for our children's children?"

The gentleness of Grandfather's words, and the timber of his voice poured cool water on the fire of Grandmother's rage. The high color in her face eased, the sparks in her eyes faded. She took a deep breath, blew out the air, and nodded to her husband.

His smiled. "I knew you would agree. Sit, my Love." He held her hand as she lowered herself to her cushion before sitting on his own cushion. "Now," he sat and looked around at the family, "would someone please pass the lentils? I confess I am quite famished!"

As Mary's father lifted the bowl and handed it to his father, a soft sigh escaped from more than one person at the table. The clatter of dishes mixed with conversation as the meal continued.

"Zebedee ben Kalev," Grandfather turned to Salome's husband, "I understand that you have a relative who is a fisherman in Capernaum. I have never been there, but I hear the area is beautiful."

"It is beautiful," Zebedee said, "especially the lake. There are some mornings when a fine mist hovers over the water, giving it a mysterious appearance. I have heard those who live in the area to boast, *Although Yahweh created seven seas, He has chosen Lake Galilee as His special delight.*"

"That does sound beautiful," Grandfather said.

"I know some might consider it foolish, but I have always wanted to become a fisherman," Zebedee grinned. "A friend of my family, Salathiel bar Pharez, is a successful fisherman in nearby Magdala. I met him when I was a child. He was kind, listening to my questions about fishing, and even offered to take me out on Lake Galilee in one of his boats."

"I want to become a fisherman, too!" John said.

"Mary," Salome extended the plate of bread, "would you like some bread?"

As she took the plate from Salome, she caught Grandmother staring at her. The older woman's face was pinched, her look resentful.

Mary sighed, realizing that Grandmother blamed her for the embarrassment she had experienced. *She will not forget it; nor will she forgive me.*

Chapter 9

"There." Mother laid a cloth over the top of the water jar and secured it around the jar's neck with a thin cord. "I believe we are done."

The dishes had been carried from the family room to the cooking area and washed. Salome wiped the crumbs from the table while Mary straightened the cushions beneath. The three women looked toward Grandmother Tzipora, who glanced around the room, before nodding.

"It is finished," Grandmother said. "Let us extinguish the lamps and join the men."

Mary blew out the lamps in the corners of the room before following her grandmother, mother, and sister to the courtyard.

The men sat on low benches surrounding a fire burning in the fire pit; although the spring days were warm, the nights still held a tinge of cold. Grandfather had recently commissioned the carpenter Jacob ben Matthan—Joseph's father—to build the benches. Grandmother had resisted, claiming benches were a waste of money, that cushions were sufficient to pad their bodies from the hard ground.

"It is not the hardness of the ground," Grandfather had grinned at her. "You are younger, my Beloved, and still move with the grace of a gazelle. I am older; however comfortable the cushions are," Grandfather had placed a hand on his back and groaned, "it is a struggle to lower my body to the ground. Once down, it is nigh on impossible to rise without help."

Grandmother had *harrumphed* in response before sitting next to him on the bench. Mary noticed over the following days that Grandmother sewed several small cushions for the seat of their bench.

Mary moved a cushion next to her parents' bench—which

happened to be the furthest from her grandparents—and sat on it. She leaned against her father's knee and looked up.

The waning moon—still a creamy orb in a clear sky—poured its soft light over Nazareth. The air was warm and still, echoing the promise of the season of rebirth.

Salome joined Zebedee, who was pointing out the *mazzaloth*—the arrangement of stars—to James and John.

Mary's father said, "The prophet Isaiah spoke of the stars." He looked between his daughters. "Do you remember what he wrote?"

"I am sorry, Father," Salome shook her head, smiling. "With two young sons, I can barely remember my name."

"The prophet wrote," Mary looked up, "'*Look at the heavens: Who created all these? He Who brings out the starry host one by one, and calls them each by name.*'"

"You are correct, Mary," her father smiled.

Grandmother snorted. "She does not have the responsibilities of Salome, her mother, or me. If Mary were a wife and mother, she would not have time to dwell on matters best left to men.

"Such as today," she folded her arms. "If she had not been—Mary, how did you explain it?—*distracted,* she would not have been wasting her time, and—"

"Enough, Wife," Grandfather cut off her words.

Mary shifted her gaze away from her grandparents, as did all the family. Grandfather's tone, and his use of *Wife* instead of *Beloved,* was an indication to all who knew him that he was speaking from his position as the patriarch. No one wanted Grandmother to see them watching while her husband spoke thus to her.

"Tzipora, we have already heard what happened today." He placed a meaty hand on the bench and pushed himself up. "Come; it is time for us to go to bed."

"Bed?" Grandmother Tzipora looked confused. "We just finished the evening meal. We just sat down. The sun has just set. Sleep is for infants and the aged, of which we are neither. We—"

Grandfather's lifted finger stopped Grandmother's words. "The prophet Moses wrote that even Yahweh rested on the seventh day. It is not the Sabbath, but if rest is good for the Almighty, it cannot be bad for us." He smiled, gently taking her arm and slipping it through his. "Come, my Beloved."

The family was silent, watching Grandfather escort Grandmother to their bed chamber. Once their door closed, all—adults and children alike—let out a deep quiet breath.

Mary's mother whispered, "I did not think that would end well." Turning to her youngest daughter, she asked, "What happened today to cause your grandmother so much displeasure?"

Mary shrugged her shoulders. "Only what John said." She briefly relayed what had occurred that morning. "I believe Grandmother Tzipora lays the blame for her being embarrassed by Rabbi Boaz at my door." Mary sighed and looked down. "I believe she also lays the blame for Grandfather's comments at my door."

She felt her father's hand on her shoulder. "Do not accept that blame on either point, Mary. You did nothing wrong."

"Father, I do not understand why Grandmother is always angry with me."

"She does not understand you," Father said. "Beyond that, my mother is concerned for you."

"Concerned? For *me*?" Mary's brows furrowed. "I do not understand."

"Your grandmother believes that the only value a girl—"

"—or a woman," Mother interjected.

Father nodded, "—or a woman has is to obey Yahweh, and to be a good wife and mother.

"To hear Father speak, Mother was not always this way. When they married, she was a happy bride, with the blessing of being loved by her husband."

"As was I," Mary's mother smiled, laying a hand on her husband's hand. "Many husbands and wives do not have that blessing."

Father lifted Mother's hand to his lips. "You speak truth, my Love." He lifted a quizzical eyebrow at her, nodding toward Mary.

Mother nodded once, her lips drawn in a tight line.

Father turned back to Mary. "This is part of the family history that you do not know. You are old enough now," he glanced towards his grandsons, and lowered his voice, "to hear it, but you must never let Mother know that we told you.

"Soon after my parents married, they learned she was expecting a child. They rejoiced, praying to Yahweh that it would be a boy, possibly even the *Messiah*."

Mary nodded. Like all the residents of Nazareth, she had been taught that when the people of Israel returned from exile in Babylon, the ancestors of King David had settled in the area that would become Nazareth. Every parent in the village—as well as Rabbi Boaz—had taught their children of the prophecy of Isaiah, that the Messiah—the one who would drive out the Romans and return Israel to the glory of King David's reign—would be the *netzer*—the branch—of Jesse, King David's father. That is where their little village of Nazareth derived its name. Because of this prophecy, all the women of child-bearing age in Nazareth believed anyone of them could give birth to the Messiah, the next king of Israel. Every expecting couple prayed for that blessing to come upon them.

"All was going well," Father continued, "until one day, during the watches of the night, Mother woke up in great pain.

"Father sent for the midwife who examined Mother and realized she was in labor. While the midwife tended to Mother, Father went to the synagogue, where he prayed for long hours. At the ninth hour, he was called home. Mother had delivered a babe.

"Father ran into their bed chamber and saw her holding a baby—a son. He sat next to her and took the babe in his arms, thanking Yahweh for their child.

"However, the baby did not cry. He barely moved. He was so small. He had no strength. His little lungs struggled to fill with air.

"As Father and Mother watched, the baby's tiny chest slowed… and stopped."

Mary's heart constricted. "How sad," she lifted a hand to wipe away tears. "Had I known…" *Yahweh, comfort my grandmother and grant her peace*, she prayed.

"My mother has never spoken of it," Father shook his head. "I learned of it from my father. He said Mother believes she had committed some sin, that she had somehow displeased Yahweh, and their baby's death was her punishment.

"A year later she learned she was once again with child. Mother was careful to follow the Law Yahweh gave to Moses; only to lose that child—a daughter—as well.

"Mother lost four more babies. Father said that, with each pregnancy, she grew more frantic to obey the Law—down to the tiniest iota—but it was not enough to save the lives of their babes.

"When Mother was carrying me, Father said she was convinced I would die as the others had. When I was born, she thought I would live only a few moments; then, only a few days; then, only a few weeks. As my days turned into months, she began to hope that perhaps Yahweh would not take me as well.

"Father said Mother persisted in following the Law with painstaking commitment. As a young boy, I remember times when Mother's teaching went beyond what was written in the Law. Father believes if I had been a daughter, she would have forced that heavy burden on me. However, being a son, Father took over teaching me about the Law, for which I am thankful."

Mary drew a shuddering breath, her eyes continuing to fill. "That explains so much about Grandmother." She shook her head. "How sad to believe that your only value—especially if you are a girl—is to obey Yahweh, else He would punish you by taking someone you loved."

"My parents did not raise me to believe thus," Mother said. "They raised me to believe that Yahweh loved me, that being a girl was His blessing to me. When your father brought me home as his wife," she placed a hand on her husband's knee, "Mother Tzipora was not pleased with the way I had been raised. She tried to change me."

"But I would not let her," Father said. "Nor did my father. My father was pleased with my wife." He turned to smile at Mother, "As am I."

Chapter 10

*F*ather," John said, "tell me the names of the stars again." His voice was tinged with the innocent self-centered persistence of a child; it was obvious events that happened before his birth held no importance to him. "When we become fishermen, I will need to know them to navigate our boat at night."

"John," Zebedee ruffled his son's hair, "patience is as important a trait for fishermen as navigating by the stars. Fish do not quickly swim into the nets." He pointed toward the northern sky. "There, do you see those stars?" He traced a pattern, "That is the mazzaloth called The Bear. Do you see it leading its cubs to the north?"

John nodded. He picked up a stick and sketched the pattern of the stars in the dirt in front of his crossed legs.

"That is right," his father said. "The Bear is mentioned in the Holy Scriptures. Do you remember the story of Job?"

John squinted his eyes, but James spoke up. "Job is the man who was good and obeyed Yahweh, yet he lost everything—including his children—and was struck with painful boils."

"You are correct, James," Zebedee continued. "After this happened, three of Job's friends came to comfort him. They tried to convince Job that what he was going through was punishment from Yahweh." He paused, glancing toward Mary and her parents—they nodded—before continuing.

"Job refused to accept their accusations. He told them that no one can prove their innocence before Yahweh. Speaking of the Almighty, Job said, *He alone stretches out the heavens and treads on the waves of the sea. He is the Maker of the Bear and the Hunter, the Seven Stars and the mazzaloth of the south."*

Mary looked to the sky where Zebedee had pointed. As a young child, her father had taught her the names of the stars; *Tzedek,* which means "justice and righteousness;" and *Heilel,* the Morning Star. He also taught her the names of the mazzaloths; *Labi,* the Lion, *Zerah,* the virgin holding the wheat, and *Taleh,* the Ram. Her father told her that the brightest star in that mazzaloth is named, *El Nath,* which means, "Elohim" and "broken or poured out." Mary shook her head; she never understood how the Almighty could be broken or poured out.

As Mary looked at the stars, twinkling in the night sky, her brother-in-law's voice faded in her ears. She heard a single, soft *voice*—she could not describe it otherwise—singing. The song did not have words; or if it did, Mary did not understand the language. Just the pure voice. After a moment, other voices joined in with the first, all singing in cadence with the twinkling of the stars, building in volume until the night sky echoed with a beautiful, glorious twinkling *song.*

She did not call her family's attention to the song. *They surely would have mentioned hearing it.* She closed her eyes, reveling in the wonder of the song, the glory of worship—for worship of Yahweh resonated within her—until a damp muzzle rubbed against her head and a wet tongue slid across the side of her face.

Chapter 11

*M*ary stood and turned in one fluid motion to see a young donkey. "Arod! What are you doing out of the stable?"

Fuzzy fur the color of ash, with black edging its ears and white muzzle, the foal shook its head and stepped over to nudge Mary's leg. In the distance, she heard the frantic bray of Aton, Arod's mother. Only a few months old, the young animal had not developed the instinctive caution of older donkeys.

"Again!" Mary's father shook his head. "This is the third time today Arod got out of the stable. I do not know what to do to keep him in."

"He is just curious," Mother smiled, reaching over to rub Arod's muzzle, "as all children are."

Mary scratched behind the donkey's ears. "He must have squeezed through the balm fence. I am surprised he did not get caught on the thorns."

"The thorns are above his head," Father stood. "Once he is taller, the balm fence will keep him inside the stable. Mary, take Arod back to the stable; there is some spare wood in our shop; I will use it to block the opening where he gets out until he is older."

As her father walked toward the shop, Mary removed the girdle tied around her waist. Fastening a loop, she slipped it over the foal's neck. "Come, little one. Your mother is anxious about you." She led the foal to the opposite side of the courtyard where the stable was located.

The fence her father had mentioned was made from planting a series of scrubby, thorny balm trees close together. The thorns on the short trees prevented Aton, and Mara the cow, from escaping, while the chickens could slip beneath the thorns' grasp to wander around the courtyard as they pleased. Mary's father had commissioned Joseph and his father, Jacob ben Matthan, to build a gate at the far corner of the fence.

Mara and the chickens—awakened from their sleep by Mary's approach—were drowsily unconcerned. "You have broken free of the stable so often," she told Arod, "the others do not care."

That was not the case for Aton. Mostly white, with spots of brown, and tall brown ears, she nudged the gate repeatedly, letting everyone know her foal was missing. She continued braying while Mary opened the gate and let the foal go to her. Withers trembling, the older donkey nuzzled Arod, while Mary removed the cloth girdle from his neck.

Rubbing the donkeys' necks and scratching behind their ears, Mary began singing the song she had heard moments before. She kept her voice soft; she did not want to call her family's attention to her singing.

Aton flicked her ears toward Mary, her trembling calmed, as she listened. Mara and the chickens lifted their heads as well.

"Do you like this song?" Mary asked them. "I heard the stars sing it."

She was wrapping the girdle around her waist when Father came, carrying several long tree branches and a coil of rope looped around his shoulder.

"These branches are for our forge," he dropped them next to the balm fence. "They are newly cut; I had them drying in the corner of our shop. They can be used here while they continue to dry."

He pointed to a spot in the lower part of the balm fence where some of the leaves were squashed together, forming a large, rough hole. On the ground nearby were some pieces of broken wood. "That is where Arod got out earlier today. I stuck that wood in the opening to block him; it obviously did not work." He picked up one of the long branches and set it in front of the hole, wedging it through some low hanging branches.

Mary helped him place several more branches in, wedging them together, until the opening was covered. Father picked up the rope and tied it around one of the branches. She helped him weave it through the branches and secured it to the gate.

"This should work for now," her father said. "Come, let us join the others. Tomorrow, I will ask Jacob ben Matthan to come and give me ideas of what we can do to keep Arod inside the stable."

They crossed to the benches and sat down. Father said, "Joseph ben Jacob stopped by on his way home from the synagogue, as you told me he would. He purchased nails for the house of the Roman overseer in Zippori."

"Yes, he was repairing the door of the synagogue when Adina and I arrived with the honey cakes for the boys," Mary said. She saw James look at her, lifting an eyebrow. *He wonders whether I am going to tell everyone what he said to Adriel ben Elron in the synagogue and what Rabbi Boaz said to him.* "The boys enjoyed the…*sweet*… reward for their hard work."

James' countenance relaxed and he smiled at her.

She nodded, smiling at him. "James, John, you enjoyed the cakes, did you not?"

"They were delicious!" John exclaimed.

James echoed his brother's enthusiasm. "Aunt Mary and Adina bat Boaz are wonderful cooks."

"Aunt Mary," John clasped his hands, "I hope you make them again!"

"I agree with James and John," Father said. "You will have to make them for us sometime." He paused. "Joseph also mentioned that you…*played* the hazzan's kinnor and *sang* with him?"

Mary picked up a stick and began drawing the outline of Aton in the dirt near her feet. Her father's tone was even, but she knew there was a question behind it.

"Aunt Mary was amazing! She played the kinnor," John lifted his arms as if he were holding the instrument and plucking the strings, "as if she had owned one her whole life."

"She and Yared bar Arieh singing the psalm was beautiful," James added. "Everyone in the synagogue grew silent, listening to them. They sounded as if they had practiced the song."

"Thank you, James," Mary said. "I love singing praises to the Most High."

"I wish I could hear you and Yared sing," Mother said.

"Grandfather should invite him to have the evening meal with us," John said. "He could ask him to bring his kinnor."

"I do not know when the hazzan would have time, John," Father said. "Yared's father told me that the hazzan has meals with many families in Nazareth," he grinned at his wife, "especially the families of girls."

"I have heard the same," Mother nodded. "The hazzan is a frequent topic of conversation among the women gathered at the well or in the marketplace. I can understand why; he is quite handsome." She laid a hand on Father's arm and smiled, "Although not as handsome as you, my Love."

"Yared is also spoken of frequently among the men of Nazareth," Zebedee said. "Adina is a wonderful daughter to Rabbi Boaz bar Penuel, but without a son, it is a blessing to Nazareth that Yared is training to one day take the rabbi's place as Leader of the Synagogue. Beyond his studies, Rabbi Boaz tells me that Yared is a hard worker. He helps care for the synagogue and the scrolls of Holy Scripture. All the men believe Yared will be a wonderful rabbi."

"I agree, he will be a wonderful rabbi," Salome said. "I have heard some parents who express an interest for him as a husband for their daughters." She lifted her hand and extended her forefinger. "There is Sarai bat Zebah," she lifted another finger, "Rachel bat Daniel," lifted another finger, "Martha bat Gilad, and," she extended her thumb, "Bityah bar Abijah. Yared would be a wonderful husband for," Salome slanted a glance at her sister, "*any* girl in Nazareth."

Mary felt color washing over her face. She focused her attention on drawing the young donkey. *That is the second time today someone has mentioned the hazzan and me and…marriage. How do you feel about Yared?* Mary asked herself. She liked Yared; how could one not like him? But that was not the question she asked of herself. *Do you feel toward him as a wife would toward a husband? Do you love him?*

Last fall, when she celebrated the fourteenth year of her birth, she reached the age when many girls married. Indeed, both her mother and sister had married during their fourteenth year.

She had often been in the marketplace, or waiting her turn at the well, and overheard the women—including the girls Salome had mentioned—discussing marriage. The girls pointed out the single men, giggling and discussing their features, their skills, their strength, their potential as a husband as if they were buying a horse. What they did was not uncommon, as most people in Nazareth considered marriage as they would bartering over a purchase in the marketplace.

Yet Mary did not look at men—nor consider husbands—the way those girls did. Yes, she hoped for marriage, prayed that Yahweh would bless her with the same marriage her parents had, as her sister—and apparently her grandparents—had. A marriage where she and her husband preferred each other; cared for each other; *loved* each other. But this type of marriage was not common among the Jewish people.

Most marriages were arranged by the parents of the bride and groom. These marriages were little more than business contracts, where position and possessions were more important than character and affection. The couple had no voice in the matter, but were informed of their upcoming betrothal by their parents. They were told that affection for your spouse might come—sometimes after years of marriage—but that was not important.

Although rare, there were marriages based on affection and love. In these cases, the young man made his preferences known to his father, who would approach the father of the young woman with his son's proposal of marriage. The two fathers would discuss the advantages of the possible union, including the mohar, the gift given to the bride's father. Traditionally, there was no set amount; it depended upon the social standing of the families. The gift was money or something of equal value to compensate the father for the loss of the daughter. The main purpose of the mohar, however, was to provide the bride with support should she become widowed.

Once the girl's father was satisfied with the details, the two men sealed the agreement with a toast of wine. The betrothal ceremony either took place immediately or, if the families wanted to prepare a celebration feast, a date was set within a few days.

During the betrothal ceremony, the father sent for his daughter to allow the young man to proclaim his affection for her and his desire for her to become his bride. In many marriages, the girl had no choice, and the father would give her away like a bag of seed. However, there were marriages where the girl was given the right to accept or reject the young man's offer.

If she accepted the proposal, the young man gave her a gift. If he were poor, it would be ten coins from the mohar. For those men who could afford something more, the groom presented his bride with a ring, saying, "Behold you are consecrated unto me with this ring, according to the laws of Moses and Israel."

The betrothal ceremony was concluded with a toast of wine, after which the fathers would discuss the marriage contract, which included the size of the dowry, as well as the details of the wedding ceremony.

The groom would assure his bride that he was going to prepare a place for her. Generally, this meant building another room onto his father's house. For some men, this might take up to a year. Once the room was ready, the groom's father would send him to the bride's home. The groom would take her to his home where the wedding ceremony and celebration took place.

Until then, the betrothal was binding. Although they did not live together, a bill of divorce was required to sever this union.

Even though they were considered husband and wife during the betrothal period, the couple was not allowed to have intimate relations nor were they allowed to be alone for more than a few moments. Whenever the couple was together, a parent, an older family member, or friend was present to provide supervision for them.

While the bridegroom built the room, the bride prepared the things she wanted to take to her new home. Each day, she waited expectantly for the sign her bridegroom was coming for her.

There was no specified time of day for the groom's return, but it typically took place at night when the workday was finished, and all their family and friends could attend the celebration. The groom and the friends he chose as his attendants would go to the bride's home.

As soon as the bride's friends and family saw them coming, they would cry out, "The bridegroom is coming!"

The bride would stop whatever she was doing to prepare. The women in her family, along with the friends she chose as her attendants, would help her don her bridal garments. She would wear her hair loose with—if she owned them—gold and jewels braided into the lengths. A long veil would be draped over her head and a crown set on top.

Her family would lead her outside where—dressed like a queen—the bride, her family, and her attendants would wait for sight of her bridegroom.

He would be dressed like a king, with a crown on his head. His friends would be carrying torches or playing tambourines and other musical instruments.

Before leaving her childhood home as an unmarried woman for the last time, the bride would receive a blessing from her parents. "You are our daughter; may you become the mother of countless thousands, and may your children's children's children rule over the nations."

Her bridegroom would escort her to his house, with her family preceding them, scattering parched grain along the path, while the groom's attendants would play their instruments and dance. As they walked through the streets, their guests—all carrying torches—would join the procession.

When they arrived at the bridegroom's home, the bride's mother, along with her sisters and attendants, would take her aside and straighten her hair and garments. Making sure her face was covered by the opaque veil, they lead her to a canopy set outside under the stars.

There the bridegroom would be waiting for her. Standing by each other's side, the couple would listen as their fathers spoke the blessings that would join them as husband and wife.

Then the wedding feast would begin. Seated at the place of honor, the newly married couple would reign as king and queen of the day. They would praise Yahweh for His blessings and would laugh at the riddles told by the steward of the feast and acknowledge the compliments paid to them.

At one point during the wedding feast, the groom would escort his bride to their wedding chamber. While their guests continued celebrating, they would consummate their marriage.

Mary's hand stilled as she closed her eyes. *Yahweh, someday I hope to be married,* she prayed. *I hope to love and be loved as my parents love; as my sister and brother-in-law love; even as my grandparents love. One day, I hope to have children.*

Yared might not be the only man in Nazareth who would be happy to have a wife who sings or draws; but what man would want a wife who hears and sees things no one else does?

11 Iyar 3757

The brilliant sun was casting long shadows over the main street of Zippori.

The city's true name was Sepphoris, but Joseph had grown up hearing it referred to as Zippori, the Hebrew word for *bird*. People in Nazareth—which lay three miles away—would point out the city, stating that it *perched like a bird* atop the edge of a hill that rose 270 cubits over the valley beneath.

It did not matter that Joseph had been working in Zippori for many months; every day he found something new that drew his attention. Lucius Septimus, the Roman overseer, had explained that King Herod not only wanted Zippori to be a political and banking capitol of the region, but he also wanted it to be the *ornament of Galilee*, filled with beautiful buildings and decorations.

Joseph had already seen men using colorful tiles to create intricate patterns on walls and even on the Roman *cardo maximus*. Joseph laughed at himself. "Joseph ben Jacob, you have spent too much time around Lucius Septimus to be thinking of the Latin *cardo* for a simple street." He had to admit the street was anything but simple; it was to be one of the main thoroughfares in Zippori, and the mosaic patterns set into it were quite beautiful.

There was much beauty in this city. *Mary would love seeing it.*

He smiled. If next week ended as he hoped—*please Yahweh, let it be so*—one day he might bring his bride here to see Zippori. There was much to see, including the king's palace, the upper city and lower city with beautiful homes and colonnaded stone-paved streets, a large reservoir, and a marketplace. Lucius Septimus said he had heard that King Herod spoke of one day building a theater here that would hold 4,000 people. Joseph shook his head. *Nazareth has about 400 people living there. I cannot imagine ten times that number sitting in one theater.*

Joseph could imagine showing Mary the buildings with beautifully carved pillars, mosaic floors and—his smile widened—even the cornice with the dentil he had built for Lucius Septimus' home.

His smile faded. There were parts of Zippori he would not want Mary to see. Shortly after Joseph began working in the city, he had explained to the Roman overseer that he would not work in any building that had artwork—he felt color wash over his face—of barely-clothed men and women. Nor would he work in a temple with artwork of their gods taking human form to mate with a woman.

Zippori was surrounded by a thick fortified wall. After his first day of work here, he had described the massive wall to his family.

"That is only wise," his father had commented. "Located where it is, Zippori is in full view of anyone, friend or foe."

His Grandfather Matthan had added, "A city set on a hill cannot be hidden." Grandfather was filled with wise sayings, either learned from his father and grandfather before him, or sayings he made up.

Joseph led Hamor, his family's donkey, who was pulling the family's cart—he had used the cart that morning to carry the finished bed-mold—past the marketplace. Here was something that Nazareth had in common with Zippori. No matter what size town—or who governed it—the marketplace was its heart, the gathering place for commerce, business, politics, or gossip. Children ran through the streets as people wandered past the booths where merchants sold a variety of merchandise, including food, herbs, oil, cloth and clothing, hair combs, jewelry, bronze mirrors, lamps, pots to cook in, or beautiful amphorae to hold beverages and precious perfumes. There were horses and camels for riding; donkeys for carrying; cages of chickens, pigeons, and doves for consumption; sheep or goats in pens; and cats and dogs running through the streets. Above the sounds of animals clucking, barking, whinnying, bleating, screeching, or braying, human voices buzzed in various dialects and languages as merchants hawked the superiority of their wares, to be countered by customers who pointed out perceived flaws. Then both parties would settle down to the rhythmic barter, offering, countering, reoffering, arguing, and offering again, until a price was agreed upon, payment exchanged, and the transaction completed.

Joseph paused near the booth of the jewelry merchant where a Roman matron was inspecting a tray of small, gold rings. Joseph fingered the folds of his girdle, where was tucked a pouch of coins. He had finished the last of his work on the home of Lucius Septimus earlier that day. The Roman overseer had been loud in his praise of Joseph's work as he counted out the coins.

"Thank you, Lucius Septimus," Joseph tried to control his features as the mound of coins in his palm grew. Most of the people in Nazareth paid in barter; few paid in coin. "You are kind."

"Kind?" The Roman snorted. "Joseph ben Jacob, you are either the humblest of men or you have no idea how skilled you are. You should consider moving to a larger city; your skill as an artisan would earn you much more there."

"Move? No, no!" Joseph shook his head as he poured the coins into a small leather pouch, secured a cord around its neck, and tucked it into the folds of his girdle. "Nazareth is my home. My family has lived here for generations. I hope one day to…raise…my own family there."

"Oh ho!" The Roman grinned. "A family? Joseph, are you considering marriage?"

Joseph's cheeks reddened.

"You are!" Lucius laughed, clapping him on the back. "Congratulations! Or how do you Jews say it? May-zeal tolv? No wait" He held up a hand, snapping fat fingers as if that action would bring the words to mind. "It is mazel tov. *Mazel tov! Did I speak that correct?"*

"That is correct," Joseph smiled, "but it is too soon to offer it."

"It might be too soon, but from your expression" Lucius grinned, "I would wager a denarius that this will not be a marriage arranged by your parents. You are drawn to a special young woman, yes?"

Joseph's smile softened as Mary's face came to mind. "You would win that wager," he said. "Yes, I am drawn to her, and she is indeed special."

"Ahhh…that is wonderful! Here," the Roman reached into his pouch and drew out another coin. *"Stop at the marketplace and buy something for this special young woman. After all, as your grandfather always says, 'A man who seeks to please his wife sows peace in the garden of his home.'"*

The Roman matron selected a ring and arranged for it to be delivered to her home. After thanking and bidding her farewell, the jewelry merchant turned toward Joseph. His smile froze as his gaze took in Joseph, his clothing soiled and dusty from the day's work, leading a donkey-drawn cart.

He thinks my appearance names me a poor laborer with no money. Joseph lifted his chin. *I am an artisan. As Father always says, "Seven years lasted the famine, but it did not come to the artisan's door."* Joseph cupped his hand over the pouch of coins hidden in his girdle. *Even Lucius Septimus said my skills would earn much more.* He nodded to the merchant. "Greetings."

"Greetings," the merchant sniffed. "What do you want?" He covered the tray of rings with a cloth, lifted it, turned away.

"I would like to see your tray of rings."

The merchant paused, eyebrows raised in a slow motion, a gesture that managed to be sarcastic, arrogant, and dismissive all at once. "My rings?" He sighed. "Look here; these rings are made from gold. Their cost would be," he took in Joseph's dirt, "beyond your ability." He looked beyond Joseph and nodded.

Glancing over his shoulder, Joseph saw a Roman soldier—dressed in red tunic and bright armor, hand on the hilt of the short sword at his side—watching him as one would watch a rat sneaking toward a pen holding chickens. Anger flared inside. *First the jewelry merchant thinks I am little more than a poor beggar. Does he now think I am a thief?*

"Joseph ben Jacob! My friend! You are still here in Zippori?

Joseph turned to see Lucius Septimus walking toward him. He bit back a smile as the countenances of both the jewelry merchant and the soldier changed with the approach of the Roman overseer. *They are surprised that Septimus would greet a common laborer as a friend.*

"Yes, Lucius Septimus; I am still here."

"I thought you would be almost home by now," he glanced at the sun. "Does not your Sabbath begin at sundown?"

"It does," Joseph replied.

The Roman looked at the merchant. "And you are at the booth of the jewelry merchant. Good, good." the overseer clapped a hand on Joseph's shoulder as he nodded to the merchant. "Greetings, Gallus Tatius," and to the solider, "Greetings, Vibius Albus. Joseph, I see you are taking my advice and purchasing a gift for that special young woman."

"Ah, yes." In one smooth motion, the merchant removed the cloth and placed the tray of rings in front of Joseph. "You wished to look at these rings, sir?"

Joseph bit back a retort and looked over the rings, making polite comments about the beauty of the rings and the quality of the workmanship.

"That is quite a compliment, Gallus." Lucius nodded his head toward Joseph. "I have met many artisans in my years overseeing King Herod's projects; yet none have been as skilled as my friend Joseph ben Jacob."

The smile on the merchant's lips was oily. "Thank you for your compliments, sir. I try to please my customers." He indicated the tray of rings. "Do you see something that you like?"

"There are several I like," Joseph said. "But my friend Lucius is presumptive in his desire to aid me. Before purchasing a ring, I should be certain the lady in question wishes to accept my proposal."

"There is no question about that," Lucius laughed. "What woman would not wish to marry Joseph ben Jacob of Nazareth?"

Joseph noted the jewelry merchant's smile fading completely as the Roman solider removed his hand from his sword, and he turned away. *It does not matter who speaks for me or the amount of money I might possess. Aside from Lucius Septimus, no one from Rome would ever be interested in anyone from Nazareth.*

Chapter 13

$\mathcal{J}$oseph's trek home was different from when he had arrived that morning in Zippori. The light clouds had changed hue and gathered in the sky.

The sky was not the only thing that had changed since that morning. With each step, thoughts fought in Joseph's brain.

"You are a skilled artisan."

"What do you want?"

"In a larger city, your skill could earn you much more."

"Their cost would be beyond your ability."

The war between feelings of appreciation and insult raged in Joseph as he walked the road that sloped from Zippori toward Nazareth.

He turned toward the path that would lead him by the olive grove—and a shortcut home—but stopped as the clouds shifted and a shaft of sunlight broke through, illuminating the figure of a young woman seated near an old tree. She was turned away from him and was too far away to clearly make out her features, or to hear if he spoke a greeting—or apparently even the sound of Hamor pulling the cart—but Joseph's heart, beating wildly in his chest, identified her.

Mary.

He watched her holding a stick and scratching at something in the dirt. Lifting his foot, he took a step toward her.

"Greetings, Joseph ben Jacob," a voice spoke softly behind him.

Whirling, he saw the rabbi walking up. Biting back a sigh, Joseph paused, controlling his gaze; it would be rude to look away from the older man, even if it were to look at Mary. "Greetings Rabbi Boaz bar Penuel."

"How fortuitous to meet you here." The rabbi paused to stroke Humor's black muzzle. "The Sabbath starts soon, and we both must get home. I was going to speak to your father about building a new stool for Adina. Just as her walking staff needing replacing because of her growth, so does her stool. Would you please tell him for me? I know between you and your father, whatever you build will be beautiful."

"Yes, of course; I will tell Father."

"Good, good. I want it as a gift for her. So, you are returning from Zippori," the older man nodded toward the city on the hill. "How is your work going?"

"It is going well," Joseph answered. *Focus on the rabbi. Do not look at Mary.* "This morning, I finished working on the home of Lucius Septimus. The Roman overseer was *kind* in his praise of my work. When I return after the Sabbath, he wants me to work on some decorations in Herod's palace, as well as decorations on other projects around the city."

"That is good. From what I hear people speak of Herod's plans for Zippori, you will have work to do for many years.

"There are those who would think of work as a curse and not a blessing," the rabbi continued, "but that is not what I read in the Holy Scriptures. They should remember that Yahweh placed Father Adam in His garden to work and tend it. Even King David wrote in his psalm, *You shall eat the fruit of the labor of your hands; you shall be blessed and it will be well with you.*"

"You speak truth, Rabbi," Joseph nodded. "Knowing there will be work for years to come is a blessing for me and…" without thinking, Joseph glanced at Mary, "and my family."

"She is drawing."

Joseph startled, his gaze shifting back to the rabbi. "What?…I… uh…pardon me, Rabbi. What do you mean?"

The older man grinned. "Joseph, as I have said before, my age does not make me blind to see that *someone* is drawn to my daughter's friend." He nodded toward Mary. "You are wondering what Mary bat Eli is doing. Am I correct?"

Joseph dropped his eyes. He felt a flush rush from his neck, covering his face, ears, and scalp. "Oh, I, uh…I am sorry, Rabbi Boaz. It is not my right to wonder about Mary bat Eli's actions."

"Joseph." The rabbi's voice was soft. "Look at me."

He raised his eyes to see a gentle smile on the older man's face.

"Joseph ben Jacob," Rabbi Boaz said, "you have nothing to apologize for. It is not wrong for a young man to think of taking a bride." He grinned. "I am correct again, am I not? You are thinking of asking your father to approach Eli ben Matthat with an offer of marriage for Mary?"

Joseph filled his lungs and nodded. "Yes, Rabbi Boaz; I am." He smiled as he looked at the young woman. "She is…everything…I have ever wanted, everything I have prayed for, in a wife. She loves Yahweh; she is an obedient daughter; she works hard, helping both her family and Adina. She is kind and gentle to everyone she meets. And she…" his words faded away as he watched her continue scratching in the ground.

"And she draws," Rabbi Boaz said. "Yahweh blessed Mary with a gift to capture images of things. I have seen a few things she has drawn; they are beautiful. She cannot afford parchment, and I doubt that her Grandmother Tzipora would permit it. From what I know, Tzipora bat Leui does not understand nor approve of Mary's gift, and would be shamed for it to become public knowledge.

"While I cannot dismiss Tzipora's authority as Mary's grandmother, I do not agree with her about Mary's gift. From what Adina tells me, Mary uses drawing—even if it is in the dirt—as a way to calm her spirit and give her mind space to think."

"She…draws." Joseph's smile faded. He looked away. "I know Mary can sing. I heard her play Yared's kinnor. Now I learn she also draws." Sadness washed over him. *What would my family think of someone drawing? Would they be shamed?* He did not think so. *But Mary's gift is beyond me. She creates something just for its beauty.* He shook his head, "Rabbi Boaz, why would she want *me* as a husband? I cannot sing. I cannot play an instrument, and I cannot draw. I am just an ordinary carpenter."

"No," the rabbi's voice took on a firm edge. "It is wrong for you to compare yourself to Yared or any other man. Joseph," Rabbi

Boaz's softened as he placed a hand on Joseph's shoulder, "let me reassure you; you are no ordinary man. You might not be an artist, but you are a skilled artisan. You might not have the ability to draw with stylus and ink, or even in the dirt, but you craft things of beauty from wood." He looked at Mary. "Yes, Mary has many *unusual* skills. The man who marries her will need to understand and accept those skills as blessings from Yahweh.

"If someone were to ask me who I thought would make a good husband for Mary bat Eli," Rabbi Boaz smiled, lifting a finger to point at Joseph, "I would name you."

Joseph's eyes widened. "You would name *me*? Not…Yared?"

"I would name you," the rabbi repeated. "Not Yared."

Wonder shot through Joseph's chest as he looked to where Mary sat, still intent on whatever she was…drawing…in the dirt. He dropped the donkey's reins and took a step toward her.

"Joseph."

Joseph paused, looking at Rabbi Boaz.

"You were not planning to speak to Mary *now*, were you?"

"I…uh…well," Joseph's brows lowered in confusion as he looked at Mary and then back at the rabbi. He lifted a hand toward the other man. "But you said…"

"While I love Mary almost as much as I love Adina," the rabbi said, "I am not her father. My blessing does not carry weight here.

"Beyond that, you might think her beautiful, but she has been sitting in the dirt. It has been fourteen years since I lost my beloved Devorah—may her memory be blessed—and I am the father of only one daughter. Yet I realize that no woman wants to hear a man ask to marry her when she is not looking her best.

"Go," the rabbi took Joseph by the shoulders and turned him toward Nazareth. "Go home," Rabbi Boaz handed him Hamor's reins, "and speak to your father about Mary." The older man grinned. "Although I have no doubt about of the outcome. I will be the first to wish you *mazel tov*."

Joseph grinned. "Do you not mean *may-zeal tolv*?"

"What?" Rabbi Boaz gave Joseph a quizzical look.

"You are not the first man to wish me mazel tov today," Joseph's grin broadened, "nor the first to speak of my marriage to," his gaze shifted toward Mary, "a special young woman."

Chapter 14

*T*he day had teased Mary.

It started out as a beautiful spring morning that called to her. She helped her sister and nephews harvest lentils and, when Salome and the boys carried the baskets of the beans to Mother and Grandmother Tzipora, Mary took a large basket of lentils to the rabbi's house. She stayed long enough to help Adina make them into a stew.

"I have often wondered how Jacob's lentil stew tasted," Adina said. "After all, his brother Esau was willing to sell his birthright in exchange for a bowl of that stew." She dipped a wooden spoon into the pot of boiling red lentils and lifted it to taste the broth. "Hmmm…it needs more spices." She picked up a fresh spoon and handed it to Mary. "What do you think?"

Mary tested the broth. "It tastes delicious, but yes, I agree; it could use a few more spices…and perhaps more garlic?"

The two girls sprinkled in a little salt, a pinch of freshly-ground cumin, followed with several crushed garlic cloves before tasting the stew again.

"There," Adina gave the pot a final stir and set the spoon aside, "that should be ready by supper. Will you stay? There will be plenty, and I know Yared loves lentil stew."

"Yared is staying at the synagogue?" Mary picked up a stick next to the fire and drew a rose blossom in the dirt.

"Yes. He is helping Father clean the room where the Holy Scriptures are stored. To do the work carefully takes several days." Adina paused. "Mary. Look at me."

Mary lifted her head and looked at her heart-sister.

Adina studied her. "You are not pleased with the opportunity of spending an evening with Yared? I thought—after that day when you sang with him in the synagogue—that you…*care*…about him."

"I do care about Yared," Mary furrowed her brow, trying to choose the right words. "But if you are asking whether I care about him more than other men…I would have to say, 'No.'"

"Well," Adina shook her head, "then I must ask forgiveness. I was wrong to speak to you about Yared as I recently have. A godly husband and marriage are blessings from Yahweh." Her lips tightened in a sad frown. "I would never make light of what I will never have."

"Oh, Adina!" Mary dropped the stick and reached over to embrace her. "Do not speak thus."

Adina laid her head on Mary's shoulder and filled her lungs with a shuddering breath.

"You have all the skills needed to make a wonderful wife," Mary whispered, "and—with Yahweh's blessings—a mother."

"Having skills would make me a good servant. It does not mean any man would choose me as a wife. I do not blame them." Adina blinked away the sheen of tears that formed in her eyes. "What man would want," her voice caught in her throat, "a wife who is crippled?"

"One who knows your value," Mary lifted the edge of her head scarf to dry her friend's eyes, "and your heart."

After pouring Adina a cup of water and helping with some of the housework—which included baking bread to go with the lentil stew—Mary bid farewell to her heart-sister. The sun was hanging low in the sky, but instead of taking the path through Nazareth to her home, she turned toward the edge of the village, where grew the grove of olive trees. Sitting under the shade of an ancient tree, she closed her eyes, feeling the wind blowing through the grove whip her head cloth and tickle her face.

I would never make light of what I will never have.

What man would want a wife who is crippled?

Mary's heart ached. Only those close to Adina knew she kept her blighted hopes veiled as would a woman in mourning. She worked hard to be a good daughter to Rabbi Boaz and to care for him and for their home. As an only child and with no living male relative, if Rabbi Boaz died, the Law Yahweh gave to Moses stated that the inheritance would go to Adina. Mary's parents had already told Rabbi Boaz that in that event, they would care for his daughter.

But what girl dreamt of being a guest in someone's house until the end of her own life?

Yahweh, please comfort my heart-sister. Mary prayed. *Let her see herself—let a godly man see Adina—as You see her.* She continued praying but, in her heart, she knew her friend would be alright. Heartache might shadow Adina's eyes, but she had a strength that made her go on.

The clouds parted, pouring sunlight over Mary's face and heart. She smiled. "Thank you, Yahweh." Picking up a stick, she drew a straight line in the dirt; then moved the stick to the top of the line and drew a short line to the right and then down. Moving over a space, she continued drawing a series of symbols. A short line over and then down. A line to the right and down, connected to another line to the right and down. Then repeated twice more. Another similar to the last three, only the first part did not connect to the second part. A line to the right and then down and curved to the left and finished with a slight curve above.

וְתִתְחַתֵּל

"*Marry?*"

Mary gasped, standing and turning in one rapid movement, holding the stick before her as a weapon.

Rabbi Boaz jumped back, both hands raised in a sign of surrender. "Mary; do not be afraid."

"Rabbi!" Mary panted, her heart beating in her throat. "You startled me."

"As I can tell," the rabbi indicated the stick still pointing at his stomach.

"Oh, forgive me," She laughed, lowering the stick. "I have often played soldiers of King David with James and John. I am certain they would have been pleased with my swift response."

"I am sure they would be," he grinned. "Had I been a Philistine, I would have either surrendered or turned and run away. But, Mary," he pointed to the lines scratched in the dirt, "you wrote וְתִתְחַתֵּל. You wrote the word, *marry.* How did you learn to write Hebrew?"

"I watched James and John practice at home. We do not have papyrus and writing tools, so they use sticks and write in the dirt to practice their lessons. When they are finished, they often leave their lesson in the dirt. When they do, I copy what they have written." She looked at the word she had written in the dirt. "It seems easy; like drawing."

"Well, your writing is quite good," the rabbi said, "better than some of my students." He paused. "If you wish, I will teach you to read and write. You could learn with Adina."

Her eyes widened. "What?"

"The evenings are long and Adina, like you, desires to learn many things. I have been teaching her to read and write. I would be happy to teach you as well."

"Rabbi!" Mary smiled. "Yes! Thank you; I would love to learn."

"Good. I will make it a point to come home early on the days you are helping Adina. And Mary," he placed a finger over his lips. "Outside of Adina, I do not see a reason to mention you learning to read and write to…*anyone*."

He means Grandmother Tzipora. Mary could imagine her Grandmother's reaction. *"She is an ordinary girl living in a small village. There is no reason for her to learn to read and write; it will not help her be a good wife and mother."* Mary nodded her head. "Thank you, Rabbi."

The rabbi pointed at the word in the dirt. "When you copy James' and John's lessons, do you know what you are writing?"

"Yes, some of the time," Mary nodded. "A few of the words."

"Such as," he pointed to the letters in the dirt, "*marry*?" He raised his eyebrows questioningly. "You do not need to respond. Your blushes answer for you."

She looked at the word written in the dirt. "Rabbi Boaz, I…do not know what to say."

"Mary, there is no need to say anything. I realize that young women," he glanced behind him at the road that led to Nazareth, "and young men, frequently think about marriage. That is not a bad thing. Yahweh created marriage to be a blessing." His smile slipped. "I pray someday Yahweh will bless my daughter with marriage."

"Amen." Her heart still ached at the memory of her hear-sister weeping. "I pray that also."

The rabbi shook his head, filled his lungs, and blew it out. "So, Mary bat Eli, is there anyone…*special*…you are drawn to?" He smiled at her.

Mary fought the urge to squirm under that penetrating smile. *"Father smiles,"* Adina had told her, *"as if he knows things that no one else knows."*

Is there anyone special? Mary wondered. *Not Yared. He is handsome, and gifted, and serves Yahweh. While those are admirable qualities, I am not* drawn *to him. So, who?*

For the second time that day, Mary contemplated a potential husband. Nazareth was small; it did not take long for her to consider and discard most of the unmarried men living there. Not that they were unworthy of marriage. It was that she was not drawn to them and did not feel they would understand her, nor understand her love for beauty and her desire to capture it in drawing or song or—she glanced at the ground—in word. *To speak truth, there are only two men in Nazareth who would understand me.* And she had just told Adina that she did not care about Yared more than other men. *That would leave…*

Her eyes widened as realization blossomed in her heart, a rainbow of colors exploding in her vision. She looked at Rabbi Boaz, who smiled and nodded.

"May I be the first to wish you mazel tov?"

Chapter 15

*J*oseph rushed to his family's carpenter shop, knowing—at this time of day—that is where he would find his father.

"Father," he spoke, touching his fingers to the *mezuzah*—the box on the doorpost that contained small scrolls of sacred scriptures—as he opened the door, "I need to speak with you."

It was then Joseph realized that his father was not alone. On the bench beneath the opened window sat Matthan ben Elihud, his father's father, and next to him was Teman bar Esau, his mother's father.

Joseph's grandfathers could have been brothers, even twins, at least in demeanor; when one spoke, it was not uncommon for the other to finish the thought. They wore their age well; taller than most men in Nazareth, they had piercing black eyes beneath bushy white brows, a full heads of white hair—although Grandfather Teman still had a few streaks of black in his beard—and ready smiles beneath long beards.

His grandfathers were good friends of each other and of Mary bat Eli's grandfathers. When the four had been young boys, after learning about the *Gibborhim*—King David's Mighty Warriors, including *The Three*—they began calling themselves, *The Four*.

"Forgive my rudeness," Joseph crossed the room to embrace his mother's father. "Greetings, Grandfather Teman," and adding the greeting for a guest, "Peace be on you," before turning to hug his father's father. "Greetings, Grandfather Matthan."

"And upon you peace, Joseph," Grandfather Teman gave the guest's response.

"I forgot that you and Grandmother Esther were spending Sabbath with us tonight," Joseph said. *How can I get Father alone to speak with him?* "How is she?"

"She is well for a woman her age. To speak truth," his mother's father grinned, "she is well for a woman half her age. Time does not affect a woman as it does a man. We men face war, work, and Romans, and we complain about our pains."

"A woman faces birthing children," Grandfather Matthan picked up the conversation, "raising children, and caring for her husband's and her family's needs, and rarely thinks of resting, much less complaining."

"I would choose war any time." Teman nudged his friend, "Do you not agree, Matthan?"

"I do agree," Joseph's father's father replied. "I would face the Philistine Goliath rather than face what my beloved Naomi has dealt with throughout her life."

Grandfather Teman grinned at their grandson. "You will learn what we mean when you take a wife, Joseph."

Joseph startled. "What?" *How do they know? Not from Rabbi Boaz. I left him standing near the olive grove.* He glanced at the faces of the older men and saw nothing in their countenance beyond the gentle humor of family elders. He felt his face redden. "Uh… pardon me, Grandfather Teman, Grandfather Matthan; but I do not understand what you mean."

"Nor will you," Grandfather Matthan replied, "until you have experienced it for yourself. Jacob," he turned to speak to his son, "use a careful hand with the chisel. You do not want to chip the edge of the bench."

"Yes, Father," Joseph's father did not change the careful movement of the tool on wood.

Grandfather Teman continued, "Especially since this bench is my gift for Esther."

"Yes, Father Teman," Joseph's father continued smoothing the edges of the bench.

"An artisan who loses focus," Grandfather Matthan lifted a thick finger, "is as blind as a rock."

Joseph looked at the floor, biting his tongue. His grandfathers generously sprinkled their conversations with words of wisdom. That the proverbs were often mixed or rarely addressed the topic at hand did not appear to bother them.

Joseph slanted a glance at his father.

Jacob looked at his father and his father-in-law and then, turning his gaze to Joseph, closed his eye in a slow wink.

Joseph gaped at his father before turning to look at his grandfathers.

As one, the two elderly men lifted their chins and, "*Humphed,*" before bursting out laughing, clapping each other on the back.

"Joseph," Grandfather Matthan grinned, "do not follow your father's example. As my revered father—may his memory be blessed—used to say, *It is a father's duty to teach his son a trade.* It appears I failed to add showing proper respect to those lessons."

"Father, pray forgive me if I have offended you," Jacob grinned. "I cannot delay if I am to finish this bench before the Sabbath."

"Then finish," Grandfather Matthan fluffed his beard. "Teman wishes to bless Esther with this bench. As I always say, *A man who seeks to please his wife…*"

Jacob and Joseph joined in as the family's patriarch finished, "*… sows peace in the garden of his home.*"

"Well," Grandfather Matthan stood, "it appears that neither my advice as a husband," his beard spread above a toothy grin, "nor my experience as a carpenter is needed here. Come, Teman. Let us move to the courtyard and enjoy a cool cup of water and leave Jacob to his task."

Joseph crossed to open the door leading into the courtyard. After the elderly men left, he returned to watch his father work.

His father extended a chisel toward Joseph. "Would you hand me the smaller chisel?"

Joseph exchanged the tools with his father.

Laying the smaller chisel against the wood, his father began smoothing the edges of the bench. "How goes your work in Zippori?"

"Good," Joseph walked to the table on the far wall and picked up the grindstone. He began sharpening the edge of the larger chisel. "I finished the work on Lucius Septimus' house. He was pleased with how the cornice looked."

"Good."

"He paid me well." He paused. "He even paid me…*extra.*"

"That is also good." More smoothing strokes along the edge. "Will you use the *extra* to purchase a ring for Mary bat Eli?"

Joseph dropped the chisel and grindstone. "M-Mary?" He stuttered, beads of sweat stinging his forehead. He bent to pick up the tool and the grindstone before continuing. "What do you mean?"

His father looked up, his beard spreading as he smiled. "Joseph, unlike your honored grandfathers, the years have not affected my eyesight. I know what I have seen."

"But I have said nothing."

"Perhaps not with words," his father's smile spreading, "but it is obvious that you are interested in Mary." He pointed the chisel he held at Joseph. "In case you are wondering, I approve. Mary bat Eli is a godly young woman of an honorable family and the daughter of my friend." Placing the chisel against the wood, his father returned his attention to working on the bench.

Joseph remained silent, pacing his breath with that of his father's. This was a difficult part of the work. Distracting his father—even for a moment—might result in irreparable damage to the wood. When his father nodded, laid down the chisel, picked up a cloth, and began wiping the bench, Joseph quietly filled his lungs.

"Father?"

His father's bushy eyebrows shifted as he glanced up at his son. "Yes?" The grin returned.

"Would you speak to Eli ben Matthat for me?"

Straightening, Joseph's father studied him.

Joseph resisted the urge to look away from the full force of his father's penetrating gaze. The same gaze he experienced when—as a boy—he had freed Grandfather Teman's prize donkey and rode him down the streets of Nazareth, pretending to be King Saul. *I am not a child asking for a copper penny to spend in the marketplace.* He lifted his chin and met his father's gaze. *I wish to bring Mary to this house as my wife.*

After a long moment, his father nodded. "After the Sabbath, I will go to Eli ben Matthat's house. If he agrees, I will suggest we wait a few days before talking to Mary. That will give you time to return to Zippori to buy a ring as well as give us time to discuss the mohar." He grinned. "My honored father might say," he lifted a gnarled finger, in imitation of Grandfather Matthan, "*Haste in buying land; hesitate in taking a wife.* But I would remind you of what King David wrote in his psalm:

"*He who finds a wife finds what is good and receives favor from the LORD.*"

"Once they hear, I think both of your grandfathers—as well as your mother and grandmothers—will agree." His grin spread into a smile as he embraced his son. "You have made a wise choice."

Chapter 16

15 Iyar 3757

*M*ary stared at her reflection, feeling as if she were in a dream. Lifting a hand, she gently smoothed the blue tunic the shade of wildflowers blooming in the fields outside of Nazareth. She fingered the cream trim on the neck and hem; she knew wealthy women had trim or designs sewn on their garments, but she had never seen—much less owned—one.

Reaching up, she touched the veil, a softer blue—almost as blue as a glorious morning sky—and as delicate as the gossamer wings of a butterfly.

I am wearing these beautiful garments. Me. Mary bat Eli. Her heart skipped. *For my betrothal ceremony.*

The last few days had rushed past like a spring windstorm driving everything that dared cross its path.

After that moment—*was it really just five days ago*—that chance encounter with Rabbi Boaz; his comments about marriage; his question about whether there was someone *special* she was drawn to; Mary had gone home with the realization erupting in her heart and mind that…*Joseph ben Jacob*…was the only man she wanted as a husband.

Everything changed in that moment.

Wherever she looked, colors swirled, pulsed, and *sang*, as if the earth itself agreed with the wonder birthed in her heart and mind. At the meal that evening, Grandmother Tzipora had no criticisms for her; perhaps because Mary sat at the table quietly, eating little, saying less.

When the family moved to the courtyard, Mary wandered toward the stable. Opening the gate, she slipped inside.

For Mary, there was something warm and comforting about the stable at night. She crossed to Mara, who welcomed her with a gentle *moo* before nudging Mary with her nose.

"All right, all right," Mary laughed, rubbing the cow's nose, and then moving up to scratch behind a brown ear. "Is that where it itches?" Mara tilted her head toward Mary with a satisfied sigh. "I guess it is. *Ooph!*"

Mary stumbled a few steps, her hands outstretched to steady herself from the force of a small head butting the back of her knee, followed by an insistent bray.

"Arod!"

The foal shook its head and moved his muzzle under Mary's hand.

Mary laughed and rubbed the animal's head. "You have no patience, young man. I was just petting Mara."

Another nuzzle.

"I have plenty of love for all of you. Greetings Aton," she spoke to the older donkey who had joined her foal in braying and nibbling Mary's shoulder, cheeks, and garment for her share of satisfying scratches. Mary shook her head. "You are as bad as your son," she laughed, rubbing Aton's brown ears.

Glancing over her shoulder, Mary leaned in to whisper into the grey ear. "Like you, I hope to have a…husband…and a family, soon."

The white ear flicked.

"I speak truth," Mary moved her hand to rub the soft white mane.

Two twitches.

"Who?" Another quick glance over her shoulder and lowered her voice even more. "Joseph ben Jacob."

Another twitch.

"When?" Mary smiled, warmth surging through her heart. "Only Yahweh knows that. But I hope…soon."

That moment came sooner than Mary expected. The next afternoon, John found her pulling weeds in their garden.

"Aunt Mary," the youngster said. "Grandfather Jacob sent me to find you. He would like to speak with you."

"Thank you, John." She stood, shaking the dirt from her robe. "I will go to his workshop."

"He is not there," the youngster said.

"Father is not in the workshop?" Mary frowned. "Where is he?"

"He and Grandmother Anne are in the family room. Great-Grandmother Tzipora wanted to be with them but," the child grinned, "Great-Grandfather Matthat made her go to the marketplace with him."

"Grandfather Matthat went *to the marketplace?*" Of all the things her nephew had told her, this concerned Mary the most. Her grandfather avoided the marketplace, often declaring he would rather do without something than ...*wade through the crowds of yelling people.* For Grandfather to take Grandmother to the marketplace could only mean something was not right. *Perhaps someone is ill and my grandparents are purchasing medicinal herbs.* "I will come at once."

When she entered the family room, Mary did not notice anything unusual. Her mother and father were seating near the table, with three cups of water in front of them, talking softly. They stopped when they saw her.

"Ah, Mary," Father said. "I see John found you."

"He did," Her brow furrowed in confusion. "Is everything alright? When John mentioned that Grandfather Matthat wanted to go to the marketplace, I was certain someone was ill, and Grandfather and Grandmother were purchasing herbs and medicines."

"No one is ill," Mother smiled. "Pray forgive us. John's age and curiosity has him noticing things that are out of the ordinary. Please," she patted the table, "join us. Your father has something to discuss with you."

"Alll…right," Mary stretched the word out. She sat, her gaze never leaving her parents. "What is it?"

"We have something important to tell you." Father glanced at Mother, who smiled and nodded. "I had a guest this morning."

"Oh," Mary said. "Who?"

"Jacob ben Matthan."

"The carpenter?"

"Yes, he had a…contract…he wished to discuss with me."

"Oh?" Mary repeated. *Why would Father need to discuss his business dealings with me?* "What contract did he wish to discuss?"

Father picked up his cup and took a sip. "A marriage contract."

Mary's eyes widened, her heart thumping around in her chest like a bird trying to escape a cage. "A…" she picked up her cup and drank deeply. Her mouth felt as if she had swallowed the desert.

"…marriage contract," Mother finished. She nudged Father's side. "Jacob, do not keep Mary waiting. Finish."

Father grinned. "Forgive me, Mary," he set his cup down. "Jacob ben Matthan came to discuss an offer of marriage from his son Joseph to…" his grin softened into a smile, "you."

"The Law gives me the right to choose a husband for you. Unlike other parents, however, I would never treat marriage as a business transaction with as you the commodity to be bartered.

"Joseph ben Jacob is a good man and the son of my friend. He obeys the Law of Yahweh, and he honors our people. Jacob and I discussed the conditions of the mohar. Joseph is not only a skilled carpenter working with his father, but he has also been working for the Romans in Zippori. According to Jacob, that extra work has built up their family's monies and, from what we hear, the work in Zippori will take years to complete. All that to say, I am satisfied that you will be cared for as Joseph's wife."

Mother laid her hand on top of Mary's. "Yet this means nothing to us if you do not wish for the union."

"Your mother speaks truth. So, my daughter," Father laid a hand on top of Mother's, "will you have Joseph as your husband?"

Mary looked at her parents, colors and song whirling around them. "Yes," she smiled. "I will have him."

The whirlwind did not stop with that announcement. That evening, after Grandfather Matthat spoke the blessing, he looked toward her.

"Mary, your father and mother tells me that you," he arched a bushy eyebrow, "are to be congratulated."

She smiled. "I am, Grandfather Matthat."

His beard spread from a toothy grin. "Ah…that is wonderful news! Mazel tov! I know how women are when it comes to a celebration. As a blessing for this special event," he nodded toward Grandmother Tzipora, who reached under the table to bring out a basket covered in cream cloth, "we have a gift for you."

Mary's brows climbed to her scalp. Gifts were rare and a gift from Grandmother Tzipora? She stood up and walked to the head of the table and looked at the basket.

"Open it, Mary," Grandmother said, her voice unusually soft.

Mary knelt by her grandmother and pulled back one edge of the cream cloth to reveal blue material. She arched a delicate brow toward her grandparents, before reaching into the basket and lifting out a blue tunic.

Mary had heard of people who purchased garments fully made, but this was the first such garment she had ever seen. The tunic was simple, with delicate cream leaves sewn along the edge of the hem and neck, yet for her it was as beautiful as a royal garment.

"Grandfather, Grandmother," Mary looked at their smiling faces. *Grandmother Tzipora smiling!* "I am without words. Thank you."

"You are welcome," Grandfather said. "Every bride deserves to have something beautiful to wear, although all I did was pay for the purchase. Grandmother chose it."

Mary controlled her expression. *Grandmother selected this beautiful garment for me? After her comments on my liking beautiful things?* She turned to the older woman. "Thank you, Grandmother Tzipora. It is beautiful."

Grandmother waved away her thanks. "As your grandfather said, every bride deserves to have something beautiful to wear." She lifted Mary's chin with a gnarled finger. "King Solomon wrote, *A wife of noble character who can find? She is worth far more than rubies.* Yahweh is blessing you with a good husband," Grandmother smiled again, "I pray you will be a good wife."

"Who knows?" Grandfather Matthat added, "Perhaps one day you will be the mother of the Messiah."

The whirlwind days continued. Shortly after sunrise the next morning, Grandmother Bithiah—her mother's mother—arrived at the house. Grandmother Tzipora gathered cleaning cloths, brushes, and soaps. The women started cleaning the house for the betrothal ceremony and cooking food for the celebration. Throughout the day, the women sent James and John to the village well to bring back jars of water. Her nephews said nothing in Grandmother's presence, but Mary heard them muttering about, "doing work meant for girls."

Late that afternoon, Mary's mother sent her to her room to bathe, giving her a bar of fragrant soap. "When Father Matthat and Mother Tzipora told me why they were going to the marketplace, I asked if they would buy a bar of soap for you. This was made with lavender oils."

Mary's eyes widened. *First beautiful garments and now fragrant soap? Will the generous gifts never end?*

Freshly bathed and her hair drying, Mary went to her parents' bed chamber, where her grandmothers, mother, Salome, and Adina—who had arrived earlier in the afternoon—were waiting.

Mary sat on a small bench in front of table with a mirror that had been Father's gift to Mother. While she watched, Adina combed through her hair and deftly braided several lengths with delicate blue ribbon she had brought. "These ribbons are a gift from Father and me."

Mary embraced her heart-sister. "Thank you," she said, and lowered her voice to add, "I look forward to the day we celebrate your betrothal."

Adina nodded, her eyes misting.

"Mary bat Eli."

Mary turned toward Grandmother Bithiah.

Mary's mother's mother was shorter than most people, although a little taller than Grandmother Tzipora, which Mary secretly felt irritated her father's mother. Wisps of white hair escaped her head covering to curl softly around dark eyes. A dove-grey tunic fell in gentle folds around her slender figure. Anyone meeting Grandmother Bithiah for the first time might think her frail, but she was healthy and strong, and—unlike Grandmother Tzipora—kind.

"Yes, Grandmother Bithiah?"

The other woman extended a cloth-lined basket. "I also have something for you."

Taking the basket, Mary moved the cover and lifted out a veil. Mary recognized the veil, although the last time she had seen it was over ten years ago when Salome wore it for her own wedding.

"Grandmother Bithiah!" Mary's breath moved the finely woven fabric. "This is…" she looked at her grandmother.

"…the same veil that my mother—may her memory be blessed—gave me to wear on my betrothal and wedding to your Grandfather Samuel."

Mother continued. "Then I wore it on my betrothal and wedding to your father."

"And I wore it on my betrothal and wedding to Zebedee," Salome added.

Grandmother Bithiah took the veil from Mary's hands. "Turn around, my child."

Mary faced the mirror and watched as her grandmother laid the veil over her head.

Grandmother stepped back as Mary's mother moved in front of her. Taking the edge of the veil she drew it across Mary's nose and secured it behind her other ear. She stepped back as Salome moved a lamp to shed light on the mirror.

Mary stared at her reflection as if in a dream. Lifting a hand, she gently smoothed the tunic, fingering the cream trim on the neck and hem. Reaching up, she touched the veil. *I am wearing these beautiful garments. Me. Mary bat Eli.* Her heart skipped. *For my betrothal ceremony.*

Mary turned on the bench to look at the women surrounding her—from her grandmothers to her mother, to her sister, and her heart-sister—their smiles radiating as the warmth of the sun, and knew she was loved.

Blinking away the tears forming in her eyes, Mary extended her arms to them. "Glory be to Yahweh, for blessing me with such a heritage of love."

Chapter 17

$\mathcal{A}$ tap at the door drew the women's attention. Mary's mother crossed to open the door. Mary's nephew James stood on the other side. "Grandmother Anne," James said, "Grandfather Eli wishes to know if Aunt Mary is ready."

Mary's mother turned to look at her. Mary looked at her reflection once more before turning toward the door. Filling her lungs, she stood. "I am ready."

"Come Bithiah bat Itamar," Grandmother Tzipora extended a hand for the other woman to precede her, "let us join our husbands."

Mary's two grandmothers left the room, followed by Salome and Adina.

Mary's mother took her arm and led her through the door, across the courtyard, and into the family room.

Fragrance permeated the room from the baskets of flowers on the tables and the lamps filled with fragrant oil—another purchase from Grandfather Matthat—flickering in the corners of the room.

Their families—as well as Rabbi Boaz and Adina—stood along the walls, all smiling at her. But the only person Mary truly saw was Joseph, standing with both of their fathers near the dining table.

He wore a cream-colored tunic with a robe, girdle, and turban in a rich brown. His eyes lit up when he saw her, his gaze holding hers as Mother escorted her crossed the room to stand next to her father. She returned his smile.

"Mary," Father said. "Joseph ben Jacob has something to ask you."

Joseph filled his lungs. "We have known each other all our lives."

Mary could feel his nearness.

"Even when I was a young boy, who considered girls something to be avoided," he exchanged grins with James and John, "I never felt that for you. In you, I have seen something different from other women. You are concerned with following the Laws of Yahweh."

Beyond Joseph's shoulder, Mary saw Grandmother Tzipora arch her eyebrow, but the older woman said nothing as Joseph continued.

"But there is more. From what I have observed, and what I have been told," he shot a glance toward Rabbi Boaz, who nodded, "beyond obeying the very letter of the Law, you want to *serve* Yahweh from your heart. You love your family, you honor our people, you are a loving friend, and you are kind to everyone."

He took another breath and lifted his face to blow air toward the ceiling, before continuing. "Mary bat Jacob, you are everything I ever wanted in," he smiled, his eyes warm on her face, "a *wife*. I care for you—no, I *love* you," he pronounced the word with caution, as if speaking a new language, "and want to become your husband."

Love. The air resonated with the word.

"Mary," Father took her hand, "as I told you the other night, although the Law gives me the right to choose a husband for you, I would never give you away as a possession." He looked at Joseph. "Joseph ben Jacob is a good man. He obeys the Laws of Yahweh, and he honors our people. His father, our families' honored elders," he grinned at the four grandfathers standing across the room, "and I have discussed the conditions of the mohar. With Joseph's skill as a carpenter—along with the extra work he is doing in Zippori—I am satisfied that you will be cared for as his wife. However," he paused, "it is not just me who needs to be satisfied," he jerked his head toward Joseph.

Mary blushed and lifted her face to Joseph, her eyes soft. "My parents," she smiled at her mother and father, "as well as my honored grandparents," grinned at the elderly couples, "have always spoken highly of you. Rabbi Boaz and my heart-sister," she smiled at Adina and her father, "also speak highly of you. I have known you all my life, and I believe you are one of the few people who understand *me*. What I feel for you, I feel for *no other man*. To use your words, I…*love* you." She smiled. "Yes, I will become your wife."

Joseph released a deep breath. He reached into his girdle and drew out a soft leather pouch.

Mary's eyes widened as he untied the strings and drew out a small golden band. Most men in Nazareth did not have the money to purchase a ring for their betrothed wife; even her mother and grandmothers did not have one. These men would give their bride a coin—or coins—from the mohar during their betrothal ceremony.

"I have spent many months working in Zippori," Joseph said. "The money I earned from that work I give to my family, as is right. However, I was hired by Lucius Septimus, the Roman overseer, to work on his house. I finished that work the other day. He was generous in his praise of my work for him, and in his pay, including paying an extra amount to buy a ring," Joseph lifted the simple gold band, "for a special young woman. If it does not fit, I will take it to the goldsmith in Zippori to adjust."

Mary removed her left hand from her father's grasp and extended it to Joseph. He slid the ring onto her second finger as he repeated the phrase that would join them, "Behold, you are consecrated unto me with this ring, according to the Laws of Moses and Israel." He smiled, adding, "I promise I will love you, provide for you, protect you, and honor you, my *wife.*"

Mary lifted her hand to look at the ring. "It fits me perfectly," she lifted her gaze to Joseph, "as do you, *my husband.*" She realized they had both spoken truthfully for although it would be months—perhaps a year—before the marriage ceremony and the consummation of their union, under the Jewish Law, they were now considered husband and wife. Only death or divorce could dissolve their bond.

"Mazel tov my children!" First Mary's father and then Joseph's father wrapped their arms around their shoulders. "May Yahweh bless you with many years of happiness and with many children."

Their families converged, with hugs, "Mazel tov!" and repeated blessing of years and children. Rabbi Boaz and Adina joined in their mazel tovs.

"Thank you, Rabbi, for your advice," Joseph grinned, "and your encouragement."

"Yes, Rabbi," Mary added. "Your wisdom opened my eyes to examine," she smiled at Joseph, "my heart."

"Ahh, you are both welcome," the rabbi smiled. "I am honored to have your confidence and trust in such a joyous matter. If I may add my own blessing," he lifted a finger, "As the prophet Isaiah wrote, *As a young man marries a young woman, so will your Builder marry you; as a bridegroom rejoices over his bride,*" he smiled at them, "*so will your God rejoice over you.*"

"Amen," Joseph said.

Mary echoed her betrothed husband.

Grandfather Matthat poured wine to toast the couple, before adding, "I know that Eli and Jacob wish to discuss the details of the dowry and the marriage contract. I understand the women have prepared food for a celebration."

"Yes, Father Matthat speaks truth." Mother crossed to hug Mary and Joseph once more, before inviting all present to join them in the courtyard to allow the betrothed couple a few minutes of privacy.

When all had left the room—with the door standing open to allow for propriety—Joseph took Mary's hand and led her to sit at the table where were placed two cups and a small amphora. Pouring wine into the cups, he handed one to her. After a sip, he set his cup on the table.

"All the bed chambers in my home are filled. My bed chamber is not big enough for two people."

Mary blushed when she noticed that he was staring at her lips hidden behind the veil.

"Ah, yes," he filled his lungs and continued. "I have spoken with Father. There are still fallen olive trees from the storm several months ago. I will begin building a room on top of my family's house. I have selected a spot on the far corner that looks out over the olive grove." He paused, "Is there anything *special* you wish included?"

Mary furrowed her brow. "Special?"

"Besides being large enough for a family," he smiled, "I know that you have a love for the beauty of Yahweh's world. I wish our bed chamber to have beautiful elements."

She set her cup down and placed her clasped hands on the table. "Joseph, you are more than a simple craftsman. You are a skilled artisan. While I can appreciate your work, I do not understand it sufficiently to request anything *special*. I will leave it to you, knowing that whatever you build will be beautiful.

"In the meantime, I will begin gathering the items we will need for our *bed chamber*." Her cheeks warmed as she spoke the word. "Mother and Salome, as well as my grandmothers, have offered to advise—as well as helping to weave and sew—whatever is needed. Adina has also offered to help; she is skilled with the loom and needle."

"If all goes according to plan, and the weather holds, our room should be finished within several months." He covered her hands with one of his. "When Father is satisfied with my work, he will send me. On that day I will come for you and take you to our home."

"I will be ready." Mary smiled into Joseph's eyes. "I will be waiting."

Part II

Chapter 18

*M*ary wiped the sweat from her brow—the summer was especially hot this year—and held her breath as she concentrated on forming the word on the tablet. With the stroke of the last letter, she blew out the air and set the stylus aside.

חישמה

"*Messiah*," Rabbi Boaz said. "You wrote that beautifully, Mary."

"Your skill with the stylus far exceeds mine," Adina said, holding her tablet—a small frame of wood filled with wax—next to Mary's.

"As your skill in weaving and sewing far exceeds mine," Mary smiled at her heart-sister. "It has almost been three months since my betrothal to Joseph yet, with your help, I now have most of the linens we will need. Plus, you have helped me sew several beautiful garments."

"A new bride needs new clothing," Adina smiled.

"Yahweh blesses each of us with unique skills," Rabbi Boaz said. "I cannot sew, weave, draw, nor bake." He lifted a date cake to take a bite. "Only a starving man would eat food I made."

"Father," Adina laughed, "you taught me the patriarch Moses wrote that a man does not live on bread alone. You are a wise man with knowledge of the Holy Scriptures. You are also a skilled teacher. Your skill will last longer than any date cake or garment Mary and I make."

"Rabbi, your daughter speaks truth," Mary said. She picked up a cake. "A teacher who tries to force a student to learn everything at once is like someone trying to eat a piece of bread—or cake— whole. It will choke him." She broke off a small piece of the cake.

"You know how to break a lesson down into smaller portions," she popped the piece of cake into her mouth and ate it, "making it easier to chew and swallow."

"Mary, with your permission, I will repeat your example to the boys during their synagogue lessons," Rabbi Boaz said. "I am certain the reference to food will make their studies easier…*if*" he grinned, "there is a plate of cakes as an example."

The girls laughed.

"Father," Adina said, "if you let me know the date, I will make certain a plate of cakes will be available."

"Rabbi, I will bring extra cakes," Mary added, "as a thank you for teaching me to write."

"That will be delicious," the older man said. "I am certain this is what the prophet Isaiah meant when he wrote, *Eat what is good, and let your soul delight in its fatness.* With these delicious cakes," he patted his stomach, "I will have no problem having the fatness in which to delight."

A knock at the door interrupted their laughter. Rabbi Boaz stood and crossed the room to answer it. "Joseph ben Jacob; greetings!" He paused and looked back at the girls.

Mary smiled. Lifting the cream-colored head cover, she placed it over her hair, draped it across her nose, and tucked the corner behind her ear. She nodded. "I am ready, Rabbi Boaz."

The rabbi stepped aside. "Joseph, please come in."

Joseph touched his fingers to the mezuzah before entering. "Greetings, Rabbi Boaz, Adina," his smile softened, "Mary."

"Greetings, Joseph," Mary returned his smile.

"Rabbi, I stopped by to let you know that the work on your stable is finished."

"Thank you," Rabbi Boaz said. "I will get the coin for payment. Please join us," he gestured toward the table. "I am teaching the girls Hebrew, and they made these delicious date cakes to enjoy with the lesson."

"Thank you," Joseph said, sitting down opposite from Mary. "As long as I am not eating the last cake."

"No," Adina lifted the plate of cakes, "there are plenty."

Joseph selected a cake and took a bite. "Hmmm…these are the best date cakes in all of Nazareth!" He smiled. "Please do not tell my mother or grandmothers I said that."

"We will tell no one," Mary smiled. "I would not wish to hurt Mother Leah, Grandmother Naomi, or Grandmother Esther." Her heart swelled, thinking of her family expanding through her betrothal to Joseph.

"How did your Hebrew lesson go this morning?" Joseph took another bite.

"It went well," Mary lifted her tablet for him to see.

"*Messiah*," Joseph read. "Your writing is much better than mine. As a boy I was certain Rabbi Boaz despaired of teaching me to write."

"Your skills lie elsewhere," Rabbi Boaz re-entered the room, "as I was telling the girls before you arrived." He sat down next to Joseph and handed him several coins. "Your father told me that working at Zippori has increased your skills as an artisan. I agree. If you were ever in larger town, your abilities would command more than a few coins.

"As carpentry comes easy for you, Mary's gift for drawing makes writing easier for her."

"As Adina's gift for weaving and sewing is a blessing for us," Mary said. "She is helping me with the linens and other things you and I will need." Her smile softened. "As I promised, everything will be ready when you come for me."

Joseph's gaze held hers. *This must be how it felt for Father Adam and Mother Eve*, Mary thought, *to be the only two people in the world.*

"*A-hem*," Rabbi Boaz cleared his throat. "I believe we were talking about the Hebrew lesson?"

Mary blushed.

"Ah, yes," Joseph grinned, looking from Mary to Adina to her father. "You learned to write *Messiah* this morning?"

"We did," Adina said. "Joseph, thank you for making these tablets for us. It is easier to write on the wax with a wooden stylus than in the dirt. And," she turned the stylus, laying it along the edge of the tablet and used its length to smooth the writing in the wax, "we can wipe away each day's lesson, to be used the next time."

"You are welcome," Joseph nodded.

Mary had told him she always left her tablet and stylus at the rabbi's house; her Grandmother Tzipora would not approve of her learning to read and write.

"I offered to make these tablets for the boys in the synagogue classes, but Rabbi Boaz said he did not think they would remember to care for them or remember to bring the tablets with them." He grinned. "Recalling my own boyhood, Rabbi Boaz knows of which he speaks. But, from my memories of studying under him, I am certain Rabbi Boaz did not merely teach you to *write* Messiah. He loved adding to the lesson with examples from scripture. I recall he particularly enjoyed teaching the Holy Scriptures with obscure meanings." He grinned at the older man. "What did he tell you?"

Mary looked at Rabbi Boaz, who nodded.

"We discussed what our parents have taught us about the Messiah," she said. "How, since the days of the patriarch Jacob, it has been prophesied that the Messiah would one day come and drive out those who have oppressed Israel and return our nation to the glory of King David's reign."

Adina added, "The prophet Samuel said Yahweh would give strength to His Messiah and break those who oppose him. Everyone in Nazareth is of the line of King David. That means any woman from here," she smiled at Mary, "could be the mother of the Messiah."

"If anyone were to ask me who I thought could be the mother of the Messiah," Rabbi Boaz smiled, pointing at the two women, "I would name either of you."

"You are kind, Rabbi," Mary smiled.

"Oh Father," Adina grinned, "of course you would name me and Mary."

"I agree with Rabbi Boaz," Joseph smiled. "I would name either of you," his eyes softened as he looked at Mary, "as one who could be the mother of the Messiah."

Chapter 19

29 Tamuz 3758

Joseph's family paused for Grandfather Matthan to speak the blessing over their morning meal.

"Blessed are You, Yahweh, Lord our God, Ruler of the Universe, Who brings forth bread from the earth.

"Blessed are You, Yahweh, Lord our God, Ruler of the Universe, Who creates the fruit of the tree.

"Blessed are You, Yahweh, Lord our God, Ruler of the Universe, Who creates the fruit of the ground.

"Blessed are You, Yahweh, Lord our God, Ruler of the Universe, Who creates varieties of nourishment.

"Blessed are You, Yahweh, Lord our God, Ruler of the Universe, at Whose word all came to be."

After the family joined in speaking, "Amen," Grandmother Naomi, his mother, his sister-in-law Mary, and his younger sister Sarah moved to the back of the room to pick up platters and bowls of food, and amphorae of water and milk, and carry them back to the table.

The house was similar to other houses in Nazareth, including Mary's. The rooms of the house formed a rectangle with an open courtyard in the center, where the cooking area, cistern, and small stable for their donkey, cows, and handful of chickens. Along the sides and back of the house were sleeping quarters for his parents and his younger sister Sarah; his father's parents, Grandfather Matthan and Grandmother Naomi; his older brother Clopas, his wife Mary bat Tovi, and their young son Samuel; and a small bed chamber for himself, which Sarah had already asked for once he brought Mary home as his bride. On the front of the house, opposite the carpenter's shop, was the main family room. With a large window to let in the morning sun, there were lamps around the room to be lit for the evening meal. In the center was a large, low table, with cushions on the floor beneath for people to sit on during meals. Along the back wall, next to the door that led to the courtyard, was a taller narrow table that held the platters and bowls for the food, as well as amphorae of water or milk.

"Joseph," Sarah handed him a bowl of cheese, "I forgot the name of the Roman festival that forbids work in Zippori for seven days."

Joseph smiled as he thanked Sarah for the food. It was hard to believe his sister was four years younger than Mary. With dark eyes in a sweet countenance and soft curls escaping her thick braid, she was the younger image of their mother. Sarah was already showing the signs and skills of nearing the age for marriage. She helped with the daily tasks of caring for the family, including preparing the meals.

"It is the festival of Apollo," he selected several pieces of cheese.

"Cheese for me!" Samuel, Joseph's four-year-old nephew, reached for the bowl.

"Samuel, do not demand." Joseph's older brother Clopas said. "You must *ask* your Uncle Joseph."

"I am sorry, Father," the youngster dropped his hands and his gaze. "I am sorry, Uncle Joseph. Please, may I have cheese?"

"Of course you may, Samuel," Joseph smiled. He lowered the bowl to allow the child to choose some cheese, before turning to hand the bowl to Clopas.

"Apollo," Sarah crossed to the other side of the table to place another bowl of cheese between Grandmother Naomi and Grandfather Matthan. "Is he the one the Romans consider the god of the sun?"

Joseph glanced at his father. Talk of pagan gods was not accepted in most Jewish homes. *I imagine Mary's grandmother Tzipora bat Leui would never allow the name of a pagan god to be mentioned in her presence, much less discussed during the family's meal.*

His father glanced at Grandfather Matthan, who nodded. "As

long as we do not follow pagan ways, it does no harm to know *some of what they believe*," he tilted his head toward Samuel, "especially as you work among the Romans."

Joseph nodded. He understood his father's unspoken message. He would not speak of the immoral activities of the pagan gods. He turned back to his sister. "Yes, Apollo is the Roman sun god. His festival is held the last six days of Tamuz and ends on the first day of Av. According to Lucius Septimus, the Romans do not work during this week, but celebrate with sacrifices to Apollo as well as games and feasts. Lucius and his wife are holding a feast at the entrance of their new home. That is one reason he was pleased I finished the dentil for their front door as quickly as I did."

"So, because of a festival to a pagan god," Clopas' wife Mary bat Tovi handed him a platter of bread, still warm from the oven, "you do not earn money for this whole week; yet you have been able to work on the bed chamber for you and your betrothed. That is a strange blessing."

"It is indeed," Joseph grinned, "but I cannot complain. I am nearly finished with *our*," he felt his cheeks redden, "bed chamber."

"Uncle Joseph, why are you blushing?" Samuel asked.

"It is a common trait for young men," Grandfather Matthan grinned as he tore a piece of bread in half, "to blush when thinking of their betrothed wife." He gave Joseph a soft wink.

Joseph's brother and father shared Grandfather Matthan's toothy grin. Clopas clapped Joseph on the back. "We all know he is looking forward to the day Father tells him that it is time to bring Mary bat Eli home as his bride."

Joseph felt his blush deepen. He did not know what to say, especially in front of his sister and nephew.

"Pay no attention to them, Joseph," Grandmother Naomi gave the three other men a stern look before turning a sweet smile to him. "We are indeed looking forward to having Mary join our family."

"Mother Naomi speaks truth," his mother handed him a cup of milk. "We look forward to the day you bring Mary home. She is a sweet young woman."

"None of my friends can say that both of their sisters-in-law are named Mary," Sarah moved to sit opposite Joseph. "When someone calls out, 'Mary,' how will we all know which one is being called?"

"The easiest solution is to use their full names," his mother said. "When you need Clopas' wife," she smiled at her daughter-in-law who was setting a bowl of figs on the table, "you will call for Mary bat Tovi. And when you need Joseph's wife, you will call for Mary bat Eli."

Sarah pursed her mouth in thought. "That sounds formal and not at all like family."

Mary laughed, as she sat opposite Clopas. "Sarah, do not worry. I am sure we will come up with an answer to this problem."

"Joseph," Grandmother Naomi took a sip of milk and set her cup down, "it is almost three months since your betrothal to Mary. You have been working every evening—and now a full week—on your bed chamber," she directed a warning look at the other men. "How soon will it be finished?"

"Soon, Grandmother," Joseph said. "The walls and floor of the room are complete, and the mortar between the stones is drying. I am almost finished with the door. After that, all that is left to build is the furniture for the room. That reminds me," he turned to his father, "we have used most of the olive wood in the shop. I will go to the grove this afternoon and harvest what is left of the tree that fell during the storm."

"Will you need help?" his father selected a fig from the bowl. "That tree was large. Even though much of it is gone, what is left is heavy."

"No," Joseph shook his head. "Thank you, but no; I do not want to take you from the work. I will hitch Hamor up to the cart to haul the wood back here; the donkey is strong enough to pull the load. Beyond that, I wish to do the work myself. When I bring Mary home as my bride, I want her to know *I* prepared the place for her."

"That will bless her," his father smiled.

"It will," his mother agreed. "I have been speaking with Anne bat Samuel."

"Oh? And what does my," Joseph grinned, "betrothed's mother say?"

"Anne tells me that, like you, Mary has been working diligently on the linens and other items for your bed chamber. When you are finished building the furniture, Anne will bring these items. If you wish, she and I will arrange them in your room. We will of course consult you and Mary."

"That would be wonderful, Mother, but there is no need to consult me. While I can build tables, stools, chests and," Joseph felt his cheeks warm again, "a bed, I do not have the skill to arrange linens and other things. I will draw a sketch of the room; you can show it to Mary to get her thoughts." His smile softened, thinking of his betrothed. "I want our bed chamber to be beautiful for her."

Chapter 20

*A*fter the meal was finished, Joseph followed his father, brother, and grandfather to their shop. Joseph grinned, recalling how quickly Grandfather Matthan responded to Grandmother Naomi's mention of needing help in their garden.

"Beloved, I cannot help," he sighed, gesturing to his son and grandsons. "As Joseph is working on his new bed chamber, Jacob and Clopas will need my help with the carpentry. We have several orders, including two plows and a yoke, which need to be finished soon." He followed the explanation with a shrug. "I am sorry. You know otherwise I would be happy to help you."

"Humph!" Grandmother Naomi crossed her arms, eyebrows lowered as she studied her husband. "I have no doubt that you would be *happy* to help me, as I recall pulling weeds is one of your favorite tasks. Samuel," she turned to the young boy, "do you want to help me pull weeds in the garden?"

"Yes, Great-Grandmother!" the child said. "Digging in the dirt is fun."

"You speak truth, Samuel," Joseph tousled his nephew's curls. "Digging in the dirt *is* fun; you never know what treasures you might find." Just as Sarah looked like a younger version of their mother, Samuel looked like a younger version of Clopas.

I wonder whether our children will look like me or like Mary? In the moments when Joseph dreamt of his coming life with Mary—which was frequent—he often wondered about the children they would have. His parents had only had two sons and a daughter. Mary's parents only had two daughters. He would love whatever children Yahweh blessed them with, but Joseph envisioned himself teaching a son the skills needed to follow in the family's trade. He imagined people saying, *"Is this not the carpenter's son?"*

"Father," he asked, "are you sure you do not need me to help with the work this morning?"

"Go," his father waved him off as he picked up an adz. "Clopas and I can manage the work. If we need help," Father lowered his voice, "your grandfather is here." He nodded toward Grandfather Matthan, who had sat down on the bench beneath the window. Hands cupping the head of his walking staff, the older man's eyes were closing.

Joseph knew Grandfather would claim it was to block the light streaming through the window; but he suspected that, in truth, it was to take a morning nap.

"I am certain," Father whispered, "that later he will tell Mother about the work *we* did today."

Joseph shared his father's toothy grin. "I am certain he will." Walking to the table for the tools, Joseph picked up a set of chisels, several cloths from the basket, and a skin filled with olive oil.

Leaving the shop, he crossed the courtyard, past the cooking area—where Mother, his sister-in-law, and his sister were washing the dishes from the meal—to the stairs that led to the roof of the house. He walked up the stairs, crossed the roof to the far corner, where was located the bed chamber he had been building for his betrothed bride. He set the tools next to three buckets. One held lime, the other sand. Joseph had mixed some of the lime and sand— along with water—in the third bucket to make mortar which he used to coat the walls and ceiling of the bed chamber.

He walked to the edge of the roof. The flecks of golden sunshine mingled with the few wispy clouds in the sky. The azure sky over-head showed no signs of rain. It was the perfect weather for building.

From this vantage point, the olive grove outside Nazareth could be seen. That grove would always hold special memories for Joseph and, he felt, for Mary. He imagined the two of them sitting here, looking over the olive grove and speaking of the events that drew them together. He would tell Mary about that day when he had come home from Zippori and had seen her sitting beneath those trees. How Rabbi Boaz had come upon him, and how their con-versation had turned to about his feelings for Mary.

"It is not wrong for a young man to think of taking a bride." Rabbi Boaz had grinned. *"I am correct again, am I not? You are thinking of asking your father to approach Eli ben Matthat with an offer of marriage for Mary?"*

Joseph's heart warmed, remembering his response. *"Yes, Rabbi Boaz; I am."* He had smiled as he looked at Mary. *"She is…everything…I have ever wanted, everything I have prayed for, in a wife. She loves Yahweh; she is an obedient daughter; she works hard, helping both her family and Adina. She is kind and gentle to everyone she meets. And she…"* He had lost his words as he watched Mary continue scratching in the ground.

"And she draws," Rabbi Boaz had said. *"Yahweh blessed Mary with a gift to capture images of things. I have seen a few things she has drawn; they are beautiful. She cannot afford papyrus; I doubt Tzipora bat Leui would permit her to purchase it. Adina tells me that Mary uses drawing—even if it is in the dirt—as a way to calm her spirit and give her mind space to think."*

Voices floating on the wind caught Joseph's attention.

"Great-Grandmother Naomi," Samuel called. "Look what I have done!"

"That is wonderful, Samuel," Joseph heard his grandmother respond. "You have drawn a bird."

Joseph glanced around; the roof top was empty and none of his family was looking his way. Walking back to the bed chamber, he squatted, lifted the bucket of sand, and gently shook it, until the surface of the sand was smooth and even. Setting the bucket down, he picked up the smallest chisel and began moving the point through the sand, forming a single wavy line; followed by other thicker wavy lines on each side; and then a series of large loops on the top.

Sitting back on his heels, he examined his drawing. *Anyone looking at it would think I had merely been scribbling in the sand. No one would know my drawing was supposed to be a flower.* He filled his lungs.

"Joseph ben Jacob, Yahweh did not give you the gift of drawing," he said. He stood and switching the small chisel for a larger one, he began smoothing the wooden frame of the door to his bed chamber. "You are an artisan," he reminded himself, "not an artist."

His hands fell into work, pausing only to exchange the larger chisel for a smaller one. His mind returned to that day in the olive grove. Rabbi Boaz had named him an artisan when he had confessed that he was not like Yared or Mary. *"Rabbi Boaz, why would she want me as a husband?"* he had asked. *"I cannot sing. I cannot play an instrument, and I cannot draw. I am just an ordinary carpenter."*

"No," the rabbi had said. *"It is wrong for you to compare yourself to Yared or any other man. Joseph,"* he had placed a hand on Joseph's shoulder, *let me reassure you; you are no ordinary man. You might not be an artist, but you are a skilled artisan. You might not have the ability to draw with stylus and ink, in wax, or even in the dirt, but you craft things of beauty from wood. Yes, Mary has many unusual skills. The man who marries her will need to accept those skills as blessings from Yahweh."*

"Yahweh," Joseph prayed, "thank You for letting Mary accept me as her betrothed husband. As I am preparing this room for our home, please prepare me. Give me the insight, the patience, and the love to understand Mary and the gifts and skills You have given her. Help me to be the husband she needs. Amen."

Chapter 21

1 Tishri 3758
Feast of Trumpets

*M*ary smiled, greeting friends with, *"Ketivah v'chatima tovah"*— "A good sealing and inscription in the Book of Life"—as her family joined the residents of Nazareth entering the synagogue for the celebration of the Feast of Trumpets.

As Grandfather Matthat, her father, and Zebedee moved into the main room of the synagogue, she followed Grandmother Tzipora, her mother, and Salome—along with James and John—up the stairs to the loft. Because they had arrived early—Grandmother insisted on being early to synagogue assemblies—they were able to find a spot next to the rail of the loft. Mary did not point out that Adina—after Rabbi Boaz escorted her up to the stool next to the rail in women's loft—always saved several places for them.

"Thank you, Adina," Mary smoothed her blue tunic with cream-colored trim and adjusted her head covering of a lighter shade of blue. These were her best garments, the ones she had worn for her betrothal. "I appreciate you saving these for us. Grandmother Tzipora would never mention it," she slanted her eyes toward the elderly lady and lowered her voice, "but I believe the main reason she insists we get here early is due to her height. If she stands behind other women, she cannot see what is going on below."

"I empathize with your honored grandmother," Adina whispered behind her smile. "I cannot stand for long periods of time. If I were sitting in the back, I would not be able to see anything either."

"Are you and Rabbi Boaz still coming to our home tonight?

Grandmother made extra honey and date cakes yesterday. She knows your father likes them."

"That is kind of her. Yes," Adina nodded. "We are looking forward to it. It is thoughtful of your family to invite us. As we do not have family in Nazareth, it is pleasant to spend days of rest with other people." She grinned. "Will Joseph and his family be there?"

"No." Mary shook her head. "It is a tradition in his family to alternate hosting a gathering at each other's homes. All of Joseph's family in Nazareth are gathering at his home this evening."

Mary turned to scan the men and older boys gathering on the main floor until she found Joseph.

Like the other men, he was dressed in his best garments, the ones he had worn to their betrothal: robe, girdle, and turban the color of oak wood over a cream-colored tunic, tassels made of blue cords and tassels attached to the corners of his garments. Joseph looked up—as if she had called his name—and caught her eye. He smiled, his gaze tender.

She returned his smile, her heart echoing the warmth in his countenance. *This is the last time I will celebrate the Feast of Trumpets as a betrothed woman.* Thoughts similar to this had become common for Mary to ponder as the time drew closer to the day Joseph would come and take her home as his bride. *Who knows; with Yahweh's blessing, perhaps this time next year, I will be carrying a child.*

Her attention was drawn to the sounds of footsteps echoing down the corridor. Everyone stood as Rabbi Boaz entered, carrying the scrolls of Holy Scripture. Yared followed, carrying a *shofar* made from a long, curled ram's horn.

After the traditional presentation of the scrolls, the two men crossed the floor to step up on the bimah. Rabbi Boaz laid the scrolls on the reading desk while Yared moved a pace away. The older man smiled, gazing around the room at the assembly of people. Lifting his arms wide, he said,

"Shout for joy to the Lord, all the earth, burst into jubilant song with music; make music to the Lord with the harp, with the harp and the sound of singing, with trumpets and the blast of the ram's horn— shout for joy before the Lord, the King."

Yared lifted the shofar, placing the smallest end on his closed lips. Filling his lungs, he blew a long, loud blast.

Its majestic sound resonated throughout the synagogue, and in Mary's heart. With the first tone of the shofar, she saw colors pulsing in the air.

As the final note died, the hazzan lowered the shofar.

"Today is the Feast of Trumpets," Rabbi Boaz said. "It is a High Holy Day, decreed by Yahweh to be celebrated on the first day of Tishri."

The rabbi opened the scroll and read, "In the book of the Law, the Lord said to Moses, *Say to the Israelites: "On the first day of the seventh month you are to have a day of sabbath rest, a sacred assembly commemorated with trumpet blasts. Do no regular work, but present a food offering to the Lord."*

"Today is a day when we celebrate and acknowledge Yahweh as the King of Heaven and of Earth."

The rabbi began teaching on the purpose of the Feast, interspersed with readings from the Holy Scripture and with Yared blowing the shofar.

As all Jewish people, Mary had heard this teaching many times, from her parents and grandparents, during the synagogue assembly each year on the Feast of Trumpets, and during times she was visiting Adina.

The synagogue assembly for this High Holy Day had three main portions. The first was a celebration of Yahweh ascending the Throne of Heaven. Yared's first trumpet blast had been to announce the crowning of Yahweh as King and the beginning of the new year.

After Rabbi Boaz finished this portion of the service, Yared lifted the shofar and blew three times—a broken sound, as if someone were crying.

"The Feast of Trumpets is also a time of divine judgment," Rabbi Boaz continued, "when the destiny of the world is fixed. On this day, we celebrate Yahweh as the sole Creator of the world, and we celebrate His ascending the Throne of Heaven and ruling over all creation. It is also on this day, we also acknowledge Yahweh as the righteous Judge Who dispenses justice for all humankind. It is on this day when Yahweh opens the Books of Life and Death for the year."

Mary had been taught that this was a time when everyone was to examine their hearts, confess their sins, and prepare for the judgement that will come on the Day of Atonement—ten days hence—when the High Priest enters the Most Holy Place in the Temple and offers sacrifice for the sins of the nation.

Bowing her head, Mary prayed, *Yahweh; Almighty God of Heaven and of Earth, may Your Name be glorified. Thank You for the blessings You have given me. Please forgive me for the times I have not been obedient to Your Law, to my parents, and to my grandparents.* She thought about the time several months ago in the olive grove, when she suppressed laughter at Grandmother Tzipora being put out of countenance at Rabbi Boaz' explanation of why Mary knew the meaning of that point in the Law Yahweh gave to Moses. *Please forgive me for the times I have been less than respectful to Grandmother Tzipora.* Even though she had not meant to be disrespectful, Mary felt it best to ask forgiveness for even unintentional sins.

She continued praying until Rabbi Boaz led the assembly in an "Amen."

Yared lifted the shofar to his lips and blew a series of thirty blasts.

"The Feast of Trumpets is when we honor Yahweh as King and Judge," Rabbi Boaz continued. "It is also when we look *with hope* to the coming of Yahweh's Chosen One, the Messiah." He extended his arms. "Oh Holy One; we await Your coming."

Lowering his arms, he looked at the assembled people. *"Leshana tovah tikatev v'tichatem"*—"May you be written and sealed for a good year."

Mary joined the others as they responded, "Amen!"

Yared lifted the shofar once again and blew a long, great blast. The horn's sound echoed in Mary's ears like a proclamation of hope.

Chapter 22

*J*oseph tried to focus on Rabbi Boaz's teaching about the Feast of Trumpets, but throughout the assembly, his attention drifted to Mary.

His heart had quickened when they exchanged glances before the assembly began. Even though the loft was filled with women and young boys, Mary stood out.

This beautiful woman is my betrothed wife. That thought still amazed him. While he considered her the most beautiful of all women he had ever seen, he recognized her beauty was more than hair, face, or figure. Her beauty was in her quiet and gentle spirit; in her desire to help others; in her affection for her family and for Adina and Rabbi Boaz; in her devotion and love for Yahweh. *This* beauty had drawn Joseph to Mary. *This* beauty made him love her. *This* beauty made him want to return that love as her husband.

He noticed movement among the women near Mary. Sarai bat Zebah, Rachel bat Daniel, Martha bat Gilad, Bityah bat Abijah—and the other young women in the loft—brightened, smiled, straightened their garments, and smoothed their head coverings as they tried to move closer to the rail. Joseph did not need to hear the echo of footsteps, nor turn his head, to know what had caused their response.

Yared ben Arieh had entered the room.

His eyes shifted back to Mary. Her hands had not moved to her garments nor hair, but her gaze shifted from him to the two men who had entered the main room.

He had lifted his chin as he turned around. *She is betrothed to me.* He stamped firmly on the momentary rekindling of—*I will not name it* jealousy—as Yared followed Rabbi Boaz as the older man circled the room, presenting the scrolls of Holy Scripture. *Mary did not respond to Yared as did the women around her. She is watching Rabbi Boaz and preparing to worship Yahweh.*

Joseph's response to Rabbi Boaz's readings, the prayers—and even to Yared blowing the shofar—was as natural as breathing, stemming from his upbringing and the years he spent in the synagogue classes. During the time of the assembly, when they recognized Yahweh as the Divine Judge, Joseph bowed his head to confess his sins.

Almighty Yahweh, may Your Name be glorified in all the earth and in my life. Thank You for Your blessings; my family—his heart swelled—*my betrothed wife.* He remembered the women's response to Yared. *Forgive me for,* he filled his lungs, *being jealous of Yared.* He remembered the day when Rabbi Boaz had told him, "It is wrong for you to compare yourself to Yared. *Yahweh,* he continued praying, *forgive me for comparing myself to Yared or to any other man. Forgive me for feeling less than what You created me to be.*

During the remainder of the assembly, Joseph felt his spirit lift, and when Rabbi Boaz spoke the final blessing, "Leshana tovah tikatev v'tichatem," he joined the others with a heart-felt, "Amen!"

Chapter 23

*T*he golden sun warmed the afternoon sky, casting shadows amongst the olive grove.

Mary walked among the ancient trees, touching gnarled trunks to steady herself as she stepped around puddles of water from a recent rain, lifting a branch to walk beneath it, noting the weight of ripened olives amongst slender, sliver-green leaves—*it will be an abundant harvest this year*—until she came to her favorite spot. Located on the edge of the grove, the trees provided shade from the sunlight but did not block the vista of nature's beauty nor the sight of Nazareth.

She sat down, placing a small basket filled with grapes and bread on the ground next to her, and sighed with pleasure. One blessing of the Feast of Trumpets was that Yahweh commanded it to be a day free from work. Grandmother Tzipora had overseen the preparation of all food the day before, including the extra food for tonight's meal, as well as small baskets of fruit and bread as a special blessing for each family member. During the meal, Grandfather Matthat reminded them that, beginning with the seventh hour on The Feast of Trumpets—when their fates are already written—until The Day of Atonement—when their fates for the coming year are to be sealed—they were to wish each other *"Gemar chatimah tovah"*—"A good final sealing." After the meal, he released the family to spend the remainder of the day resting as they wished. "For me," he would grin, picking up his basket of grapes and bread, "that means a nap."

For Mary, resting meant walking in the olive grove. After changing into a brown tunic and green head covering—she would never wear her best garments to sit beneath a tree—she walked down the ravine outside of Nazareth and up the slope to the olive grove.

Leaning against the tree's trunk, her gaze sought the location of Joseph's home across the ravine on the edge of the village. On top was the frame of a new room. *Our bed chamber,* she smiled. Squinting, she thought saw movement near the room and waved. When she had spoken to Joseph after the synagogue assembly that morning, he had asked how she was spending her afternoon. After she told him she wanted to rest in the olive grove, he confided he would be carving something special.

"It does not violate Yahweh's Law; carving is as restful for me," he smiled, "as drawing is restful to you."

"I will look for you," she smiled shyly, "and wave."

He returned her smile. "I will wave to you."

During the five months of their betrothment, according to tradition, she and Joseph had never spent time alone. They frequently visited between their homes where, under the supervision of their families, they spent time getting to know each other better and making plans for their future. When his family had come to her home, she had shown Joseph and his parents some of the things she and Adina had made or items she was gathering for their bed chamber. When her family visited Joseph's home, he had escorted her and her parents up the stairs to the roof and showed them the nearly completed room. He did not open the door for her to see inside, nor did she expect it. That would happen once Joseph came to take her home as his wife.

Of course, Mary's smile widened into a grin, *Joseph will not come for me without first notifying our families.* During the visits, she had noted the older women of their families whispering behind their hands. Her mother would often ask Mother Leah to step outside to see their garden. On several occasions, Grandmother Naomi invited Grandmother Tzipora to accompany her to the marketplace to purchase spices for a particular meal. During the times their families were together, Mary would focus her attention on other things, knowing the women of their families were discussing the details of their wedding celebration.

Once their bed chamber was finished and the details of the wedding feast ready, Father Jacob would send Joseph for her.

She picked a grape from the basket. "Thank You, Yahweh," she whispered, "for the beauty of this holy day. For the time when we celebrate You as our King and our Righteous Judge. Thank You for the hope of our coming Messiah. Thank You for Your blessings of life," her eyes swept the vista, "for the beauty of Your creation," she looked at the house on the edge of Nazareth, "and for family. Amen."

She ate a few grapes, relishing the fruits' sweet, refreshing taste. Out of the corner of her eye, a movement caught her attention; a butterfly flitted down to land near a small puddle of water.

The creature's delicate wings were iridescent blue with silver tips, the blue reminiscent of the cords and tassels the men wore on the corners of their garments. She smiled. With Adina's help, she had woven a prayer shawl in those colors for Joseph. She planned to give it to him during their wedding celebration.

Moving so as not to startle the butterfly, she shifted to a kneeling position, picked up a stick, and began drawing. *I wish I had brought my wax tablet and stylus with me. I could have shown my drawing of this butterfly to Joseph.* She smiled, imagining his encouraging words, praising her ability, making light-hearted comments about her ability to draw and his lack of artistic skill.

Thank You, Yahweh, for Joseph. Thank You that he understands my love of the beauty You created and my desire to capture it in drawing.

Sandal-clad feet beneath the hem of a white robe appeared in front of her.

She dropped the stick and sat upright on her knees, keeping her gaze lowered, waiting for Grandmother's blistering chastisement.

"Greetings."

Mary gasped at the deep, resonate voice. Her head snapped up, eyes widening at the sight of the man standing before her.

Taller and broader than any man she had ever seen, his bearing was that of a warrior. But it was not just his form that startled her. Dressed in luminous white garments, his hair whipped wildly from a noble brow, although the leaves of the trees around them were still. She could not name the color of his eyes, but every part of the man was as white as his garments, his skin shimmering a radiant light as if from within, making the sun behind him appear dim.

Mary fell backwards and—her terrified gaze never leaving the man—scrabbled behind the trunk of the olive tree. The icy grip of panic froze her to the spot where she cowered. She would have screamed, except her throat had constricted too much to produce sound. *Yahweh, protect me, Yahweh protect me.*

"Mary." The man's voice resounded as if he were a multitude instead of one. "Do not be afraid." He extended a shining hand.

Mary shrunk back. "What…" she rasped "Who are you?"

"I am Gabriel."

"Gabriel?" Her brow furrowed. "You are named for the angel Yahweh sent to the prophet Daniel?"

"I am," the man lifted his hand to place it on his chest, his smile was gentle, "Gabriel."

She gaped, as realization washed over her.

The angel—for that is what this luminous being was—smiled. "Greetings, you who are highly favored. The Lord is with you."

"Highly favored? The Lord is with—me?" She ran her tongue over her lips. "I do not understand."

"Come, Mary. Sit." The angel pointed to the spot near her basket.

Keeping a wary eye on the angelic being, Mary moved to where the shining hand pointed. She picked up the basket and held it against her, as if trying to draw comfort from the simple earthbound object, absently noticing the butterfly had not flown away, but was crawling over the grapes and bread. "You are Gabriel, the messenger of Yahweh?"

The angel nodded, smiling. "I am."

"What do you want with me?"

"Do not be afraid, Mary," the angel's countenance softened. "You have found favor with Yahweh. You will conceive and give birth to a Son, and you are to call Him Jesus. He will be great," the angelic voice echoed, "and will be called the Son of the Most High. The Lord God will give Him the throne of His father David, and He will reign over Jacob's descendants forever; His kingdom will never end."

With the angel's first words, Mary's brow slanted downward again—as if he were speaking an unknown language—but as he continued, her eyes widened, and her mouth gaped. *The Son of the Most High. The throne of His father David…that can only be…* Her heart threatened to beat out of her chest. "Do you mean," she dropped the basket into her lap and leaned forward, "I am to be… the mother of…the Messiah?"

"You are."

Me! Lifting her hands, she cupped her cheeks, rocking in wonderment. *I am going to be the mother of the Messiah. I am going to be the mother of the Messiah. Wait…Gabriel did not mention…* She looked up at the angel. "…and Joseph will be…his father?"

The angel shook his head. "No."

"I do not understand," she frowned. "I am betrothed to Joseph… we have not…how will this be," she blushed, "since I am a virgin?"

"The Holy Spirit will come on you," the angel said, "and the power of the Most High will overshadow you. So, the Holy One to be born will be called the Son of Yahweh."

She shook her head, trying to understand how this all could be possible. As she opened her mouth, the angel continued. "Even Elizabeth, your relative, is going to have a child in her old age, and she who was said to be unable to conceive is in her sixth month."

"Elizabeth?" Mary smiled. *She and Zechariah have prayed for a child for years,* "is going to have a child?"

"Yes," Gabriel nodded. "For no word from God will ever fail."

The Son of the Most High. Elizabeth is with child. The mother of the Messiah. What will I say? How will I explain it? Thousands of questions swirled through her mind, finally settling on one statement Gabriel made. *"The Lord is with you."* If Yahweh chose her, if He was with her, then nothing else mattered.

Setting the basket aside, Mary knelt. "I am the Lord's servant." She lowered her eyes, extending her arms to each side. "May your word to me be fulfilled."

The butterfly spread its delicate wings and flew to land on her outstretched hand. A moment later, another butterfly joined it; then another. She looked upwards as a myriad of butterflies joined the first one, swirling around the angel and her, their wings brushing her skin, her hair, the clapping of a thousand wings breaking the silence, sounding like water cascading over a waterfall. Mary felt wonder permeate her being, a warmth coursing from her heart to her abdomen.

As the butterflies swirled skyward, Gabriel extended brilliant white wings, like those of a majestic eagle, and ascended in a cloud of shimmering, delicate wings.

Chapter 24

*T*he golden sun warmed the afternoon sky, the fluffy clouds casting shadows over Nazareth and Joseph's home.

Joseph had chosen a spot on the rooftop near the room he had built for Mary and himself—*our bed chamber*, he smiled—where he could look across the ravine to the olive grove outside Nazareth.

He sat on a small stool behind a wooden chest. On a small table nearby were his tools, a skin filled with oil, several rags, along with a jar filled with water, a cup, and a small basket. Yesterday, the women of his family—like all the women in Nazareth—had not only prepared the food for today's feast and tonight's family gathering, but had also made extra food for their family. Each person in his household had baskets filled with bread and cheese. After the meal, when Grandfather Matthan released the family with, "Gemar chatimah tovah," he encouraged everyone to spend the day resting. For most of Joseph's family, that meant napping in their bed chambers. Sarah had mentioned wanting to spend time sewing decorative trim on one of her tunics. *Sarah is becoming quite a young woman*, he smiled, imagining his sister quietly sewing, compared to several years ago, when his sister considered needlework something to be avoided.

Joseph lifted a hand to shield his eyes as he squinted at the olive grove. He thought he saw movement and waved. When he had spoken to Mary after the synagogue assembly that morning, she told him she planned to spend time in the olive grove. He had confided spending the afternoon carving something special. He remembered her smile when he explained that carving was as restful to him as drawing was to her.

That something special was the wooden chest in front of him.

There had been a small amount of olive wood left after he had built their bed frame. He decided to use the wood to build a decorative chest for Mary. It was too small to store garments, but perhaps Mary would want to use it to store her comb and ties for her hair, or maybe her tablet and stylus for drawing. It was simple in shape and design. However, knowing his betrothed bride's love for beautiful things, he had decided to carve roses on the corners of the lid. He was almost finished with the last rose. His plan was to leave the chest in their bed chamber and give it to Mary during their wedding celebration.

"Thank You, Yahweh, for Mary. For a betrothed wife who loves You, who wants to serve You, and to be a blessing to those around her. I know that one day, should You bless us with children," he smiled, "she will be a wonderful mother."

Setting aside the small chisel, he tilted his chin upward, stretched his neck, and rubbed his eyes. As he lowered his face, movement caught his attention.

Looking closer, he saw someone running—almost stumbling—down the slope from the olive grove, waving their arms.

Mary!

Panic shot through him like an arrow from a warrior's bow. Knocking over his stool as he jumped up, he grabbed the largest chisel from the table. He had not seen anyone chasing Mary, but that did not mean she was not in danger. Lions could hide among the trees and rocks, and a viper's bite could kill in moments. Whether creature or man, Joseph was prepared to defend Mary from whatever had sent her running toward him. Darting across the rooftop, he took the stairs two at a time, raced across the courtyard, and through the door of his home. Turning, he ran toward the ravine and his beloved.

Nazareth was less than a Sabbath's day journey from end to end—and Joseph's home was on the edge of the village—but Joseph felt as if he were running all the way to Zippori. His heart raced, blood pounding in his ears, his prayers spilling over his lips keeping cadence with his feet, "Yahweh protect her. Yahweh protect her. Yahweh protect her." As he drew closer, he could see Mary holding the edge of her garments with one hand, while waving the other hand as she called,

"Joseph! Joseph!"

Joseph reached her in the bottom of the ravine. "Mary, Mary, do not worry. I am here." In one swift movement, he grabbed her by the arms and shoved her behind him as he turned—chisel held before him as a weapon—to face whatever was following. He could not see anyone or anything. "Mary," he asked over his shoulder, "where is it? What are you running from? A snake? A lion?"

"No." She stepped away from him, bent over—placing her hands on her knees—and drew in deep, ragged breaths. "No," she shook her head and straightened. "I wanted to tell you what *he* told me."

"He?" He scanned the area of the ravine, the slope, to the edge of the tree line, but he could see no one. "Mary, I do not see anyone. Where is he?"

Mary filled her lungs and blew them out. "He is gone."

"Gone? Where did he go?"

She lifted a hand to point upwards. "There."

"There?" Joseph's brows creased in confusion. "What do you mean?"

"He ascended," Mary's face took on a look of wonder, "into the sky."

Joseph's brows crept upwards. "He did *what*?"

"The angel," Mary looked upward, "ascended into the sky."

He shook his head. "The…angel?" He spoke the words as if he pronounced them for the first time.

"Yes," Mary lowered her head to meet his gaze. "An angel."

"Mary," he shoved the chisel behind the folds of his girdle and rubbed his eyes, "what are you saying?"

"Joseph," she smiled, "the angel Gabriel appeared to me."

Joseph caught his breath, his eyes widening, as Mary spoke of butterflies, the winged angel, and his message.

When she got to the end, she paused and waited.

He frowned, looking at Mary.

"Joseph?" she echoed his frown. "Say something."

"What," he shook his head again, "…should I say? What you tell me is beyond belief."

"I agree it is hard to believe," Mary laughed. "I was there, and I still have difficulty believing it, and not just his message about me." She shook her head. "Even though Elizabeth and Zechariah are in their old age, they are to be blessed with a child.

"I spoke with the angel Gabriel. I am to be," she extended her hands before her, palms up, "the mother of the *Messiah*. And we are to name Him…"

"No! Mary!" Joseph lifted a hand, stopping her words. "The only ones to name a child are his mother and father. From what *you* say the angel told you, *I* am to have nothing to do with *your* conceiving this child. If I am not to be His *father*, how can I name him?"

"The angel said that Yahweh—"

"Stop!" he clapped his hands in front of her face.

Mary blinked. "Joseph," confusion covered her countenance, "do you not believe me?"

"Believe?" He frowned. "Believe? You tell me an angel appears to you, tells you that," he swept his hand toward the village, "of *all* the women in Nazareth, *you* have been chosen to be the mother of the Messiah."

"Yes," she nodded, "but—"

"And that is not all," he cut her off. "Not only are *you* to be this child's mother. *Yahweh* is to be His father."

"Yes," she spoke the word slowly, her gaze never leaving his face.

"The Messiah is not going to be the son of a man—He is not going to be the child of my body—but the Son of Yahweh?"

"Yes," she nodded.

"And the *angel Gabriel* told you this."

"Yes. Joseph," her brows slanted in a frown. "You believe me, do you not? You and Rabbi Boaz both said you believed either Adina or I could be the mother of the Messiah."

"*After* I took you home as my bride," he flung up his hands. "*After*! This," he pointed toward the olive grove, "is a fantastical tale such as one would hear in Zippori. You are suggesting that Yahweh," he pivoted, jabbing a finger toward the city set on the hill, "is like the pagan Roman gods who take the form of a man and impregnant human women."

"No!" Mary gasped. "Joseph, how could you think I would suggest such…such…"

"Blasphemy?" Joseph frowned. "How could I think you would suggest such *blasphemy*? I will tell you how. You have gone *mad!*" The word echoed between the slopes of the ravine.

Chapter 25

*L*ook, Rabbi Boaz!" John pointed toward the night sky. "There is Tzedek, and there is the mazzaloth of Labi, the lion. The lion is the symbol of the tribe of Judah. That is the tribe of King David." He thumbed his chest. "It is our tribe too, because our family is descended from King David."

Even though Mary's heart was breaking, she shared a smile with Adina over John's comments. *Such innocence, taking pride in his family lineage.*

"John, the lion is the symbol of all the residents of Nazareth," James huffed, crossing his arms, "because everyone in Nazareth is descended from King David."

"You are both correct, John ben Zebedee," the rabbi nodded. "The prophet Moses mentioned a lion when he wrote about Father Jacob blessing his sons."

Adina leaned over to whisper to Mary. "Father is ever the teacher. Even though the preparation for celebrating the Feast of Trumpets fatigues him, Father loves any opportunity to share his knowledge."

Mary had arrived home late in the late afternoon. Weary in body and spirit, her heart heavy, her mind filled with the weight of Gabriel's appearance and Joseph's response, all she wanted was to seek her bed to ponder the thoughts that had attacked her as she walked home. *Did I really see the angel Gabriel? I am truly to be the mother of the Messiah? Gabriel said the power of Yahweh will overshadow me; what will that feel like? Joseph does not believe me.* Tears trembled on her lashes. *He thinks I am mad. What will he do? What will he say? How can I convince him I am not insane?*

But she could not spend the rest of the day alternating between weeping and sleeping. Rabbi Boaz and Adina were due to arrive for the evening meal. She whispered, "Yahweh, help me," before going to her room to wash away her dirt and tears, change into fresh garments, and re-braid her hair before going to help lay out the food they had cooked yesterday.

Her family's attention was focused on preparing for their guests. No one noticed her reserved demeanor, nor asked about her afternoon, for which Mary was thankful. *What could I tell them? If my betrothed husband does not believe me, how can I expect my family to believe what he called a fantastical tale?*

Rabbi Boaz and Adina arrived as the setting sun was casting long shadows over their home. Taking a deep breath and holding it for a moment, she exhaled slowly, smiled, and joined her family in the custom of welcoming their guests.

After Grandfather Matthat welcomed Rabbi Boaz and Adina to their home, the guests sat on a small bench near the door to remove their shoes. James offered them a basin of water to wash their feet and John offered the towels to dry them. Once they retied their sandals, Grandfather Matthat picked up a small amphora and poured a drop of olive oil onto their heads. Grandmother Tzipora followed by offering cups of cool water. Mary's mother and father completed the act of honoring guests by helping them stand and kissing their cheeks.

While Rabbi Boaz spoke to Zebedee and Salome, Mary embraced Adina. "Welcome, my heart-sister."

"What is wrong?" Adina whispered into Mary's ear. "You seem… sad. Did something happen?"

What do I tell her? 'The Angel Gabriel appeared to me and told me I was to be the mother of the Messiah, and when I told Joseph, he thought I am insane.' I cannot tell her that. Yet, I will not lie. All that passed through her mind in the beat of her heart. "I am just fatigued."

"Ah…" Adina smiled. "Much goes into preparing for the Feast of Trumpets. When the Holy Ten Days of Awe come in the midst of preparing for your wedding, I can understand how it would be fatiguing."

Any other conversation was cut off by Grandmother inviting their guests to the table. Mary led Adina to a cushion next to hers at the end of the table. During the preparation for the evening, Grandmother Tzipora had insisted that Adina, being a guest, should sit at the head of the table near her, but Grandfather Matthat had intervened.

"Beloved, Rabbi Boaz and Adina are more than guests; they are as family. While I have no doubt Adina would politely join in a conversation about the harvest," he turned to grin at Mary, "I am certain she would prefer talking with Mary about things close to the heart of younger women."

Grandfather spoke the blessing over the simple meal; platters of bread, and bowls of cheese, grapes, and cucumbers placed around the table, along with jars of water and milk. Adina and Rabbi Boaz had brought a large platter of honey cakes Adina had baked the day before. The conversation was as light as the meal; comments about the morning's assembly, how each had spent their afternoon, and news about their neighbors.

After the meal, Grandfather invited everyone to the courtyard, to sit around the fire. The new moon was a creamy sliver amongst brilliant stars scattered across the black expanse of the sky. It was then John had drawn Rabbi Boaz's attention to the stars, pointing out the mazzaloth of Labi, followed by James reminding his younger brother that everyone in Nazareth was descended from King David.

"You are both correct, sons of Zebedee," the rabbi had nodded. "The prophet Moses mentioned a lion when he wrote about Father Jacob blessing his sons."

"Rabbi Boaz, is that when Father Jacob was very old?" James asked.

The rabbi nodded. "You are correct, James. Moses wrote of the time Father Jacob was about to die. He had called his sons to bless them and to tell them what would happen to each of them in the days to come. His blessings were filled with wonderous imagery; some encouraging, others less than encouraging. When it came Judah's turn, Father Jacob described his son as a lion.

He extended his arms wide. "*You are a lion's cub, Judah,*" the rabbi's voice carried across the courtyard, "*you return from the prey, my son. Like a lion he crouches and lies down, like a lioness—who dares to* rouse him? *The scepter will not depart from Judah, nor the ruler's staff from between his feet, until he to whom it belongs shall come and the obedience of the nations shall be his.*"

He lowered his arms. "Many of our people's elders and Teachers of the Law believe that, in speaking to his son Judah, Father Jacob was prophesying about the coming of the Messiah."

Mary's heart skipped at the rabbi's last word. *Will it always be thus, my heart leaping at any mention of Messiah?*

The conversation drifted back to discussions of events important to Nazareth. When it came time for Rabbi Boaz and Adina to leave, Mary's father would not hear of them walking home. He hitched Aton to their wagon, and he and Zebedee drove their guests back to their house.

After bidding farewell to their guests with the traditional, "A good final sealing," Mary's mother draped an arm across her shoulder. "I have not had time to speak privately with you, but you look tired."

Mary laid her head on her mother's shoulder. "I am tired, Mother."

"Is it the plans for the wedding? Are they too much for you? You do not wish to get ill. I will ask your father to speak with Joseph and ask him—"

"No!" Mary cut off her mother, "Uh, I mean…there is no need for Father to speak to Joseph." *That cannot be allowed to happen. I do not know what Joseph would tell Father.*

Mother's brown furrowed. "You are certain?"

"I am certain. Please, Mother. As you say, I am just tired."

"Then you must rest."

"I will. Good night, Mother."

"Good night," her mother kissed her forehead, "my sweet Mary."

Mary crossed the empty courtyard to her bed chamber. Placing her hand on the door, she saw the ring on her finger. Wearied by far more than what had been the longest day of her entire life, she turned to lean against the door and slide down to the ground. Tilting her head to stare at the sky, she relived each moment of the afternoon: The butterfly. The appearance of Gabriel. *You have found favor with Yahweh. You will conceive and give birth to a Son, and you are to call Him Jesus.* Her questions. *Elizabeth is with child.* Running to Joseph. Telling him the news. His reaction. *Blasphemy?" You have gone mad!*

Tears flowed down her cheeks as she remembered the stabbing pain from Joseph's accusation. "Yahweh, please help me," she whispered. "Please show me what I must do, what I can say to convince Joseph that I am neither lying nor mad." She remembered her last words to Gabriel. Wiping away the tears, she looked upward. "Yahweh, I am Your servant." She lifted her arms as a babe would to her parent. "May Your word to me be fulfilled."

Mary's eyes widened as, once again, she heard the single, soft *voice* singing the unknown language. It was the same song she had heard months before; first the one voice, to be joined by other voices. It had the timbre of Gabriel's voice. It sounded like the rush of the wings of countless butterflies. For a timeless moment, the sadness of her meeting with Joseph washed away. A refreshing balm poured deep into her soul, echoing the angel's announcement, "The Lord is with you."

Chapter 26

Gatherings were a joy for Joseph's family. Even though they saw each other frequently—in each other's homes, in the marketplace, during synagogue assemblies, or just passing in the streets—whenever they were all together, there was lots of food, fun, laughter, and stories that began with, "Do you remember when…?" From what Joseph could tell of his limited experience with Mary's family, their gatherings were not as joyful, due—in his opinion—to her Grandmother Tzipora. He had looked forward to the day when Mary could experience joy and laughter without fear of chastisement.

Joseph moved amongst his family—the ones who lived in his home as well as his grandparents, aunts, uncles, and cousins from his mother's side—smiling, talking, even eating, as if nothing were wrong. As if his life had not been shattered as an alabastron struck by a mallet.

After his family left with a flurry of embraces and well-wishes for "A good final sealing," Joseph bid his parents a good night and crossed the courtyard to walk up to the roof. Walking to the edge of his house, he picked up the stool he had knocked over in his haste to reach Mary. Setting it against the outer wall of the nearly completed room—*Will it ever be our bed chamber*—he slumped down on it.

His face ached from the smile plastered against his face all afternoon, holding back the scream that demanded release. Joseph clasped his head between his hands, as if he could squeeze out the memory of the events between himself and Mary.

Seeing Mary running toward him. Fearful that she was being chased by a lion or snake. *Would that it had been a lion. I would have willingly died fighting it.*

Mary's announcement. "I spoke with the angel Gabriel."

An angel?

"I am to be the mother of the Messiah."

That I could believe. As Rabbi Boaz said, if anyone were to ask him who could be the mother of the Messiah, he would name Adina or Mary,

But that was not all.

"*The child will be the Son of Yahweh,*" Mary had said. "*We are to call him…*"

He had cut her off. "*I am to have nothing to do with your conceiving this child.*" He had retorted. "*If I am not to be his father, how can I name him?*"

It was the first time he had ever spoken harshly to Mary. His stomach wrenched as if twisted by a blacksmith's pincher. *I likened her story to one told of the pagan Roman gods.* But the shock and pain on Mary's face when she asked how he could believe such a thing did not stop his words.

"*How could I think you would suggest such blasphemy? I will tell you how. You have gone mad!*"

It repeated in his mind. *Angel. Mother of the Messiah. Son of Yahweh. I am not to be his father. I cannot name him. Pagan Roman gods. Blasphemy? You have gone mad!*

As painful as the events of the afternoon were, what threatened to destroy Joseph was the thought, *What do I do now? Yahweh,* he prayed, *as much as I love her, how can I marry a woman who is either a blasphemer or insane?*

Chapter 27

10 Tishri 3758
The Day of Atonement

$\mathcal{M}$ary woke to threads of sunlight tickling her eyes. Through slitted lids, she saw light peeking through the shutters and slanting across her bed chamber. *Praise Yahweh for sunlight.* It had rained steadily for the last nine days. She stifled a yawn and closed her eyes again, wishing for just a little more sleep.

Yet, she knew she could not stay in bed. Although the Law Yahweh gave Moses stated the Day of Atonement was to be a day of rest from work, her family would join the other residents of Nazareth at the synagogue assembly for the readings of scriptures concerning the Holy Day. It did not matter that Adina would save spaces for them in the loft as she always did; Grandmother Tzipora would insist they arrive early.

I need to arise and dress.

Mary took a breath as shallow as a puddle after a brief rain. *That feels alright.* She drew in a bit more air. *That feels alright.* Sighing softly, she breathed in deeply, relishing the fresh air, drinking in more, until a wave of nausea lashed back.

In one swift movement, she turned, grabbed the bucket she had placed on the floor, and emptied her stomach. After an eternity of retching, she set the bucket down, patted the table next to her bed to locate the bowl that held a damp cloth, and rolled onto her back to wipe her mouth with a trembling hand.

It had been nine days since the Feast of Trumpets and Gabriel's visit. That moment—from drawing the butterfly, to Gabriel appearing, her terror, his announcement, her response, his ascension amidst the swirling cloud of butterflies—was etched in her mind as deeply as the fissures in the bark of the olive tree she had crouched behind when she first saw Gabriel. She smiled at her choice of protection. *As if that ancient tree could shield me from an angel sent from Yahweh.*

Although it had been less than a month—not time enough for her to miss her monthly flow—Mary was noticing changes in her body. She tired easily and would retire to her bed chamber whenever possible for a quick nap. She had bouts of dizziness. She was hungry all the time, yet certain foods—such as those seasoned with coriander, dill, or garlic—would trigger nausea. Nausea was as a common companion, provoked from many things; smells, quick movement, even deep breaths.

She thought she was keeping these changes hidden, but her mother had noticed.

The Law Yahweh gave to Moses required everyone to fast on the Day of Atonement. In preparation for the fast, on the night before—like other Jewish families—her family consumed a large meal. Grandmother Tzipora had overseen the meal preparation; it took most of the day.

After Grandfather Matthat had spoken the blessing, the family filled their plates from bowls of cheese, lentils, cucumbers, and leeks, and several platters of bread. Mary had put some of each food on her plate, but she ate only a small amount of cheese and a piece of bread.

"Mary," Mother had stood, and picked up an empty platter covered with breadcrumbs, "would you please help me refill everyone's cups?"

"Yes, Mother." Mary had lifted an empty bowl that had held cucumbers, and crossed the room to the tables next to the door. Setting the bowl on the table, she had turned to reach for the amphora of milk.

"What is wrong?" Mother's voice had been low, even though the room resonated with laughter and conversation.

A thrill of alarm had shot up Mary's spine. What does Mother mean? What does she know? Has Joseph spoken to her and Father? *She had developed a sudden interest in a chip at the base of the amphora. "I do not know what you mean."*

Mother had taken her time filling the smaller amphorae with water from the large one in the center of the table. "We cooked a large meal in preparation for tomorrow's fast, yet you have eaten almost nothing." *Her brows lowered. "Are you ill?"*

"No, Mother, I am not ill." Mary remembered controlling her features, thinking, That is not a lie. Pregnancy is not an illness. *"I am weary. We have been working all day preparing for tomorrow."*

"That is true," Mother had set the amphora down, *"but I think it is more than fatigue."* She began re-arranging the honey cakes on a platter. *"Since your betrothal, you have been working hard to prepare for the day Joseph comes for you. Indeed, you both have been working hard, so hard that you have not seen Joseph since the Feast of Trumpets. It is not wrong to miss your betrothed husband."*

The morning following Mary's encounter with Gabriel and her disastrous meeting with Joseph, he had sent a message to her father. It read:

"Joseph bar Jacob to Eli ben Matthat, Anne bat Samuel, and Mary bat Eli.

Greetings.

There is a special project in Zippori that will take me many hours to complete. I will be spending long days in Zippori and will be arriving home too late to visit with Mary. I will see her and you all on the Day of Atonement."

Mary had gazed at the floor while her father read Joseph's note, doing her best to control her features. Her family expressed concern, knowing she would be saddened to not see her betrothed husband for ten days. She could not let her family know that not seeing Joseph for a time was a relief. She did not know how he would react to her nor what he would say. Beyond his response to me, Mary had confessed to herself, I do not know how I would respond to Joseph.

"You speak truth, Mother." Mary had kept her gaze on the amphora. *"I miss seeing Joseph, but mostly I am weary."*

"You will see him tomorrow morning at the synagogue. After we return home from the assembly, go to your room and rest. Or," Mother had lifted the plate of honey cakes, *"go to the olive grove. I know you love spending time there."*

Mary had lifted the amphora. "Yes, Mother." Turning, she had crossed to the table to fill Grandfather Matthat's and then Grandmother

Tzipora's cups. She continued filling her family's cups, relieved her mother had not pressed the matter.

"Get up, Mary. You do not wish to further alarm your mother."

She got out of bed and crossed to the small table that held a jar of water and a basin. She removed her sleeping garment and set it aside. Lifting the small bar of fragrant soap that had been a gift from her mother, she washed her face and body and patted dry with a towel before moving to the small bench where she had laid out the garments she had worn to her betrothal and to the assembly on the Feast of Trumpets; the blue tunic with cream colored trim on the neck and hem.

Slipping the tunic on, she laid the girdle aside, not wanting to add pressure to her tender stomach. She sat on the bench to tie her sandals, before turning to pick up her comb and work through her dark tresses. After combing out the tangles, she braided her hair and secured the end with a small ribbon.

Reaching over to the edge of the table, she picked up the soft blue veil, as delicate as the gossamer wings of the butterflies she had seen ten days before. She draped it over her head and stood to cross to the door.

Mary took a careful breath and placed her hand on her abdomen. *You will conceive and give birth to a son.* Having had time to think about it, she was certain that she conceived the babe on that afternoon Gabriel visited her. She had spent the last nine days wondering what will happen when her pregnancy became obvious. What will happen if Joseph refuses to take her home as his bride? What will he say to her parents? Will he declare that he is divorcing her because she is insane? If he divorces her, she will be cast off, shunned by all who know her.

If Joseph declares she is a blasphemer, there is only one response. She will be stoned.

Almighty Yahweh, Gabriel said I had found favor with You. She moved her hand softly across her abdomen, *Thank You for the honor of being the mother of Your Son. Help me know what to do next. Right now, Joseph and I are the only ones who know. That will not last for long. Please let me know how to share this news with others. Please let* someone *believe me. Please give me the wisdom and strength to prepare for the birth of Your Son. Almighty Yahweh, above all; I want to be found worthy by You.*

Chapter 28

The sky mocked Joseph. Since the day following the Feast of Trumpets—the day that changed his life forever—clouds gathered in the sky like an ominous grey mountain over the village of Nazareth, the wind howling around the corners of buildings.

Not today. On the morning of the Day of Atonement, instead of weeping from the weight of sin being presented that day in the Holy of Holies, Joseph woke to see wispy clouds in an azure sky.

Nine days prior, the storm that threated as he walked toward Zippori broke as he entered the city. The lightening was blinding, the thunder deafening, the rain pouring between the torn flesh of the clouds, washing mud and debris over the mosaic tiles of the Roman streets.

The storm suited Joseph. The other workers would do whatever they could to work indoors. Not him; he wanted to face the fury that raged around him, that echoed the storm raging in his head, his heart, his soul.

In his note to Mary and her parents, he had explained there was a special project in Zippori that would take long days of many hours to complete. What he did not explain was the project was his need for space, his need for time to think and to pray. Spending long days in Zippori would grant him time to decide what to do next in response to Mary's incredible announcement.

Lucius Septimus had been surprised by Joseph's request to work outside during the storm.

"Joseph ben Jacob, you should not tempt Jupiter," the overseer cringed as thunder crashed overhead.

"I do not fear your pagan gods," Joseph adjusted the bag of tools over his shoulder.

"Then you should fear your own Yahweh. Whether Roman or Jewish, an angry deity is not to be dismissed."

"If Yahweh wishes to strike me, there is nothing I can to do prevent Him." Noting the shock on the overseer's face, Joseph relaxed. "Forgive me, Lucius Septimus. I have…decisions…to make and need time alone to ponder them. Working outside will grant that time."

"As you wish." The Roman lifted his hands, palms facing Joseph. "Have you any experience with carving marble?"

"I have some experience."

"Good, then you can work on the columns at the entrance to the public bath. Herod wants a dozen columns, six on either side of the doors. The columns are ready, but before they can be set in place, the decorative capitals need to be carved." He crossed to his desk, rummaged through a stack of parchments with drawings, selected one, and handed it to Joseph. "Here is the design."

Joseph studied the drawing, asked a few questions, before putting it into his bag. "I will begin at once."

"Be careful, Joseph," The Roman laid a hand on his shoulder. "I will pray for your God and mine to have mercy on you."

Adjusting his head covering to shield his face, Joseph stepped out into the storm and turned down the street leading toward the baths. Despite his declaration, he cringed as the storm seethed around him. *Is Lucius correct? Did I anger Yahweh? Did He send this storm as a punishment?* Remembering the Day of Atonement—the day of judgement—was but nine days away, Joseph responded as he had been trained from childhood. *Yahweh, please reveal my sin and forgive me.* While he would never claim to know the mind of the Almighty, Joseph felt his sin stemmed from his indecision toward Mary.

With every step, he relived that moment with Mary in the ravine between his home and the olive grove. Her wild story of butterflies, of the angel Gabriel, and his message. *"I am to be the mother of the Messiah,"* she had said, her countenance shining with awe, *"and we are to name Him…"*

He had cut off her words. He had retorted if *he* were not to be the father, he could have *nothing* to do with naming the child.

She had tried explaining again, but he had cut her off once more. She had reminded him that he had agreed with Rabbi Boaz that either she or Adina could be the mother of the Messiah.

"After I took you home as my bride," he had flung up his hands. He had called her story fantastical, comparing it to something that one would hear about the pagan Roman gods.

"No!" Mary had gasped. "Joseph, how could you think I would suggest such…such…"

"Blasphemy?" he had finished her sentence. *"How could I think you would suggest such blasphemy? I will tell you how. You have gone mad!"*

The word had echoed around them. It still echoed in his heart and mind. No matter how he looked at it, no matter the hours—both waking and sleeping—pondering it, there were only two conclusions. Either Mary was blasphemous, or she was mad.

If she were speaking blasphemy—and what else would likening Yahweh to the licentious Roman gods be but blasphemous—the Law given to Moses had only one penalty.

Death.

If she were guilty of blasphemy, it was his responsibility to accuse her of this crime before the elders of the village. If she confessed to this sin, Mary—his beautiful, sweet Mary—would be taken outside of Nazareth, possibly the very ravine where the nightmare between them had taken place. All of the residents in their village, every man, woman, child, her family, his family—even he himself—would stone her.

That was too horrifying an event for Joseph to even think about, much less face. He would rather die than harm Mary.

The only other conclusion was that she was mad. But how could she be insane? She had never shown any signs of having lost touch with reality. Such knowledge would not have been kept a secret in their little village. Surely Rabbi Boaz would have known; she was a close friend—a heart-sister—to Adina. If Mary's parents had known, they would have refused his proposal of marriage.

If Mary were insane, could she be helped? King Saul had been tormented by an evil spirit and could only be helped by the harp music of David bar Jesse, who would later himself become king. But Mary did not have bouts of insanity. Yes, her drawing was certainly *unusual,* but was it a sign of insanity? He did not think so, but he had no knowledge of such things. Could she be treated? Nazareth was a little village; they did not have a skilled doctor. Even if they did, he would have to tell their families what she had told him.

Yahweh, why? What have I done, what sin have I committed? I love Mary; I do not want to lose her, to sacrifice her. Father Abraham was obedient to Your command to sacrifice his only son Isaac. Do You want me to give up Mary? Am I wrong to love her? Am I selfish to want to want her as my wife?

By the time he arrived at the public bath, Joseph was wet and frustrated and no closer to an answer than he had been that morning.

He had spent every minute of the last nine days wrestling with his memories, wrestling with himself—and just as Father Jacob— wrestling with Yahweh.

Joseph thought by leaving home before dawn and arriving long after sunset, he would hide his struggle from those around him. But he had not hid it from everyone.

"Joseph, you are spending more time in Zippori than in Nazareth," Lucius Septimus had come to inspect the work on the bath yesterday afternoon. "I would wager by the time you arrive home, there is little left of the day to visit with your betrothed."

"She knows why I am spending so much time here," Joseph said. *That is not a lie. I have no doubt that Mary knows the reason I am staying away.*

"Ah, whatever she might say," the overseer wagged a finger, "I am certain she thinks otherwise. Providing for a wife is a good thing but, from my experience, women who are happily married want to spend time with their husband. Tomorrow is a special Jewish Holy Day, is it not?"

Joseph nodded. "It is the Day of Atonement."

"That is it. You—along with all the other Jewish artisans—will not be working. Joseph, you have finished your work here. Go home," he waved his hands as if shooing chickens. "Eat. Rest. See your betrothed. That will refresh your soul."

Joseph gathered his tools and walked home in the pouring rain. After changing into dry clothes, he joined his family at the table. Not that he wanted to eat, but because he knew to do otherwise would cause unwanted comments and questions. When the meal was over, he went to his bed chamber and fell into a dreamless sleep.

When Joseph awoke that morning, the golden sky mocked him. As he followed his family to the synagogue, he knew three things.

He would see Mary that morning.

He had not decided what he would do in response to what she had told him.

Whatever happened, his dream of a life with Mary was over.

Chapter 29

*M*ary saw Joseph enter the main room of the synagogue with the men of his family.

He was dressed in his best garments, as was everyone present, but that was to be expected. Every Jewish child was taught to honor Yahweh by wearing their best garments when they went to the synagogue and especially on High Holy Days.

The difference for Joseph—and for herself—was that their garments were the ones they had worn for their betrothal celebration.

The heavy lines in his brow, the dark circles under his eyes, and his downturned lips—unusual for Joseph, who was known for his happy demeanor—gave evidence that he was tired and unhappy. *The blame is mine.* Her heart ached. *He has been working long hours because of me.* She had no illusions about the *work* he had mentioned in the note he had sent nine days ago.

He wanted to be away from me.

As if sensing her gaze, Joseph turned and looked up at her.

Mary gave him a gentle smile, lifting her hand in greeting.

He stared at her, lips drawn in a tight line, before nodding and turning as Rabbi Boaz and Yared entered the room.

Everyone stood as Rabbi Boaz entered, carrying the scrolls of Holy Scripture. Yared followed, carrying a shofar made from a long, curled ram's horn.

After the traditional presentation of the scrolls, the two men crossed the floor to step up on the bimah. Rabbi Boaz laid the scrolls on the reading desk while Yared moved a pace away. The older man smiled, gazing around the room at the assembly of people. Lifting his arms wide, he said,

"Hear, O Israel: The Lord our God, the Lord is One. Love the Lord

your God with all your heart and with all your soul and with all your strength. Amen."

As the rabbi spoke the first word, Mary—along with everyone in the synagogue—joined in speaking the *Shema*. From childhood, she had been taught this was the most important prayer of the Jewish people, forming the center of Jewish belief and worship.

After Rabbi Boaz spoke the "Amen," he gestured for everyone to sit, waiting while the elders and the elderly and the frail were offered the places of honor in the main room of the synagogue. Stools were also placed in the women's loft for the elderly and infirmed. There was an empty stool near Adina, ostensibly for Grandmother Tzipora; yet, Mary's grandmother refused to take it, declaring that she would not dishonor Yahweh by sitting during synagogue assemblies.

Mary—fatigue, hunger, and nausea battling within her—longed to sit on the stool. However, that would draw her grandmother's displeasure and unwanted questions from her mother. She grasped the rail to steady herself, thankful that her sleeve covered her whitened knuckles, and tried to focus on the rabbi's words.

Rabbi Boaz began by reminding everyone that the Day of Atonement completed the Days of Awe, which had begun on the Feast of Trumpets, when God inscribes each person's fate for the coming year into the Book of Life. During the Days of Awe, every Jew sought to examine their lives, amend their behavior, confess their sins, and seek Yahweh's forgiveness.

"The Day of Atonement is the one time during the year when the High Priest enters the Holy of Holies, into the very presence of Yahweh," the rabbi bowed his head, placing his hands on his turban in reverence, "as a representative of the Jewish people."

Mary—and everyone present—followed the rabbi's act of reverence.

He continued, explaining what the Law given to Moses commanded concerning the events of the Day of Atonement. The Law centered solely around the High Priest and his careful preparation in representing the nation of Israel before Yahweh in the Temple in Jerusalem

On the Day of Atonement, the High Priest would remove his costly priestly garments and bathe in the ceremonial mikvah before donning simple, pristine white linen garments, which symbolized repentance.

The High Priest would sacrifice a young bull and a ram on the altar as a sin offering for himself and for the other priests, before walking to the Holy Place where were located the altar of incense, the seven-branched candelabrum, and the table of shewbread. Taking a censer of glowing coals from the altar and two handfuls of crushed sweet incense, the High Priest would continue to the center of the room, to the Veil of the Temple.

The Veil of the Temple—stretching the height and width of the room and as thick as a man's hand—was made of fine linen and blue, purple, and scarlet yarn with figures of cherubim embroidered onto it. The Veil prevented men from carelessly entering into the heart of the Temple, the Holy of Holies, where resided the Holy Presence of Yahweh.

Passing through the Veil, the High Priest would enter the Holy of Holies. Walls covered in gold and floors of a marble whose blue tinge gave it the impression of moving water, in the center of the room was the Ark of the Covenant with the Mercy Seat, the golden lid with two Cherubim placed on either end. It was here that the Presence of Yahweh resided.

Once inside the Holy of Holies, the High Priest would light the incense to create a cloud to cover his eyes from a direct view of Yahweh. Standing before the Ark of the Covenant, the High Priest would sprinkle the sacrificial blood on the Mercy Seat and the floor before the Ark of the Covenant, praying and making atonement for his sins and for the sins of the whole nation of Israel.

Opening one of the scrolls on the reading desk, Rabbi Boaz said, "Speaking through the Prophet Ezekiel, Yahweh said,

"I will give you a new heart and put a new spirit in you; I will remove from you your heart of stone and give you a heart of flesh."

Turning to another scroll, the rabbi said, "Speaking through the Prophet Jeremiah, Yahweh said,

"'The days are coming,' declares the Lord, 'when I will make a new

covenant with the people of Israel and with the people of Judah. It will not be like the covenant I made with their ancestors when I took them by the hand to lead them out of Egypt, because they broke My covenant, though I was a husband to them,' declares the Lord. 'This is the covenant I will make with the people of Israel after that time,' declares the Lord. 'I will put My law in their minds and write it on their hearts. I will be their God, and they will be My people. No longer will they teach their neighbor, or say to one another, "Know the Lord," because they will all know Me, from the least of them to the greatest,' declares the Lord. 'For I will forgive their wickedness and will remember their sins no more."

"Through the blood of the sacrifice," Rabbi Boaz lifted his eyes to look at the assembled people, "Yahweh is graciously providing a way for sinful people to come into His presence."

Lifting his arms to either side, Rabbi Boaz led the people in speaking the Shema once more, *"Hear, O Israel: The Lord our God, the Lord is One. Love the Lord your God with all your heart and with all your soul and with all your strength. Amen."*

Rabbi Boaz nodded to Yared, who lifted the shofar to his lips and blew a single long, loud blast.

Chapter 30

*J*oseph joined the others in speaking the final Shema. No matter what he was going through—no matter what he was feeling—acknowledging the sovereignty of Yahweh was first and foremost.

After Yared blew the long blast on the shofar, the men around Joseph turned to greet each other, commenting on the assembly, the ending of the Ten Days of Awe, and the coming harvest. Except for his family, Joseph greeted no one. His mind was elsewhere.

He had sensed Mary's presence the moment he entered the main room of the synagogue; without conscious thought, he had turned to look up at her.

His heart had leapt at the sight of her beautiful face, but his response was crushed by her pale, wan countenance, the dark smudges beneath her eyes, the tightness of her smile. *The blame is mine,* he chided himself. *You have not contacted her in nine days save for the brief note sent on the morning after the Feast of Trumpets. Her announcement might have been wild and unexpected, yet she is your betrothed wife; she deserves better than your silence.*

The only reason he could give in response was that he had still not made up his mind. Though he had spent days wrestling with his spirit—and even felt he wrestled with Yahweh—his prayers had not been answered. While Rabbi Boaz spoke about the holiest day of the year, Joseph's battle continued on the one question in his heart and mind.

Does Yahweh want me to divorce Mary?

The Law given to Moses allowed a man to divorce a wife by presenting her with a certificate of divorce. If the wife had not been unfaithful to him, the husband had to return the mohar to her. If his wife had been unfaithful, he could divorce her in front of the elders in a court setting and keep the mohar. In all cases, the divorced woman would be free to marry another man—although she could never remarry her first husband—but what honorable man would want to marry her? In the end, the divorced woman would be shunned by her family and community.

Joseph refused to imagine Mary being unfaithful to him. Indeed, from Mary's wild announcement, she would conceive this child without being unfaithful to him. *"The Holy Spirit will come on you,"* she said the angel had told her, *"and the power of the Most High will overshadow you."*

That thought had wrenched Joseph's gut and haunted his days and nights. The idea Yahweh would behave like the pagan gods to impregnant a woman. No matter how Joseph looked at it, that statement was blasphemous. If he publicly denounced Mary's words as blasphemy, she would be stoned.

No. I cannot believe Mary would intentionally speak blasphemy. He frowned. *I will not publicly denounce her for such.* That left him with only one thought; Mary had lost her sanity. *And neither will I publicly humiliate her by pronouncing her as insane.*

Yahweh, forgive me, Joseph prayed as Yared blew the long blast on the shofar, *but I still do not know what You want me to do.*

"Joseph, Joseph," his father placed a hand on his shoulder.

Joseph shook his head, his attention refocused on his father's face. His father, Grandfather Matthan, Grandfather Teman, and his brother Clopas stood nearby, watching him, while the men of Nazareth were walking toward the door.

"Are you alright?" A frown gathered on his father's face, his unwavering gaze searching his face.

Joseph nodded. "I am fine, Father. I have been," he filled his lungs and blew out the air, "seeking Yahweh on a matter."

"This is a good day to seek the Almighty's guidance," Grandfather Matthan said.

"Is it something you wish to speak with us about?" Grandfather Teman asked.

"No, no, no," Joseph spread his hands. "I thank you, but this is something I need to do on my own."

"As you wish," his father said, "but come, it is time to leave."

Joseph turned to follow the men leaving the synagogue. As he reached the foot of the stairs, he looked up to see Mary on the bottom step, her face barely a cubit away from him. Her skin was the color of cold wood ash left over after a hot fire. She lifted her eyes to his, her gaze wide and startled.

With both of their families—with the residents of Nazareth—surrounding them and watching, there was little he could do.

He spread his lips in a tight smile. "Mary."

Chapter 31

$\mathcal{M}$ary followed her mother, Grandmother Tzipora, Grandmother Bithiah, and Salome as they joined the women and children walking down the stairs from the synagogue loft.

She was not feeling well, she was lightheaded, and she grasped the rail, focusing on taking each step as the room reeled. As she reached the last step stairs, she paused, taking a shallow breath. *Thank you, Yahweh,* and lifted her head to see Joseph standing not a hand's breath away.

He stared at her for an unbearable moment, before stretching his lips in a tight smile. "Mary."

Her eyes widen. *Joseph! I have missed you! I have wanted to see you. I have wanted to talk to you. But not here, not with our families, our friends—with everyone in Nazareth—watching. What do I say? What will you say next? What will you do? How will I respond? Our families are surrounding us. Yahweh, please help me. I just want to go home.*

All that flashed through her mind in the time it took for her to say, "Joseph," before the room went dark.

Chapter 32

Four days later

Joseph sat on one of the low benches surrounding the fire pit at Mary's home, watching the languid flames of the newly lit fire struggle to gain strength.

He barely listened to the conversation amongst the men sitting around the fire pit. His father and Mary's father, their grandparents, his brother, Mary's brother-in-law, and even Rabbi Boaz discussing the recent holy days, the potential of the coming harvest, even the weather turning cooler. Yet, he was aware the conversation was a mask to cover their concern for what had happened at the synagogue four days prior; what had happened to Mary.

Since his life-altering encounter with Mary in the ravine, Joseph had intentionally avoided seeing his betrothed. He needed time to ponder, to pray, and to determine what Yahweh wanted him to do in response to her fantastical announcement. In all of that pondering, he never imagined what had happened on the Day of Atonement.

When Mary fainted, he instinctively reached out and caught her, causing a rippling gasp around them. Even though they were betrothed, to touch Mary—even when she was unconscious, and they were in a public place—was frowned upon by many.

"Remove your hands from her!" Tzipora bat Leui stepped over to them, trying to pull Mary out of his arms. *As if I would molest her in the synagogue, in the presence of our families and friends.*

"Leave her alone." He pivoted, shielding Mary's unconscious body from her grandmother.

The older woman startled. As the matriarch of Mary's family, she was unaccustomed to having anyone defy her will. Brows lowered, she opened her mouth. "What—"

"Stop, Wife." Matthat ben Levi placed a hand on her shoulder.

"Matthat," she sputtered, "he has no right—"

"He has every right," Mary's grandfather responded. "He is her betrothed husband." He looked at Joseph and nodded.

Joseph returned the nod, before scooping Mary up in his arms.

His action caused a flurry of activity.

Joseph crossed to one of the step-like benches along with wall and laid Mary on it. He removed his sleeveless robe, folded it, and placed it gently beneath her head.

Rabbi Boaz sent Yared for a cup and amphora of water.

"Water?" Mary's grandmother sputtered. "Rabbi, you would have Mary violate Yahweh's Law concerning fasting on the Day of Atonement?"

Rabbi Boaz turned to the older woman. "Tzipora bat Leui," he smiled, "I honor your concern for the Law, but I do not agree with your interpretation. Yahweh would not want those who are ill to fast."

Mary began to stir, moaning a bit.

Mary's mother knelt by her daughter. "Shhh…" she whispered. "Lie quietly."

"Zebedee," Mary's father turned to his son-in-law, "run to the house and hitch Aton up to the wagon. Drive it back."

"I will go with you," Salome said to her husband. "James, John, you come with us. While your father hitches the donkey up to the wagon, you can gather blankets to spread in the bed of the wagon. Then you can begin building up the fire and help me gather things we will need for your Aunt Mary."

"I will stay here," Grandmother Tzipora frowned.

"I will escort you home, Beloved," Grandfather Matthat took her hand. "Once there, I will offer whatever help you and Salome need. Eli and Anne will remain here with Joseph." He turned to look at Joseph. "Take care of her."

"I will." Joseph nodded. "Thank you." He looked at his parents. "Father, Mother—"

"With Eli's permission," his father turned to Mary's father, "we will all go to their house to offer our help."

"Thank you." He turned toward his mother's mother. "Grandmother Esther, do you think you can help Mary?" His grandmother was skilled with medicinal herbs. She had treated his family many times and people from Nazareth frequently called on her for help with illnesses.

Joseph's grandmother laid a hand on his shoulder. "Your grandfather and I will go to our house. I will gather my herbs and meet you at Eli and Anne's house."

"Thank you," Mary's father said. "We appreciate your help."

All of this took place in less than a minute. As Yared was returning with the amphora and cup, Rabbi Boaz turned to the residents of Nazareth who were still in the synagogue, gaping with curiosity.

"Friends," he spread his arms wide, "thank you for your concern for Mary bat Eli. As you can see, she is beginning to wake, and her family is attending to her. Please, go home; enjoy the rest of this beautiful day. Should Mary come to your mind, take a moment and pray for her."

Adina removed her headcloth, poured water from the amphora over it, and handed it to Mary's mother. "What else can I do? Father and I were to come to your house to break the fast with your family, but we can stay home."

"No," Mary's mother smiled softly. "Please come. I am certain Mary would want to have her heart-sister by her side."

"Come, Adina," Rabbi Boaz said. "We will go to our house and get the honey and date cakes you prepared yesterday. I know they are everyone's favorite."

Joseph bent and picked up a stick and poked the fire, sending sparks shooting upwards, as if attacking the fire would remedy the situation of what was happening to Mary.

He had ridden on the wagon bench next to Eli and Zebedee, his eyes never leaving his betrothed. After they arrived at Mary's house, he jumped out, rushed to back of the wagon, and lifted

Mary. The movement caused her to moan. He turned to hand her to her father. *I might claim the right as her betrothed to catch her when she fainted, but I will not enter her bed chamber before we are fully married…*if *that ever happens.*

While Zebedee tended to the donkey and wagon, Joseph followed Mary's parents through the door of their house, into the courtyard, to the door of Mary's bed chamber. He watched as the women going to and from Mary's bed chamber stepped aside for Mary's father to carry her inside.

After a few moments, Eli exited the room, and crossed to stand next to Joseph. "Do not worry," he placed a hand on Joseph's shoulder. "My mother and daughter had everything ready for our arrival. Your grandmother has brought her herbs. Mary has the combined wisdom and care of all the women in our family."

Joseph glanced at the other man. A frown was gathering on Eli's face, his unwavering gaze on the door of his daughter's bed chamber. *His face gives lie to his words,* Joseph thought.

As if feeling Joseph's gaze, Mary's father turned to face him. "Come," Eli took a deep breath and patted Joseph's shoulder, "let us sit and wait. The women will have an answer soon."

Joseph followed Eli across the courtyard to the fire pit, where the men of both their families—along with Rabbi Boaz—were gathered. Matthat ben Levi was overseeing James and John as they tended the fire. Salome was filling a large bowl with steaming water heated in an earthenware pot set over the coals. Straightening, she gave them a nod—her face tight—and turned to carry the bowl to her sister's bed chamber.

Joseph's father joined him. "How is Mary?"

"I do not know, Father." He looked around. "Where is Mother?"

"Doing what every woman does in anxious times," his father smiled briefly, "seeing to the food. Your Grandmother Esther is in Mary's bed chamber, but the room is too small for the women from both of our families. Your mother suggested that she—along with the rest of the women of our family—set out food in the main room to eat once the sun sets and the fast for the Day of Atonement is broken." Lifting a hand to shield his eyes, he glanced at the sun slanting in the courtyard. "It is not much longer. Hopefully, by the time the fast is broken, Mary will feel well enough to join us."

Joseph nodded. "Hopefully." He refused to point out that his father's smile was as tight as Salome's. *He is trying to lift my spirits.* "Father, Eli ben Matthat, if you will excuse me, I am going to sit."

Crossing to the opposite side of the fire pit, Joseph chose a bench where he could see the door to Mary's bed chamber.

The morning following the Day of Atonement, Joseph had sent a message with one of the artisans from Nazareth to Lucius Septimus, explaining why he was not going to be in Zippori. The Roman overseer had sent a note back, encouraging Joseph to stay with his betrothed, and ending with, *"I will say a prayer to our gods and to your Yahweh for her healing."*

Since that day, Joseph had come to Mary's house every morning and stayed until the setting sun washed the evening sky in streaks of orange, red, and gold.

Mary's sister Salome—who was overseeing the meals—greeted him each morning and offered him milk, cheese, and bread, still warm from the oven. He would thank her, take some food—it would have been rude to refuse; Joseph realized that Mary's sister needed to do something to help—and cross the courtyard to the fire pit. After greeting the men in Mary's family and Rabbi Boaz— who had accompanied Adina every day to be by her heart-sister's side—Joseph would sit on the bench and watch the flow of women going in and out of Mary's bed chamber.

He made no pretense to join in the men's conversation, and no one tried to engage him. All he could think of was what was going on behind that door.

What caused Mary to faint? In the quiet of the synagogue, she had opened her eyes once, gave him a weak smile, and had whispered, "Joseph," before closing her eyes again. On the journey home, he had sat where he could see her. At one point, the swaying of the wagon appeared to cause Mary discomfort; she had lifted Adina's dampened headcloth to her mouth, moaning.

What will she say to her family? Will she mention seeing Gabriel? Will she tell them what the angel said to her? Will she tell them she is carrying a child? Will they wonder if it is my child? Despite everything that had happened, Joseph realized two things: He still loved Mary, and he still did not know what to do.

He took his stick and began writing in the dirt.

חישמה Messiah.

"I spoke with the angel Gabriel," she had told him. *"I am to be the mother of the Messiah."*

No. Joseph frowned. *It cannot be true.*

"Messiah."

Joseph startled, jabbing the stick into the dirt, smearing his writing. He looked up to see Rabbi Boaz standing at his shoulder.

"Forgive me, Joseph. I did not mean to startle you."

"It is nothing, Rabbi."

"It *is* something," The older man sat down next to him. "We are all concerned about Mary, but none more than you." He glanced down at the dirt and smiled. "'Messiah.' Even smeared, your writing has improved since you were a boy coming to synagogue classes." He glanced around before continuing in a lowered tone. "I must assume that *someone's* interest in learning to write has inspired you, true?"

Joseph tried to imitate the rabbi's smile, but knew it was a weak copy. "True." An idea occurred to him. Since the Feast of Trumpets, Joseph had wanted to seek wisdom from someone he trusted, but did not know how to bring up the subject. Now he had an opportunity. "Rabbi, may I ask you a question," he pointed toward the word written in the dirt, "about the Messiah?"

"The Messiah?" The rabbi lifted bushy white eyebrows.

"Yes. If you do not mind. It will give me something," he gestured toward Mary's bed chamber, "to distract my mind."

"Ahhh…" the rabbi relaxed. "I understand. Yes, of course. What do you want to know about the Messiah?"

"What do you think will be the circumstances surrounding the coming of the Messiah?"

The rabbi lifted his hands to clasp them beneath his face, palms together, thumbs under his chin, forefingers touching his mouth.

"Over the years, but especially during the Ten Days of Awe, I have frequently pondered the coming of the Messiah.

"When I was young like you, I studied in the Temple in Jerusalem. One of my teachers was considered an expert on the prophecies concerning of the Messiah. Being young, I was convinced that I understood exactly what the prophecies in the Holy Scripture meant concerning the Messiah. What I believed surely was the only one true interpretation. My teacher would frequently say, "Prophecy is hidden in mystery. What we *think* about any prophecy does not mean it is what Yahweh *meant* when He spoke it to the prophets."

"Now that I am older, I realize he was correct. It is difficult to understand prophecy, especially the prophecy concerning the Messiah. For instance, there are different prophecies concerning where the Messiah will be born. The Prophet Hosea wrote: *For out of Egypt will I call my Son.*

"Many Teachers of the Law believe that scripture is a prophecy in reference to the Messiah, but how can the Messiah come from Egypt? *We,*" he stretched his arms wide, "believe that the Messiah will be born of a woman from Nazareth. Yet, none of the women of our community have ever traveled to—much less lived in—Egypt.

"The Prophet Isaiah wrote: *But you, Bethlehem Ephrathah, though you are small among the clans of Judah, out of you will come for Me one who will be ruler over Israel, whose origins are from of old, from ancient times.*

"Now that is easier for us," the rabbi smiled. "We believe the Messiah will reign on David's throne. Bethlehem was the hometown of King David. As we are David's descendants, it is also the ancestral home of everyone who lives in Nazareth."

"Yes," Joseph said, turning toward the older man. "The Messiah will be born of the line of David. He will be ruler over Israel. But *how* will he be…" Joseph caught himself. *I almost asked, "How will he be conceived? That will bring up questions I do not wish to pursue.* "…known? How will we know him?"

The rabbi did not appear to notice Joseph's hesitation. "Ah, Joseph," he smiled. "That is a question I do not think anyone knows, not even the Teachers of the Law at the Temple in Jerusalem. When it comes to prophecy, we would do best to remember that some things are beyond our understanding. Remember what Yahweh said through the Prophet Isaiah: *'For My thoughts are not your thoughts, neither are Your ways my ways,' declares the Lord. 'As the heavens are higher than the earth, so are My ways higher than your ways and My thoughts than your thoughts.'"*

Joseph opened his mouth to ask another question when he noticed Mary's mother walking toward them. Her eyes wide, her mouth set, she clutched her older daughter Salome's hand on one side, and her own mother's hand on the other, both women mirroring Anne's expression. His Grandmother Esther walked next to Tzipora bat Leui. His grandmother's gaze was sad, but Mary's grandmother's arms were crossed beneath her chest, frown set, eyebrows downturned. Adina followed the women, crossed to stand next to her father, and lifted the edge of her head covering to wipe her eyes.

Joseph stood, as did Rabbi Boaz and all the men around the campfire. Mary's father crossed to his wife.

"Beloved, how is she?"

Mary's mother took a shuddering breath, blinking away the sheen of tears that had gathered in her eyes, before shaking her head. "I do not know." She extended her hands, gesturing toward her mother and mother-in-law. "*We* do not know. She is weak. She cannot stand. The illness is causing…" she glanced at Joseph, "*delirium.* She rejects all offer of food and vomits the teas Esther bat Yachin made from medicinal herbs. Whatever is wrong with Mary is beyond our knowledge."

Joseph slumped down on the bench, as Eli wrapped his arms around his wife. She trembled for a moment and then collapsed against her husband, weeping.

"I do not understand," Eli said. "Surely it is nothing more than weakness from the fast?"

"It is *more* than weakness from the fast, my son," Tzipora bat Leui said. "I have warned Mary, I have warned both of you," she glared at her son and daughter-in-law. "You allowed Mary freedoms that went against Yahweh's Law. Now He is punishing her."

"No!" Eli said. "You are wrong, Mother."

The older woman gasped. "You speak *thus* to me?"

"I do." Eli lifted his head, meeting his mother's gaze. "You are wrong. This is not Yahweh's punishment. Mary loves Yahweh and seeks to serve Him in all she does."

His mother bristled. "If that is true, if your daughter is as upright as you claim, then what is wrong with her?" She folded her arms, favoring her son with a thin smile.

"Enough, Wife." Matthat ben Levi crossed to his wife. "You have spoken enough."

"Matthat—" she began, but her words were cut off by his upraised hand in front of her face.

"I said, you have spoken enough." He turned to his Joseph's grandmother. "Esther bat Yachin, you do not know what is wrong?"

Grandmother Esther shook her head. "No. I am sorry; it is beyond my knowledge."

"Then we will look to those who have the more knowledge." He turned to Rabbi Boaz. "Rabbi? Is there anyone in nearby villages who is skilled in medicine?"

The rabbi shook his head. "There is no one near Nazareth who is skilled in medicine. That is why, when Adina was an infant, we wrote to…" his words trailed off, his gaze turned inward, a smile hovering around his mouth.

"What?" Eli asked. "Rabbi, you are thinking of something. What is it?"

Rabbi Boaz looked at Mary's parents. "Do you recall when Adina was an infant, and we were seeking help for her foot?"

Eli's eyes widened. "Yes." He looked at his wife, who nodded. "We sent a letter to our kinswoman Elizabeth and her husband Zechariah."

Joseph controlled his expression as the mention of Mary's kinswoman caused memories of the nightmare in the ravine to wash over him.

"Zechariah bar Barach was kind enough to consult with a physician in Jerusalem on Adina's behalf," Rabbi Boaz said. "He wrote back with advice on what could be done for Adina. Perhaps, if we wrote a letter to Zechariah bar Barach, he could consult a physician on Mary's behalf."

"No." Joseph stood. He blanched under the combined gaze of all present. *For two weeks, I have prayed, asking Yahweh to help me know what to do about Mary. Perhaps this is His answer. A physician will be able to know whether her fantastical announcements are caused from an illness. If illness…please Yahweh; let it be an illness that can be treated. If it is not an illness, I will take that as a sign You want me to divorce Mary.* All of that flashed through his mind in the time it took him to stand. "We will not only send a *letter* to Zechariah bar Barach and Elizabeth bat Shelomoh." He lifted his chin. "We will send *Mary*."

Chapter 33

*J*oseph ben Jacob," Lucius Septimus' eyes widened, "you wish to ask *my* advice? You! Kalev!" he pointed over Joseph's shoulder to a boy walking down the street, carrying a basket of *tesserae*, small colorful tiles. "You are not paid to take a relaxing stroll down the cardo. The workers need those tesserae for the mosaic pictures in the theater. *Perge modo!* Hurry up!" He turned back to Joseph. "My apologies. Now, you need my advice on what matter? Certainly not on your craft; you are one of the most skilled artisans in Zippori, unlike some," he spit out a crude name at the back of the boy now hurrying down the street. "No insult to you and your people, but many workers are as not as committed to working unsupervised as you are. And I cannot imagine your need for advice would be on matters of religion."

"You are correct on both counts." Joseph smiled—the first time in several weeks—at the surprise on the overseer's face. "My question has to do with traveling.

"You have traveled with your wife many times between Rome and Zippori." Without going into detail, he explained that Mary needed to travel to her relative's home in Ein Kerem to consult a physician. "I have traveled to Jerusalem only a few times, but it has always been with a large number of our people, for safety. Mary will be traveling with only our rabbi and his daughter. They will need to travel with a caravan for protection."

Once the decision had been made to send Mary to her kinswoman, the family wasted no time. The following day, Rabbi Boaz arranged for Eli's letter to be taken to Elizabeth and Zechariah asking for their help in find a physician for Mary.

The next decision: Who would go with Mary? Mary had never traveled anywhere that took longer than a few hours on foot. Beyond being ill, she would need to travel three or four days with someone who would be a trusted chaperone.

Rabbi Boaz offered the solution. "It has been several years since a physician examined Adina's foot. Adina and I will escort Mary to Ein Kerem and ask the physician to examine both of them."

"Rabbi, we know you love Mary," Eli protested, "but there is no need for you to take time from your work in the synagogue to make this journey. She is our daughter."

"Eli, please allow me to do this," the rabbi said. "After my wife Devorah—may her memory be blessed—died, you and Anne stepped in to help me care for Adina.

"Beyond wishing to repay your generous act, there are several reasons I wish to go to Jerusalem. I have not been to the Holy City since Rabbi Joshua ben Sie was chosen as High Priest. I feel I should introduce myself to the High Priest as the Rabbi of Nazareth. While I am at the Temple, I will offer a sacrifice and pray for Mary.

"After the physician examines Mary and Adina, my daughter and I will travel on to Jerusalem. I will write to the Leader of a Synagogue close to the Temple and arrange for us to stay in a guest chamber.

"When I was younger, I studied at the Temple; several of my fellow-students are now Teachers of the Law. This journey will allow me to visit with my friends and any of my instructors who are still living." He smiled. "There were also some *interesting* people at the Temple who were not teachers or priests. Simeon ben Anaiah was not a teacher or priest, but he was considered a wise and devout man. I enjoyed talking with him about the Holy Scriptures." He grinned. "He spent many hours in the Temple's Court of Women."

"In the Court of Women?" Eli asked. "Why would he be there and not the Court of Men?"

"The Court of Women is where new parents bring their babies to be dedicated," Rabbi Boaz said. "He told many people Yahweh had revealed to him that he would not die until he had seen the

Lord's Messiah. As the Messiah has not come," he slanted a glance at Joseph, "I assume Simeon ben Anaiah is still among the living."

"How will you travel?" Mary's grandfather Matthat asked. "No one we know is traveling to the hill country of Judah or Jerusalem now. With thieves lurking along the trade routes, no one ever travels alone."

"Beyond that, we will have to find a conveyance for the girls to ride in," Mary's mother said. "With Mary's illness and Adina's foot, neither girl can walk."

"I will ask Lucius Septimus," Joseph said. "There is a caravan that frequently comes to Zippori, with deliveries and correspondence from Jerusalem and Rome. I am certain the caravan owner will know what we can do to arrange for Rabbi Boaz, Adina, and Mary to travel with his caravan."

The next time he was in Zippori, Joseph approached the Roman overseer with the question of arranging travel with the caravan. "I would also be thankful for any other advice you might have."

The Roman's countenance brightened. "I know exactly what to do. I will speak with the owners of the caravan about your honored rabbi, his daughter, and your betrothed traveling with them. I would also be honored if you would allow me to offer you the use of my camel and palanquin for your betrothed and the rabbi's daughter to ride."

"Lucius Septimus!" Now it was Joseph's turn to be surprised. "I do not know how to respond to such generosity. I would, of course, pay you for the use of your animal."

"No, no, no," he waved his hands. "There is no need. Since we have finished our home—in great part to your skills—my wife Ovidia is content to remain in Zippori; she travels only rarely. Our camel, Gobba, has grown fat from sleeping in his stable. If you will provide his food and water, you would be doing *me* a favor to exercise him. My wife has no plans to travel again until the spring; there will be plenty of time for the camel to be returned."

"You are most kind," Joseph said. "Do you know when the caravan is expected? It is imperative for Mary to be examined by a physician soon."

"Your Yahweh must be pleased with you," the Roman replied. "The caravan is expected today or tomorrow. I will introduce you to Jacob ben Reuben, who is related to the merchants who own the caravan." He laid a hand on Joseph's shoulder. "I know you are concerned over your betrothed's health. With your Yahweh's blessings, she will soon recover and come back to Nazareth and to you."

"Amen," Joseph nodded, his lips stretching into a thin smile. *Almighty Yahweh; please heal Mary. Elsewise, show me how to divorce her without bringing her shame.* "May it be as you speak."

Chapter 34

24 Tishri 3758

"Fishermen are not the only ones to navigate by the stars," Jacob ben Rueben said.

"Truly?" Rabbi Boaz replied.

Adina grinned at Mary. She leaned in—keeping her eyes on the young man speaking with her father—and whispered to Mary. "Jacob ben Reuben might be training to be one of the owners of the caravan, but I would wager he does not know more about the stars than Father. Yet, Father listens as if he never heard this information before."

"Rabbi Boaz is known for being a wise teacher and a gracious man."

Adina nodded. "He is indeed. As much as he loves teaching, Father delights in finding someone who loves sharing knowledge."

Mary sat back against the pillow in the palanquin and watched the elderly rabbi and the young merchant discuss the stars in the onyx sky. *To think we have only known Jacob ben Reuben for less than a week.*

Joseph had come to her house five days prior. She was still in her bed chamber fighting the nausea and weakness. Her parents told her that Lucius Septimus had introduced Joseph to Jacob ben Reuben from Bethany. Jacob was related to the owners of a caravan that traveled to distant lands and returned with camels laden with merchandise. They also carried supplies for the overseer and workers in Zippori.

"I have arranged for Mary, Adina, and Rabbi Boaz to travel with this caravan to the home of Elizabeth bat Shelomoh and Zechariah bar Barach in Ein Kerem," Joseph had told them, adding that the Roman overseer had been kind enough to offer his camel for the girls. "Lucius Septimus said it has a palanquin with curtains to shield Mary and Adina."

The next day, Joseph escorted her father and Rabbi Boaz to Zippori to meet this young man from Bethany. While they were gone, Mary's mother—supervised by Grandmother Tzipora—had packed what Mary would need for the journey. Joseph had brought a basket from his Grandmother Esther filled with medicinal herbs for Mary.

The following day, she bid farewell to her family. After Grandfather Matthat had spoken a prayer for a safe journey, he embraced her. "Be safe. Come back to us soon."

"I will, Grandfather Matthat."

"Convey our love to Elizabeth and Zechariah." Grandfather Samuel embraced her.

"I will, Grandfather Samuel."

After embracing her, Grandmother Bithiah had handed her a sealed jar. "Give these olives to Elizabeth. She prefers olives from Nazareth."

"Yes, Grandmother Bithiah."

"Remember to be of help to Elizabeth bat Shelomoh and Zechariah bar Barach." Grandmother Tzipora lifted a finger in front of Mary's face, "and obey the Law Yahweh gave to Moses."

"I will, Grandmother Tzipora."

Mary had received blessings and embraces from Salome, Zebedee, and even her nephews, who bemoaned aloud wishing *they could travel in a caravan.*

Mary wiped away tears as she embraced her parents. "I do not know when I will see you again."

"Yahweh knows," her father had swallowed hard. "We will trust the timing to Him."

"Take care of yourself." Her mother had lifted the edge of her head covering to wipe away tears. "We will pray for you. We love you."

"I love you too." Mary blinked, tears trembling on her lashes. "I pray for you all."

She held the edge of her woven garments, the color of ripened wheat, while her father helped her climb into the back of Joseph's cart next to Adina. Her mother handed them a basket of food and several skins of water. Her father had given Rabbi Boaz a pouch of coins to help with any unforeseen expenses.

Joseph climbed onto the seat of the carriage, gathered the reins, and gently slapped them against Hamor's rump. Mary waved to her family as they called blessings and farewells and pledges for letters.

The sun was casting long shadows when they had reached the caravan outside the walls of Zippori. The caravan would leave as the sun set; beyond using the stars as a guide, everyone knew only fools and madmen faced the desert's full heat willingly. Mary had seen several men armed with short swords and bows and arrows patrolling the caravan; thieves hunted the trade routes, looking for easy targets.

While Joseph had gone to find Jacob ben Reuben, Rabbi Boaz helped the girls out of the wagon and then untied the reins to Sefina, his donkey. When they were children, Adina had misunderstood her father and thought he had named the grey animal after her.

In a few moments, Joseph returned with Jacob ben Reuben. Of an age with Joseph, he was taller than most men, even Yared, with long limbs and a strong body. His dark beard curled around an angular jaw, and dark hair sprung mane-like around his face. His white garments were long and loose, allowing air to flow beneath them, cooling his body.

"Greetings Rabbi Boaz bar Penuel; peace on you," he bowed his head, placing an open hand against his chest before turning to the girls. "Adina bat Boaz, Mary bat Eli. Peace on you. Welcome. I am honored that Lucius Septimus would recommend our humble caravan to you."

Mary slanted a glance at her heart-sister, thankful their veils—worn to protect most of their faces from the dust—covered their astonished smiles. From what Mary could see, the *humble* caravan contained numerous camels and donkeys, some with well-tooled saddles on their backs, and others bearing heavy bags of various sizes. On the way from Nazareth, Joseph had told them that Jacob ben Reuben's caravans traveled to distant lands, returning with costly perfumes and spices; flax and other textiles, including silk from the legendary lands of the far east; *terra sigilata* pottery; tall, slender Grecian *amphorae* to hold water or wine; precious and semi-precious stones; gold and silver fashioned into cups, bowls, plates, and jewelry. Jacob ben Reuben's caravans had the trust of rulers and would carry correspondence between cities.

"And on you peace, Jacob ben Reuben," Rabbi Boaz returned the gesture of greeting. "We are thankful you have room for us with your noble caravan."

"Rabbi, Joseph ben Jacob tells me that you are a wise and knowledgeable teacher. I look forward to speaking with you. My mothers' relatives—who own this caravan—are skilled in the matters of buying and selling, but not in much else. My elder brother Joktan would be surprised to hear me confess that I miss conversing with someone who speaks of more than the cost of merchandise."

"I would be honored to speak with you."

"Wonderful." Jacob turned when one of his men called his name. "If you will excuse me, I must see to the needs of my people. We will leave shortly," he nodded before leaving.

"A pleasant young man," Rabbi Boaz smiled. "I look forward to getting to know him better."

Joseph led them to where the animals were lined up, stopping next to a camel the color of the desert sand, with large dark eyes fringed by thick, black lashes. A bright yellow, square palanquin was secured to its back. Cushions were placed inside the palanquin for Adina and Mary to recline against, and four poles supported a red awning with yellow curtains draped on each side, to provide privacy and protection from dust storms.

"Oh my!" Mary gasped. Accustomed to walking everywhere and only occasionally riding in the cart, she was startled by a conveyance worthy of a queen. "Joseph," she had turned to him, eyes wide, "we are to ride in this?"

"You are." He smiled.

Warmth spread in her heart. *This is first time he has smiled easily at me since the Feast of Trumpets.* "Please thank Lucius Septimus for us. He has been most generous."

"I will relay your gratitude."

"Joseph," Adina had laid a hand on the camel's shiny coat, "what is its name?"

"Gobba." He pointed out the bag of grain to feed the animal and a container for holding its water. "Jacob ben Reuben said you will be stopping by areas where there is water. I will secure the camel's reins to the back of the rabbi's saddle; Gobba will follow Sefina, allowing you and Mary to rest and not worry about guiding the camel. If all goes according to plan, Jacob ben Reuben said you will arrive in Ein Kerem in three to four days."

Rabbi Boaz helped Joseph secure the bags containing Mary's and Adina's belongings onto the camel before placing a hand on Adina's arm. "Joseph, there is no need to bother with Gobba's reins; Adina will help me secure them to Sefina's saddle." Mary saw his gaze slant from his daughter's face toward her and Joseph.

"Of course, Father."

Mary smiled as Adina followed her father the few steps to their donkey. *How kind of Rabbi Boaz to allow Joseph and me time for a private word while still acting as chaperone.* She turned back to Joseph, her gaze hesitant, her smile shy. "I know my parents have thanked you for arranging this journey, but I also wish to add my thanks."

"You are my betrothed wife," he gazed into her eyes. "I want everything to be…well…with you."

Mary's smile slipped, uncertain whether he meant he wanted her to recover from the physical weakness or from what he considered a mental weakness. She lifted her chin, pinning her smile. *I will not think poorly of my betrothed.* "Thank you. I also wish…everything… to be well with me…and with us." *Yahweh, please let it be so. Please allow Joseph to one day believe me.*

He nodded once. "I will send letters to you."

"I will send letters to you, as well."

Rabbi Joseph and Adina returned. "Jacob ben Reuben is signaling; it appears time for the caravan to leave."

Joseph laid a hand on Gobba's shoulder and pressed downward as Lucius Septimus had showed him. The camel squawked as he knelt. Joseph and the rabbi helped Adina and Mary climb into the palanquin. Joseph had kept his hand on the camel while the rabbi climbed onto Sefina. Then he stepped back, gazing at Mary.

Mary had stretched her lips in a thin smile, until she saw Rabbi Boaz lift his hands. She bowed her head as he prayed the same prayer Grandfather Matthat had prayed.

"May it be Your will, Lord, our God and the God of our ancestors,
that You lead us toward peace, guide our footsteps toward peace,
that we are supported in peace, and make us reach
our desired destination for life, gladness, and peace.
May You rescue us from the hand of every foe and ambush,
from robbers and wild beasts on the journey, and from all
manner of punishments that assemble to come to earth.
May You send blessing in our handiwork,
and grant us grace, kindness, and mercy
in Your eyes and in the eyes of all who see us.
May You hear the sound of our humble request
because You are God Who hears prayer requests.
Blessed are You, Lord, Who hears prayer. Amen."

After speaking their farewells, Rabbi Boaz added, "Remember; all that Yahweh does is done for the best," before gathering Sefina's reins and clicking to Gobba, who stood with another squawk. Adina turned away to study the line of animals before them.

Mary gazed down at Joseph once more, tears gathering in her eyes. "Farewell, Joseph."

The muscles in Joseph's throat worked, his eyes never leaving hers. "Farewell, Mary."

As the caravan moved forward, Mary's eyes never left Joseph's, until she could no longer see him. She turned around, drew a shuddering breath, her eyes misting.

Yahweh, guide my footsteps back to Nazareth and to Joseph.

Chapter 35

*F*or the last three days, they had traveled during the night, the full moon lighting up the desert as bright as lamps in the corners of a room. They would stop to set up camp when the sun shot streaks of gold through pink clouds, hinting of warm days to come.

Despite the excitement of traveling in a caravan, Mary expected to fall asleep in the elegant palanquin. However, she had not considered how Gobba's undulating movement would exacerbate the tenderness of her stomach. She laid back against thick pillows, a damp cloth to wipe her face and mouth at her side, along with a skin of water and a small basket with bread; she had discovered that eating small amounts of food kept the extreme nausea at bay. While she focused on not vomiting, Adina kept her apprised of interesting sites and entertained her with a running commentary on the conversations between her father and the young merchant.

After attending to his responsibilities with the caravan, Jacob ben Reuben had dropped back that first night to ride with them, conversing with Rabbi Boaz about things that—as Adina whispered to Mary—were dear to a scholar's heart; the Holy Scriptures, the history of their people, world events, and stars.

"Rabbi, I am certain you are familiar with the mazzaloth known as Labi," the younger man pointed to an arrangement of stars, "the Lion?"

"I am," Rabbi Boaz said, "although I believe you are more familiar with the stars than I am, as they guide you on your journeys."

"They do indeed," the younger man smiled. "When I was younger, during the warm season, my family—as I am certain most families do—spent evenings outside enjoying the cooling breezes. My father would point out the stars and teach me and my brother their names.

"When I began traveling with my mother's relatives, I learned what other nations also named the stars." He pointed toward one star. "That star—the one we know as *Tzedek*—is known to the Romans as *Jupiter* named after the father of their gods." He pointed to another star. "That star—the one we call *Heilel*—the Romans call *Venus*. The mazzaloth we call *Zerah*," he pointed to another group of stars, "they call *Virgo*, the Virgin, and our *Taleh*," he pointed to a different group of stars, "they call *Aries*, the Ram.

"Since I began traveling by night, I have watched the stars move in what I have come to consider as a sky journey, similar to our caravan. Sometimes, they make their trek alone, as if they are the only star in sky. Other times, it appears they travel close to each other. Sometimes, it appears they reach a destination and, after stopping to sojourn there for a time, turn around and return to the place they started."

"Your description of the sky journey is fitting," Rabbi Boaz said. "I have noticed some of these patterns as well. Now that I have the privilege of watching them through the night, I will keep watch for their sky journeys in the future.

"You mentioned your mother's relatives are merchants. Are your father and his family also merchants?"

"No, Rabbi," Jacob grinned, his teeth glinting in the moonlight. "My family is descended from the priestly tribe of Levi. My father serves as a priest in the Temple in Jerusalem, as did our ancestors before him. I was training to join them, as my older brother Joktan was already doing.

"Seven years ago, when I turned twelve, relatives of my mother came to our home for a visit." He grinned. "Unlike my priestly relatives with their somber raiment and staid conversations, these men are merchants who travel to far-off, exotic places.

"Listening to the tales of their journeys mesmerized me; I asked them many questions. I was elated when they invited me to travel with them on their next journey. It was to Greece." Jacob turned to the older man. "Have you ever traveled there?"

"I have not had that pleasure," Rabbi Boaz replied. "The farthest I have traveled was to Jerusalem." His smile was self-deprecating. "I fear I am like your *somber* relatives; I trained in the Temple."

Jacob laughed. "From what I have learned of you, I would not liken you to my priestly relatives, especially not my older brother. Joktan is but three years older than me, yet as far back as I can remember, he has always behaved as if he were one of the seventy members of the *Sanhedrin*, the highest religious council of our people. Joktan adheres strictly to the Law given by Moses and frequently comments on what he perceives as failings with me, with our family, even our own parents."

Mary shook her head. *His brother sounds like my Grandmother Tzipora.*

"I was not surprised when Joktan expressed his opinion to our father of my traveling to Greece." The young man crossed his arms, frowning. 'Jacob should not be allowed to travel to these lands,'" he pitched his voice in a deeper range. "'Who knows what might happen to him, what pagan ideas or habits he might pick up from the Gentiles? Nothing but tragedy can come from this action. No,'" Jacob swiped his hands wide, "'he should stay here and continue studying for the priesthood.'"

Mary raised her eyebrows, glancing at Adina. *His brother would speak thus to their father?*

"Since you *are* a merchant," Rabbi Boaz said, "I must conclude your honored father did not agree with your older brother?"

"No, praise Yahweh, my father did not," the younger man laughed. "He and Mother allowed me to go with my relatives, feeling that one journey would satiate my thirst for adventure, and I would return home to resume my studies.

"However, that journey proved to be more. I have always had a natural gift for bartering at the marketplace. My mother's relatives showed me how to use that gift to buy and sell goods on a larger scale. Once I returned home, they approached my father; I soon left my priestly studies and joined them, learning how to become a merchant."

"From what Joseph ben Jacob tells me he learned from Lucius Septimus, you have prospered as a merchant."

"The Roman overseer is kind to say as much," the young man smiled. "My relatives speak of making me a full partner one day soon."

As the conversation shifted to the history of their people, Mary nibbled a piece of bread and took a sip of water. She settled back on the pillows and glanced at Adina; her heart-sister was sleeping. She whispered a prayer for her family, for Joseph, and for Jesus, her unborn son. Although she had not yet missed her monthly flow, there were other physical symptoms besides the nausea that pointed to a pregnancy. She also prayed for the strength to do what Yahweh wanted of her, adding, "Please send someone who believes me. Amen," and drifted off to sleep.

She woke when the undulating movement of the camel stopped. She sat up, as did Adina, rubbing their eyes and looking to see the caravan was camping near a stand of sycamore fig trees within sight of a city.

"Jacob ben Reuben told me the Gentiles calls the city Scythopolis," Rabbi Boaz explained after greeting them. "You would know it as Beth Shan."

Even though they did not attend classes in the synagogue as the boys did, from her childhood, Mary—as Adina—had been taught the history of their people. When she was a young child, her family had camped near this city one year when they journeyed to Jerusalem to celebrate Passover. She remembered *playing war* with the other children in their group, some pretending to be Philistine soldiers and other pretending to be Israelite soldiers.

Now, it was more than child's play. It was there on Mount Gilboa, the large mountain on the west, where the battle took place. The three sons of King Saul were killed in that battle, but Saul was severely wounded. To avoid being captured, he fell on his sword.

The Philistines fastened the bodies of Saul and his sons to the walls of Beth Shan. The men of Jabesh Gilead marched to the city, recovered the bodies of Saul and his sons, and buried their bones under a tamarisk tree in Jabesh.

After he learned of the death of Saul and his sons, David—who would follow Saul on the throne—wrote a lament with the recurring line, *"How the mighty have fallen."*

As a child, it was an exciting story told to children; now it was more. Mary shook her head. *So much death and sadness.*

Rabbi Boaz had Gobba kneel as Joseph had shown him, and held his daughter's and Mary's hands as they stepped out of palanquin. After securing the camel's and donkey's reins, they provided the animals with food and water before setting up their tents beneath the shade of a tree.

The rabbi pointed to the lush expanse surrounding them. "Despite the sorrow our people experienced at this place, this is a beautiful area. I have heard some people say, *If Yahweh's first garden is located in the land of Israel, then its gate is Beth Shan.*"

After sharing a light morning meal of bread and white cheese, Rabbi Boaz retired to his tent, and Mary and Adina laid down in their tent. Within moments, Adina was sleeping. Mary sighed, wishing sleep would come as easily to her; even weak from the nausea, she wondered whether she would be able to sleep in the daytime. She reached in her bag and drew out her stylus and tablet of wax wrapped in its cloth. Adina had brought them so Mary would be able to continue practicing her writing.

She wrote "Messiah" several times and then sketched what she remembered of Gabriel. Holding it at arm's length, she examined her work. *I cannot believe I have seen an angel. Will anyone ever believe me?*

She glanced at her sleeping heart-sister before sighing, turning her stylus flat, and wiping away the image of the celestial being.

She re-covered the tablet with the cloth, tucked it and the stylus back into her bag, and laid down on her pillow. Within moments of whispering her prayer, she fell asleep to dream of butterflies and stars swirling in the sky.

Chapter 36

*T*he sun hung low as Joseph walked home from Zippori, a warm breeze blowing wispy clouds across the clear sky. The only thought he gave to the weather was to pray that Mary, Adina, and Rabbi Boaz had experienced such weather. *With these conditions, they might have already reached Ein Kerem.*

Passing the olive grove, he noted the trees were heavy with fruit. Within a few days, the residents of Nazareth would gather to harvest the olives. After spreading sheets on the ground beneath the trees, everyone would grab a stick to beat the branches, causing the ripened olives to drop. The children, squealing with delight, would run around with baskets and bags, gathering the fruit.

He smiled, remember the times of harvest from his youth, and wondering whether he would watch his own children join in the celebration of the harvest. *Only if Mary is healed,* his smile faded, *and returns to me.*

Will we ever come back to this place together? He looked around at the grove, remembering how much had happened there.

It was there, in this grove, he had seen Mary sitting under a tree scratching a stick in the dirt. *"She is drawing,"* Rabbi Boaz had told him. Moments later, the rabbi followed with the observation that Joseph was attracted to Mary.

He looked at the ravine, frowning. It was there he had run to meet Mary, fearful she was being chased by a wild animal or a person. It was there—he gritted his teeth—she had said, *"The angel Gabriel appeared to me...I am to be the mother of the Messiah."* It was there he refused to believe her wild story, denouncing it as either blasphemy or insanity. It was there his life changed forever.

"Aaaaiiiiieeeee!" Throwing his head back, screaming at the sky.

"Why?!" He shook clinched fists, crying out in fury. "Why did this happen? Why did Mary tell me such an outrageous story? Why did I respond as I did? Yahweh, why did You allow her to become ill? Yahweh," he dropped to his knees, opening his fists, and extending his arms wide in supplication, "Almighty Yahweh; please let it be an illness. I could not bear it to be anything else.

"Please heal Mary," he pled. "If this illness is Your way to force me to release her from our betrothal, then I will. Just please heal her.

"And heal my heart; for if You want me to divorce Mary," he grasped his head with both hands, rocking back and forth as tears blinded him, "I will never love another."

Chapter 37

*A*s the early dawn folded across the land in ribbons of pink and lavender, Jacob ben Reuben rode up on his donkey. After exchanging greetings, he added, "We should reach the end of your journey and the home of Mary bat Eli's family before the third hour."

"Truly?" Adina asked. "It feels like only yesterday we left Zippori."

"Perhaps the seeming speed of the passing days is because you and Mary made the journey whilst sitting on thick pillows in a palanquin," Rabbi Boaz grinned. "Unlike some of us who," he grimaced as he shifted in the saddle, "had less comfortable means of travel."

Mary bit back a smile as Adina gasped, "Father!"

Jacob threw his head back, roaring with laughter. "Rabbi Boaz, if I had had teachers such as yourself, I might not have left studying for the priesthood."

"If you had," the older man smiled, "we might never have met, and we would not have had such a pleasant journey. I am certain your older brother would disagree with me, but I believe there are many ways to serve Yahweh."

"You are an astute man, Rabbi. I have been honored you traveled with my humble caravan. I hope we have an opportunity to meet again. I would enjoy more conversations."

As the young man rode away, Rabbi Boaz turned to them. "Mary, I hope I have not scandalized you," he grinned, "as I did my daughter."

"No, Rabbi," Mary returned his grin. "You remind me of my Grandfather Matthat. He often says things that *scandalize* my grandmother. I confess, like Adina, I am surprised at how quickly our journey has passed."

"I am thankful you have made the journey without much discomfort," he said.

"I am also thankful for that," Mary said. "I seem to feel somewhat better over the last few days. If it were not for what everyone did to arrange this journey, I would send word to the physician that I do not need to see him." She explained how small amounts of food and water helped keep the nausea at bay. "Adina has made sure I had a supply of bread and water."

"We both enjoyed Adina's bread," the rabbi smiled at his daughter before continuing. "While I am sorry for the circumstances, it has been pleasant to journey with you and Adina. I have wanted to take her to see Jerusalem."

"For me as well, Rabbi," Mary smiled. "My family traveled to Jerusalem when I was too young to care about history. Now, to see the land of our fathers has been a rare treat."

"To think that we camped near Ben Shan," Adina's eyes widened, "and the next day the lovely springs of Aenon near Salim, and yesterday the ruins of Jericho. It is amazing to think of what happened in these places."

Yes; so many battles, Mary thought. *So many people died, even kings and princes. King David did not die in battle, but he faced many challenges.* She slipped her hand beneath her robe to place it on her stomach. *I have focused on myself and wondering if anyone will ever believe that I am to be the mother of the Messiah. But one day, my son will grow up. As the Messiah, he will face the Romans. They will not relinquish control of Israel simply because Jesus tells them to leave. What challenges will he face to return Israel to the glory of King David's reign? What battles will he fight?*

As the caravan followed the road leading toward Ein Kerem, Mary prayed Yahweh's hand to be on her unborn son.

Less than an hour later, Adina drew her father's attention to something glinting in the distant.

"That is the Temple of Yahweh in Jerusalem." Ever the teacher, Rabbi Boaz reminded Mary and Adina of the history of the edifice.

Originally built by King Solomon—according to the instructions given to his father King David by Yahweh—the Temple stood for over 350 years before it was destroyed, pillaged, and burned by King Nebuchadnezzar of Babylon. He had carried all its treasures—and the people of Judah—to Babylon. Later, under the supervision of the priest and scribe Ezra, and even later under Nehemiah—who had been appointed by the Persian King to be Governor over Jerusalem—the Temple was rebuilt, although it did not have the grandeur of the original Temple.

About forty years ago, Herod the Great was appointed by Rome to be King over Israel—and for the past twenty years he had worked on restoring the Temple to its former glory. Though not yet completed, the new Temple was broader and taller than the original. Rising eleven stories, it was covered on all sides with massive plates of gold.

It was this gold that Adina and Mary saw gleaming in the sunlight while they were still too far away to see the City of David.

The goods in Jacob ben Reuben's caravan were destined for the Xystus Market, Jerusalem's large marketplace, located a short distance from the Temple in the northeastern corner of the Upper City. The young man told Rabbi Boaz he had arranged for one of his workers to oversee the delivery of their merchandise while he escorted the rabbi and the girls on to Ein Kerem.

Rabbi Boaz tried to convince Jacob that it was not necessary, but the young merchant would have none of it.

"This caravan is as my home," he said, "and those who travel with it are my guests. I will not dishonor a guest by asking them to wander unaccompanied to an unknown destination. Beyond that, I promised you, Joseph ben Jacob, and Eli ben Matthat I would see you three safely to Ein Kerem. It is less than a Sabbath Day's journey. By the time I am back in Jerusalem," he grinned, "my workers should have unloaded the camels."

When the caravan turned toward Jerusalem, Jacob ben Reuben led Rabbi Boaz, Adina, and Mary southwest. Soon, the road led upward into the hill country region of the tribe of Judah and the small village of Ein Kerem. Rabbi Boaz pointed out several springs, explaining Ein Kerem means, *Spring of the Vineyard.*

They stopped near some boys tending a vegetable garden to ask for directions to the home of Zechariah bar Barach. They boys—wide-eyed at the camel and its elegant palanquin—pointed toward a street leading up the hill to the furthest edge of the village. "The l-l-last house," one boy stuttered.

A few minutes later, Jacob ben Reuben and Rabbi Boaz were knocking on the door of a house shadowed amongst several ancient cypress trees. The men advised Mary and Adina to stay in the palanquin until they were certain they had the correct house.

"The young lads appeared awestruck at what I am certain they thought were royal ladies," the merchant grinned. "It would not surprise me if, in their bemusement, they directed us to the wrong house."

The door opened, and an elderly man stepped into the sunlight. "Greetings," he bowed, opened hand on his chest. "I am Jacob ben Reuben and this," he indicated the man at his side, "is Rabbi Boaz bar Penuel from Nazareth."

As the man opened his mouth, a woman rushed past him. Half the height of the elderly man, her hair—the color of a dove—fell in a thick braid over her shoulder. That was not what caused Jacob, the rabbi, and Adina to gape as the young boys had a few minutes earlier. It was the sight of her creamy tunic flowing over the pronounced curves of her stomach.

Mary's heart raced to see living evidence of Gabriel's message, but bit the inside of her cheek to keep from laughing. *Apparently in his correspondence with my parents and Rabbi Boaz, my kinsman Zechariah neglected to mention that Elizabeth was with child.*

Her cousin lifted the edge of her tunic as she hurried to the camel. "Mary! Greetings!"

"Greetings, Elizabeth," she smiled at her kinswoman.

Elizabeth caught her breath. She lifted her hands to her swollen belly, her gaze turning inward, focusing on—*something*—before lifting awed eyes to Mary's face. "You are…" her words froze as she noticed the others staring, before continuing, "uh…have…arrived. Zechariah and I have been keeping watch since dawn."

She gave her head a little shake and turned to the others. "Forgive me for being rude. We have been anxious to see our kinswoman. Please, be welcome to our home."

"Father," Adina said, "since we have come to the right house, could Mary and I please get down? As comfortable as the palanquin is, I confess, I am ready to walk."

"I am certain you are," Rabbi Boaz laughed. Crossing to Gobba, he had the camel kneel.

After he helped her out of the palanquin, Mary hurried over to embrace her cousin. "Elizabeth! It is so good to see you." She turned to embrace Zechariah. "It is good to see you, Zechariah." She lifted an eyebrow at his silence.

"You must forgive my husband," Elizabeth laid a hand on his arm. "He is unable to speak right now."

Mary controlled her expression, as did her traveling companions; it would be rude to question such an unusual comment. She introduced the rabbi and Adina, and then indicated the merchant. "This is Jacob ben Reuben. We traveled from Nazareth to Ein Kerem with his caravan." She turned to her kinswoman. "This is my cousin, Elizabeth bat Shelomoh and her husband, Zechariah bar Barach."

"Greetings, Rabbi Boaz bar Penuel, Adina bat Boaz, and Jacob ben Reuben," Elizabeth said. "Peace be on you."

The rabbi bowed his head, placing a hand on his chest as he returned the traditional response of a guest, "And on you peace, Zechariah bar Barach and Elizabeth bat Shelomoh, I am thankful for the opportunity to meet in person although—from our correspondence through the years—I feel as if I know you." He drew Adina forward. "Your help in seeking wisdom from the physician for my daughter was a blessing beyond measure."

Adina echoed her father's greeting. "For years I have wanted to extend my thanks as well. It is because of your aid that I walk without much discomfort."

"We are honored to have been a part of your healing," Elizabeth said before turning to the merchant. "Jacob ben Reuben, thank you for bringing our kinswoman and her friends safely to our home."

"I was honored to have the pleasure of traveling with them."

"If you all will follow me," the older woman said, "I have prepared food and drink for your arrival."

"Elizabeth bat Shelomoh, Zechariah bar Barach," the young man laid a hand on his chest, "I ask your pardon in turning down your gracious offer, but I must return to Jerusalem. As worthy as our workers are—and as much as I jested about their unloading our merchandise—my esteemed relatives taught me, *Who does not work shall not eat.* I always desire to set an example for those we employ."

"We understand," Elizabeth smiled, "and honor your desire to be an exemplary manager. Should Yahweh bring you back to Ein Kerem, we would be blessed to have you eat from our humble table."

"I would be honored to sit at your table. Rabbi Boaz bar Penuel," he turned, laying a hand on his chest, and bowing his head, "Adina bat Boaz, Mary bat Eli; it was a blessing to have you travel with my humble caravan." He gave the rabbi the directions to the building in Jerusalem his relatives used as a place of business. "Go there when you are ready to return to Nazareth. Perhaps Yahweh will bless us with the joy of traveling together in the future."

"I pray that as well, Jacob ben Reuben," the rabbi smiled. "We have enjoyed getting to know you. I know I speak for my daughter and Mary bat Eli when I say that whenever we look at the stars and their journeys, we will think of you. May Yahweh bless you now and in the coming years."

"Amen to that." The young man climbed onto his donkey. "Fare you well." Turning his donkey, he rode down the road toward Jerusalem.

"Jacob ben Reuben seems like a pleasant young man," Elizabeth said before turning to her guests. "Now, if you would follow me, I have bed chambers prepared for each of you, along with a meal. Once you have eaten, I am certain you wish to rest."

"Thank you, Elizabeth bat Shelomoh," Rabbi Boaz said. "It will be nice to lie on a bed."

The rabbi, Adina, and Mary shook the folds of their garments before touching their fingers to the mezuzah, and stepping into the front room. They sat on a small bench placed near the door and—as all guests do upon entering a home—removed their sandals, placing them in an empty basket.

"It is our honor to have you visit our humble home," Elizabeth said as Zechariah moved to the table next to Mary, where a small basin of water, three towels, an amphora, and three cups were placed. Lifting the basin, he knelt and placed it on the floor in front of their guests to wash her feet. In homes of wealthy people, this task was done by a servant; in homes without servants, the guests washed their own feet.

After drying their feet with the towel and retying their sandals, Zechariah removed the bowl, amphora, and towels, before pouring a small amount of olive oil onto each guest's head. Elizabeth offered them a cup of cool water. Zechariah helped the rabbi stand, as Elizabeth did Mary and Adina, and leaned forward to kiss their guests' cheek.

The rabbi thanked Zechariah and Elizabeth for the acts of honoring their guests. Adina stood and looked around. "This is a lovely room."

The house had been in Zechariah's family for several generations. It was similar to most houses in Israel, built in a rectangle with an open courtyard in the center, where the cooking area, cistern, and small stable for their donkey, cow, and several chickens. Along the sides and back of the house were bed chambers; however, as Zechariah was the last living member of his family—with the exception of his and Elizabeth's bed chamber—all the sleeping quarters were reserved for guests. One thing was different; this house had a mikvah.

Zechariah led Gobba to their stable as Elizabeth escorted their guests across the courtyard to their bed chambers. She drew her guests' attention to the fact that, due to the house being positioned on the upper edge of the tree-covered ravine, in the distance they could see the Temple of Yahweh gleaming in the sunlight.

Elizabeth had prepared three of their larger guest rooms with the considerations of their guests in mind. The walls of each room were bare, with a single window facing toward the courtyard. The bed was a thick pallet set on a wooden frame and covered with linens Elizabeth had woven herself. Next to the bed was a low table with a cup and pitcher of water. Beneath the window was a small table with a bowl, pitcher of water, a bar of homemade soap, and a towel.

In Rabbi Boaz's room was a table with several scrolls. "My

husband," Elizabeth grinned at Zechariah, "feels all scholars enjoy reading before they sleep."

"He is correct," the rabbi smiled. "I will thank Zechariah bar Barach for this consideration."

Adina's room was next to her father. It also had the bed, and tables, but it had something else. Next to the bed was a small bench with an upright piece of wood on one side.

"This is called a *chair*," Elizabeth explained. "My husband saw one of these in the marketplace and purchased it for his honored grandmother—may her memory be blessed. We thought it would be helpful for Adina bat Boaz while she was here."

"How kind of both of you to think of me," Adina sat on the chair, cautiously rocking side to side on the seat and leaning against the upright piece of wood, before inviting her father and Mary to test it.

"Please take however long you need to wash and change your clothes," Elizabeth said. "Once I have shown Mary her room, I will finish preparing the meal for you."

Elizabeth led Mary to a room on the long wall of the courtyard. The room was similar to Adina's, but with a stool instead of a chair. Elizabeth peered out the door, closed it, and turned to take Mary's hands in her own.

"Blessed are you among women," she cried out, before gasping and covering her mouth with a hand. She glanced at the door, and continued in a lower voice. "Blessed is the child you will bear! But why am I so favored, that the mother of my Lord should come to me?"

Mary clapped a hand to her mouth, her eyebrows climbing to her head covering. "You…*know*…about…*my baby?*"

Elizabeth nodded.

"How? I said nothing."

"As soon as the sound of your greeting reached my ears," Elizabeth laid a hand on her own swollen stomach, "the babe in my womb leapt for joy." She wrapped her arms around Mary. "Blessed is she who has believed that the Lord would fulfill His promises to her!"

"You *know!*" Mary's voice cracked on the last word. She stepped away from her kinswoman and, lifting her hands to her face, dissolved into tears. *Elizabeth knows!* Mary's heart raced. *I do not have to convince her to believe what Gabriel told me.* The room exploded in a sunburst of light and colors. *Someone believes!* She heard—just as when the angel had ascended—the clapping of a thousand wings, their sound as that of a cascading waterfall. *Thank You, Yahweh, for answering my prayers!*

Raising her head, she extended her arms, "My soul glorifies the Lord and my spirit rejoices in God my Savior," she wiped away the tears pooling in her eyes, "for He has been mindful of the humble state of His servant. From now on all generations will call me blessed, for the Mighty One has done great things for me—Holy is His name."

She stepped over to Elizabeth, grasping her hands, and twirling the two of them in a circle. "His mercy extends to those who fear Him, from generation to generation. He has performed mighty deeds with His arm; He has scattered those who are proud in their inmost thoughts. He has brought down rulers from their thrones but has lifted up the humble. He has filled the hungry with good things but has sent the rich away empty."

She stopped and embraced her kinswoman. "He has helped His servant Israel, remembering to be merciful to Abraham and his descendants forever, just as He promised our ancestors."

Chapter 38

Nazareth

Joseph's family was finishing the morning meal when a knock came at their door. His father went to answer it, then returned. "Joseph, Rabbi Boaz has returned and would like to speak with you."

"Jacob," his mother frowned, "why did you not invite the rabbi inside instead of leaving him to stand in the cold weather?"

"Leah, I did invite him in," he grinned at his wife, "but he had no place to leave the camel."

"Ah," Joseph wiped his mouth with a cloth before standing, "Rabbi Boaz must be returning the camel Lucius Septimus loaned us for the journey."

"Camel?" Little Samuel squealed, before turning to his parents. "Please, may I go look at the camel?"

Mary bat Tovi looked at her husband, who smiled and nodded. "Yes, Samuel," she turned to their son, "you can go look at the camel, but," she lifted a finger, "be calm. The animal does not know you and you would not wish to frighten it."

"I will!" The child jumped up and ran from the room.

"I will watch him," Sarah stood and hurried after the boy.

The adults exchanged grins. Although Sarah now proclaimed that—as she was ten years of age—she was no longer a child, she had not succeeded in hiding her childlike enthusiasm.

Joseph did not have to caution Samuel nor Sarah about being calm; the presence of an animal whose shoulder height was taller than all the men in Nazareth was daunting. Rabbi Boaz held Gobba's reins so that the animal's head was lowered. Samuel was stroking the camel's forehead. Sarah was running a hand along the palanquin's bright material.

"Rabbi Boaz, what was it like to ride in a palanquin?" she asked

"You will have to ask Adina that question," the rabbi smiled, "as she and Mary bat Eli rode in the palanquin. I rode our donkey, Sefina. Ah, greetings Joseph. I am glad to find you still at home. I came early so you could take Gobba back when you went to Zippori."

"Greetings Rabbi Boaz," Joseph said. "You were wise in your timing." He glanced up at the sky; the sun was hidden behind a grey blanket of clouds. "I will be leaving for Zippori soon."

"Please offer our thanks to Lucius Septimus. Adina asked if you would give him this basket of oat cakes she made for him. Having the camel and its elegant palanquin made the journey easier for Adina and Mary."

"He will be pleased to hear that, and I know he will enjoy Adina's cakes." Joseph set the basket on the floor of the palanquin. "How is…" he looked at his sister and nephew. Samuel and Sarah appeared to still be enthralled with the camel, but Joseph noticed Sarah's head tilted toward him and the rabbi. He hesitated asking about Mary before them; as his Grandfather Teman would say, 'Words spoken in the presence of small birds fly on the wings of the wind.' *I would not wish to provide fodder for questions amongst my family.* "Sarah, please take Samuel inside. I need a moment to speak privately with Rabbi Boaz."

"Yes, Joseph. Come, Samuel." His sister took the boy's hand. When the child pursed his lips in a frown, she added, "Mother said she was going to teach me how to make almond cakes today. I will need someone to try them for me."

Samuel brightened. From her lessons in cooking, Sarah showed promise of being a skilled baker. "I would be happy to try them." He turned and hurried through the door, all but dragging Sarah with him. As she passed through the door, Sarah turned to grin at Joseph.

Joseph burst out laughing; the rabbi joined him.

"They are good children," the rabbi said.

"They are indeed," Joseph said, "although Sarah is growing quickly.

It will not be much longer before she is ready for betrothal. Speaking of betrothal," he turned back to the rabbi, "how is Mary?"

"The journey was a challenge for her. From what I could observe, she spent many hours fighting off waves of nausea. Adina cared for Mary, making sure she had food and water, as well as tending her when the nausea overcame her.

"After we arrived in Ein Kerem, a physician came to examine Elizabeth bat Shelomoh." He smiled. "Neither Adina nor I were aware that Mary's kinswoman was with child."

Joseph's eyes widened. *My kinswoman Elizabeth is with child,* Mary had told him.

The rabbi shook his head. "Yahweh's blessings never cease to amaze me. Mary did not appear to be surprised; I assume her parents had their reasons for not sharing this news with us.

"Nonetheless, a physician regularly comes to examine Elizabeth, which I assume it is due to her age. Zechariah and Elizabeth had sent word to him, asking if he would examine both Adina and Mary." He smiled. "The physician gave Adina a good report, for which I am thankful.

"Adina and I stepped aside while the physician examined Elizabeth and Mary." His smile faded. "Joseph, I am sorry. I know you had hoped—we all had hoped—the physician would prescribe a medicine which would cure Mary, allowing her to return to Nazareth with Adina and me. That did not happen. From what I understand, the physician will continue to examine Mary whenever he comes to see Elizabeth." He placed a hand on Joseph's shoulder. "As my grandmother—may her memory be blessed—used to say, *Where there is life, there is hope.*

"Mary felt well enough to sit at table with us that night and again the following morning. Zechariah bar Barach drove Adina and me in their carriage to the synagogue in Jerusalem where I had arranged for guest rooms. He then went with us to the Temple, where we offered sacrifices for Mary's healing.

"When we went back to Ein Kerem to get Gobba," the rabbi reached into the folds of his girdle and brought out a scroll of papyrus. "Zechariah bar Barach wrote this letter and Elizabeth asked me to give it to you. He wrote another I gave to Mary's parents."

"Thank you," Joseph took the letter and tucked it in the folds of his girdle. He did not wish to read it in the rabbi's presence. "I will read it later," he glanced up at the sky, "but I must leave for Zippori."

"Ride the camel," the rabbi grinned. "He will carry you to Zippori faster than you could lead him."

"That is wise." Joseph took the camel's reins and listened while the rabbi explained how to guide the animal. "Thank you again, Rabbi, for everything you have done for Mary."

"Of course," the rabbi smiled. "We all love Mary, although not as much as you."

Joseph had Gobba kneel and climbed into the palanquin, turning the animal toward Zippori. He grinned at the gapping expressions of the people who saw him riding in such a royal manner through the streets of Nazareth.

Once on the road leading to Zippori, Joseph drew out the letter. Unrolling the scroll, he read:

To Joseph ben Jacob
From Zechariah bar Barach
Greetings.
Mary bat Eli asked me to write this letter to you.
She, along with Rabbi Boaz bar Penuel and his daughter Adina bat Boaz, arrived two days ago. She was weary, which is to be expected after a long journey.
Our physician came the next day to examine my wife Elizabeth. I am pleased to share the news with you; after many years of praying, Yahweh has blessed us. Elizabeth is with child.

Joseph's eyebrows climbed to his forehead once again. *"Elizabeth and Zechariah are to be blessed with a child in their old age,"* Mary had told him. He shook his head; surely he had mis-remembered the events of that day in the ravine. He continued reading.

We waited to share this news with our family and friends. Due to her age, my wife did not experience the normal signs of a woman conceiving.

Joseph frowned. He knew the cessation of a woman's monthly flow was the sign of conception. *How would Zechariah and Elizabeth know she was with child?* He glanced at the road; he could see Zippori. He needed to hurry to finish Zechariah's letter.

We decided to wait until she felt the babe move before announcing it. That happened recently; indeed, when Mary arrived, my wife felt the babe move. Now we are excited for all to know that Yahweh has blessed us. Rabbi Boaz bar Penuel has also carried a letter to Mary's family, sharing this news.

Because of Elizabeth's age, we felt it best for her to be examined regularly by a physician. We had arranged, when he came, to examine Adina bat Boaz and Mary. He had a good report for Adina. Unfortunately, he did not find anything unusual that would cause the discomfort Mary is feeling. He felt something in Mary's life was causing great distress, which resulted in the nausea and weakness she has experienced. Elizabeth promised to care for Mary. We are praying she will soon recover her strength and will return to Nazareth and you.

In the Law Yahweh gave Moses, the Almighty said, "Worship the Lord your God, and His blessing will be on your food and water. I will take away sickness from among you, and none will miscarry or be barren in your land." *Since Elizabeth conceived, we have prayed this promise over her; we will begin praying it over Mary.*

Mary sends her affection.

Blessings on you.

Zechariah bar Barach

Joseph re-rolled the papyrus and tucked it into the folds of his girdle. Zechariah had not mentioned Mary's strange announcement. But then, Rabbi Boaz and Adina were present. She probably would not mention her story of the angel in their presence. *"The physician felt something in Mary's life was causing great distress, which resulted in the weakness and nausea she has experienced."*

That is my fault. He let out a long breath. *I did not believe her story—how* could *I believe such an implausible story—and it resulted in Mary being sick. It is all my fault. Even if she is healed and returns to Nazareth, would she still wish to be my betrothed?*

As Gobba entered the main street of Zippori, Joseph whispered, "Almighty Yahweh, be with Mary. Please heal her. I will do whatever You want, even divorce her," his heart felt rock-heavy, "just heal her."

Chapter 39

Ein Kerem
A month later

*T*o think that I am not the only person to be visited by the angel Gabriel," Mary shaped another mound of dough between her palms and slapped it on the dome of the fire pit.

Although Zechariah and Elizabeth's house had a fire pit similar to most homes in Nazareth, shortly after Elizabeth conceived, Zechariah had the potter in Ein Kerem build the low domed oven similar to the one in Rabbi Boaz's house.

It had been a month since Mary had arrived at Ein Kerem. Every day, the weakness and nausea eased more, and she had slipped into a natural routine of helping Elizabeth. At first Elizabeth would not hear of it, declaring that Mary was a guest, and *she* was perfectly capable of doing her house work.

"Please allow this, Elizabeth. Grandmother Tzipora's last admonition was for me to be of help to you and Zechariah."

Elizabeth humphed. "That sounds like something Tzipora bat Leui would say. Fine," she shrugged. "I would not want your grandmother to be displeased with you, although," she lifted a finger, "I will not allow you to do more work than I. You are earlier in your pregnancy than I am and you suffered from weakness and nausea, although we praise Yahweh that you are daily getting better," she turned to Zechariah, "do we not, husband?"

The elderly man sitting nearby, nodded vigorously. He picked up a wax tablet and stylus similar to Mary's and wrote something. He turned the tablet around for the women to see.

"Praise be to Yahweh," Elizabeth read.

Mary was not surprised to learn that, like Rabbi Boaz and Adina, Zechariah taught Elizabeth to read. When she told her two elderly relatives she was learning to write, they were pleased to continue teaching her. She also learned what Elizabeth called Zechariah's *gesture speaking*. To keep from having to write all their communication down, Elizabeth and Zechariah had devised a series of hand motions to represent simple language.

The evening after Rabbi Boaz and Adina left, Mary told Elizabeth and Zechariah about Gabriel's visit to her. It was a relief to tell someone about the angel's message. She was surprised to learn that Zechariah had also been visited by the angel Gabriel. Because of Zechariah's inability to speak, Elizabeth told Mary what happened. It was as exciting a visitation as her own.

Zechariah was one of 18,000 priests who served in the Temple of Yahweh in Jerusalem. There were 24 divisions of priests; Zechariah was of the division of Abijah. In addition to serving in the Temple during holy festivals, he—along with the other priests—would also serve one week twice a year.

On the day seven months ago, for the first and only time—as his name would not be drawn again—Zechariah had been chosen to burn the incense as part of the morning sacrifice.

While Mary knew the priests had daily prescribed responsibilities in the Holy Temple, she was not familiar with what most of them were. With Zechariah using the gesture speaking and writing details on his tablet, Elizabeth explained what had happened on that particular morning.

Each day, there were about fifty priests serving in the Temple. In the morning, they were divided into two groups. Their first task was to inspect the Temple courtyards. Afterwards, the priests met and marched in two columns to the Chamber of Hewn Stone, the room where the Sanhedrin—the highest religious council of the Jewish people—would meet. Here, the day's duties were assigned by casting lot, according to the proverb written by King Solomon: *The lot is cast into the lap, but its every decision is from the* Lord.

Lots were cast to determine which priest would stir the coals that still glowed on the altar of burnt offering from the previous day; or the priests who would take part in that day's sacrifice; or those who would trim the wicks of the golden seven-branched candlestick in the Holy Place and replenish the oil; or lastly, those who tended the altar of incense.

The final preparation was to bring out the sacrificial lamb for the *Tamid,* the perpetual sacrifice that was offered daily at the third hour and again at the ninth hour. Once the animal had been inspected and prepared for sacrifice, the gates were opened and the worshippers—including Elizabeth—had come into the Temple courtyard. After the lamb was sacrificed, the officiating priest, standing on the east side of the altar, sprinkled the lamb's blood onto the two sides of the altar.

While this was happening, the other chosen priests were preparing everything in the Holy Place, where was located the seven-branched candelabrum, the table of shewbread, and the altar of incense. Here, in the Holy Place, the most solemn of the day's ceremonies would take place, that of offering the incense, which symbolized Israel's prayers being accepted by God.

"You can imagine how honored we were," Elizabeth said, "to learn Zechariah had been selected to burn the incense and to pray for our people."

Mary shook her head in wonder. "That is indeed an honor, but I confess I am not surprised. Zechariah is known to be an honorable man, who walks blamelessly before the Lord." She turned to smile at the elderly man and was surprised to see Zachariah drop his head and lift a hand to wipe away tears. "Elizabeth," she lowered her voice, "have I said something amiss?"

"No, you have not," Elizabeth stood up with a groan, hand pressing on her back, and waddled over to hand Zechariah a cloth to wipe his eyes. She kissed his brow before crossing to a worktable where she poured three cups of water. She handed one to Zechariah before returning to the baking area and handed a cup to Mary. "My husband is ashamed of what happened in the Holy Place."

"What?" Mary slanted a glance at her elderly relative through lowered lashes as she sipped the water.

Elizabeth eased herself down by the oven and took a sip of water before continuing the story.

Having been selected to burn the incense, Zechariah's first task was to choose two priests to help him in this sacred service. The first helper removed what had been left on the altar of incense from the previous evening's service. Then, speaking prayers, he walked backward away from the altar. The second helper then came forward and spread live coals taken from that morning's burnt offering; after which, he also worshipped and retired.

As Elizabeth—along with the other worshippers and priests waited outside—Zechariah now stood alone in the Holy Place, illumined only by the seven-branched candlestick. In front of him, toward the heavy Veil that hung before the Holy of Holies, was the golden altar of incense, on which the red coals glowed. To his right was the Table of Shewbread; to his left was the golden candlestick.

"Then it was time for Zechariah to burn the incense," Elizabeth set down her cup. "He walked forward and spread the incense on the altar. A cloud of smoke from the incense formed and moved upward, filling the Holy Place with a fragrant cloud. Zechariah waited until he was sure that the incense was burning well.

"At that point he bowed in worship. After his prayers, he would have stood and reverently left the Holy Place, except something wonderous happened." She turned to look at her husband. Zechariah nodded.

"What I have told you about the sacrifices I know because it is tradition and commonly known. What happened next I learned from Zechariah's writings and from his gesture speaking.

"As I said, after Zechariah was certain the incense was burning properly, he knelt in prayer. While he was worshipping, he felt—a presence."

"A presence?" Mary asked, remembering her own experience. Kneeling to draw the butterfly, and then seeing the sandal-clad feet beneath the hem of a white robe appear in front of her. *If I had not been focused on drawing, would I have sensed the angel's presence?*

Elizabeth nodded. "Yes, that is what he wrote. He was kneeling in front of the altar of incense, when he felt a presence.

"Looking up, he saw a man standing on the right side of the altar of incense; but the man was unlike any man Zechariah had ever seen before." She looked at her husband, who nodded his head vigorously.

Zechariah stood, lifting his hands far above his head and then stretching them out to either side.

"The man was taller and broader than any man we knew," Elizabeth said,

"Yes!" Mary said. "He was taller than Gobba the camel and appeared to be stronger than the Judge Samson. The way he carried himself reminded me of a warrior."

Zechariah nodded vigorously. He touched his clothes and hair, then turned his head away, shielding his eyes with his hands.

Elizabeth nodded and turned back to Mary. "He said the man wore garments which were whiter than snow and glowed."

"Yes!" Mary jumped up to cross to Zechariah. "His garments, his hair, and even his skin were white and shining as if lit from within. His hair whipped wildly about his face, as if from a storm, but no wind was blowing."

The elderly man's eyes widened, and he nodded again. He patted the air in front of him in a crawling motion.

"Zechariah said he terrified and crawled beneath the table for the shewbread."

"I crawled away," Mary laughed, "to hide behind a tree."

"Zechariah said the man spoke, yet it sounded as if others were in the room with them."

"That is how it sounded to me," Mary said. "His voice echoed as if a multitude of people were speaking instead of just him."

Zechariah pointed to himself, then patted the air in a calming motion.

"The man told Zechariah not to be afraid," Elizabeth said.

"He told me that as well," Mary laughed, "as if that would ease me. I asked him, 'Who are you?'" Placing her hand on her chest as the angel had, she said, "He told me, 'I am Gabriel.' I asked, 'You are named for the angel Yahweh sent to the prophet Daniel?'" Her eyes widened as her focus turned inward, to that afternoon on the Feast of Trumpets. "He said, 'I…am…Gabriel.' Her gaze returned to her kin. "That is when I realized *who* was standing before me."

Elizabeth gestured toward her husband. "The angel did not tell Zechariah his name," she sighed, "at least not at first. After telling him to not be afraid, the man told Zechariah that our prayers had been heard." She laid a hand on her swollen stomach. "He said, 'Your wife Elizabeth will bear you a son, and you are to call him John.'" She looked at Mary, "He went on to say that our *son*," she smiled in wonder, "will be a joy and delight to us and that many will rejoice because of his birth." She laughed, "Zechariah said he thought, *'Of course that would be a wonderous delight and joy to us; we have prayed for a child for decades.'*

"The man went on to say that our son will be great in the sight of the Lord. He said our son was never to drink wine or fermented drink, and that he would be filled with Yahweh's Holy Spirit before he is even born. The man said that our son will bring back many of the people of Israel to the Lord our God." She closed her eyes, smiling, and continued speaking. "He said our son will go on *before* the Lord, in the spirit and power of the prophet Elijah, to turn the hearts of the parents to their children and the disobedient to the wisdom of the righteous—to make ready a people prepared for the Lord."

Mary heard a ragged gasp, and looked to see Zechariah weeping, his face in his hands, groaning as his shoulders shook.

Elizabeth stood and hurried to her embrace her husband, shushing him as one would a child.

"Elizabeth, I do not understand," Mary said. "Why is Zechariah weeping? What you have told me sounds much like what I experienced. This is a wonderful pronouncement; you are not only to have a son, but he is also to be a mighty servant of Yahweh."

Elizabeth wiped her husband's eyes again and, picking up his cup, encouraged him to take a sip of water. She crossed to Mary and, taking her hand, led her back to sit by the oven. "You spoke truth; much of yours and Zechariah's story were the same. But that is where the similarities end. Mary, what did you say after Gabriel told you that you were to be the mother of the Messiah?"

"When I understood that Joseph was not to be the father of my son," Mary smoothed her hand across her abdomen, remembering that moment, "I said, 'I do not understand. I am betrothed to Joseph, but we have not...'" she glanced at Elizabeth and Zechariah. "I said, 'I do not understand how this will be, as I am,' she felt herself blushing to the roots of her hair, 'a virgin?'"

"*That* is where your story and Zechariah's differ," tears pooled in her kinswoman's eyes. Elizabeth looked at her husband. His eyes were still red-rimmed, but the despondent look was gone, replaced by calm determination. He nodded. Elizabeth gave Mary a tremulous smile.

"Your question to Gabriel revealed understandable confusion. Yet, after hearing the angel's message, after hearing that our prayers were to be answered," Elizabeth drew a shuddering breath, her eyes misting, "Zechariah asked, 'How can I be sure of this? I am an old man and my wife is well along in years.'"

Mary gasped, eyes wide. *Zechariah had faced Yahweh's angel. Yet, when told of the promised child, Zechariah did not believe?*

Elizabeth nodded. "You understand. You had never been with a man, yet you did not question Yahweh's word. My husband did not believe.

"The man told Zechariah, 'I am Gabriel.'"

Mary glanced at Zechariah. Her elderly kinsman shuddered as if reliving the memory.

"That is when Zechariah realized he was in the presence of an angel. He said, 'I am Gabriel, I *stand* in the presence of Yahweh. I have been sent to tell you this good news. Now, you will be silent and not able to speak until the day this happens, because you did not believe my words, which *will* come true at their appointed time.'"

"Oh Elizabeth, Zechariah," Mary's eyes were filling, "I am so sorry. How you must have felt, what you must have thought."

"It was terrible," Elizabeth said. "It does not take long for a priest to burn the incense. When Zechariah lingered in the Temple, I—along with the worshippers with me—began to wonder. Then when he came out," she wiped her eyes, "and he could not speak, people began saying, 'He had a vision,' while others said, 'He is being punished by Yahweh.'" Elizabeth shook her head. "It was later, when we were home, when he got his tablet and wrote the story of what happened.

"After we had grown accustomed to his inability to speak, and we developed ways to communicate, we began wondering about the angel's message. To think that, after all these years, *I would finally conceive.*" She glanced at her husband and lowered her voice. "It had been years since I had a monthly flow. We did not know how we would *know* I was with child. I remained secluded for months, to protect myself, to protect the child, and to avoid our neighbor's questions about what happened to Zechariah.

"In my fifth month," Elizabeth laid a hand on her abdomen, smiling. "I felt the babe move. At first, it felt like a butterfly brushing against my stomach. A week later, it felt like a small *thump.* The day you arrived, when you spoke my name, our babe *leapt* as if for joy!" She reached over, took Mary's hand to lay it on her own abdomen. "It was as if our son, John," she leaned over to lay a hand on Mary's abdomen, "*recognized* your son, Jesus."

Mary smiled, nodding.

"The Lord has done this for me," Elizabeth smiled, tears sparkling in her eyes. "In these days He has shown His favor and taken away my disgrace among the people."

Mary smiled. "The Lord has blessed both of you. You love each other, and now you are going to be parents. Everyone will be thrilled to see Yahweh's answer to your prayers." Her smile faded. "Joseph did not believe when I told him. He thought my story was a result of madness or..." tears stung her eyes, "blasphemy."

Elizabeth took Mary's hand and squeezed. "Trust all to Yahweh." She looked at her husband, who nodded, smiling. "As Zechariah says, 'All that Yahweh does is done for the best.'"

Mary laughed, blinking away the tears "That is what Rabbi Boaz says."

Zechariah picked up his tablet and stylus. After writing for a moment, he turned the tablet toward them.

"Your rabbi is a wise man," Elizabeth read. She erupted in laughter.

Mary joined her kinswoman. *Thank you, Yahweh, for bringing me to Elizabeth and Zechariah's home. They are a blessing to me, and to my son...Your Son.*

Chapter 40

Nazareth
A month later

The sun hung golden in the midafternoon sky as Joseph walked home from Zippori. He had finished his work early and even though he asked for something else to do—anything to keep his mind focused away from what might be happening to Mary—Lucius Septimus had sent him home.

"Joseph ben Jacob, since your betrothed wife left for Ein Kerem, you have arrived in Zippori before the other workers and have been the last one to leave." The overseer laid a plump hand on Joseph's shoulder. "You will not help her by wearing yourself out. I know your people enjoy repeating the wise sayings of your elders, so I tell you what my father's father would say, *Fatigue damages even the most skilled artisan as surely as a dull chisel damages marble.*"

"I am fine. I can still—" Joseph protested, only to be cut off by the large Roman.

"You are not fine. You are exhausted. Joseph; you need to rest." He picked up Joseph's bag of tools and handed it to him, before grasping Joseph's shoulders and turning him toward the street leading out of Zippori. "Go home. Be with your family. Eat. Rest."

By the time he had left Zippori and began walking down the road toward Nazareth, Joseph realized Lucius was right. His eyes felt weighted, and his feet felt as if they were shackled. He stumbled along the road, tripping over his own sandals. *I just need to rest.*

He hesitated when he came to the path that would lead him to the olive grove and the shortcut home. Since that day, a month ago, when he screamed out to Yahweh, Joseph had avoided the olive grove. Two weeks prior, when the residents of Nazareth gathered to celebrate the olive harvest, he had stayed away, informing his family he had extra work to do in Zippori.

If I take the shorter way through the olive grove, I will arrive home earlier, and be able to rest. His lips turned down. *If I arrive home early, I will face questions from my family I do not wish to answer nor have the strength to avoid.* He filled his lungs with a deep sigh. *I just want to rest.*

His battle with fatigue won out; he turned toward the olive grove. *Just for a few minutes.*

He walked to the tree where he had seen Mary kneeling and scratching a stick in the dirt. He turned and leaned against the tree, sliding down against the trunk until he was seated on the ground. The branches provided a deep, soothing shade.

He glanced at the road he had been walking on. It was there Rabbi Boaz had said, "*She is drawing,*" followed with the observation he knew Joseph was attracted to Mary.

Joseph took a deep breath and turned his head to look at the ravine. It was there he had run to Mary, fearful for her safety. It was there—his heart ached—she had said, "*The angel Gabriel appeared to me…I am to be the mother of the Messiah.*" Tears filled his eyes as he relived that day; refusing to believe her story, claiming it stemmed from blasphemy or insanity. It was there, a month ago, he had screamed out his pain and frustration, pleading with Yahweh, promising to divorce Mary if the Almighty would just heal her.

Joseph looked up, tears streaming into his beard. *I made a vow with the Almighty, and I will keep it.* He wept until his eyes were dry and his chest burned.

He felt a light sensation on his right hand. Looking down, he saw a butterfly with delicate wings of iridescent blue and silver tips crawling across the back of his hand. *Mary had spoken of butterflies.* Joseph held his breath, watching the creature when, out of the corner of his eye, he saw sandal-clad feet beneath a white robe near him.

Joseph caught his breath and sat up, certain someone from Nazareth had seen him weeping like a babe. He wiped his face with the palms of his hands and looked up, eyes widening at the sight of the man standing before him.

He was taller and larger than any man Joseph had seen, either in Nazareth and Zippori, with the bearing of the Roman soldiers. But it was the blinding light shimmering from his garments, his skin, and his wild hair that identified him.

This has to be the angel who appeared to Mary. This had to be Gabriel.

"Greetings."

Joseph shifted to prostrate himself before the angel of the Lord, hands covering his head, bracing himself, certain the Almighty had sent the angelic being to strike him for being slow in keeping his promise to release Mary from their betrothal.

"Joseph, son of David." Gabriel's voice echoed across the ravine and back, as if he were a multitude of heavenly beings. "Do not be afraid."

Joseph frowned into the dirt, uncertain how to *not be afraid* while facing divine judgement. Shock shot through him like lightening through a storm cloud as a hand touched his shoulder. "Rise."

Lifting his eyes above his fingers, he noted the angel was unarmed…and was smiling. Gabriel gave a single nod of his head. "Rise. Sit."

Eyes never leaving the angel, Joseph shifted and sat against the tree. He lifted his bag of tools, not as a means to protect himself, but to draw comfort from something of this world.

"You are Gabriel," he whispered, "the messenger of Yahweh? The one who visited Mary?"

The angel nodded again. "I am Gabriel."

"What do you want with me?"

"Joseph, son of David," the angel's countenance softened, "do not be afraid to take Mary home as your wife, because what is conceived in her is from the Holy Spirit. She will give birth to a Son, and *you* are to give Him the name Jesus, because He will save His people from their sins."

With the angel's first words, Joseph's brows climbed to his head covering. *Take Mary home as your bride.* His heart leapt. *I can marry her.* As Gabriel continued, Joseph's jaw dropped, he frowned; he heard the words the angel spoke, but they made no sense to him. "Mary is…" he licked his lips, "truly with child?"

"She is."

"And no *man*," he blushed, realizing what he was about to ask," is the child's father?"

The angel nodded. "The child was conceived by the Holy Spirit of Yahweh."

Joseph shook his head in wonder. *Mary is with child, yet she is still a virgin. Yet…* He licked his lips again. "*I* am to name him?" *If the angel strikes me for imprudent questions, so be it; I have to know.*

"*You* are to name him Jesus."

Joseph realized by naming the child, he would be announcing to all that he was the child's father. It had been three months since the Feast of Trumpets, when Mary was visited by Gabriel. Even if they married tomorrow, she would give birth in six months' time. By his naming the child, all who knew them would assume they had been intimate before their wedding ceremony. Joseph lifted his chin. *Yahweh has given me the command—the honor—of naming His Son. I care not what men will think of me, of us.*

He remembered the rest of the Gabriel's words and looked at the angel again, "I do not understand what you said, *He will save His people from their sins.* The Messiah is to drive the Romans from our land, ascend the throne of David, and restore Israel to the glory of David's reign. Your words sound as if the Child—as if Jesus—will not be a warrior like King David, but will be like the prophets of old."

The angel looked at him, but said nothing.

He is not going to answer me. No; the angel spoke Yahweh's words not his own. Rabbi Boaz always said, "All that Yahweh does is done for the best." Yahweh answered my prayer concerning Mary; I will trust the rest to Him.

Setting his tool bag aside, he knelt, extending his arms to each side, and bowed his head. "I will do all the Lord has commanded."

The butterfly spread its delicate wings and flew to land on his outstretched hand. A moment later, another butterfly joined it; then another. He looked upwards as a myriad of butterflies joined the first one, swirling around the angel and himself, their wings brushing his skin, his beard, the clapping of their wings sounding like a waterfall.

As the butterflies swirled skyward, Gabriel was instantly within a breath of Joseph's face. "Joseph, awake!" The angel's eyes blazed like fire, his voice boomed in Joseph's ears, echoing across the sky as Gabriel disappeared.

Joseph sat up gasping, looking around. He was in alone in the olive grove.

Chapter 41

Ein Kerem
A month later

ook, John," Zechariah pointed toward the night sky, "that is the mazzaloth Tzedek."

"Zechariah," Elizabeth laughed, "our son is but a babe. All he knows or cares about is eating, sleeping, having dry clothing," she rubbed her nose against the infant's nose, "and being held."

"He will not always be so young," Zechariah reached to take the babe in his arms. "One day he will fulfill the word Yahweh spoke through the angel Gabriel." He looked in the baby's face. "My son, the angel said you will go before the Lord, in the spirit and power of the prophet Elijah, to turn the hearts of the parents to their children and the disobedient to the wisdom of the righteous—to make ready a people prepared for the Lord. There is much you will need to learn to be prepared for your calling, including being trained in ordinary things, like watching the stars at night." He adjusted John in his arms, so the babe was facing upward. "Do you see?" he pointed to the stars. "That is the mazzaloth Tzedek."

Elizabeth crossed her arms, eyebrows lowered, until she glanced at Mary; then the women burst out laughing.

"Husband," Elizabeth said, "you are incorrigible."

"And you," he leaned over the babe to kiss Elizabeth's cheek, "are my heart's delight." He turned to Mary. "What did you say the merchant Jacob ben Reuben told you about the names the Romans called the star arrangements?"

"He said the star we know as Tzedek is called Jupiter by the Romans, after the father of their gods." She pointed to another star, "The one we all Heilel, the Romans call Venus." She pointed to an arrangement of stars. "The mazzaloth we call Zerah, they call Virgo, the Virgin." She pointed to a different mazzaloth, "Our Taleh, the Romans call Aries, the Ram."

Mary told Elizabeth and Zechariah about Jacob ben Reuben's *star journey*. "If you look," she pointed to the stars, "Tzedek is closer to Zerah than when I first arrived in Ein Kerem."

John began wailing, flailing tiny fists as he announced his displeasure to his parents and Mary.

"Poor baby," Elizabeth reached for him, but Zechariah, held out his hand, palm facing her.

"No, stay, Wife. You have fed him; I will take him to his bed." Zechariah leaned over to allow Elizabeth to kiss John's tiny brow before he carried the baby into the house, talking to the child.

"John, you probably will not remember but, during the celebration of your circumcision, our rabbi wanted to name you after me. Rabbi Kalev bar Gilad is an honorable and godly man, but he is old—older than your father. Rabbi Kalev forgot by naming you after me, your name would have been Zechariah ben Zechariah." He nuzzled his son's head. "Or would you have preferred Zechariah bar Zechariah." He threw his head back, laughing, and continuing talking to John as he carried the infant into the house.

"Zechariah is a good father," Mary smiled.

"He is indeed," Elizabeth said. "And he is a good husband. I am blessed," she smiled at Mary, "as you will be."

Mary's smile slipped, thinking about Joseph. "I hope what you say will be true."

"Remember what the prophet Jeremiah wrote," Elizabeth laid a hand on Mary's knee. *For I know the plans I have for you, declares the Lord, plans to prosper you and not to harm you, plans to give you hope and a future.*

"Yahweh has chosen you to be the mother of His Son. He will provide all you need to accomplish His plans for you."

Mary nodded. "You speak truth, Elizabeth." She smiled. "Look at how He has fulfilled His promise to you and Zechariah." She laughed. "I still remember the expressions on the faces of everyone at the ceremony of circumcision when you announced your son's name was to be John."

Elizabeth joined in Mary's laughter. "You are the only one who knows about the angel Gabriel visiting Zechariah in the Temple. While that day provided fodder for the gossips, once Zechariah returned home from Jerusalem, most people forgot he came out of the Holy Place unable to speak. Indeed, our local friends assumed he had suffered what King David wrote about in his psalm, *May my tongue cling to the roof of my mouth.*" She grinned, "Do you remember how the neighbors looked when Zechariah spoke for the first time since that day in the Temple?"

Mary laughed, clapping her hands. "That was a memorable day."

After a quick and easy labor, Elizabeth gave birth to a son. On the eighth day, their friends gathered to celebrate the ceremony of circumcision. When it came time to name him, Rabbi Kalev was going to name him after Zechariah.

"No!" Elizabeth had said. "He is to be called John."

The elderly rabbi insisted, saying, "But there is no one among your relatives who is named John. He should be named after his father."

When Elizabeth refused, the rabbi turned to Zechariah and made signs to him—Mary smiled, *As if Zechariah could not hear—*asking what name he wished to give the child.

Zechariah asked for his writing tablet. Because Elizabeth was holding the baby, Mary brought the tablet to Zechariah. He wrote something and then turned it for all to see.

Rabbi Kalev read aloud, "His name is John."

Before those present could close their gaping mouths, Zechariah stood. "Praise be to Yahweh, the God of Israel," he said, his voice raspy, "for He has come to His people and redeemed them." He set the tablet down and crossed to stand in next to Elizabeth. "He has raised up a horn of salvation for us in the house of His servant David as He spoke through His holy prophets of long ago, for salvation from our enemies and from the hand of all who hate us, to show mercy to our ancestors and to remember His holy covenant that He promised to Father Abraham. A promise to rescue us from our enemies, and to enable us to serve Him all our days without fear in holiness and righteousness before Him."

Taking John from Elizabeth, Zechariah lifted the babe to be face-to-face with him. "And you, my son, will be called a prophet of the Most High," his voice grew stronger with each word. "You will prepare the way for the Lord's Messiah, to give His people the knowledge of salvation through the forgiveness of their sins, because of Yahweh's tender mercies. Through this, the rising sun will come to us from Heaven to shine on those living in darkness and—in the shadow of death—to guide our feet into the path of peace."

That news of that event spread through Ein Kerem. Their neighbors would stop by with food, as if Elizabeth was too weak or Mary had no knowledge of cooking. After thanking them for their kindness, Elizabeth would invite them to see John.

"I struggle not to laugh," Elizabeth said. "They mean well, but they all gaze at John as if the babe will perform a miracle in front of them." She smiled, laying a hand on Mary's arm. "Could you imagine how they would react if they knew they were in the presence of the mother of the Messiah?"

Mary laughed. "I am thankful you and Zechariah know, but I would not wish to draw attention to myself," she laid a hand on her abdomen, "or my son by sharing my story, especially with strangers. I will leave that revelation to Yahweh."

"You are wise," Elizabeth smiled. "Have you given more thought to our offer to stay here?"

Over the time she had been in Ein Kerem, Mary's nausea and weakness had eased. She had missed her monthly flow and had experienced other signs that conception had taken place. She believed—and Elizabeth and Zechariah agreed—it occurred on the afternoon of the Feast of Trumpets when the angel Gabriel appeared to her.

She had sent letters to her parents, informing them of her

recovery. She also sent letters to Joseph. Her parents replied, but not Joseph. She wondered what he would do. *Will he divorce me?*

The previous evening, Elizabeth and Zechariah had offered a solution. If Joseph divorces her, which would bring shame on her family, she should live with them.

"It might be wise," Zechariah had said, "for your son to be raised near Jerusalem."

"We have empty rooms in our home," Elizabeth had said. "As John is to *prepare the way* for your Jesus, we could raise them together."

"I could arrange for both our sons to be trained in the Law Yahweh gave to Moses," Zechariah added, "as well as the skills needed to rule a nation."

"Zechariah," Elizabeth said, "imagine how excited Anna bat Phanuel and Simeon ben Anaiah will be to see our sons." She turned to Mary. "If you go to the Temple when we present John, you will see Anna. She is an elderly widow; her husband died after they had been married only seven years. Can you imagine losing your husband?" She wiped a tear from her eye. "That was many years ago; Anna is now eighty-four years old and considered by all who know her to be a prophetess. She never leaves the Temple now, but spends days and nights praying, fasting, and worshipping."

Zechariah nodded. "I see Anna bat Phanuel every time I am in the Temple. Elizabeth spoke of Simeon ben Anaiah. He is a friend. Like Anna, he is elderly," he grinned, "even older than I. Simeon has waited many years for the Consolation of Israel. He has said Yahweh's Holy Spirit revealed to him that he would not die before he had seen the Lord's Messiah."

Mary's eyes widened. *It is not only to me to whom Yahweh revealed the coming of His Messiah. There is Zechariah, Anna bat Phanuel, and Simeon ben Anaiah. So many people have heard and are waiting to meet Jesus.* She slid her hand across her abdomen. *If only Joseph were one of those people.*

Chapter 42

A month later

*J*oseph walked up the stairs that led to the roof of his home and crossed to the far corner, where was located the bed chamber he had been building for Mary and himself. He dropped the tools, cloths, and skin of oil next to the small stool behind a wooden table before walking to the edge of the roof.

The flecks of golden sunshine dotted the sky over the ravine and olive grove. He closed his eyes, filled his lungs, and released the air. After all those months, there was a peace in this place, in his heart.

He turned and walked back to the bed chamber. Opening the door, he stepped inside, and picked up the small wooden chest he had built for Mary, the one he planned to give her during their wedding celebration. He had not worked on the chest since the afternoon of the Feast of Trumpets. Carrying it outside, he placed it on the table, sat on the stool, and picked up a tiny chisel. All that was left was to go over the fine details of the roses before rubbing it with olive oil.

He fell into the rhythm of work, feeling the pleasure of creating something of beauty for someone he loved. When he was satisfied with the details of the wooden roses, he set the chisel aside, opened the skin of oil, and tipped it over the cloth.

"Joseph."

Joseph startled and stood—knocking over the stool, dropping the cloth, and spilling oil over the top of the chest—and turned to see Mary's father standing at the top of the stairs.

"Eli bat Matthat." He closed the skin of oil and set it aside. "I-I did not hear you."

"Forgive me," Eli crossed the roof to Joseph. "I did not mean to

203

startle you. I was walking by your house, when I looked up and saw you. I did not realize you would be home today. I understand you spend most days in Zippori."

"I…uh…" Joseph focused on wiping up the oil trickling over the side of the chest, "do spend many days in Zippori. However, this is the Roman festival of Saturnalia. The Romans in Zippori are celebrating with many unusual traditions, including a public feast and the giving of gifts. Lucius Septimus chose to celebrate by *giving* the workers and artisans a day off of work."

"That is an interesting celebration," Eli looked at the bed chamber, the small chest Joseph had been working on, and frowned. "Joseph, I wish to speak with you."

"I…see. Please sit," Joseph set the stool aright and placed it near Eli, before stepping inside the bed chamber to get another stool. Once he was seated, he looked at Mary's father. "Is it about Mary?"

Eli studied him. "It is."

"I have received the letters from Zechariah bar Barach. He says Mary is getting better. He also said that his wife Elizabeth bat Shelomoh…" Joseph did not know how to finish.

"Elizabeth has given birth to a son."

Joseph nodded. "Zechariah bar Barach wrote us of their news. Mazel tov. I understand they have wanted a child for many years." *What is it you wish to speak about?*

"They have," Eli smiled. "This is a wonderful blessing for them. We received a letter from Zechariah today. It has been thirty days since their son was born; they are presenting their new son at the Temple in ten days." His smile faded and he looked at Joseph. "My wife and I are going to Ein Kerem to celebrate with them."

"That will be…a joyous time." *Did you come to talk to me about this baby?*

"When Anne and I return to Nazareth, we are bringing Mary home with us. Joseph, when your father approached me with your offer of marriage to Mary, I believed you cared for her. We do not know what happened on the Day of Atonement to cause her to become ill. Indeed, her mother and I noticed she was not feeling well shortly after the Feast of Trumpets.

"At your suggestion, we sent her to Elizabeth and Zechariah, in the hopes a physician would diagnose the illness and prescribe a cure.

"Zechariah writes that the physician could not find anything to cause Mary's illness, nor could he say whether it will return.

"It has been three months since Mary has been gone. During this time, we have not seen you, we have not heard from you. I have seen your father several times, and he says you work from sunrise to sunset, yet he has said nothing about you," he glanced at the bed chamber, "continuing to prepare for your wedding.

"There would be many in Nazareth who would understand if you were concerned about whatever caused her unknown illness, or," his eyes narrowed, "if you were *afraid* to bring Mary home as your bride. They would not condemn you for," his mouth pulled down in distaste, "*divorcing* her."

He straightened, crossed his arms, and stared at Joseph. "Joseph ben Jacob, Mary's mother and I want to know," he filled his lungs and blew out the air, "what are your intentions toward our daughter?"

He wants to know if I am afraid. I was. Joseph frowned, realizing he had never been afraid Mary had been unfaithful to him. But fear? *Yes. I was afraid. I was afraid that—for whatever reason—she was blasphemous or she had lost her sanity. I pled with Yahweh, promising I would divorce Mary if He would heal her. When the letters from Zechariah stating she was getting better, I avoided making a decision. I was afraid, because I still loved her.*

Joseph looked across the rooftop, beyond the ravine, to the olive grove. He remembered the butterfly landing on his hand. The angel Gabriel appearing, *"Joseph, son of David,"* he had said, *"do not be* afraid *to take Mary home as your wife, because what is conceived in her is from the Holy Spirit. She will give birth to a Son, and you are to give Him the name Jesus, because He will save His people from their sins."*

He realized Mary's father was watching him, still waiting for his answer.

What are your intentions?

Joseph blew out his breath, dropped the soiled cloth, and stood. "Eli ben Matthat, my intentions are to go with you," he smiled, "and bring Mary home as my wife."

Chapter 43

Ten days later

*M*ary, I cannot tell you what a blessing it is to have you here, helping me with the house," Elizabeth said, adjusting the blanket around John. "I never realized how much time it takes to care for a newborn."

"I cannot tell you what a blessing it is to have you helping with the cooking," Zechariah grinned, reaching for another piece of bread.

The sun was a soft gold rising in the eastern sky. They were sitting around the table in the courtyard where Mary had placed bowls of white cheese and dates, a pitcher of goat's milk, cups, and a platter of bread, still warm from the oven.

Mary—like Elizabeth—was dressed in a simple tunic, her hair falling in waves to her waist.

"John demands much of his mother's attention and time. If you were not here," he grinned, "I would have to learn to cook."

"Zechariah is skilled in many areas, but cooking is not one of them," Elizabeth laughed.

Mary joined in their laughter. "I am glad to help, but to speak truth, it is a blessing to me to do something to thank you. I spent so many weeks praying," she laid her hand on Elizabeth's arm, "someone would believe me. Coming here was the answer to my prayer. It never occurred to me to be thankful for the weakness and nausea that brought me here."

They heard a knock at the door.

Elizabeth frowned. "Who can that be at this hour?"

"I will find out," Zechariah stood and walked into the house. A few minutes later, he returned escorting two people.

Mary's eyes widened. "Mother! Father!" She jumped up and ran to embrace her parents. Only then did she realize a third person was with them. *Joseph!* Her heart leapt. She smiled until she noticed he was staring at her lips. Blushing, she realized she was unveiled in the presence of her betrothed.

She was uncertain what to do, when she felt something soft in her hand. She looked to see Elizabeth handing her a linen veil.

While her parents "Oooed" and "Awwed" over John, Mary turned to drape the veil over her head. Lifting the edge of the fabric, she draped it across her nose, and tucked behind her right ear.

She filled her lungs and turned to face her family and betrothed. "We did not know you were coming." She noticed Elizabeth and Zechariah exchanging looks with her parents. She sniffed, lifting her chin. "*I* did not know you were coming."

"We received word from your parents only yesterday," Zechariah grinned. "We thought to keep the knowledge secret, thinking it would be a pleasant surprise for you."

Mary's eyes crinkled as she grinned. "Well, it was." She turned to her parents, "You must tell me—"

Elizabeth interrupted, "Before they do, I am certain they are fatigued from their journey. Husband, did you properly welcome our guests to our home?"

"I did, although it was brief, as *someone*," Zechariah slanted a glance toward Joseph, "appeared to be anxious for the welcome to end."

Mary noticed color cover Joseph's face. She was thankful her veil hid her smile; she would never wish to embarrass her betrothed. Her smile faded as memories of their last encounters washed over her.

"Come," Elizabeth extended a hand, indicating the table. "Please sit. I am certain you are hungry. I know you will enjoy it; Mary prepared the meal."

The next few minutes were spent getting more cups for milk, passing the food, talking about their journey, as well as family and friends in Nazareth.

"Everyone sends their love," Father looked at his wife and winked. "Even your Grandmother Tzipora."

"They are thankful to hear you are feeling better," Mother said. "Rabbi Boaz and Adina asked me to tell you they look forward to seeing you soon."

"We were blessed by Lucius Septimus' generosity in allowing Joseph have time away from work, as well as the loan of his camel and his wife's palanquin for your mother."

"Gobba is here?" Mary grinned.

"He is," Father grinned. "Your mother enjoyed riding in the palanquin."

"It was comfortable," Mother straightened, lifting her chin, imitating a haughty look. "I felt quite regal."

Everyone laughed.

When Mary lifted the plate of bread to her parents, her mother shook her head. "They are delicious, but I confess, I am quite fatigued."

"I am certain you are." Elizabeth handed John to Zechariah. "Husband, if you will lay John in his bed, I will escort Eli and Anne to our guest chamber. Mary, why do you not show Joseph our garden? When I have your parents settled in their bed chamber, we will return and escort him to his bed chamber."

Mary's eyebrows rose, surprised at Elizabeth's suggestion that she be alone with Joseph, even if he was her betrothed. Glancing at her parents, they nodded.

"We will rest," Father said, "and speak with you later."

She stood and turned to Joseph. "If...if you will follow me."

He nodded.

She led him to the far end of the courtyard, through a small gate, to the walled area where Elizabeth grew herbs, fruit, vegetables, and even fragrant flowers.

After admiring the garden, Joseph asked, "Is there a place where we may sit?"

"Certainly," Mary led him to a bench beneath the shade of a palm tree. She sat and busied herself smoothing her garments, then glanced at him through lowered lashes

Joseph walked a few paces away, turned, and walked back before squatting in front of her. He looked into her eyes. "*I* am to name Him...*Jesus*."

Mary gasped, her eyes widening as Joseph smiled at her. "What?" She licked her lips, uncertain how to continue.

"Gabriel told me."

Her heart flew up in her throat and beat wildly. "Gabriel?"

"Yes." He took her hands in his. "The angel—Gabriel."

Mary's spirit soared in response to the colors glinting around them as Joseph told her of the olive grove, the butterfly, and the angelic dream.

Chapter 44

I cannot believe I have been here for three months," Mary poured water into her mother's and Elizabeth's cups, before handing a plate of cakes made from oats and raisins. Setting down the plate, she selected a cake for herself.

"I cannot believe the change in you," her mother smiled. "When you left Nazareth, you could barely sit up, much less eat anything without being ill."

"I can imagine how anxious you were for her," Elizabeth lifted the shawl to check John, who was nursing contentedly. "If anything happened to John, I do not know what I would do."

"We did not know either. We praise Yahweh Joseph suggested sending Mary to you and Zechariah." She lifted her cup to take a drink.

Mary glanced at Elizabeth and smiled. She lifted her own cup to hide her expression as her mother set her cup on the table. *Will anyone beyond Joseph, Elizabeth, and Zechariah ever know our story?* She thought it best to change the topic. "I wonder how long the men will be gone?"

"Who knows?" Elizabeth lifted John to her shoulder and patted his back. "Eli and Joseph need to buy supplies for your journey back to Nazareth."

"We do not need much," Mary's mother said. "Even with a camel, we do not have room to store much."

"Ah, but my husband is with them," Elizabeth grinned. "Zechariah is intrigued by the things he finds in the Xystus Market. It is common for him to wander among the booths for hours."

From her relatives' descriptions, the Xystus was larger than the market in Nazareth, or even Zippori. Located in the northeast corner of the Upper City, it was convenient to the Holy Temple, King Herod's palace, and the homes of many wealthy people. From numerous booths, merchants sold fish, spices, honey, wine, oil—both for cooking and lamps—vegetables and fruit, balms and other medicinal supplies, cooking pots, and dishes, linen and wool, costly apparel, ivory, ebony, gold, silver, and precious stones. At the far end of the marketplace were pens for animals; chickens, pigeons and other birds, sheep or goats, camels, and donkeys.

"Well, at least the day is pleasant," Mary's mother looked out the window toward the sky. "It feels more like spring and less like mid-winter."

"Our winters are milder here than in Nazareth," Elizabeth said. "I confess, I will be surprised if the men return before late afternoon." She glanced at John, "Ahh…he is sleeping. Anne, Mary, if you will excuse me, I am going to take him to our bed chamber. I have learned I should take advantage of John sleeping to also lie down and rest."

"Of course," Mary's mother held the sleeping baby while Elizabeth stood. "Mary and I will clear the meal and wash the dishes."

"Thank you," Elizabeth smiled. "I do not know what I will do once you have left. It has been pleasant to have another woman in the house."

"We will miss you, too," Mary hugged her, careful not to disturb the sleeping baby, "but we are not leaving until after John's presentation in the Temple. You and Zechariah will have to come visit us in Nazareth."

She and her mother gathered the cups and dishes and carried them to the cooking area. After storing the remaining food and washing the dishes, Mary turned to her mother. "What would you like to do?"

"If you do not mind, I believe I will follow Elizabeth's example and take a nap. I still have not recovered from traveling at night." She leaned over to kiss Mary's forehead. "Why do you not go to your bed chamber?"

"I think that is a wonderful idea. I might take the opportunity to bathe."

Once in her room, Mary removed her tunic before crossing to the wash table to pour water into the bowl. She lifted a bar of perfumed soap to her nose and smiled. Zechariah knew Elizabeth loved flowers, and he would purchase bars of fragrant soap from the Xystus Market. She had given Mary one of these bars of soap. *Zechariah is an attentive husband.* She smiled. *I believe Joseph will be the same.*

After bathing, she leaned her hair over the bowl to wash it. Rubbing her hair with a linen towel, she sat on the bench, picked up the comb, and began working it through her dark tresses.

I wonder whether Jesus will have wavy hair. She braided her hair, before slipping on a light-weight garment and crossed to her bed to lie down.

She fell quickly into a deep sleep—something Elizabeth told her was common for expectant mothers—when the sound of someone knocking on her door startled her awake.

"Mary! Mary!"

"Mother?" She sat up. "Is something amiss"

"No. Please let me in!"

Mary stumbled across the room to light the lamp before crossing to open the door. Her mother stood in the doorway, holding a basket covered with a cloth. Mary yawned, idly noticing her mother was wearing festive garments. "Mother, what is it?"

"You must hurry," her mother entered the room, closed the door, and crossed to the bed, where she set the basket down.

"Hurry?" Mary scratched her head. "For what?"

"He is coming!"

"Who is coming?"

"Joseph!"

"Joseph? What do you mean?"

Mother grinned and removed the cloth covering the basket.

Mary crossed the floor and glanced inside the basket. She looked at her mother, her eyes sparkling with tears.

Mother nodded.

Mary lifted out a veil of soft blue—as blue as a spring morning—and as delicate as the gossamer wings of the butterflies she saw in the olive grove. Beneath the veil was a blue tunic the shade of wildflowers that grew in the fields outside Nazareth, with cream trim on the neck and hem. These were her betrothal garments.

"Mother," Mary licked her lips, "does this mean…"

"Yes," her mother embraced her. "Joseph is coming to take you home as his bride."

Today is my wedding day!

"But there is more."

"More?" Mary's eyes widened.

Mother crossed the floor and opened the door.

Elizabeth stood outside, holding a small chest and a mirror. "May we enter?" she smiled.

"*We?*" Mary lifted an eyebrow questioningly and then gasped as Elizabeth stepped aside to reveal Adina standing behind her.

Mary ran over to embrace her heart-sister. "Adina! You are here! I do not understand! Is Rabbi Boaz—"

"Father is here, waiting with Joseph." She grinned. "When we learned Joseph was coming with your parents with the intention of bringing you home as his bride, your parents invited us to accompany them."

"I knew you would wish your heart-sister to be your bridal attendant," Mother smiled.

"I do," Mary said, "but where have you been?"

"Father and I have stayed the last several days in the guest chambers at the synagogue near the Temple."

Mary turned to her mother and Elizabeth. "Is this *why* the men went to Jerusalem today?"

Elizabeth grinned, "Getting Rabbi Boaz and Adina was the main reason they went to Jerusalem, but I sent a list of items for Zechariah to purchase. I did not have everything needed for a wedding feast."

Mary clapped her hands to her cheeks. "A wedding feast…our wedding feast?"

Mother grinned and drew her into an embrace. "Yes, my daughter; *your* wedding feast." She held her at arm's length. "But you must hurry. Your bridegroom is preparing himself to come for you soon."

Mary laughed and turned to the three most important women in her life. She extended her arms to each side. "Please help me get ready."

Elizabeth set the chest and mirror on the side table while her mother and Adina helped her don her wedding garments and tied the sandals to her feet. Leading her to sit on the bench, her mother unbound her braid and combed her long, dark waves. Elizabeth opened the chest she had carried and drew out jewels and a small golden crown.

"I wore these for my wedding to Zechariah. I would be honored if you wore them today."

Mary wiped away the tears spilling from her eyes and nodded. Elizabeth braided the jewels into her hair and Adina braided the lengths of blue ribbon she and Rabbi Boaz had given her for her betrothal. Then Mother draped the veil over her head placed the golden crown on top.

Mother helped her to stand while Adina held the mirror so she could see her reflection. "Oh…my…" Mary said. "I look like…"

"A bride," Mother blinked away tears and embraced her.

"You are beautiful, my heart-sister," Adina embraced her.

"I am thankful you and Rabbi Boaz were able to be here," Mary said. "I could not imagine my wedding day without you present."

"I am thankful to be here as well, and that you and Joseph will be in Nazareth for," she grinned, "*my betrothal.*"

"What?" Mary's eyes widened. "You are to be betrothed?"

Adina nodded.

"Who?"

"Yared."

"Yared ben Arieh…our hazzan?"

"Yes," Adina smiled.

"I did not think this day could be filled with any more surprises," Mary embraced Adina, "nor more joy. When did this happen?"

A knock at the door drew their attention.

"You will have to wait for my story," Adina said. "Today is your day; yours and Joseph's."

Mary and Adina followed Mother across the floor while Elizabeth opened the door.

Mary's father was waiting, dressed in festive garments, and holding a small lamp. His beard spread in a toothy grin when he saw her. "Ah, my little Mary," he embraced her. "You look beautiful. How do you feel?"

"Bemused. A few days ago, I wondered if I would ever see Joseph again. Now he is here; now *this* is happening."

Father laughed. "I confess I believe men have it easier than women when it comes to the marriage ceremony. It is the bride's responsibility to be ready for the bridegroom *whenever he comes,* while the bridegroom—and his father—decide when that day will be." He turned and took her arm, while Mother stepped to take her other arm. "Now, come."

They waited as Mother, Elizabeth, and Adina lit small lamps and left the room. Her mother stepped to Mary's other side and, along with her father, led Mary out of her room. Stars were blazing in the clear evening sky, providing a soft luminous light as they walked across the courtyard, through the gate to the small garden. Lamps filled with fragrant oil were placed around the garden and beneath a canopy decorated with ribbons.

Mary turned to Elizabeth. "You were supposed to be sleeping."

Elizabeth grinned. "I can sleep any time, but it is not every day I decorate my home for a marriage ceremony."

They walked to the bench, which was covered with a soft blue cloth. *It was here that Joseph told me about Gabriel visiting him in his dream.* Adina and Elizabeth straightened her garments, while Mother smoothed her veil before she sat. Then they all arranged themselves around her and waited.

Soon, Mary heard the faint sound of a tambourine. A moment, Zechariah entered the garden—grinning broadly and playing the instrument with one hand while holding John in his other arm—followed by Rabbi Boaz, and then Joseph.

Joseph wore the same garments he had worn for their betrothal; a cream-colored tunic, with a robe and girdle in rich brown; on his head was a golden crown. Joseph's eyes lit up when he saw her, his gaze holding hers as he followed the other men across the garden to the bench.

Mother and Father helped Mary to stand, while Adina and Elizabeth straightened her garments. Her parents moved to stand between her and Joseph. Father lifted Mary's hand and Mother placed hers on top. Together, her spoke the traditional blessing over Mary—

"You are our daughter; may you become the mother of countless thousands and may your children's children's children rule over the nations."

When they stepped aside, Joseph extended his hand to her. "I have come for you, my bride," he smiled.

She returned his smile as she took his hand. "I am ready for you, my husband."

He escorted her to the canopy where they listened to Rabbi Boaz, her father, and Zechariah—who stood in for Joseph's father as well as being his attendant—as they spoke the blessings and words that would complete their wedding.

The feast was evident of Elizabeth and Zechariah's planning. The main room of the house was fragrant from the oil lamps burning brightly in the corners of the room.

"Flowers might not be blooming now," Elizabeth said, "but Zechariah did not allow that to deter him."

"It is beautiful," Mary embraced Elizabeth and then Zechariah.

"We will have another feast once we have returned to Nazareth," Mother said.

"There is no need," Mary protested. "This is perfect."

"Perhaps, but our family and Joseph's family wish to celebrate your marriage," her father grinned, "You would not wish to deny your Grandmother Tzipora the opportunity to speak praise of the bride."

Zechariah and Mary's father escorted them to the place of honor at the table. There, seated side by side, they reigned as king and queen of the day. They listened as Rabbi Boaz praised Yahweh for His blessings, and laughed as Zechariah—now acting as the steward of the feast—told riddles. She smiled when her father and Rabbi Boaz praised them for obeying the Law, loving their family and friends, honoring their people, and wishing to serve Yahweh.

The feast continued. Mary smiled as she watched those she loved, laughing, singing, and rejoicing as they celebrated.

"Mary?" she heard Joseph spoke her name.

She turned to see him smiling at her. He stood and extended his hand. "Arise my darling, my beautiful one, come with me."

She flushed when she heard him speak King Solomon's love poem. In ordinary circumstances, this would have been when the bride and groom would go to the bridal chamber and consummate their marriage She glanced at her parents; they were smiling and nodding at her and Joseph.

She looked up into his face and smiled. She slipped her hand into his and stood. "I am my beloved's," she whispered the Beloved's response, "and my beloved is mine."

Zechariah stood and began telling jokes. Mary glanced at Elizabeth, who nodded at her and then laughed at her husband. Her parents, Rabbi Boaz, and Adina joined in laughing at Zechariah.

Mary was thankful her family's attention was distracted as she and Joseph left the room and walked into the night. He led her across the courtyard to open the door of his bed chamber. He extended his hand for her to enter. "My bride," he smiled.

Her heart swelled within her chest. "My husband," she said as she stepped through the door.

The room was slightly larger than the one she slept in. Flames dancing over the lamp stand gave off scented perfume. Beneath the shuttered window was a wash table with a bowl and pitcher and folded linen towels. The bed—a thick pallet, covered in linens, on a wooden frame—was on the other wall. Next to it was a small table holding two cups, an amphorae, a bowl of grapes, and a plate of oat cakes.

Mary walked around the room, noting Elizabeth's touch in turning a guest room into a bridal chamber. She turned to Joseph.

"Elizabeth and Zechariah have been most generous in celebrating our marriage," Joseph said. "They told me when they received your parents' message that I was coming with them and why, they began preparing." He smiled. "They said they considered you the daughter they would never have."

He turned and walked to the window. "That first night after your parents and I arrived, Zechariah joined Elizabeth as they escorted me to this bed chamber." He stared out at the sky. "They told me they knew about what…Gabriel told you." He filled his lungs and blew out the air." I told them of my dream, about what the angel told me."

He crossed the floor and took her hands. "Gabriel told me the *babe* in your womb is Yahweh's Messiah, conceived by the Holy Spirit. When we announce that you are with child, when *I* name him, everyone will believe he is *my* son. However, between us, we will know otherwise."

Her brows lowered. "I do not understand."

"Mary, you were…" color washed over Joseph's face, "…a virgin when the Holy Spirit placed the babe in your womb. I will not do anything to change that."

Mary flushed. "You mean…?"

Joseph let out a long breath. "I mean we will not consummate our marriage until *after* the message Gabriel spoke has been fulfilled."

Chapter 45

"It has been only two days since we left Ein Kerem," Mary's eyes were bright with tears, "and I miss Elizabeth and Zechariah and baby John as if it has been months."

"Do not be sad, Beloved," Joseph leaned over to wipe a tear from her cheek. "I promise; we will return to see them."

"Thank you, Beloved," she glanced at her parents, who were talking with Rabbi Boaz. Adina had already retired to the tent she shared with her father. Mary leaned toward him. "I want Elizabeth and Zechariah to see our Jesus when he is born."

"They will," he whispered. He grinned. "I think Elizabeth and Zechariah were blessed by the parting gift you gave them."

"I think so too," she laughed.

Joseph loved hearing her laugh; it sounded like bells.

When he had gone to Jerusalem to the marketplace with Mary's father and Zechariah, he had purchased several sheets of papyrus for Mary to practice her writing. She had taken one sheet and, dipping a sharpened stick into the ashes from the fire pit, had drawn a picture of baby John. She had given the picture to Elizabeth and Zechariah the night before they left. Their praise of Mary's gift filled Joseph's heart. *Thank you, Yahweh, for sending Mary to Elizabeth and Zechariah. They have been a healing balm to my Beloved's soul.*

"However, I am looking forward to being back in Nazareth," Mary brightened. "To think; Adina and Yared are to be betrothed! How often have I prayed for my heart-sister, that some man would *see her* and *love her*," she reached over to lay a hand on his, "as *you* love me."

Once the caravan—they had been blessed to travel back with Jacob ben Reuben—had left Jerusalem, one of the first things Mary did was demand to hear of Adina's betrothal to the hazzan. "To be honest," she had said, "I believed he would marry Sarai bat Zebah. Her father is the seller of purple; as his only child, she will have a rich inheritance."

"I confess I believed he would as well," Adina had said.

"Beyond being the daughter of a wealthy man," Mary's mother had said, "she is pretty."

"I never thought that," Mary's father had said.

The three women had turned to him, lifting inquisitive brows. "Oh?" Anne had looked at Eli. "And what made you think otherwise?"

"I never thought that because," Eli had grinned, "it was clear Yared was smitten."

Joseph had felt it best to support his father-in-law. "Eli speaks truth." He turned to grin at Adina. "It was clear Yared was *smitten*."

Adina had blushed rosily.

"While I consider my daughter beautiful," Rabbi Boaz had said, "I am thankful Yared saw her other traits. After his father approached me with a proposal of marriage, I asked Yared why he wanted to marry Adina.

"He looked at me as if I were not thinking clearly." The rabbi had grinned at his daughter. "He told me not only do you obey the Law, but you seek to serve Yahweh by helping to care for the synagogue. He said you not only love our family and friends, but you love the people in our community. Those are traits Yared considers necessary for the wife of a future rabbi. Beyond that, Yared also told me he thinks you have an unusual and graceful beauty."

"Yared speaks truth," Mary had smiled at Adina. "You are graceful and beautiful. He is the one I have prayed for you; a man who knows your true value and your heart."

Mary had spoken to Joseph about wanting to help with Adina and Yared's betrothal celebration.

"I want it to be as beautiful as ours was," she smiled at him.

"Of course you should help," Joseph told her. "She is your heart-sister." *When you smile at me that way, my Wife, I cannot deny you anything.*

"Mary," her mother called, "we forgot what Simeon ben Anaiah said about babies. Something about hope."

They had met Elizabeth and Zechariah's elderly friend the evening before they left Ein Kerem. Shorter than Mary's father, face heavily lined with wrinkles, hair and beard whiter than snow, Simeon was well-versed many topics. After wishing him and Mary mazel tov on their marriage, he spent his time discussing the Law with Rabbi Boaz and Zechariah, as knowledgeable in the Law Yahweh gave to Moses as any Temple-trained priest. He shared ideas with Mary's mother on fighting grasshoppers eating the plants in the garden, and praised John's strength when the infant grasped Simeon's finger.

"Mother, Simeon ben Anaiah said every baby's birth is the birth of *hope*."

"Yes, that is what he said," Mary's mother said. "What a beautiful comment. I want to remember and share it with expectant parents in Nazareth."

"I agree…ahhhh-hhaaaaa," Mary covered her mouth as she stifled a yawn.

Joseph's beard stretched into a toothy grin as he stood and extended a hand. "My Beloved, you should follow your heart-sister's example and retire to our tent. You are weary."

After bidding his wife's parents and Rabbi Boaz a good rest, and checking to see that Gobba and the donkeys were settled, he followed Mary into their tent. She had changed into a light sleeveless tunic and was braiding her hair. He helped her unroll the thick pad they used as a bed. Helping Mary lie down, he waited until she turned on her side before slipping into his night garments and stretching out next to her.

Mary turned and laid her head on his shoulder. Although he had stated they would not consummate their marriage until after she had given birth, marriage allowed them the freedom to touch each other's hands, to lie next to each other, and even kiss.

"Joseph?"

"Yes, my Beloved?"

"Once we are home, and announce that I am with child, people will think I conceived shortly after our marriage."

"Yes."

"From what Elizabeth told me, my body will not grow big for a while, especially since it is my first baby."

"I know not these things. I will trust what Elizabeth tells you."

"Joseph?" she yawned again.

"Yes, my Beloved?"

"What will we do once the baby is born? As I count the months, he should be born in Tamuz. Everyone will see he is a not a tiny baby born too soon and wonder."

"Do not concern yourself, Beloved." Joseph pulled her closer and kissed her brow. "We will leave that to Yahweh."

Chapter 46

18 Iyar, 3758

"Joseph," Mary whispered.

Silence.

"Joseph," she raised her voice a little.

"Chhauuucccckkk…" her husband's snore was deep and unbroken.

Mary shook his shoulder gently. Then shook it a little harder. "Joseph!"

"What?! Huh?!" Joseph sat straight up. His hair stuck out from his head, and his eyes were glazed and confused from sleep. He turned toward her. "Mary, what is it? Are you alright?" he asked in the anxious tones of a first-time father-to-be.

Mary smiled. "I am fine," she said. "I just need to get up."

Joseph's eyebrows shot up. "Again?"

"Yes, again."

"You got up a short time ago."

Mary lowered her brows in mock anger. "And if you want to eat your morning meal," she pointed to the window, where streaks of light peeked through, "you need to help me up."

Joseph glanced at the window, where dust motes danced on the light peeking around the edges of the shutter. "It is morning already?" he asked, as he stood up and bent to help Mary up from their bed.

"I am sorry I woke you so many times last night," she smiled. "Being late in my pregnancy has made it is difficult to get up out of bed without help."

He helped her straighten the coverings of their bed and then sat on it, while Mary crossed to the wash table beneath the window. He would wash and dress after she was finished.

Joseph was pleased with how their bed chamber looked. There were two windows on the walls that faced the corner of the house, allowing sunlight to shine over their bed, a thick pallet on a wooden frame. Their bed was covered by a blue and cream stripped covering Adina had woven as a marriage gift. Besides a bowl and pitcher, the wash table held a stack of towels and a comb he had carved for her. On the table next to their bed were two cups, an amphorae of water, and the small rose chest he had carved for Mary. Beneath the other window were two larger chests that held their clothes.

After washing her face, Mary dipped a split twig into a small container of salt and scrubbed her teeth. Choosing a clean tunic from the chest, she slipped it over her head.

He washed his face while she picked up the comb, and began working it through her waist-length locks. When her hair was free from tangles, she braided it again, and took a short length of ribbon from the rose chest to secure the ends. She sat on the bed and bent over to pick up her sandal. And stopped. She could not reach them.

She sighed and smiled at him. "Joseph," she said, "would you please help me?"

He grinned at her, wiped his face and beard dry, and moved to tie the leather sandals on her feet. "How would you get along without me?" he asked.

"I know not," she replied. "Yahweh indeed blessed me with a kind and helpful husband." She stood up. "You have time to finish dressing while I help Mother Leah, Grandmother Naomi, Mary bat Tovi, and Sarah with the morning meal. With the Sabbath beginning tonight, we have to prepare extra food."

Joseph helped her down the stairs and watched as she walked awkwardly across the courtyard, her hand rubbing the lower part of her back. He turned to climb the stairs and crossed the rooftop to the area near their bed chamber.

For the past five months, this spot had been a haven for Mary and him. Knowing how much his wife—*I love being able to call her my wife*—was drawn to the nature Yahweh created, he had the potter, Ephraim bar Ovid, make several deep clay pots. Joseph filled them with soil and placed them near their bed chamber. In these pots, Mary grew fragrant herbs and wildflowers she dug up from the fields around Nazareth.

Near the pots was a couch he had built similar to one they had seen in Zippori. Shortly after they had arrived back in Nazareth, Mary said she wanted to thank Lucius Septimus for allowing Joseph time to travel to Ein Kerem, and for letting them borrow Gobba.

Joseph was pleased to note Mary's composure; many Jewish people would not step foot in the home of a Gentile. Yet, when she met Lucius Septimus and his wife Ovidia, Mary had been polite and gracious, both in her thanks and in her admiration of their home. He noted she was especially interested in the Romans' couch. Several weeks later, he surprised her by building one.

It looked like a bench large enough for two people. On one side it had an upright carved piece of wood to lean your back against and carved pieces of wood on either end to rest your arm. Mary had sewn a cushion and stuffed it with odd pieces of fabric and placed it on the bench for them to sit.

He set this couch next to their bed chamber, turned so they could see the olive grove. They spent many early mornings sitting on this couch, looking over the olive grove, and speaking of the events that drew them together. At night, they would sit here and look up at the stars. Mary told him about the time she heard what she called the *star song*.

"The stars were brilliant in the night sky," she recalled. "As I looked at them, I *heard* a single, soft voice." She lifted her shoulders in a shrug. "I do not know how else to describe it. This voice was singing, but not in a language I understood. It was joined by another and then another, until the sky was filled with the beauty of this song."

He shook his head, pondering the unique gifts Mary possessed. On their journey home from Ein Kerem, she told him she *heard* colors or *saw* sounds. He grinned, remembering she had also told him what happened as she listened to the star song.

"I closed my eyes, listening to this beautiful, wonderous twinkling song, when suddenly I felt a damp muzzle rub my head and a wet tongue lick my face." She had laughed, describing how Arod had escaped from the stable.

That donkey had proven adventurous. Last month, they had awakened at dawn to a braying. Arod had pushed through the stable and wandered through the streets of Nazareth to Joseph's house.

"He must miss you," Joseph had said, although they never determined how the animal knew where Mary now lived.

Mary had taken Arod back to her family's house, only to have the animal show up again the next morning. Between their families, they never knew from day to day where the animal would be.

Joseph laughed, shaking his head. "Yahweh, thank You for the joy of having Mary as my wife."

The smell of bread baking interrupted his thoughts. He entered their bed chamber to finish dressing for the day. Reaching into the chest for his garments, he lifted a prayer shawl and laid it on their bed. Just as he had made the rose chest as a marriage gift for Mary, with Adina's help, she had made this beautiful prayer shawl for him. He saved it to wear on special occasions, Sabbaths, and holy days.

Mary reached over to set a bowl of cheese on the table when she gasped, "Oooph!" She leaned back, placing a hand on her rib.

"Mary, what is wrong?" Joseph's mother said.

"There is nothing wrong, Mother Naomi," Mary smiled. *I love being able to call this godly woman my mother-in-law.* She rubbed her swollen abdomen. "The babe decided he needed more room to move."

"*He* decided?" Sarah laughed. "You always speak of the babe as if you *know* it is a son. You *could* have a daughter."

"Sarah, mothers often have a sense of these things," Grandmother Leah smiled as she set a bowl of dates on the table.

"It happened to me," Mary bat Tovi removed bread from inside the dome of the fire pit and slapped on more dough. "When I was carrying Samuel, I *sensed* he was a boy."

"I hope one day you will both have girls," Sarah grinned, "and will have the *sense* not to name them *Mary*." She sighed dramatically. "I cannot imagine having four Marys in our home."

The women burst out laughing.

Mary smiled. *How blessed to be part of a family that laughs.*

Joseph—along with the other workers from Nazareth—left Zippori early, in order to be home in time for the Sabbath service. After washing and changing into his good clothes, he tied the prayer shawl around his waist. He helped Mary—who was dressed in a soft green tunic that flowed gently over her swelling abdomen—down the stairs and across the courtyard, and joined his family walking to the synagogue.

They met Mary's family at the door of the synagogue. After greeting them with hugs and, "Shabbat Shalom," Mother inquired about Mary's health.

"She is fine," Grandmother Tzipora surprised Mary by smiling. "Yahweh heard our prayers and healed Mary, then blessed her with a husband, and now," she placed a hand on Mary's abdomen, "with a child."

Mary glanced at Joseph, who smiled. "That was a blessing, Grandmother Tzipora."

Following the women of their family—along with Samuel, James, and John—Mary walked up the stairs to the loft, where Adina was waiting for them.

Wearing a tunic the color of ripened wheat with a cream head covering, Adina also wore a necklace made with ten golden coins. This was her betrothal gift from Yared.

As usual, Adina was sitting on a stool and had saved several spots for them, including a stool next to her for Mary.

"Sabbat Shalom, my heart-sister," Mary hugged Adina, "thank you for this stool." She smoothed her garments before sitting with a sigh.

"How are you feeling?" Adina asked.

"If you are asking whether I have any more bouts of nausea, no—thank Yahweh—I do not. From what I have heard from every woman who has ever been with child, what I am experiencing is normal. I tire easily, I eat a lot, and I," she leaned over to whisper in Adina's ears, "I pass water frequently."

Adina lifted a hand to cover her grin, glancing at the women around them. "That must be…uncomfortable."

"Well, it is inconvenient, as you will one day—with Yahweh's blessings—understand," Mary grinned. "However, as all the older women in our families have experienced it, they are understanding and offer much advice and help."

Their attention was drawn to the sounds of footsteps echoing down the corridor. Everyone stood as Rabbi Boaz and Yared entered, carrying the scrolls of Holy Scripture

After the traditional presentation of the scrolls, the two men crossed the floor to step up on the bimah. Rabbi Boaz laid the scrolls on the reading desk while Yared moved a pace away. The older man smiled, gazing around the room at the assembly of people. Lifting his arms wide, he said, "Shabbat Shalom."

Mary joined everyone in responding, "Shabbat Shalom."

After the opening prayer, Rabbi Boaz led everyone in speaking the *Shema*. "Hear O Israel! The Lord our God, the Lord is One."

When everyone was seated, the Rabbi continued. "Today, one of our young men—Joseph ben Jacob," he smiled, "will read from the Holy Scriptures."

Mary gasped at the honor bestowed on her husband. She looked down at Joseph, who caught her eye and smiled. He nodded at Rabbi Boaz before turning to walk to the reading desk. He closed his eyes for a moment, before whispering to Rabbi Boaz and Yared, who unrolled the scrolls and then moved a pace away.

Joseph looked up at Mary before he filled his lungs. "From the prophet Isaiah.

For a Child will be born to us, a Son will be given to us;
And the government will rest on His shoulders;
And His name will be called Wonderful Counselor,
Mighty God, Eternal Father, Prince of Peace.
There will be no end to the increase of His government or of peace,
On the throne of David and over His kingdom, To establish it

*and to uphold it with justice and righteousness
from then on and forevermore.
The zeal of the LORD of Hosts will accomplish this."*

With Joseph's first words from the Holy Scripture, Mary saw colors pulsing in the air, just as when Yared had blown the shofar on the Feast of Trumpets. When Joseph finished reading, Mary—along with everyone present—waited to hear what he would say about the scripture.

Joseph lifted his hands and pointed to the scroll. "What we have all been taught about the prophet's words," he smiled at Rabbi Boaz, "is that it is prophecy concerning the Messiah. When He—the Messiah—comes, He will be great," he looked up to the loft and smiled at Mary, "and will be called the Son of the Most High." He extended his arms to each side. "May He come soon."

"Amen," Rabbi Boaz said. "May He come soon." He turned and gestured to the assembled people.

Mary stood with the others and repeated. "Amen. May He come soon."

Rabbi Boaz thanked Joseph and smiled as he returned to stand with his family. "Thank you again, Joseph ben Jacob, for the reading of the Holy Scriptures. This passage from the prophet Isaiah does bring hope," his smile slipped, "which is what we need now. Please," he patted the air, "be seated."

Mary looked at Adina, who was frowning as she gazed at her father. She turned to Mary, lifted her shoulders, and shook her head.

When the assembly was seated and quiet, Rabbi Boaz reached into the folds of his girdle, and drew out a scroll. Lifting the paper, he said, "This message arrived today; it is from Rome."

A collective groan rose from the people, followed by whispered grumbling. Nothing that came from Rome was ever good news to the Jewish people.

"What does Caesar Augustus want now?" Grandfather Matthat asked.

"Another census," Rabbi Boaz frowned, "I expect to prepare for another tax."

Grumbling rippled among the people.

Jesse bar Naum, the town elder, stood. "We already pay three taxes." He lifted his fingers, to tick off each name. "To Herod, to Rome, and to the Temple."

More grumbling.

"This tax is not just for the Jewish people, nor is it to be paid now." Rabbi Boaz unrolled the document he held. "This decree from Caesar Augustus states that *all* the people in the inhabited world will taxed. In order to know how many people are under his rule—and what monies will be collected from this tax—Caesar Augustus has decreed that everyone will go to their own town—to the town of their fathers—to register and be counted."

Another groan rose from the people.

"Rabbi Boaz," Haran ben Reuel, the town elder, stood. "This registration Caesar decreed means everyone here will have to travel to the town of our ancestor, King David. To register for this tax," he extended his arms wide, "everyone in Nazareth will have to travel to Bethlehem."

Chapter 47

30 Sivan, 3758

*W*hen the sun rises," Joseph handed Mary a skin of water, "we will be in Bethlehem."

"Praise Yahweh for that," Mary she took a drink and handed the skin back to Joseph. "I am fatigued."

"I am sorry we were late in traveling to register for the census." He took a drink and secured the skin before returning it to the bag hanging from Aton's back. "If we had gone when arranged, you would be resting at home instead of riding a donkey outside of Bethlehem."

Mary moved Arod closer to Aton and placed her hand on Joseph's arm. "Beloved, do not apologize because your skills were needed in Zippori."

He shook his head. "I felt sorry for Lucius Septimus. Everyone—Jew and Gentile alike—have to register for this census. Like us, many people had to travel to the town of their fathers. *However,* Herod sent word to Lucius that the work on Zippori would continue on schedule."

"At least you were able to finish your portion of the work. *Oooff!*" she gasped as Arod stumbled in a hole in the road.

"Mary!" Joseph guided Aton over to Arod. "Are you alright?"

"Yes, I am fine." She patted the donkey's grey neck. "I imagine he is tired of just walking. I think we all are tired, but the donkeys more so; we are riding, while they carry us."

After the shock of the news from Rome wore off—as well as the accompanying grumbling—the residents of Nazareth made plans to travel to Bethlehem. To avoid leaving their homes empty, their animals and fields unattended, and their work paused, each family in Nazareth divided themselves to travel in rotation.

Joseph's Grandfather Matthan and Grandmother Naomi traveled to Bethlehem along with other neighbors. In addition to registering their names in the census, they arranged for a room for the rest of their family members to stay in when it came their turn to travel to Bethlehem. When Joseph's grandparents returned to Nazareth, his parents and his sister Sarah went next, followed by his brother Clopas, sister-in-law Mary, and nephew Samuel.

Because of the shortage of workers, by the time Joseph finished his task in Zippori, all of his family—as well as Mary's family—had left for Bethlehem and returned to Nazareth.

Mary's parents had come to see them before they left, bringing extra food, skins of water, and blankets for her to sit on to make the journey easier.

After sharing tips for traveling, Mary's father said, "Take Aton and Arod for the journey."

"Both of your donkeys?" Mary lifted her eyebrows. "Will you not need them?"

"Your father can use our Hamor whenever he needs," Joseph's father said.

Mary saw their fathers exchange looks with their mothers. "Father, Mother; Joseph and I do not need both donkeys for this journey. We can take Aton."

"And then Arod would break out of the stall and follow you," Father grinned.

"Then we will take Arod," she countered. "Joseph and I can take turns riding."

"Mary, if you and Joseph were traveling alone, you could take turns walking," his mother said, "however that is not the case. I praise Yahweh you and Joseph will be traveling with a caravan. Beyond that, you will not be borrowing Gobba for this journey. You are great with child; you need to be as comfortable as possible." She looked at Mary's mother. "Anne, do you not agree?"

"Leah speaks truth," Mary's mother smiled. "You were born in Elul. The days before your birth were not as hot as what we are experiencing now. I was miserable and I was not traveling away from Nazareth."

"Please, Mary, take the donkeys," her father said. "It will make your mothers happier, which will make our lives," he grinned at Joseph's father, "much easier."

Mary soon realized their mothers were correct. Even though the caravan traveled at night, the heat lessened only a little after sundown. However, even with the extra blankets to sit on, riding a donkey for long hours was difficult. Whenever the caravan stopped, Joseph would lift her down so she could stretch and walk around for a few minutes.

Even with the discomfort, the time away from family allowed them privacy to speak of the events of the past year and ponder the future.

"I am an artisan," Joseph helped Mary lie down in their tent and stretched out next to her. "I have no knowledge of kingship nor being a warrior."

"When I was traveling to Ein Kerem," Mary laid her head on his shoulder, "we passed many places of historic battles. All my life, I heard the stories of the battles our ancestors fought, but they were just stories. Now, seeing these places, and knowing who our son will be," she placed a hand on her swollen abdomen, "made me wonder what will happen to him. Even as Yahweh's Messiah, what will he do, what will he face, what battles will he fight, to drive the Romans out of Israel?"

Joseph drew her close. "We will pray for Yahweh to protect him and to guide him. Remember what Rabbi Boaz always said, *All that Yahweh does is done for the best.*"

There were also moments of wonder. The evening before, as they started on the night's journey, Mary looked up and gasped.

"Mary, what is it? Are you alright?"

"Forgive me, Joseph, I am fine." She pointed upward. "Look at those two stars. I know that one is Tzedek, but I do not know the name of the other. Look at how close they are. They almost look like one star, the biggest star I have ever seen."

"And the brightest star as well," Joseph said. "I know Jacob ben

Reuben mentioned what he called the *star journey,* but this is different." He shook his head, "It has a sense of being…something more…something portentous."

The stars were still bright in the night sky when the caravan arrived at the road leading up to Bethlehem. After bidding farewell to the caravan owners, they turned their donkeys to begin the ascent to the Town of David.

"I heard our family and friends speak of going up to Bethlehem," Mary said. "I wondered how they could travel south from Nazareth and yet be going up to Bethlehem. Now that I see the road, I understand what they meant."

Located five miles south of Jerusalem, the little town was built on a gray limestone ridge over 1600 cubits high, making it higher than Jerusalem or Nazareth. The ridge had a summit at each end and a valley in the middle like a saddle between the summits.

Ever the artisan, Joseph commented, "The shape of the summit and valley makes Bethlehem looks like the amphitheater they are building in Zippori."

"Just think of the history of our people that happened here," Mary looked around as the entered the little town. "Rachel, wife of Father Jacob, is buried here. Ruth, the great-grandmother of King David, left her native land of Moab to come here with her mother-in-law Naomi."

"And King David was born here," Joseph grinned, "which is why we are here."

Mary straightened, her stomach feeling like a hand squeezing to make a fist. She bit back a moan, not wanting Joseph to notice. *This is surely caused by fatigue from traveling.* She blew out a soft breath as the pain eased.

After asking directions from a man walking down the street, Joseph found the house with the room Grandfather Matthan had rented for the family. He knocked on the door, and an elderly man answered, looking beyond Joseph to Mary.

She held a hand to her abdomen as another tightening grew. She clamped her mouth shut. *We are here. We will be in our room soon, and I can rest.*

"I am Joseph ben Jacob and this is my wife. My grandfather," Joseph said, "is Matthan ben Elihud. He rented a room for our family to use for the census."

"I am sorry," the man shook his head. "The room is no longer available."

"What do you mean?" Joseph frowned, "My grandfather made arrangements."

"It has been over two weeks since any of your family came to Bethlehem," the man said. "I assumed they no longer needed the room. I have rented it to another family."

Mary's eyes widened as the tightening grew followed by what felt like a poke in the lower part of her abdomen. A moment later, water gushed from between her legs.

She had been raised around animals; she had witnessed Arod being born. She had been certain she would know when it was her time. *How do I tell Joseph? I do not wish to worry him.* Then another wave of pain hit, she cried out one word. "Joseph!"

Running back to her, he saw the blankets beneath her were wet. "Mary, are you—" but stopped when she doubled over, crying out.

"What is wrong with your wife," the man asked. "Is she ill?"

"She is not ill," Joseph spat. "She is in labor. Please, do you know of another person who has a room? We need to be private."

"Private?' the man sneered. "All of Bethlehem is filled with travelers coming for the census. Every room in my house is rented. I even have people sleeping on my floor. There is no room for anyone else, much less room for *privacy.*"

Joseph did not even wait for the man to shut the door. He turned and ran to the house across the street to bang on the door, pleading for a place for Mary. The owner of that house told the same story; travelers took up all available space. Joseph dragged the donkeys down the street of the small town, knocking at each door.

Mary gasped as a pain, sharp as a knife, cut through her. "Joseph, *please help me.*"

He dropped the donkeys' reins and lifted Mary from Arod's back. Grasping the two sets of reins, he continued walking, dragging the animals behind.

She heard him praying, "Yahweh, please help Mary, Yahweh, help Mary. Please help me. Help me find a place."

There was one building at the end of the street. Joseph carried Mary up the house and kicked at the bottom of the door, calling out for someone to help.

The door opened to reveal an older man holding a lamp. He took one look at them and said, "My house is full, but there is a small place out back where I keep a few animals. It is warm and private."

Joseph looked at her, "Mary?"

She nodded into his shoulder, moaning as another pain hit.

"Thank you," Joseph told the man. "That will be fine."

"Just a moment," the man said. He stepped back into the house and returned with several blankets and another lamp. He led the way around the house to a small cave dug into the hill. Inside were several donkeys, a cow and her calf, and some chickens were sleeping. A tall wooden loft kept bundles of hay out of the animals reach.

The man set the lamp and blankets on the ground, climbed up the loft, and tossed down armloads of fresh hay. Climbing down, he arranged the hay into a pile and covered it with the blankets. "I am sorry your wife has to give birth in a humble stable," he said. "Please allow me to water and feed your donkeys."

"Thank you," Joseph said as he laid Mary down on the bed and opened the skin of water to give her a drink.

"Is there anything else I can do for you?" the man asked.

Joseph stood. "Will you direct me to the midwife?"

"No," Mary grabbed his hands. "Joseph, do not leave me."

"Mary, I know nothing about birthing a child."

"Joseph, *please!*" Mary arched her back as another pain hit.

Joseph filled his lungs and turned to the man. "Thank you. We do not need anything else now."

The man nodded. "My wife and I will be praying for you and your wife."

After he left, Mary gasped out instructions to Joseph.

He plumped up the hay behind for her to sit up against. He found two long pieces of rope and tied them to the corner of the loft so they dangled above Mary's head, before knotting the ends.

With each pain, Mary would reach up, pull on the knotted ends, and straighten her body to allow the baby room to move downward. Between pains, she would collapse against the hay to rest.

The morning slipped into afternoon, and then into night. Time lost all meaning to her; all she knew was the ebbing and waning of the pains. Between the pains, Joseph wiped her face, gave her sips of water, and whispered his love and prayers.

At one point, Mary felt a change in her body. Leaning forward, she grabbed her knees. With each pain, she lowered her head and chest toward her knees, filled her lungs, and pushed, working with with the pains to birth the baby. In between the pains, Mary told Joseph how to hold the babe and cut the cord when she pushed him out.

Mary felt a massive pain forming. She filled her lungs, grabbed her knees, and pushed, holding that position until she felt the babe slip from her body. She fell against the hay as she heard him take his first breath and begin wailing.

Joseph laughed with relief as tears filled his eyes. "Thank you Yahweh!" He lifted the babe and laid him on Mary's chest. He covered them both with the edge of the blanket she was lying on. The babe continued to cry—strong, healthy cries.

"Oh, sweet baby! Sweet baby Jesus!" Mary stroked his back, shooshing him softly. When she lifted her hand to stroke his cheek, the babe turned to take her finger into his mouth. "Poor Babe," Mary laughed. "You are hungry." Reaching beneath the blanket and adjusting her tunic, she led the babe's mouth to her breast. His cries subsided as he settled down and began nursing.

Mary looked at Joseph. He was covered in sweat—as she was—and looked as exhausted as she felt. Her eyes widened. *I can see Joseph.* She looked at the nursing babe. *I can see Jesus.* She looked at the lamp; it was dark, having run out of oil hours earlier. She turned to look toward the night sky. It was long after the new moon had risen at the feet of Zerah the Virgin, yet the stable was bathed in a warm light. It was as if Tzedek, the other star—and all the star journeys in the night sky—had stopped over the stable to celebrate Jesus' birth.

As she looked at the sky, she heard a single, soft *voice*. "Joseph," she whispered, "do you hear it? Do you hear the song?"

He tilted his head to listen, then he looked at her, his eyes widening. "I hear it!"

Mary's heart soared as another voice joined the first, then another, building in volume until the night sky echoed with a beautiful, glorious twinkling *song*.

When the last echo softened, Joseph looked at Mary.

"Are you…well?"

Mary smiled—weary—and nodded. "I am well."

He looked around the stable. He found a manger—a feeding trough—that he carried to set near Mary. "It is not a proper bed for a king," he told her, "but it is what Yahweh has provided for now." He spread an armload of fresh hay in it and then looked at her. "Can I do anything for you?"

"I would like to clean myself and swaddle the babe," she said.

"You wash yourself and change."

He laid his palm against his chest. "I will clean and swaddle the babe."

"Joseph," Mary's eyes widened. "I did not bring anything to use as swaddling cloths." She blinked back tears. "I am sorry; I was not prepared to give birth. I have brought nothing for him."

"You do not need to apologize, Beloved. It matters not what we use, whatever I pull out of the bag will be his swaddling cloth." He smiled at her. "It will be what Yahweh has provided for now."

Crossing the stable to their donkeys, he opened the bag across Arod's back that held Mary's possessions. Reaching into the bag, he pulled out several cloths for cleaning, a bar of soap, a fresh tunic, and…frowned when he felt something hard. He looked in the bag, and then at Mary, who smiled. Reaching inside, he lifted out the small wooden chest he had carved. "You brought *this*?" he asked. "Why?"

"You made it for me," she said, "not because it was useful, but because it was beautiful. I keep special things inside. I wanted to bring it with me."

He shook his head. "You are a wonder." He put the chest back in the bag and handed her the garment, the cleaning items, and a skin of water. "Now something for swaddling." Crossing to Aton, he lifted the bag containing his possessions. "As I said," he grinned, "whatever I pull out will be what Yahweh has provided for his swaddling cloths." Reaching inside, he pulled out the first thing his fingers closed around.

"Joseph! It is your prayer shawl." Mary looked from him to the sleeping baby.

He shook his head. "I said the first thing." He closed the bag and turned to her, the blue and white cloth in his hands. "What would be more appropriate to wrap the Messiah—the Son of Yahweh—in," he said, "than a prayer shawl?"

He bathed the infant and followed Mary's instructions to swaddle him, and then helped her lay the sleeping babe on top of the hay in the manger.

After changing the soiled hay under Mary for fresh, Joseph laid down next to her and covered both of them with a clean blanket. Speaking a prayer of thanksgiving, he kissed her brow.

"Rest, my Beloved."

"Rest, my Beloved," Mary responded, laying her head on his shoulder. She fell into a deep sleep, with dreams of pulsing, singing stars and woke to the simple cry of her baby.

She sat up and reached into the manger to lift Jesus out. Setting him to nurse, she covered them both with the blanket. She studied his face, his tiny ears, nose, fat cheeks, his plump mouth moving as he nursed. When she reached out to touch his thick, soft hair, he opened his eyes and looked at her. She smiled at him, certain he would fall asleep after he finished nursing, but he did not. He stared at her, dark eyes studying her face, until he finally closed his eyes and fell asleep.

"Sir?" A voice called from outside. The dawn light cast a shadow of a man on the floor of the stable.

Joseph awoke and stood in one fluid movement, shielding Mary and the babe from the newcomer. "Who is it?"

"It is I. Gershom bar Moshe; I am the owner of the house. "How… is your wife?" he asked.

Joseph crossed to the door. "She is fine, thank you," he said. "She gave birth to a son."

"Mazel tov! May Yahweh bless your family." The old man paused. "Sir, there are some men—shepherds—who want to see the child."

Joseph frowned. "What?"

"A group of shepherds just arrived at my house," Gershom explained. "They said they heard a babe had been born here and wanted to see him. I do not know how they knew, but I told them to leave you alone. Then they told me their story, and I thought I should ask you."

"Their story?" Joseph asked. "What happened?"

"I should let them tell you," Gershom said. "If you wish, I will get them."

"Yes, of course," Joseph said.

"Joseph?" Mary called.

He crossed the floor and knelt by her, giving her a drink of water.

"What is happening?" she asked, her voice weak with fatigue.

"The owner of the house said that shepherds have arrived, wanting to see the babe."

The elderly man returned, leading six men. Dressed in the rough garments of shepherds, the men were hesitant and wide-eyed as they entered. When they saw the sleeping babe, they gasped and fell to their knees.

"It is the babe!" one of them said.

"Just as we were told," another agreed.

Mary and Joseph looked at each other and then at the shepherds. "Who told you about our baby?" Joseph asked.

The shepherds looked at each other as though uncertain what to say. Finally, the one who spoke first turned to the young couple. "An...*angel*," he whispered. "We were watching our flocks nearby. It was an ordinary night, when suddenly a man appeared *in the sky.* Only, he wasn't a man..."

"He was huge!" A young boy interrupted, stretching his arms above his head. "Taller than Goliath must have been, with a robe that was blinding white. And he had massive wings like an eagle."

"Benjamin, please, let me tell the story," the older shepherd said.

He turned back to Mary and Joseph. "I am Ilai bar Abijah; this is my son Benjamin. As he said, an angel appeared. I am not ashamed to say that we were terrified. We cried out and fell to the ground. This…angel…told us not to be afraid. Then he said he had, *good news that will cause great joy to all people. It will be for everyone in the world.* He said, *Today, in the Town of David, a Savior has been born. He is the Messiah. You will know it is him when you find a newborn babe lying in manger.*

"Suddenly the whole sky was filled with other angels, all singing and worshipping Yahweh, and proclaiming peace on those who love Him. I have never heard anything like it; it sounded like all of creation was singing. Then they turned and—flew—upwards. We had to come and find the child this angel spoke of." The shepherd peered at the sleeping baby. "And here he is, just as the angel said."

Mary looked at Joseph, who nodded. She tucked the prayer cloth around Jesus, who squirmed for a moment, and then settled in his mother's arms. She gently extended the baby toward the shepherds. "You may touch him," she said. "It is as the angel said. He is for everyone. He is for you."

Chapter 48

12 Av, 3758

"Look John," Zechariah lifted his son over the bed where Mary had laid Jesus. "This is Jesus ben Joseph. He is not only your relative, he is also," he glanced toward the owners of the house, who were in the next room and lowered his voice, "Yahweh's Messiah. *You* are to be his prophet, preparing the way for him." John looked at the sleeping baby, frowned, then turned to extend chubby arms to his mother.

"Husband," Elizabeth laughed, taking John from his father, "he is barely eight months old himself. All he cares about is eating, sleeping, and playing." She reached into her bag and pulled out a soft ball made of cloth and handed it to her son.

Joseph laughed as John shook the ball, causing a wooden rattle. "What is making the noise?" he asked.

"Elizabeth sewed several small pieces of wood inside the ball," Zechariah said. "John loves shaking it," he grinned as his son stuck the ball in his mouth, "and chewing on it."

"He plays with it for hours," Elizabeth said.

"That is a wonderful idea," Mary said. "Joseph, we should make one of these balls for Jesus when he is older."

"We will," Joseph looked out the window at the slant of the sun rising in the eastern sky, "but we must leave soon if we wish to arrive at the Temple early."

"Joseph speaks truth," Zechariah said. "There is always a long line of parents waiting to present their babies."

"At least we do not have to walk to Jerusalem," Mary said. "Thank you, Elizabeth and Zechariah, for bringing your wagon."

"You are welcome," Elizabeth said. "It makes it easier to travel with a baby. You will see how the motion of the swaying wagon will lull the boys to sleep."

After helping the women and babies into the back of the wagon, the men climbed onto the wagon bench. Gathering the reins, Zechariah turned the donkey and drove down the streets of Bethlehem and onto the road leading to Jerusalem.

"I am happy you and Zechariah are going to be with us today," Mary smiled.

"We are pleased to be with you," Elizabeth said, "especially since your families were unable to come."

The morning after Jesus was born, Joseph spoke with Gershom bar Moshe about arranging to send a message to Zechariah and Elizabeth as well as messages to their families. After Joseph gave the messages and coin for their delivery, the older man told him, "One of my guests have left. There is now an empty room in my house. Please bring your wife and son inside."

"Thank you," Joseph smiled. "You have been most kind to us."

Leaving Mary and the baby to the ministrations of Gershom's wife Hannah bat Reuel—cooing over Jesus and promising to prepare a hearty meal for the young couple—Joseph went back to the stable to tend to Arod and Aton.

Opening the bag of food for the donkeys, he noted their supply was low.

I will have to purchase more food for them…as well as supplies for Mary, the baby, and me.

He frowned, contemplating all the items they would need if they were to stay much longer.

He noticed the disarray in the stable, lingering evidence of what had occurred last night; the pile of soiled hay, the ropes dangling from the loft, the manger moved nearer to the *bed* where he and Mary had finally slept. Bending, he grabbed an armload of hay. *The least I can do is restore order to the stable.* Carrying the soiled hay outside, he prayed, "Yahweh, You sent Gershom to provide a place for us yesterday. Please provide for us again."

Once the stable was cleaned, Joseph sought out Gershom. The older man was trying to repair the broken leg on a bench. It was obvious from his expression that the repair was not going as desired.

"Do you need help?" Joseph asked.

The man laughed derisively. "I am a simple farmer, not a carpenter. I need someone who knows what they are doing."

Joseph smiled. "Sir, I am a carpenter. Please allow me to repair the bench as a thank you for your kindness to my family."

"Gladly," Gershom handed him the mallet

Within a short time, the bench was repaired.

Gershom examined Joseph's work. "This is well done," he said. "You are more than a simple carpenter." He eyed Joseph. "How long are you planning to stay in Bethlehem?"

"My wife and had planned to be here only long enough to register for the census. Now, we need to wait forty days until our son has been circumcised and we have presented the offering for Mary's purification rites."

"I have other things that need repairing," Gershom said. "What if you do this work in exchange for staying in our room and eating meals with us?"

"Yes, thank you."

"I will ask if any of our neighbors need work to be done. I do not imagine you will become wealthy, but perhaps you will be able to earn the money for your present needs and for your journey back to your home.

"Thank you, Sir."

"Please call me *Gershom*." The man extended his hand.

Joseph nodded, taking the man's hand and shaking it. "Gershom. I am Joseph. Thank you. As you were last night, you are once again," he smiled, "an answer to prayer."

Several days later, a message arrived from Zechariah, filled with mazel tovs and the promise he and Elizabeth would come when they presented Jesus in the Temple.

Messages also arrived from both of their families, concerned by Jesus' early arrival.

"Our parents wrote they are praying Yahweh will protect our son and help him grow strong," Mary told Elizabeth. "They also wrote that, due to everyone recently traveling to register for the census, they do not have monies to come to Bethlehem right now. They are pleased you and Zechariah are near and will be with us today as we celebrate Jesus' presentation in the Temple. They look forward to meeting Jesus when we return to Nazareth." Mary smoothed the blanket around Jesus. "My prayer is he will not grow *too* much, as our families will be surprised if he is not the size of a small baby born early."

"Leave that to Yahweh," Elizabeth patted Mary's arm. "He has provided for you thus far; He will provide for you—and for Jesus—in the coming days."

"That is what Joseph continually tells me," Mary smiled. "With the work he has now, we have been able to buy what we and Jesus needs, but little more." She glanced at her husband's back, and then lowered her voice. "To speak truth, we have only enough monies to present two small doves."

The Law Yahweh gave Moses stated that when a woman gave birth, she would be ceremonially unclean for forty days for a son and twice that time for a daughter. When the time was complete, she was to bring an offering to the Temple; a year-old lamb for a burnt offering and a young pigeon or a dove for a sin offering. If she could not afford a lamb, she was to bring two doves or two young pigeons, one for a burnt offering and the other for a sin offering.

Soon, Zechariah was driving the wagon through the gate into Jerusalem, up the streets, and stopping in front of the Holy Temple of Yahweh. Mary had come here as a child with her parents, and again only months ago when she came with Zechariah and Elizabeth when they came for Elizabeth's purification rites and to present John in the Temple.

It felt different this time; Mary stared wide-eyed at the grandeur of the City of David as if seeing it for the first time. *Will this be where Jesus will rule from? Will Joseph and I live here when He is King?*

While Zechariah arranged for their wagon and donkey to be

kept in a nearby stable, Joseph helped her and Elizabeth down from the wagon. She smoothed her garments before turning to lift Jesus—who was sleepily opening his eyes—from the wagon bed.

Once Zechariah rejoined them, Joseph placed his hand beneath Mary's elbow as Zechariah and Elizabeth led the way through Solomon's Porch, the East Gate, the Court of Women, and up fifteen steps to the Gate of Nicanor where parents were already waiting to present their newborns to be dedicated to Yahweh and to present the offering for the rite of purification.

"It is good we came early," Zechariah said. "It is almost time for the morning Tamid sacrifice," Zechariah said. "After that, the Temple courts will fill with people."

Mary gently bounced Jesus in her arms. "I want to remember everything," she whispered to Joseph, "every little detail."

From a distance—even as far away as Bethlehem—the gold on the Temple walls gleamed as if it had captured the sunlight. Now, steps away, to be close to this much wealth was more than Mary could comprehend. Yet, people walked past it as if it were an unimportant, everyday occurrence.

The Temple court was filled with parents bringing their infants; some—like herself and Joseph—were dressed in simple garments while others wore rich raiment. Priests in somber black robes walked among the courtyard, nodding to their acquaintances, discussing world events, or details of the Law Yahweh gave to Moses.

"Elizabeth, you stay with Mary," Zechariah said, "and I will take Joseph to the Court of Gentiles, where the animals for sacrifice are sold."

Several minutes later, the men returned. Joseph held a wooden cage which held two doves.

Zechariah pointed to a spot in a shaded corner of the court. "Elizabeth and I will wait there while you present your offering."

Mary and Joseph joined the line of parents and babies. When it was their time, Joseph gave their names to the scribe in attendance, "We are here to present our first-born son to Yahweh. His name is Jesus," he smiled at Mary, "bar Joseph."

"Mazel tov." the scribe's smile was as wooden as his offer of congratulations. He dipped his stylus in the ink well and entered their names onto a scroll. "You may present your offering."

Joseph stepped up to the priest and gave him the cage with the doves.

The priest's smile was filled with warmth. "Mazel tov on your son. As the Word of Yahweh says, *Every first-born male that opens the womb shall be called holy to the Lord.* Amen."

"Amen," Mary and Joseph smiled.

They turned and walked to where Elizabeth and Zechariah were talking to a man. "Joseph," Mary's smile widened, "it is Simeon ben Anaiah."

The elderly man's beard spread in a toothy grin. "Ah, the carpenter and his bride. Joseph ben Jacob, Mary bat Eli. How wonderful to see you again."

"We are happy to see you as well, Simeon ben Anaiah," Joseph said.

"And from what Zechariah and Elizabeth tells me," the older man indicated the bundle in Mary's arms, "this is your birth of hope. I love babies. May I see him?" He lowered his voice. "I promise not to wake him."

"Certainly, you may see him." Mary lifted the edge of the cloth from Jesus' face.

"Ahhhh…" Simeon's smile broadened and then froze. His expression changed, his eyes widening, blinking, as if a blind man seeing for the first time. Without asking permission, he slid his hands beneath the baby, lifting Jesus from Mary's arms. "Praise be to the Most High God!" he cried aloud.

The people in the court surrounding them turned to watch the elderly man weeping, kissing Jesus' forehead, and crying praise to Yahweh.

"Now Lord," he looked upwards, "as You have promised, You may now let Your servant depart in peace." He looked down to stroke Jesus' face. "For my eyes have seen Your salvation, which You prepared in the sight of all nations; a light for revelation to the Gentiles and the glory of Your people Israel."

Mary stared at Joseph, uncertain how to respond.

Simeon turned back to them. "Blessings on you both," he placed

Jesus back in Mary's arms. "This child is destined to cause the falling and rising of many in Israel, and to be a sign that will be spoken against, so that the thoughts of many hearts will be revealed." His smile faded as he looked into Mary's eyes and whispered, "And a sword will pierce your own soul too."

"Uh…, thank—" Mary's response was interrupted.

"Praise be to Yahweh!" A woman—the oldest person Mary had ever seen—walked up to them. She peered at the baby in Mary's arms and turned, lifting her arms. "Praise be to the Most High God."

"It is Anna bat Phanuel," Elizabeth's whisper was echoed by others around the court. "This is she whom we told you about," she said to Mary and Joseph. "The one who is considered a prophetess."

Mary's eyes widened as the elderly woman hurried to the people in the Temple court, crying praise to Yahweh, pointing to her baby and proclaiming Jesus as the promised redemption of Jerusalem, of Israel, and the world.

20 Tevet 3759

"Look, Mama," John pointed a chubby finger upward, "*tars.*"

"You are right, John, those are *stars,*" Elizabeth enunciated the word. "They are big stars. That one," she pointed to the sky, "is called Tzedek."

"Tuzz-deck," the child repeated.

Joseph grinned as Elizabeth continued teaching John the names of the stars and mazzaloths. Mary was sitting near the fire, holding Jesus on her lap while drawing pictures in the dirt, as Hannah refilled cups of milk and offered a plate of warm oat cakes to everyone.

"Gershom," Joseph said, "you and Hannah have been a blessing from Yahweh to us." Due to the older man's recommendation, over the last six months, many people in Bethlehem had hired Joseph to repair or build things for them. As a result, Joseph was able to buy the things they needed, as well as save money toward going back to Nazareth.

The months in Bethlehem had also allowed them several opportunities to visit with Zechariah and Elizabeth. When Gershom learned this week was Zechariah's time to serve in the Temple, he invited Zechariah and Elizabeth to stay in their home. "This will allow you to see your kin once more," he had told Joseph, "before you and Mary return to Nazareth."

After swallowing the last bite of cake, Gershom dusted his hands, and stood. "I will check the lock on the door once more and then Hannah and I will retire for the night."

After wishing everyone a good night, Hannah and Gershom crossed the courtyard to their bed chamber.

"Zechariah, these last few days have been a joy for us." Joseph continued watching their wives playing with their sons. "We have enjoyed being with you and Elizabeth. It is a relief to have someone to speak with who *knows* all that happened to us, and *who* Jesus is. We will miss you and Elizabeth."

"Hmmm."

Joseph turned to look at Zechariah. The older man's eyes had lost their focus; he was staring into the distance as though he were alone. "Zechariah?"

"What? Oh. Forgive me, Joseph," the older man straightened. "I have been…distracted."

"I could see that. I am sorry about your friend, Simeon."

That afternoon, when Zechariah returned from the Temple, he had told them Simeon ben Anaiah had died.

"Thank you," Zechariah said. "Simeon was a righteous and devout man and a good friend." He filled his lungs. "I will miss him."

"May your memories grant you peace," Joseph said. "But you also seemed *worried*."

Zechariah glanced at the women, and then lowered his voice. "Herod sent for the High Priest today."

Joseph's eyebrows slanted downward. "It is never a good thing to be called to Herod's presence. Did you learn what he wanted from Rabbi Joshua ben Sie?

"Apparently, Herod had some unexpected guests—Magi from the Eastern School."

"What?"

The magi were known even to those from remote towns like Nazareth. From Babylon, magi were wealthy men of noble birth who had been educated in the Eastern School, a center of learning which included training in the natural order of the world. Magi were respected, influencing rulers and authorities throughout the world.

"*Magi* came to Jerusalem?"

Zechariah nodded. "According to Rabbi Joshua, they went to Herod's palace and asked to see the new King of the Jews."

"What?" Joseph stood.

"Joseph," Mary turned to the men, "what is it?"

Elizabeth turned as well. "Husband, what has happened?"

Zechariah looked at Joseph, who nodded. Looking at the closed door to Gershom and Hannah's bed chamber, he beckoned to the women. "Come closer," he lowered his voice.

The women stood and carried the babies to sit near their husbands.

Zechariah repeated what had occurred in Jerusalem. The arrival of the magi to Herod's palace, asking to see the new King of the Jews. "Herod sent for the High Priest and other Teachers of the Law. When they arrived at the palace, he asked them where," he looked at Jesus in Mary's arms, "the Messiah was to be born."

"What?" Mary leaned toward Joseph. "What did they say?"

Zechariah shook his head. "They told Herod the Messiah was to be born in Bethlehem in Judea, and then added what the prophet Micah wrote:

"But you, Bethlehem Ephrathah,
though you are small among the clans of Judah,
out of you will come for Me
One who will be ruler over Israel,
Whose origins are from of old,
from ancient times."

"Oh no," Elizabeth said. "Husband, what does this mean?"

Zechariah looked at Joseph. "It means you and Mary should leave."

"What?" Joseph frowned.

"From what I heard, Herod was not pleased with the teacher's answers. Better to trust a hungry lion than Herod," Zechariah said. "All of Jerusalem know he is insane. He killed his wife, he killed his own children because he thought they were planning to steal his throne." He looked at the two babies. "He would not hesitate to kill others." He put an arm around Elizabeth's shoulder. "We should leave as well."

"We are going back to Nazareth in a few days," Joseph said.

"We are going home once Joseph and Mary leave," Elizabeth said.

Zechariah shook his head. "That is not far enough nor soon enough."

"Where should we go?" Joseph asked.

"Anywhere outside of Herod's dominion," Zechariah said. "The Roman Emperor would be displeased if Herod tried to reach outside the boundaries given him."

"Where would that be?" Mary hugged Jesus closer.

Zechariah shrugged his shoulders. "Gaul is far away. Or Egypt; it is under Roman rule, but outside of Herod's authority. There are communities of Jewish people who have lived there since Nebuchadnezzar conquered Jerusalem."

"Zechariah," Joseph pulled Mary close. "We have enough money to go to Nazareth, but no further."

Zechariah clasped Joseph's forearm. "We will pray for Yahweh's guidance."

"Shhh!" Joseph put a finger to his lips as he lifted his head to listen.

He heard the sound of animals walking, the creaking of harnesses and saddles, and men's voices, growing closer and louder until, whoever it was, stopped in front of the house. A moment later, someone knocked at the door.

"It is thieves!" Elizabeth whispered.

"Wife," Zechariah grinned for the first time that night, "thieves would be quieter and nor would they knock on the door."

Joseph stood and crossed the courtyard to knock on Gershom's bed chamber. A moment later, the man—dressed in a sleeping tunic—opened the door. "Joseph," he yawned, "is something amiss?"

Joseph gestured in the direction of the street. "Someone is knocking on your door."

"Who would be coming to my house this late?" Gershom said. "The registration for Caesar's census is over."

"I do not know," Joseph said. He followed, Zechariah joining them, as Gershom crossed the courtyard to the cooking area. Getting several of Hannah's long knives, Gershom handed one to Joseph and Zechariah before walking into the front room in the house. Once inside, Gershom lit one of the lamps as the knock was repeated.

Bracing his feet, Gershom looked at Joseph and Zechariah, who nodded.

"Who is it?" he called out.

"Sir," a man answered. "It is Ilai bar Abijah. I came here with my son and our friends the night the baby was born in your stable. Please, Sir, I have brought more men who are asking about the child."

Joseph's brows climbed to his scalp. He looked at Zechariah. "Could it be Herod's soldiers?" he whispered.

"If it were Herod's soldiers, they would not have waited once the man identified the house."

Gershom paused and then called through the door, "Ilai, who told you about the baby born in the stable?"

"An angel."

Gershom looked at Joseph, who nodded, before setting the knife down. He grasped the wooden bolt across the door and slid it back.

When he opened the door, Joseph saw Ilai and his young son, Benjamin; beyond them were six men. The three men in the front—wearing robes of heavy linen shot through with gold and silver thread gleaming in the moonlight—were obviously wealthy. Each man held a box covered with what appeared to be gems. The other three men who, from their garments appeared to be servants, held the reins of tall camels or donkeys.

"Greetings, Ilai bar Abijah," Gershom glanced at the men behind the shepherd. "What brings you to my home at this hour of the night?"

The shepherd extended his hand to the men with him. "These noble men were traveling from Jerusalem and stopped to ask directions from us."

Before his father could say more, Benjamin stepped forward. Placing his opened palm to the side of his mouth, he spoke in a whisper that Joseph felt could be heard in Jerusalem. "I…think… they…are…*kings!*"

Ilai rolled his eyes as he laid a hand on his son's shoulder and pulled him back. "Benjamin, what did King Solomon write about speaking in his proverbs?"

The boy lowered his gaze, clasped his hands, and replied, *"Even a fool who keeps silent is considered wise; when he closes his lips, he is deemed intelligent."* He glanced at the three guests. "I am sorry."

"Benjamin bar Ilai, no apology is needed," the man closest to them smiled at the boy. His voice was cultured, but with a foreign accent. "We are honored you would consider us royalty." He looked at Gershom, Joseph, and Zechariah.

Gershom exchanged grins with the newcomers before turning to the shepherd and his son. "Thank you for bringing these men to my home, Ilai and Benjamin."

"Yes, thank you," the first man reached into the folds of his girdle and drew out a coin to give to the shepherd. "Please consider this as gratitude for your help."

"No, Sir," Ilai folded his hands against his waist. "We were honored that Yahweh sent an angel to tell us of the birth of the Messiah. We would not take coin for helping others to see the child. Come, Benjamin." After bidding farewell, the shepherd led his son down the street of Bethlehem.

"I have seen many things in my life," the first man watched the father and son disappear into the night, "but I have never seen a man refuse coin." Shaking his head, he turned, placing his opened hand on his chest. "I am Gathaspa Kagpha Larvandad and these," he extended his hand to the two men next to him, "are my friends and traveling companions, Melichior Karsudan Badadakharida and Balthassar Gushnasaph Hormisdas."

"Greetings, peace be on you," Gershom said. After identifying himself, he introduced Joseph and Zechariah. He stepped back, extending a hand toward the front room. "Welcome to my home. Please come in."

"And on you peace," Gathaspa returned the response of a guest. "Thank you." He turned to their servants. "Wait here."

"If you wish, your servants may take the animals to my stable in the back."

"Thank you," the magus said. "That would be a kindness." After giving further instructions to the servants, he and his companions stepped into the room.

Joseph waited while Gershom extended the courtesies due a guest. He glanced at Zechariah, lifting an eyebrow. *Gershom behaves as if noble people often visit his home.* After washing their feet, anointing their heads, offering cups of cool water, followed by kissing their cheeks, Gershom asked, "Why is my home blessed to receive such honored guests?"

"It is we who are honored," Gathaspa placed his opened palm on his chest and lowered his head in a single nod. "As Ilai bar Abijah, and his son said," his beard spread wide from a grin, "we are looking for the new King of the Jews."

Gershom indicated Joseph, "I believe you are looking for the son of my friend, Joseph bar Jacob."

Joseph was not certain how to address the strangers. He copied the stranger's actions, placing an opened hand on his chest and bowing his head. "Greetings." He indicated Zechariah, "This is Zechariah bar Barach, who is my kinsman and a priest of Yahweh."

Joseph was thankful when Zechariah took a step toward the strangers.

"Greetings," Zechariah repeated Joseph's actions. "As my kinsman said, I serve in Yahweh's Temple in Jerusalem. I was there today. There was word King Herod had esteemed visitors from the Eastern School."

"We have the honor to receive training in the Eastern School," Gathaspa said.

"We spoke with Herodes Magnus this day," the magi named Melichior said.

"He who was appointed King of the Jews by the Roman Senate," the magus named Balthassar said, "is *not* whom we seek."

"Gershom?" Hannah stepped into the room. Her gaze was as calm as her husband's.

"This is my wife, Hannah bat Reuel," Gershom said and introduced the newcomers.

Hannah smiled. "Welcome to our home. If you would please come to our courtyard, we have laid out food and beverage for you."

Joseph grinned, imaging the women hurriedly laying out food for such noble guests.

They escorted their guests to the fire, where Mary and Elizabeth were waiting with Hannah; both mothers held their sons covered against their shoulders.

Zechariah drew Elizabeth forward. "This is my wife, Elizabeth bat Shelomoh and our son, John."

Joseph took Mary's elbow and drew her forward. "This is my wife, Mary bat Eli, and our son, Jesus."

Joseph and Zechariah helped Gershom bring benches for their guests, while Hannah, Mary, and Elizabeth offered them bread, cheese, oat cakes, and cups of milk.

Once the magi had eaten their fill and thanked them for their hospitality, the three couples sat down. Mary and Elizabeth holding their sleeping babies across their laps.

Zechariah indicated the magi. "Elizabeth, Mary, these are the men who went to Herod's palace today."

"As my friend mentioned to your honored husbands," Melichior said, "he who was appointed King of the Jews by the Roman Senate, is *not* whom we seek."

"We have traveled from our land to meet the true King of the Jews," Balthassar lifted his hand to point skyward, "the one whose star shines over this little town."

"Balthassar, it is not a single star," Melichior said," but multiple stars." He pointed toward the sky. "That star is known to the Romans as Jupiter." His tone reminded Joseph of Rabbi Boaz when he was teaching the synagogue classes. "The second one is called *Sharu* in our land and *Regulus* by the Romans; both names mean *king*. Behind them was the grouping—I believe you call these *mazzaloth*—known as *The Lion*. Several months ago, these stars came together to form the brightest star we have never seen." His eyes widened as his voice shrank to a whisper. "It riveted our attention."

Balthasar grinned before addressing his companion. "Melichior, I am certain these noble people do not wish to hear a lecture on the stars."

Gathaspa smiled. "You must forgive our friend. Although we travel to many places and study many languages in order to learn many things, Melichior drinks in knowledge as a thirsty man drinks water. His is a gifted teacher, and his passion is the stars. There are many nights when he disregards sleep in exchange for studying the sky.

"Last year, in our month *Arah Tisritum*, which I believe your people call…," he turned to Balthassar.

"*Tishri*," the magus said.

"Yes, thank you, my friend. It was in your month known as Tishri. These stars and mazzaloths came together to form what would have appeared to those not knowledgeable in the heavenlies as one large star. Since the joining of the stars was in the mazzaloth of The Lion, we determined it must mean a king had been born."

Melichior lifted his forefinger, "A king born to the *Lion of Judah*, which we understand represents the Jewish people."

"We determined to come and see for ourselves this new king that the heavens proclaimed," Gathaspa said. "When we arrived in Jerusalem, we went to the palace of Herod." He paused at the look that passed between the Jews. "Ah…I see from your expressions you do not trust King Herod; after meeting him, neither do we. But we did not know this before we entered his palace, where we assumed a new king would be born.

"Herod was surprised by our story and assured us that no king had been born to his household."

Balthassar took up the story. "One of Herod's advisors reminded him of the…Messiah, I think was the name…a king whose coming was prophesied by your ancient holy men."

"Herod called for the Leaders of your Temple and asked them about the Messiah. They told us that the prophecies stated that the Messiah would be born in Bethlehem. And so we came to this little town, where the star," he pointed skyward, "had stopped. However, we did not know which house. We saw some shepherds, stopped to ask if they knew where to find the new king who had been born. The shepherd named Ilai bar Abijah told us about the king who had been born in Tammuz."

The magi looked at the baby sleeping in Mary and Elizabeth's laps.

Zechariah, Elizabeth, Gershom, and Hannah looked at Mary and Joseph.

Mary looked at Joseph, who nodded.

Joseph crossed to Mary and helped her stand. She extended her baby to the magi. "His name is Jesus ben," she smiled at her husband, "Joseph."

The magi looked at the baby and then each other, before slipping off the benches to kneel in the dirt. The expression on their faces changed from calm assurance to awed humility.

"It is *he*," Gathaspa said in hushed tones.

"The one born as King of the Jews," Balthassar murmured.

"As the stars told us," Melichior whispered.

Joseph stared at the magi—kneeling in the dirt in front of his wife and child—and then looked at the others. From their wide-eyed stares, it was apparent that they were all surprised by the response of the noble men.

"Please," Gathaspa looked at Mary and Joseph, "we brought gifts for the new king. May we present them?"

Mary lifted an eyebrow at Joseph, who nodded. "We would be honored," she smiled.

Joseph thought the night had produced enough surprises, but he realized he was wrong. His bit his lips to keep from gaping as, in turn, each magus opened the jewel-encrusted boxes they held.

"I bring gold, the royal metal," Gathaspa opened his box to reveal golden nuggets, "in honor of his kingship."

"I bring frankincense, used to make sacred incense," Melichior opened his box to reveal small pieces of dark brown resin, "as the King of the Jews would lead his people in worship before Yahweh."

"I bring myrrh, the ointment of burial," Balthassar opened his box to reveal an amphora, the length of his hand and filled with a milky liquid, "as every good King is willing to die for his people."

Joseph gazed at the gifts of the magi. *Any one of these are worth more than I would ever earn in a lifetime. With these, we can travel wherever we need, to protect Jesus.* He looked at Zechariah, who nodded, as if hearing his thoughts. *This is what Yahweh has provided.*

"Thank you," he took each gift and placed it next to Mary. "My wife and I accept these gifts on behalf of our son Jesus," he looked at everyone and then smiled at Mary, "the King of the Jews."

After the presentation of their gifts, the magi stood. "It is late and we do not wish to keep you from your sleep," Gathaspa said. "Is there an inn nearby?"

"No, I am sorry," Gershom said. "Bethlehem does not have an inn." He quickly told the story of the night Jesus was born.

"Mary bat Eli gave birth to the new King of the Jews in the stable where our servants are waiting with our animals?" Melichior asked.

Gershom nodded.

"Then, if you will allow us to hire it from you," Balthassar said, "we would be honored to sleep there."

Gershom's eyebrows climbed to his scalp. "You wish to sleep in my stable?"

Gathaspa looked at his companions, who nodded. "What was worthy to be the birthplace of the King of Kings, is an honor for us."

Joseph went with Gershom to lead the magi to the stable. By the time he returned to their bed chamber, Mary had finished nursing Jesus. Her exuberant questions and comments gave evidence of her joy at the thought of returning to their families in Nazareth.

"I still cannot believe what happened tonight," Mary laid Jesus on the small pallet next to their bed, stretched out next to him, and reached over to pat his back. "With this money, we will be able to help our families once we are back home.

"Can you imagine what Adina will say when we tell her we met magi? That they slept in the stable where Jesus was born? *Ahhhhh—hhhh*," she yawned.

"Uh…yes," Joseph said as he removed his sandals. *I will have to tell her what Zechariah told me about Herod.*

He looked at his wife; her eyes were closed, her hand still on the baby's back. He smiled, *But not now,* and lifted her hand, to place it next to her face. Laying down next to her, he kissed her cheek.

"Yahweh, thank You for Your blessings," he whispered, "and for Your provisions." He filled his lungs and blew out the air, "And give me wisdom to know what You want me to do next. Amen."

The sound that woke Joseph was unlike anything he had ever heard. He propped up on his elbow and tilted his head to listen. It was a growl; no, it was a scream; no it was a roar; it was wail.

Whatever it was—it was coming from nearby!

He turned to get out of bed, only to find he was lying on a blanket covering a mound of hay. He frowned, looking around. Above them was the tall wooden loft that kept bundles of hay out of the reach of the animals. In the corner Arod and Aton were huddled with another donkey, a cow and her calf, while the chickens ran between the animals' legs; the stable was filled with squawking, braying, snorting and mooing.

Next to him, Mary was asleep and, beyond her, was the manager where Jesus was sleeping, swaddled in his prayer shawl, the light shining on the manager.

He jumped when a crash of lightning lit the night sky, followed by a scream resounding through the streets, the scream of a feral animal hungry for blood. He looked at the bed of hay; Mary continued to sleep as did Jesus in the manger.

He stood and hurried to calm the animals, then turned to see a man standing in the door of the stable.

Taller and broader than any man Joseph had seen, the man was facing away from him and the stable. In his right hand he held a massive sword reflecting the stars' light as if it were on fire.

Joseph approached the man to speak to him, but froze at the sight of what was happening in the streets of Bethlehem.

Other men—similar to the one who stood before Joseph—were fighting what appeared to be…*Nephilim*, the creatures of old. Dark creatures, larger than Goliath, some with multiple limbs or heads, some with legs or horns of an animal, even some with massive wings.

The creatures' opponents were like the man standing in front of Joseph. Tall, muscular, blinding light shimmering from their garments; their skin, and wild hair identified *what* they were without turning toward Joseph—*angels*.

Angels and the dark creatures fought with a skill and animosity honed from eons of battle. As fearful as these beings were, it was the monster in their midst that caused Joseph to gape like a man who had swallowed his tongue.

Taller than the houses, it was an enormous horned dragon with a long serpentine neck, crocodile teeth, claws as sharp as knives, and a tail that swept down trees.

As the angels fought the creatures of darkness—lightning sparking from their swords—the dragon screamed as it ripped roofs off houses, digging through the rooms with its claws and pointed snout, and devouring whatever—or whomever—it grabbed.

Louder than the dragon's screams was the wail as that of a woman crying out in deepest misery and loss.

Joseph looked up and noticed the night sky was as black as tar; not one star could be seen. *What was the source of light shining on Jesus?* He turned and walked to the manger. His eyebrows rose as he realized light was not shining *on* Jesus; it was emanating *from* Jesus.

Mary turned in her sleep, moaning and weeping. "Joseph," she whimpered. "Help us."

He crossed to Mary, and stooped, laying a hand on her. "Shhh… Beloved," he whispered. "Do not be afraid."

He hunted through the stable for something he could use as a weapon. He found a chisel, as long as the sword in the angel's hand. Lifting the tool, he stepped toward the door of the stable, determined to defend Mary and Jesus.

"Joseph." Gabriel appeared in front of him. "You must go."

"Go?" Joseph shook his head. "No, I will defend my family. I will fight these creatures of Gehenna."

"No," eyes blazing, Gabriel touched the chisel in Joseph's hand. The tool shattered, knocking Joseph to the ground. "This battle is not yours to fight," the angel said.

"Get up and take the child and his mother to Egypt. Stay there until I tell you, for Herod is searching for the child to kill him."

Gabriel was instantly within a breath of Joseph's face. "Joseph— awake!" The angel's eyes blazed like fire, his voice boomed in Joseph's ears.

Joseph sat up, gasping, looking around. Sunlight was peeking through the shutters on the window. He was in their bed chamber in Gershom's house. Mary was sleeping in bed next to him, her hand beneath her cheek. Jesus was sleeping on the pallet next to his mother.

Joseph ben Jacob," Gathaspa asked, "may we have a word with you?"

The magi were waiting while their servants finished packing the camels and donkeys, including a basket of oat cakes Hannah bat Reuel had prepared for the morning meal.

"Certainly," Joseph bowed his head and followed the three magi to the corner of the house.

Looking around to make sure they were private, Gathaspa said, "We did not wish to worry your wife, but you should know before we left Herod's palace, he asked once we found the new King of the Jews, to return and tell him where he was."

"Herod said he wished to come and see the child too," Balthassar added. He looked at his two companions, who nodded. "Last night, we all had the same dream. We were warned not to go back to Herod. We will return to our country by another route. Be careful, Joseph ben Jacob."

"Thank you," Joseph said. "I, too, had a dream last night. An angel told me to take Mary and the baby and go to Egypt and stay there until Yahweh tells us. He said Herod would try to find the baby to kill him."

"Then go," Melichior said, lifting a hand in blessing, "and may you and your family be guided and protected until the time for you to return."

Chapter 50

The next evening

$\mathcal{I}$ do not know when we will see you again, little one," Elizabeth lifted Jesus to kiss his cheek. "Take good care of your mother. Listen to your father. Grow to be a strong man of Yahweh."

Mary picked up John and hugged him. "I will miss you as well. I had hoped you and Jesus would grow close and help each other prepare for your future." She kissed his cheek. "We will trust that to Yahweh."

After the magi left, Joseph spoke with Zechariah, before telling Mary and Elizabeth their news.

"We are going to Egypt and not Nazareth?" Mary's eyes widened.

"We are going to Nazareth and not our home?" Elizabeth echoed Mary's expression.

Joseph told them he had a dream—without giving the details of what he saw—that Gabriel had said they were to go to Egypt. "He said he would tell us when it was safe to return."

Mary's next question, "What about Arod and Aton? They belong to my parents," was answered by Zechariah.

"Elizabeth and I will go to our home, pack what we need, and then travel to Nazareth. We will take your parents' donkeys back to them, along with any letters you wish to send. We will answer all their questions as best we can, *without* saying anything about angels or dreams."

While Mary and Elizabeth packed their things, Joseph and Zechariah went to the Xystus Market, to arrange to travel with two different caravans, and to purchase items for their journeys. Joseph returned with a donkey, a camel, and a palanquin.

"Joseph!" Mary gasped. "Why did you purchase a camel?"

"We are going to be traveling further than our other journeys," he said. "The camel and palanquin will be comfortable for you and Jesus. Once we get to Egypt, we can sell the camel if we wish and keep the donkey. We still have nearly all of the gold from the magus Gathaspa. Here," he handed Mary the pouch, "put the remainder in your rose box with the magi's other gifts."

Mary opened the carved box and set the gold next to the container of frankincense and the amphora of myrrh, wrapped in Joseph's prayer shawl. After giving the box to Joseph to put in the palanquin, she picked Jesus up to see the camel.

"Look Jesus," Mary guided the baby's hand to rub the animal's nose. "This is a camel. *Ca—mel.* Joseph, what is its name?"

"Jero."

"Jero. Jesus, can you say, *Ja-Roh?*"

"Mary, I also have a gift for you." Joseph extended a box to her.

"A gift for me?" She handed Jesus to Joseph and took the box. Lifting the lid, she looked inside. "Joseph," she breathed. Reaching in, she lifted out a stylus, sheets of papyrus, and a sealed bottle of ink.

"You learned to draw and write in the dirt," Joseph said. "When we presented Jesus in the Temple, you told me you wanted to remember everything. I wanted to give you something that will last longer than scribbling in the sand. Now you can write your memories of this time."

"Joseph, we have a baby and, if Yahweh blesses us, "she smiled at him, "we will have more children. Right now, caring for Jesus and for us takes all of my time.

"One day, I will write down my memories of this time. For now," Mary placed her hand on her chest, "I will treasure all these things in my heart."

Author's Note

When I read stories in the Bible, I wonder about how or why the people said or did certain things. How did Noah gather the animals into the ark? Why would Rebekah and Isaac favor one son over the other? Why did Balak not run screaming in terror when the donkey spoke to him? What did Mary think when Gabriel appeared to her? What did Joseph think when Mary told him she—as a virgin—was to give birth to the Son of God? What did Peter think when he was walking on the water? Who could afford perfume that cost a year's wages?

Perhaps because of their "moment in time" nature, the people in these Bible stories are often viewed as iconic figures on a stained-glass window. David was a courageous young boy. Solomon was the wisest of all. Peter was brash and impulsive. Mary had an uneventful pregnancy. Joseph had no concerns about raising the Son of God. Martha fretted over a meal while Mary sat peacefully at Jesus' feet. People misunderstood Who Jesus of Nazareth truly was.

But these people were more than a boy with five stones; a man with a floating zoo; parents who played favorites; a couple with an unexpected—albeit unique—pregnancy; a disciple who acted before thinking; a woman with an expensive bottle of cologne; or people following the teacher from Nazareth. They had flaws and strengths, likes and dislikes, favorite foods, hopes and fears, pride, and insecurities.

Just like us.

One reason I like writing biblical novels is when I view these people as simple humans, when I research their time period and culture, the Bible stories come alive, and I glimpse possible answers to some of my questions.

The inspiration for this story came in 1982, when our first child, Rachael, was born on Christmas Eve. When reading the birth story from Luke the next morning, I was drawn to the verse, "Mary treasured all these things in her heart." Having that connection with Jesus' mother, I have pondered Mary and Joseph for many years and often wanted to tell their story.

When I started thinking and researching for this book, I knew I wanted to write the characters as I did for my *Sisters Of Lazarus* series. I wanted these characters to be ordinary people chosen by God for an extraordinary task. In addition, I wanted them to have traits a modern reader would understand and empathize.

Living near Nashville, Tennessee, has allowed me the opportunity to meet many creative people in the music, film, and publishing industries, as well as graphic designers, painters, dancers, and even a sculptress. While pondering a unique trait for Mary, I decided to make her artistic. A creative ability would be something unique for a woman of that time; I believe it would also help her to see God in a different way—the way many of my artist friends see God.

I shared this idea with my husband Mike, mentioning that Mary would draw in the dirt. One reason was due to lack of money for papyrus and ink. A second reason was it would help her keep her ability a secret out of concern most people would not understand. Mike—a fount of inspiration and wisdom for me—suggested whenever Mary needed time to think, she would stoop down and draw in the dirt. The thought of Jesus growing up watching His mother do that was amazing!

While pondering Mary a few days later, my friend Mary-Kathryn Cunningham came to mind. Mary-Kathryn is a synesthete. Synesthesia is a neurological condition in which stimulation of one sensory or cognitive pathway (for example, hearing) leads to automatic, involuntary experiences in a second sensory or cognitive pathway (such as vision). This may, for instance, take the form of hearing music and simultaneously sensing the sound as swirls or patterns of color.

For my story, I knew Mary had to be a synesthete.

If you would like to learn more about the research I used for different aspects of this book—including information about synesthesia—visit my website: www.paulakparker.com. Under the "Musings" tab is the page "Biblical Fiction Glossary, Useful Information, and Research."

Finally—and this is a big request—if you liked this story, would you please consider leaving a review on your favorite online bookstore, social media platform, or blog? I love this story and want as many readers as possible to discover it; your voice can reach people I cannot. Leave a review and tell a friend. The best compliment you can give an author is to recommend their book to your friends and family.

Thank you, dear reader, for giving your time to read this book. Stories need an audience. It means a lot that you trusted me to entertain, and hopefully inspire, you with this story.

Blessings,
Paula K. Parker

Acknowledgements

I have a confession.

I have read books and closed the cover without reading the author's acknowledgements. After all, I didn't know the people and didn't care that they had any part in the creation of the book. All I wanted to do was flip past the page and move on to the next story.

Now that I have been on the other side of the book creation process, I realize a book is one child that takes a village. The conception of the story might take place in the author's imagination, but it takes a team of behind-the-scenes people to carry it through to the published state. Not to mention the author's family, who selflessly sacrificed so he or she could craft their story.

Therefore, please take a moment to allow me to publicly acknowledge and thank these people.

Thank you to everyone who read my *Sisters of Lazarus* series, and then encouraged me to write more biblical novels. Your enthusiasm, your kind comments, and readers' reviews, your recommendation to your acquaintances were a blessing and balm to my heart. I wish I could list each of you by name, but alas, there is not sufficient space.

Thank you, Malcolm Down. Even though we no longer work together professionally, your belief in my writing and your comments made me realize that it was possible for me to be an author.

Thank you, Rick Larson, for sharing information from your research about the Star of Bethlehem and the Christ Quake. Your research led me on a path that opened up ideas about Mary and Joseph and the birth of Jesus I had never considered before.

Thank you, Tracy H. Sugg, for sharing your knowledge as a gifted artist, and your enthusiasm for my work. Thanks for suggesting I include the Slaughter of the Innocents.

Thank you Mary-Kathryn Cunningham for sharing your experience being a synesthete.

Thank you, Donna Williams, Marian Rizzo, Mary-Kathryn Cunningham, Susan K. Stewart, and Tracy H. Sugg for your humbling endorsements of this book.

Thank you, David Warren, for your friendship, your immense talent, and generous nature. The book cover is simply breathtaking.

To my mother, Helen Jones, thank you for always believing in me and my ability, and for being one of my biggest fans. To Jean Parker, thank for your encouragement and for being the best mother-in-law ever.

To my children: Rachael, Anna, Joshua, Bethany, and Mary; my three sons-in-law, Nathan, Billy and John; and my grandchildren: Isabella, Penelope, Aubrey, Harrison, William, Charlotte, Eleanor, and Josie. You are everything I've ever prayed for and one of the reasons I do what I do.

To Mike, my best friend, the father of my children, the best husband a woman could ever have, and now my publisher. Thank you for the love, support, encouragement, and courage to pursue our dreams and chart a course into untested waters.

Of course, I cannot end an acknowledgement page without thanking the One who loves me more than anyone in the world, Who sacrificed His life for me, Who daily reminds me *I am worth so much more*, and Who holds my life in His hands; my Lord and Savior, Jesus Christ.

About the Author

*E*arly training in music and theater led Paula K. Parker to a life-long love for the arts. This passion eventually brought her to Nashville, Tennessee, where she—along with her writer husband, Mike—helped establish local community theaters, Carpenter's Playhouse and Springhouse Theatre Company.

Paula co-authored *YHWH: The Flood, The Fish & The Giant* and *YESHUA: The King, The Demon & The Traitor* with New York Times Best-selling novelist, GP Taylor, before penning her own bestselling novel, *Sisters of Lazarus: Beauty Unveiled,* and its sequels, *Glory Revealed: Sisters of Lazarus Book 2* and *Grace Extended: Sisters of Lazarus Book 3*

An internationally acclaimed playwright, Paula has written numerous short sketches, one-acts and full-length plays, including *The Sam Jones Story*, a historical play commissioned by Nashville's Summer Lights Foundation, and her popular adaptations of several of Jane Austen's classic novels, including; *Jane Austen's Pride & Prejudice, Jane Austen's Sense & Sensibility* and *Jane Austen's EMMA*.

To learn more about Paula and her writing, visit her online at

www.PaulaKParker.com

www.ingramcontent.com/pod-product-compliance
Lightning Source LLC
Chambersburg PA
CBHW050824190726
48286CB00007B/1983